A MYTH OF ROME

ESTHER FRIESNER

CHILD OF THE EAGLE

A Baen Books Original

Baen Publishing Enterprises
P.O. Box 1403
Riverdale, NY 10471

ISBN: 0-671-87725-9

Cover art by Gary Ruddell

Distributed by Simon & Schuster
1230 Avenue of the Americas
New York, NY 10020

Printed in the United States of America

DEDICATION

For my father, David R. Friesner, with heartfelt gratitude for his support and inspiration.

ACKNOWLEDGMENT

Special thanks to David Drake, for his invaluable help with this book.

CHAPTER ONE

The dagger was sacred to his family. Some said it was the same blade that brought down the tyrant's son while other hands saw to humbling King Tarquin himself. Brutus held the old, awkward length of black steel across the palms of both hands, studying every chip and crack and pitting of the metal as if he were an augur seeking the future's path through a haze of blood.

When he looked up, he was in the Senate house. The dagger was still naked to the sight of anyone who might care to look his way, yet no one remarked on it. He thought this was very strange. He spied Cassius in conversation with Dolabella and a third man whose face was unfamiliar to him. Cassius swore he'd revealed the names of all the conspirators, brought them all together under one roof so that when the hour to strike came, each man would know the face of his friend. Why was he speaking with strangers at this late hour? Didn't he know what he risked?

Suddenly there came a clamor from the entry: *Caesar! Caesar comes!* The cheers and shouts of the mob that followed in his wake, little scavenger fish swimming under the great shark's fins, invaded the cool, shadowed grandeur of the Senate.

A steady hand, came the whisper in his ear. *I know you have a steady heart.* It was Cassius' voice, though the man himself was still plainly visible a good spear-cast away. Brutus tried to hold onto the mask that was his face, afraid to let even the minor emotion of startlement betray him.

But there were too many marvels battering at the doors of his senses. Caesar was in his chair. He had not crossed the floor of the Senate; he was simply *there*. Antony was nowhere to be seen. One of the conspirators had detained him outside, on some plausible premise. Good. At least

1

that much of the plan was still in place. He found it hard to accommodate his life to surprises.

And then the signal. A voice rang out calling all willing hands to the noble cause of breaking the new tyrant's yoke before it settled too firmly on Roma Mater's shoulders. *Save the mother who nourished you, noble men!* He dashed forward to add his blade to the melee of plunging steel over Caesar's body, raised it high, brought it down—

Stood alone.

Unwounded, unmarked, untouched, Caesar lay naked at his feet. He could see every inch of the man's body: the scars of old encounters healed both dark and white, the stringy lines of muscle, the skin tanned leathery by southern suns and northern seas. The skin was whole. There were no fresh wounds.

He looked to left and right: The Senate house was empty. The shouts of the crowd outside had died. Not a sound penetrated the hall. Only Pompey's statue stood for witness. It was as if the rest of the conspiracy had taken wing, transformed by the intervention of some god of the old tales into swans or hawks or vultures, leaving the slaying of the old eagle entirely in Brutus' hands.

He looked down.

Well, my son? Caesar's voice would outlive his years. It held a young man's strength, and the power to work wonders. Caesar's eyes held him captive in their unblinking black gaze. *What will you do?*

"My duty," he said simply, without even the hesitation of a breath, and the black dagger sank itself full-length in Caesar's heart.

The old man died. Task done, Brutus turned to go, to find where the others had flown. A shock of agony slammed into his chest. Unbidden, his hand rose to lay itself over the pain—

—and found blood, and the dagger's hilt, and greater pain. He fell to the floor of the Senate house, the stone cold along his spine. Above him, Pompey's sculpted face still stared out at nothingness. He turned his head to the side and met Caesar's death-glazed eyes. The old man leered, a rictus of the grave.

Then, against all possibility, the blue lips moved: *And now, my son? What will you do now?* The corpse opened its mouth in laughter that became a scream.

Brutus sat bolt upright on his bed, shivering with sweat, Caesar's death-cry on his own lips. When the heaving of his belly stilled enough to let him move without fear of spewing up last night's frugal dinner, he set his bare feet on the chill tiles, tossed a light mantle over his night tunic, and crept into his own garden like a common thief.

What did it mean, the evil dream? He believed in the here and now; he mistrusted visions. He paced the length of the peristyle like the captive beasts brought in from Africa Province for the games. Back and forth, back and forth, beating away the fury and the panic and the fear with the whip of constant motion. At last he regained command of himself, drawing in long, deep, slow breaths, one after the other.

The night was beautiful around him. He embraced that beauty. He had schooled himself to ignore the lesser physical discomforts, and so the chill that would have sent another man back for footwear and a heavier mantle only served to refresh him. The many scents of the garden were a welcome distraction from the dream.

"Ivory or horn?" he murmured to himself as he stooped to pluck a flower. Its head was closed against the night; he could not tell by the heaven's light what sort it might reveal itself to be when it opened, rich in fragrance or valued only for its loveliness.

"Do you need to know the future so badly, Brutus?" asked a voice behind him.

He whirled, tense as a scent-taken hound, his body springing into a Roman soldier's unshakable stance for a standing fight. His eyes probed the shadows.

"I am here."

Now the voice came from behind him again. A second time he spun to face its source and saw only the gray shapes of plants, the walls of the house, the pale candle of a statue he had brought into the garden to please his wife. It was the figure of a young Greek boy, holding a pet sparrow to his laughing cheek. The bloodless starlight drank the simple joy from the stone face, giving the lovingly carved features a sly and sinister cast.

A slender hand, warmer white against the marble, stroked the boy's rounded thigh. The lady smiled, looking up into that frozen face, staring at the stone sparrow pressed against it. "Here is one lad who won't need to study how to be cruel to his lover," she said.

"Who are you?" Brutus asked. He did not raise his voice; it was only a woman. He would feel more than a fool if he roused the servants for this. She was dressed like a proper Roman matron, her mantle drawn up in a hood over her head. With her face concealed and revealed by chance, he could not accurately guess her age. She sounded young. "How did you come into my house?"

Her laughter ran over him like a mountain waterfall, clear and icy cold. "No door closes to me." She reached up and drew back her mantle.

If he had seen a face like hers before, it was in dreams with gentler wakings than the one he'd suffered through this night. He remembered being a lad, just free of the striped toga of childhood, mooning over his mind's own image of long-dead Lucretia, beautiful and strong. King Tarquin's son raped her, sure of her silence after, but she would not let the crime go unpunished, unavenged. She had not hesitated to take her own life as a pledge to her true testimony, even though she was only a woman. She turned her dishonor into a sword to cut the throats of kings.

This woman was Lucretia come again. There had been much talk in the streets these past few days of wonders.

Brutus did not believe in portents touching on what he and the rest had planned to do, but he could hear of such events without needing to believe in them. If men could carry living fire in their hands unhurt and the night sky be filled with uncanny lights and noises, why could this not be the ghost of old Roma's noblest woman? And why should she not come to him?

Then the lady said, "You are discourteous, Brutus. I have heard you are spare of speech, but this—! I see by your eyes that you have already judged me and decided on a verdict. Is speech between us unnecessary?"

He shook his head. It felt heavy, as if the fumes of the Delphic priestess' tripod had stolen into his brain. "I know—" He hesitated. "I know who I *think* you are. I don't know who you might truly be."

"You always were a careful man." She gave him an approving look. "You do not rush headlong into the pit until you have first scouted the edge of it for a ladder. They had much to do to convince you to become one of their party, Cassius and the rest."

She spoke of his friend and the other conspirators so calmly. How much did she know, and how had any woman come into possession of the knowledge? He had kept his own counsel after the decision was made to join the plot, for Roma's sake. Only Portia knew, but his wife was no ordinary woman. Brutus was too wise to the world's ways to expect to find another of her sex and strength in these times. This woman, whoever she might be, was no Portia, and his reason sneered at the fancy that had made him think—even for a moment—that she was the woman of his ideals. No matter how her beauty opened him to the heart, he knew each generation could raise up only one Lucretia.

"Who sent you?" he demanded, threat creeping wolflike into his voice. "Who are you? Speak!"

"Here is all I am." Her hands fluttered to her shoulders like doves, her gown falling to a spill of fine wool at her feet. She stepped free of it and came into his arms. "Do you need to know more?"

Her arms were around his neck, the perfume of her skin the scent of the garden itself, the garden in full bloom under the spring's quickening sun. When her lips parted to his, he thought he tasted honey.

He shoved her away to arm's length without ceremony, though his head reeled and his mouth burned. "Whose whore, then, if you won't tell me your own name?"

Her eyes, of a blue that tugged at the skirts of his memory, grew wide, the sooty lashes almost sweeping the gull-wing brows. Her lips compressed themselves around the one word—*whore?*—without sounding it even to a whisper. Then: "You care too much for names, Brutus. It was a name that set your feet on the path of parricide."

"My father is dead," Brutus replied stiffly. "It was Pompey's pleasure that he die."

"Pompey? You used to treat the man like the foul air that gusts from a tannery. If he passed you in the street, you drew aside your toga as though the very touch of his shadow on your clothes was an unspeakable pollution. And yet you stood with Pompey at Pharsalia. Why?"

"I stood with the cause, not the man."

"Then why do you stand with the man now, and not the cause?"

His face tightened in a look of honest puzzlement. "What are you babbling about? Why are you here? To what good? If you come from Cassius or one of the others, you do our design no good by keeping me awake at this hour."

"And if I come from one who knows of your plans and yet would see Caesar live?" Her brows lifted, her gaze probed his soul.

"Rubbish. Armed men would come with you, then. There would be no need for—" He waved one hand rapidly, nervously at her flaunting nakedness, as if the gesture could dismiss the fact.

She was relishing all this; she could not hide her pleasure. "Did you never think that some who know your intentions and oppose them have no means to summon armed men? And some have no need of them at all." She folded her hands behind her back as if she were a child called upon to recite and strolled back to the statue of the boy and the sparrow. "You will not escape my question by diverting me. I want an answer: Why do you stand with the man?"

At the end of all patience, Brutus thundered, "What man?" He no longer cared if he roused the household. All he had left was the desperate need to banish this woman, with her beauty and her fire, before he saw his sleep-robbed self caught up in her madness.

"The man they wish to make you: Junius Brutus, the man who brought down the kings." A sudden stern look eclipsed her mask of gentleness. "Junius Brutus the paragon, the whip with which they drive you where they will, like an ox. You are called Brutus—you who care so much for names!—but must you allow them to reduce you to a brute beast because it is their pleasure?"

"They thought Junius Brutus was thickwitted, so he earned the name," Brutus replied evenly, trying to hold back his anger. She could say what she liked about him, to his face, but he would not stand for any tongue to soil his holy ancestor's name. "His actions proved their error. The name is one I bear with pride, no matter what it means."

"If you act with Cassius, it will come to mean the lowest form of treachery. Caesar spared your life after Pharsalia, pardoned Cassius on your word, favored you over him for the praetorship of city—"

"Put on some clothes," Brutus told her, thin-lipped. "If you've come to plead with me for Caesar's life, don't expect me to listen to your words when my mind is preoccupied."

She gave him a searching look, mischievous. "Would

you clothe all statues, then? Or is it only my body that can turn you from stone to flesh? You don't *look* much like Galatea."

He threw his own mantle in her face.

"Very well. To please you." She settled it over her shoulders, but contrived to drape it so that she was almost as naked as before. "What will you do to please me?"

Brutus did not answer. He searched the shadows, anticipating the arrival of the slaves his shout must have awakened. Where were they? For that matter, where was Portia? He had slept apart from her these past few nights, unwilling to have his own troubled thoughts break her rest as well. She had objected, but on this he stood firm. She claimed she slept fitfully without him, yet neither his shout of temper at this intruder nor his earlier cry of fear on awakening had brought her running. The air of the garden, of the whole house seemed thick as oil, like the air of dreams where a fleeing man breaks his heart to run but can not seem to lift one foot before the other. It caught and smothered all sounds.

The woman made an impatient noise and cast aside the mantle. "The sun comes," she said. "I want your sworn oath before the first rays touch the sparrow's wing." She pointed at the statue of the Greek boy.

"My oath to withdraw from the conspiracy?"

"Your oath to thwart it, and to save Caesar. You, to whom Duty is the greatest god, you will give me your oath to do a son's loyal duty and save your father's life!"

He gaped at her. For the first time since her coming it did not matter whether she went clothed or bare before him. Her words had blanked all else from his mind. "My father," he said slowly, "is dead."

"Servilia's husband is dead," the woman replied.

She reached her hands up to the wealth of coiled and interwoven plaits adorning her head and withdrew two pins. Hair bronze and gold as autumn sunlight tumbled over her shoulders while Brutus' rational mind objected that only two small pins could never have restrained so much.

He would have protested, but she gave him no time. Like a panther she leaped towards him, holding the pins. She was all insanity, a Bacchante with streaming hair, and she sank the glittering points into his eyes.

He collapsed beneath her, arms crossed before his eyes too late to ward off the attack. He felt nothing when the pins drove home, but knew the darkness they brought.

Darkness, and out of darkness a cool, gray glow. Shades walked through it, men of rank and honor, wearing the toga of senators. He was in the Senate house again, only now the faces were either wholly unfamiliar to him or younger versions of faces he did know. It was strange to see this man or that with the gloss of youth still on him, when Brutus only knew him as wrinkled, balding, with brown spots covering the crinkled skin.

Two men stood up, locked in hot debate. He heard the name *Catiline* flying from their lips, plain to hear, as well as slipping in whispers from the mouths of the other senators. Brutus shuddered at the name. Traitor to his birth, to his class, to all that was sacred to the Republic, Catiline had conspired to murder the consuls, to bring back the bloodbaths of Sulla's time.

Traitor, Brutus thought. *But one whose plots were uncovered in time.*

And if they had succeeded? She was even there, in his thoughts, in his visions. *You who are a man of virtue, tell me this: If a bad cause triumphs, is victory purification enough?*

Bodiless, he could not close his ears against her words. Eyeless, he could not help but watch the men at their debate. One was his uncle Cato, the other Caesar. The argument between them kindled, filling the Senate house with the pent energy of a thunderstorm about to break. There had been some rumor linking Caesar himself to

Catiline's filthy doings, which added more sparks to the tinder. Every eye present was fixed on the pair.

Then a slave came in carrying a message. He was Caesar's slave and he handed the note to his master as he must have delivered a score and more of the same. If the words contained the seeds of mourning or joy, it was all one to him. Caesar took the note, dismissed the man, and began to read it to himself.

Cato seized upon this simple act as a means to humiliate his rival, or in the best of worlds to bring him down. These were uncertain times: Who could say for sure whether the names of all of Catiline's fellow-traitors were known? On the basis of such a small scrap, Cato accused Caesar of correspondence with the enemy, demanded that the contents of the note be made public, here and now. A general cry went up from the assembly, backing him.

Caesar regarded Cato and his hunting pack with the same unruffled expression that many men had come to know and dread. He offered up the note to Cato freely. Brutus' uncle read it, his brow darkening. Here was no conspiracy against the state. Here were only the tender, intimate words of a woman to her lover, writing of pleasures shared, pleasures anticipated, urging his swift return to her arms. And that woman Cato's own sister, Servilia. He threw the note back at Caesar. "Keep it, you drunkard," he snarled, and redfaced, returned to the debate at hand.

A breeze sweet with myrtle stroked Brutus' cheek. He was in his garden again, his sight restored. There was a bench beside the wall, a painted marble bench that stood near the espaliered pear tree that bore only a handful of small, hard fruits each season. He found himself seated there, with the woman beside him.

"Why do you think he spared you after Pharsalia?" she murmured. "Why do you think he has shown you so many favors? He knows. So do you, every time you see your face reflected in the surface of a pool of water. To cut him down and be called traitor is one thing; to be a parricide is worse."

"No." He pushed himself up from the bench and staggered to the pool in the center of the garden. Across the small expanse of water, the statue of the Greek boy flirted with him in vain. He sank to hands and knees and leaned forward, a strange Narcissus, staring and staring at the face the waters gave back to him. He saw what he had often seen before, and as often denied: Though the lips were a trifle fuller, the features softer than the old eagle's campaign-hardened looks, there was still too great a resemblance to be ignored. He recalled the whisperings among the slaves when he was a boy, that certain way his named father would study him when he thought the child was not looking, his mother's peculiar manner with him—part fondness, part embarrassment—that he saw her assume with no other child.

"Lies," he muttered. "Lies. Ivory-gate dreams."

A dainty foot touched his hand. He looked up, scaling her entrancing body with his eyes. "What will you do?" she asked, Caesar's words.

He fell back onto his haunches and took a breath that searched beneath the skin of fear to find his center. What would he do, unable now to deny whose son he was? Roman law reserved the worst of deaths for the man who killed his father, and the scorpion-whips of the Furies loved to feast on the bodies of kin-slayers. What would he do?

Then he recalled those other words that had come to him likewise in the dream: *I know you have a steady heart.*

"If he knows I am his son, if I know him for my father, it changes nothing." He made himself sound strong. "Junius Brutus killed his own sons when they conspired to bring back the Tarquin kings. He did what needed to be done, for the sake of Roma's freedom; I will not do less, not even if Caesar is my father. He's still a man who hungers to be king, and for once—may the gods help us—he is a man with the power to make it so. Marius, Sulla, Pompey, all had the armed men to back them, but Caesar's power is greater than the sword."

"Your fears are mine," she said. "When men depend on force to take their desires, that I can understand; that I can fight. But when they find other ways to conquer— " She shook her head.

"Then why would you have me spare him?"

"Because if I share your greatest fear, I also share your greatest love."

She knelt beside him and swept her fingertips over the surface of the pool.

Afterwards, lying on his back, looking up into a sky where stars paled and faded into the dawnlight, he could not say for certain what he had seen in the water. It was like those dreams whose effects lingered though their images were lost. If he tried hard, he could recapture some of it.

He remembered fire. First it was the flames of Caesar's pyre in the Campus Martius. Someone spoke over the body—was it his face or Antony's he saw, or was it both by turns? The people set up a terrible wailing. Some seized burning brands from the pyre and ran with them through the streets, crying for vengeance.

He remembered blood. Armies marched against one another, more wars of Roman against Roman, while the city herself lay bleeding. Then rising from a pool of blood, a crown: The kingly crown that he and the others would have kept from Caesar's head at sword's point. The blood worked a strange magic on the crown, softening the gold until it ran into a new shape, the shape of the laurel wreath that all Romans recognized as a mark of honor, but never as a threat.

The blood trickled away as a man's head emerged from the pool beneath the crown. Brutus could not discern the face, streaked with red, but the power of the vision made a soothsayer of him. In the eyes he could read the deeds of the man.

Deeds! Vileness, atrocity, infamy, Roma shamed. Old men in the robes of senators huddled together in fear like rain-drenched chickens, powerless phantoms escaped from Hades' realm. Toadstool palaces sprang from the seven hills, excessive, gaudy as seaport whores. Within their walls were luxury and dissipation to outdo any Brutus had seen or heard tell of in oriental realms. The gods of Roma and all they stood for languished, the streets filled with the triumphal processions of foreign cults, their temples and too-smooth-faced priests crowding out the native faith and virtues of the old Romans. It was all noise and spectacle, hollow as a blown egg.

And through all this, Brutus saw the face of the man who wore the simple wreath shift shape, reform, change from one face to many, each following each until all became a blur. The wreath was the only thing that remained unchanged.

Brutus felt cold earth under his back. He closed his eyes, not wanting to remember more. But it was no use: Not all the training of boyhood, youth and manhood could leave him master over his own memory. It brought forth what it willed.

This one portion of the seeing he remembered perfectly, above all others: The man's head sank back into the pool of blood, leaving the wreath to float upon the surface. Two gnarled hands raised it, dripping, from the blood. An aged woman, clad in beggar's rags, stood holding out the laurel wreath of victory. Tears streamed from her eyes in torrents, but could not wash the crimson stains from the gold.

Not one king! she cried in a voice that cracked with despair. *Not one of them to claim that hated title, yet without it they were still kings in fact, kings in deed. What does a word matter? Still he was killed for the sake of a word. They killed him, they said, to save the Republic;*

the·Republic that is as dead as he. As I. She let the crown fall into the dust. *They found a different word to serve them:* Imperator! *Now jackals fight over my bones. Let me perish.*

She tore away her dark mantle and showed the scrawny body of a crone, but where the sagging breasts should be, Brutus saw instead the many teats of a she-wolf. Roma Mater lifted her face to the heavens and howled.

"*No!*" He sprang up as he had started from the dream, this time with a shriek that should have woken all his household and the neighbors too. The echoes of it died without a single hint of stirring from the house. Not even the watchdog in his kennel barked.

Smooth hands slipped over his shoulders, drawing him down into the woman's lap. He let himself be cradled against the softness of her breast like an infant. "I swear to you by any oath you care to name that I have shown you the truth," she said. "Bring his death and this is how it will be for Roma."

For a time he could not speak. His mind was too stunned. He had been schooled in the Stoic tenets of acceptance, but he would wager that none of the old masters ever had to accept a night like this. She stroked his brow, her fingers wet. He touched the dampness and held his own fingers in front of his face to see if she had anointed him with water or blood. They were clean.

"I have decided," he said, and he swore the oath she asked. The thought of what he had done took possession of his body and he shuddered in every limb.

"Hush," she breathed, and took him into her arms more sweetly. He clung to her at first because he was overwhelmed by what he had promised her. To save Caesar! How? Even if he withheld his blade, the others would not turn back from the task. He saw it as hopeless, knew he would die with Caesar as the dream had foretold. Perhaps that would be best. His life until this had been lived by decisions and certainties, the unquestioned demands of virtue. Now he had lost all that to a vision and a woman unlike any other. He held her to him more tightly and loved her as if this taking of the body's joy were his last reality.

They did not linger in each other's embrace when they were done. She helped him rise from the earth and led him around the garden pool to where the Greek boy still cupped his pretty sparrow. She stroked the stone wings with her fingertips as the first true light touched it.

The wing fluttered, colored, fledged, and the living sparrow took to the air, twittering. Brutus followed its flight, his soul lost to the miracle.

When he looked back from the sparrow's escape, she was gone.

He walked slowly back into the house. He did not see the hooded figure watching him from the shelter of the peristyle.

CHAPTER TWO

The Senate had been called to meet in the portico of the theater which Pompey had had built for the greater beauty of Roma. It was not the place of Brutus' dream, which gave him a pang of uncertainty. "Ivory or horn?" he murmured to himself as he mingled with his fellows in the shadow of Pompey's statue.

"Did you say something?" Cassius asked, keen-eared as the fox he so closely resembled.

"Nothing that matters." He felt the weight of his concealed shortsword press against his side. He had left the dagger at home. He did not think it was fit to bring the sacred blade with him now, when his purpose was so different, and as for the end his new plans might have—

If a spirit could shrug, his did. What would be, would be. He might dream dreams and see otherworldly visions, but he had no illusions. The conspiracy relied on the fact that once their blades were raised against Caesar, the other senators would not interfere, some because they sympathized wholeheartedly with the assassination of the tyrant, some out of plain fear to fall with Caesar. If he turned on his former allies, they would not waste much time in cutting him down. Oh, his name and reputation might have been what galvanized the conspiracy, but once it was all set in motion he would find that respect makes poor armor. He was only one man.

For the fifth time that morning he wondered whether he had done a wise thing in not commanding his slaves to stand by him in this, or the freedmen clients who depended so heavily on his favors. They owed him service; what greater one could they provide than helping save his life while he saved Caesar's?

Again the answer came, unchanged: He could not do it. If he died in spite of their support, what would become

16

of them? Slaves and freedmen who laid hands on patricians faced a stern judgement, sterner yet if Brutus' plan failed. A triumphant conspiracy would not make Caesar's mistake of pardoning foes too freely. He knew that that was not Cassius' way, at least. He could not drag innocent men into a fight that wasn't theirs, where they had nothing to gain and all to lose. That was not *his* way.

"You don't look well." Cassius spoke softly, with a challenge in his voice.

"I'm fine. I—Portia had a restless night. I had to comfort her." The lies came freely; his soul cringed.

Cassius chuckled and laid a hand on Brutus' shoulder. "She'll sleep more securely tonight, I promise you. And I confess, so will I."

"Your son looked very much the man this morning." Brutus changed the subject quickly, if not artfully.

It didn't seem to matter. Cassius beamed at Brutus' mention of the lad, who an hour or so earlier had gone through the rites signifying his departure from boyhood. The ceremony marking the boy's fourteenth year took place in the forum, under the eyes of Brutus, many of the conspiracy, and several other friends, relatives and well-wishers. Tradition called for there to be a party later, in Cassius' house. A party! Brutus hoped that his nephew hadn't had his heart set on it.

Cassius spoke as if he were any ordinary patrician father whose only purpose in the Senate this day was to take pride in his son: "I admit it will take me by surprise a time or two, seeing him without the *bulla* round his neck, and wearing a grown man's toga instead of a child's. I caught Junia weeping over him last night while he slept."

"Weeping?" Brutus frowned. "There's only one way to keep a boy from growing into a man. If she'd considered that, she wouldn't have wept."

"You're too hard on your sister," Cassius chided. "That, or Portia's spoiled you for all other women."

Brutus said nothing, remembering last night and the

nameless woman. Just thinking about her made the blood run hot beneath his skin. As deep as his affection for Portia lay rooted to his bones, he had never felt such desire for her. Portia's embraces satisfied him; this woman's touch left him ravening. Discreetly he reached inside his toga to run his fingers over as strange a charm as ever a man carried who did not believe in such trinkets: A sparrow's feather.

"Don't tell me you expect Junia to be a philosopher too," Cassius pressed. He was never one to let go of an argument. "Your sister puts on a solemn matron's face in public, but she's as foolishly tenderhearted as any woman behind our walls. I'm glad she wasn't with us in the forum when he received his first shave. There was hardly anything worth reaping in that field; the barber nicked him, trying to find something worth scraping off. It bled, but he kept his toga clean and he didn't make a sound. You can be proud of your nephew, my friend."

"Sometimes I think there's little sense in these old rituals," Brutus said quietly. Before Cassius could question him, a petitioner approached with praetor's business for Brutus to settle. He gave himself up gratefully to hearing out the fellow's case.

The sun climbed. Caesar did not come. The senators milled about, some hearing petitions, some making plans to dine together, some gossiping, some silent. Only the silent ones failed to make some comment about Caesar's absence.

"I hear tell that when he made a sacrifice the other day, they found that the beast had no heart," one remarked to his neighbor, within Brutus' hearing.

"That's an evil omen," the other said, making a hasty gesture to ward off ill luck. "We might as well not look to see him here today."

"Don't be so sure. Caesar treats portents the way he treats women: They're fair if it suits him to say they're fair. If it's his pleasure to be here, he'll come; otherwise, he'll use that omen as a convenient excuse for his absence."

"Why would he want to be absent? He's the one who called for this meeting!"

The first senator turned his hands palm upwards. "I've given up trying to read Caesar's purpose these days. You know the talk: He wants to make himself king."

Again his comrade made the warding sign. "Roma rid herself of kings long ago; to reinstate them would be sacrilege."

Laughter met those words. "You exaggerate! If it were such sacrilege, why is there a prophecy in the Sybilline books saying that we'll never conquer the Parthians unless we are led by a king?"

The other man shook his head. "The *surviving* Sybilline books," he stressed.

"You're as picky as an old woman. Well, perhaps today we'll reach a decision to satisfy everyone. I understand we're to consider giving Caesar a crown—"

"Jupiter—!"

"Calm yourself; Roma's safe. He'd only wear the diadem outside of Italy, in the provinces, where they're used to kings."

"Are you sure of this?" the other asked earnestly.

The first spread his empty hands once more. "As sure as I am of anything I hear tell of. I do know that Caesar himself has refused to accept a crown on Roman soil more than once, before today, publicly."

"Because the people showed themselves against it."

"Then I hope today's decision pleases them as well as you. For myself, I couldn't care less." Their conversation turned to other matters, and Brutus himself was distracted by yet another petitioner.

When he had a moment free from the demands of his office, he glanced around to see how the others were bearing up under Caesar's delay. If his own feelings were any gauge, each man must be in agonies of impatience to have the enterprise over and done with, and that quickly.

Fear of discovery, fear of reprisals, a thousand uncertainties all formed their own conspiracy to feed upon the spirits of the men who would kill Caesar.

Under the circumstances, they were doing well. Brutus noted some of them—praetors like himself—hearing cases calmly and patiently. Their faces betrayed nothing, their decisions were given as if their sole purpose in coming to the Senate today was to render this service to the citizens.

"Astonishing," he said under his breath. It had taken all of Cassius' powers of compulsion to turn a pack of grumbling malcontents into a group of men united in their cause. Like a ropemaker, Cassius had to plait many fragile threads into a single cord without allowing any to escape his hand. For this task, every thread must be kept taut, and until the work was done there was always the danger that one would spring loose or snap altogether. But this rope seemed likely to hold strong until it dropped around Caesar's neck.

So Brutus thought. Cassius beckoned to him. Their duties had separated them, but now the true leader of the conspiracy made terse signs with his hand, commanding Brutus' attention. A third sharer in the plot stood with Cassius: Casca. Brutus had never cared much for the man.

Casca looked pale and ill, and Cassius' thin lips were pressed together hard. "What's wrong?" Brutus asked.

"It seems that you're a traitor to our cause," Cassius said softly.

The magic that had touched the carved sparrow took its price: Brutus turned to stone in its place. A score of reactions raced through his head—denial, counteraccusation, admission, flight. Not one showed on his face. He waited—unmoved, unmoving—his eyes resting steadily on Casca's. He could count the drops of sweat on the man's brow and follow one that lost its hold, trickling down into Casca's eyes, making him blink and wipe it away. The only thought he could force into words was: *So this is how it ends.*

Then Casca burst into speech: "Don't say it that way, Cassius. Don't I feel like enough of a fool? I was wrong to tell you about the incident in the first place."

"What incident?" Brutus asked, wondering what Cassius and Casca would say if they could see how his knees shook with sudden weakness beneath the purple-striped toga. Cassius allowed himself a thin flash of teeth to stand in place of a smile. "Some fellow or other accosted our friend Casca here and said—"

"He said we'd kept the secret from him, but that you'd told him everything," Casca blurted to Brutus. "What was I to think?"

"To *think*," Cassius stressed. "That was what you were supposed to do. I don't think I care to know how close you came to revealing everything." He shook his head almost imperceptibly over Casca's near-fatal blunder.

"But what *did* the man mean?" Brutus asked.

Casca snorted. "He wanted to know how I was suddenly rich enough to stand for the post of aedile. By Mercury, some of these old owls meddle worse than women!" He huffed and puffed himself up with enough indignation to cover his embarrassment.

"And some of these geese squawk too readily." Cassius made it clear that this was no joke. His eyes were winter seas. Casca deflated like a pierced bladder; he shivered and moved away.

"You can't blame him," Brutus said for Cassius' ears alone. "When a man is on edge, the shadow of the ax looks very much like the ax itself. He sees it fall his way and jumps aside."

"You've been reading your Plato again," Cassius replied indifferently. "We didn't come here today to discuss philosophy." He cast a sharp look past Pompey's statue to the entryway of the portico. "Curse it, what's keeping him?" His left hand, knotted in the folds of his toga, clenched so tightly that the knuckles were white.

Before he could answer, another man descended upon

them. Brutus recognized the senator Popilius Laenas, but he was unprepared for the heartiness of the greeting he and Cassius now received. Embracing them both warmly, the man insinuated his head between theirs and whispered, "My wishes are with you. May all your plans succeed, but soon. What you mean to do is no longer secret." Having said this, he uttered a false laugh like a donkey's bray and sailed off to greet other senators.

"Well!" Cassius took a deep breath between gritted teeth and let it out in a whistle. "Fortuna is on our side so much, at least: That Casca was nowhere near to hear that! He might have run off straightaway to Caesar's house to throw himself on the tyrant's mercy."

A mercy you and I both have enjoyed, Brutus thought. Cassius settled the folds of his toga carefully and remarked, "I think we'll all be the better for it if I keep him under my eye from now on." He went to put his words into effect at once.

Brutus watched him go, then glanced to where Popilius Laenas was presently in conversation with Trebonius. He wondered what was being said. *If the fool well-wishes every one of us—of them—in the same way he did Cassius and me, surely one will snap. 'What you mean to do is no longer secret', oh yes, there's what a fearful man needs to hear! Pour those words in the right ears and all plots against Caesar's life will crumble and scatter to the four winds like crumbs of stale bread. There will be no need for me to do anything at all to save Caesar. Perhaps it was enough that I gave my oath to—to the gods alone know whom. I can't deny their presence in all this; she was no common messenger. And since all the wonders of last night must have come from the gods, I can see their works in this day's events too. My part is accomplished: The intention can be as good as the deed, where the gods are concerned. The scent of a burning sacrifice nourishes them the same as the beast's body.*

A stir from the entryway drew Brutus' attention. He

saw one of the slaves from his own house crossing the floor, a haggard look about him. The fellow scanned the faces of all the senators present, searching for his master, his own expression urgent and reluctant at the same time. Whatever word he brought, it was not good.

Brutus felt his stomach shrink, but by this time he had practiced maintaining the shell of calm for so long that it was second nature. He hailed the slave in a clear, firm voice. "Here, Dion." For a time master and man stood eyeing one another as if this were their first meeting.

He's as reluctant to tell me his news as I am to hear it, Brutus thought. He forced himself to scowl and demand, "Don't just stand there: Speak. What have you—?"

"She's dead, Master!" The words burst from Dion's lips at the same time that the tears burst from his eyes. "Our mistress is dead!"

An invisible pilum drove into Brutus' heart. His breathing became shallow, every breath sending red flashes over his sight. Fighting the icy current that battered his spirit down, he held the edge of his toga like a lifeline and asked, "How did it happen?" His voice was as controlled and measured as if he were standing in judgement over the household watchdog for stealing meat from the cooks.

Dion's eyes widened a little, searching his master's face for some indication of human grief. His expression darkened with disapproval, but only slightly—it was not a slave's place to judge his master openly by word or sign.

Clever Dion, Brutus thought. *And what shall I call myself for keeping this mask frozen over a torn heart? Clever too, or merely well disciplined? Or am I just . . . dead? I have no hope of fulfilling my oath to save Caesar. When he comes—if he ever comes—all I can offer is a token: My willingness to shed my blood with his. My feet are already on the road to Avernus, following my wife.*

He came out of his thoughts, realizing that the slave had been speaking to him for a while. He tried to glean what information he could from the few last words Dion spoke:

"—fell, and her women raised a cry. One of them sent me here to tell you. The neighbors are at your door, all speaking of it. Master, I—"

"Trouble?" Cassius was at Brutus' back so suddenly that Brutus jerked aside, as if to face an assault.

"My wife—Portia is dead."

Cassius' hand clamped over Brutus' hard as a boarhound's grip. "You're sure?"

"My mistress was nervous all morning," Dion spoke up. "She kept sending one of us after the other to the forum for word of our master. I myself came here twice already. Each time we came home not knowing what to tell her: We saw Master tending to affairs, nothing extraordinary. Still she wouldn't be still, rushing back and forth inside the house, until at last—so Chrysilla came running to tell me—she collapsed and all her women set up a cry that she was dead."

"The alarms of women . . ." Cassius flavored the words with scorn. He lowered his voice almost to the point of inaudibility and commanded Brutus, "You will not leave us now."

Brutus jerked his hand free of Cassius' grip. "Go home, Dion," he told the slave. "I will follow." To Cassius he said in the same placid, matter-of-fact tone, "I know my duty."

Cassius inclined his head, the ghost of a reverence. "I spoke too harshly."

"Until Caesar comes, nothing will take me from this place. If my wife is dead, well then, my rushing home will not bring her back from the shades. I'm no Orpheus." He turned his face from Cassius, sick of the man.

"You're pale enough to pass for one of Pluto's subjects." Cassius' voice was as insinuating as himself. "Go outside and see whether there's any news of Caesar. The air will revive you."

Brutus' look was a hawk's. "Are you so concerned for my welfare, or do you just enjoy giving orders?"

"I—" For a moment Brutus enjoyed the rare treat of watching Cassius quail. "I meant nothing ill by it. I only thought you might—"

"I'll go." Brutus left without another word. It took all his effort not to run into the blessed daylight. For the past few hours he had felt the weight of gigantic, unseen things pressing down upon his shoulders, presences he could not name reaching out with hands of smoke to stop his breath. Outside the theatre portico the air was freer, lively with the noise and bustle of Roma. But the air could not blow away the dread shrouding him, and the daylight could not reach into the cavern where his soul huddled alone.

Portia . . . He did not weep. He wondered at this. His chest ached, torn from within, but there were no tears. He recalled cold nights in camp when men traded tales of how during really freezing weather a ghastly numbness would creep slowly up their bodies, turning them to stone by inches. *Call* this *cold next to that? This is nothing!* they would conclude, trying to keep the cold off by laughing it away.

Brutus touched his heart. Beside this, even the petrifying chill of campfire legends would pall.

"Master! Master!" Dion came running through the crowds, shouldering and shoving his way back to Brutus' side.

"I told you to go home," Brutus said sternly.

"Master, I was, I *was* going home. But I had not gone far before I saw little Hiero, the cook's son, racing towards me. When I made him stop and questioned him, he told me wonderful news: She lives! Our mistress is not dead. They sent him from the house after me to tell you so. It was only a faint, but her women were so frightened by it that they assumed—"

Brutus raised one hand to stay Dion's clattering tongue. "What became of the boy?"

"Hiero?" Dion shrugged. "I sent him back to the house again."

"You will both be rewarded." There was nothing in Brutus' words to hint that he understood well enough Dion's true motives in sending the boy back: Good news from only one mouth, the thanks-gift for it paid into only one purse. Nevertheless, the slave colored up scarlet and begged leave to go home.

Brutus had no sooner granted this than his eye caught a peculiar figure loitering near the theatre building itself. It was a man, very closely muffled up, though the weather didn't demand such protection. He slumped against the wall, his stylus hastily scribbling over a child's wax tablets. he was so engrossed in his own work that he was unaware when Brutus stole up beside him and cast a look over what he was writing: It was a letter to Caesar, warning him of the conspiracy, naming names.

"Caesar will not read your message if it comes to his hand so humbly, Artemidorus," he said. "Couldn't you afford the papyrus?"

The man jumped, hugging the tablets to his chest. "My life—" he gasped. His eyes bulged with terror, darted over Brutus' hands, seeking the expected dagger.

"Peace." Brutus knew it was a useless word as well as he knew this poor, shuddering fellow. Artemidorus of Cnidos was no warrior; he was a teacher of logic, and therefore all the more likely to fly to pieces when his orderly perception of the world was set on end by some unexpected occurrence. "Stop shaking. Take your warning for Caesar and go away. There is only one life in danger today, and it's not yours."

The Cnidian stammered something—thanks and disavowal all jumbled together—and fled without waiting for a second invitation. Brutus rubbed his chin. *Yes, it's better if you run away, my friend. Better that than stand to see your brush with courage turn futile before your eyes. Caesar would never have read your warning in time—I know him. He's always so beset by petitioners on these public occasions that he invariably passes their notes to his servants and looks to them later. Your intentions were good, but sometimes the gods refuse to be satisfied with anything less than a true sacrifice. I was a fool to believe anything else.*

The street noises grew louder. Brutus craned his head in the direction of the mounting clamor. He could just see the top of a litter pushing its way down the street, and given the swarming crowds around it he didn't have to wait to hear the name the people shouted to know who rode within.

So he's come.

Someone laid a hand on his back. "I would never have marked you for an impatient man, Brutus." Antony's high-browed face, full of bluff good humor as always, favored Brutus with a broad smile. "What business do you have with Caesar today, that it can't wait for him to come into the Senate? Waylaying him in the streets like this, it must be something out of the ordinary."

Brutus took in Antony at a glance. There was much about him that revolted Brutus' austere nature: the drinking bouts, the liking for childish pranks, the countless dalliances with other men's wives. Some would call the man generous, but it was all generosity done for show. In Brutus' opinion here was a wastrel, a prodigal, one who had never known the meaning of *enough* in anything, least of all wine. Still, here was also a man of strength and courage in battle, devoted to Caesar. He could use Antony.

"Truthfully, I was waiting for you," Brutus said. *A chance,* he thought. *Here is the gods' own gift. All I must do is take it.*

"Is that so?" Antony's large eyes blinked slowly. "Walk with me into the Senate, then. We can talk better there, without the distractions of the street."

"No!" Only after the word flew from lips, almost a shout,

did Brutus realize how sharply he'd spoken. Caesar's litter was stopping before the theatre portico. He imagined he could see Cassius' ravening face peering out, tense yet satisfied, a sliver of white in the shadows. "Here."

Antony shook his head. "I'm wanted inside. Caesar slept poorly last night, and Calpurnia worse. He's here over her objections, if that's not too weak a word to put to the scene in his house all this morning. Poor woman! It's courting misfortune to repeat what she dreamed. I'll only tell you that she summoned enough soothsayers to rewrite the lost Sybilline books, every one of them entreating Caesar not to leave the house today."

"Yet here he is," Brutus murmured.

Antony shrugged. "He wasn't afraid of dreams, but seeing as his wife was almost out of her mind with fear, he would have humored her."

"That's the worst thing you can do with women," a third voice cut in. "Never give them their way on trifles." Decimus Brutus Albinus wedged himself squarely between Brutus and Antony. "Bow to one whim and you've got to bow to all. And if word of how you indulge the creatures reaches the ears of rational men—" His laughter was coarse and loud. "I've done Caesar a great service today."

"For which Caesar will thank you tomorrow, Albinus," Brutus said easily. He knew this other Brutus well: a fellow-conspirator, despite the fact that Caesar held him in such trust that he was named second heir in the dictator's will. So rumor said, at any rate.

"He will, if he can." Albinus was a poor actor. He gave the words too much ironic relish.

Toad, Brutus thought. If he had still counted himself as one of the plot, he would be pondering the best way to slit Albinus' stupid throat if the chance presented. As he was now, he knew he could not waste time on such fancies. Albinus' assigned task was to make sure Caesar arrived and then to keep Antony out of the way until the task was done. As if he had read Brutus' mind, Albinus began to draw Antony into conversation.

Caesar had descended from his litter. Brutus saw some of the senators coming out to meet the dictator. Among them was Popilius Laenas, who had been so effusive in his whispered support for the conspirators' plot. Now he was bent on greeting Caesar just as effusively, demanding the great man's attention.

They're speaking, Brutus observed closely. *Rather it's Laenas speaking, Caesar paying close attention. What's the man saying? Were all his protests of support a sham so that he might reveal the conspiracy?* He noted Cassius, who had also come a little way out of the portico to oversee Caesar's arrival. The man's face was a smear of ash with two burning coals for eyes.

Coals igniting a fire, Roma ablaze . . .

But no. If Laenas had told Caesar anything touching on the conspiracy, the dictator didn't seem to care whether he lived or died. His dignity upon him as always, Caesar gave the senator one of those diplomatic half-smiles of his, the sort he reserved for highly placed fools. In the center of the mob, Caesar was entering the portico.

"Albinus, I need a service," Brutus said, trying not to let his speech run out as fast as the beating of his heart. "Go to Cassius for me and tell him that the news I had was false: Portia is alive."

"Why don't you tell him yourself?" Albinus was on guard. With Casca, he was another of Cassius' taut strings overdue to snap.

The other man's doubts had a peculiar effect on Brutus. He disliked being questioned like this. It lessened who he was, who he knew himself to be. "I have business I must discuss with Antony," he said severely. "Cassius knows this."

"Ahhh. I see." Albinus rolled his eyes from Antony to Brutus, then towards the Senate house. Caesar was well inside by this time. "I am happy for the—the change in

the news." He squeezed Brutus' forearm and scuttled
off to join the others.

"Was it my fancy, or is there something odd about
Albinus today?" Antony scratched his head.

Brutus seized his arm and yanked it down, forcing the
man to face him. "Antony, are you armed?" he gritted.

Antony goggled at him. If this was his first run-in with
a lunatic, he didn't like it. "Armed?" he repeated vacantly.

Brutus had neither words nor time to waste. He plucked
aside his toga to show Caesar's Master of the Horse the
shortsword he himself carried. "There are more like this
in there," he said, nodding towards the portico. "All of
them ready, at the signal, to shed Caesar's blood. If you're
armed, we'll have a chance to stop them. We may die
doing it, but I'm resolved to die before I allow Caesar's
death."

"Caesar . . ." Antony's eyes were losing light, as if
someone had dealt him a stupefying blow to the skull.
"I'll bring men—" He tried to go.

Brutus' grip on that beefy arm tightened. "There is no
time. *Are* you armed?" Antony nodded. "Are you with
me?" Another nod. "Then come."

He strode back towards the portico, Antony stumbling
after. "Who are they? How many—?"

"Don't worry; you'll know them. They'll show themselves
at the given word."

"But—but if the first blow kills Caesar—"

"Caesar won't be an easy killing. Let's face one thing
at a time. Stay out of sight until you hear my shout. You
and I are supposed to be outside; they think I'm talking
with you to keep you from being on hand to rescue Caesar."

No longer overwhelmed by shock, Antony's military
bearing was back. This time his nod was crisp. "Surprise
is with us as much as with them. May Fortuna be with
us too."

Brutus did not reply. He left Antony standing out of
sight, hugging the outer facade of a pillar. The shadow

of the entryway fell over Brutus' face, daylight to his back. If Albinus had delivered his message to Cassius, no one would be looking to see him. Oh, Cassius would be fuming, most likely, to have his original arrangements overridden like this. He might be storing up a stream of choice words to mete out afterwards.

In the way the human mind has of focussing on trifles in the midst of disasters, Brutus realized that he really didn't like Cassius' self-righteous harangues at all. For that reason alone, he felt confident he had made the right decision on that night of vision and flame.

Caesar was in his chair, a host of petitioners surrounding him. Cassius pressed close on the right side, with Casca stationed behind the chair, along with Pontius Aquila and Marcus Spurius. Albinus and Servilius Galba were at the left, with a fidgety Cinna more than a sword's-reach off behind him. Tillius Cimber had the dictator's attention as he stood humbly before him, half-stooped as if on the point of falling to his knees. The brothers Bucolianus and Caecilius backed Cimber, and were themselves in turn crowded by Rubrius Ruga and Minitius Minus Basilus. Trebonius and Ligarius were edging their way closer to the group from opposite directions as Cimber's voice rose ever louder, ever more eloquent.

"—my brother. I beg of you, O Caesar, reconsider. Your generosity is already as far-famed as your military exploits. Mercy is no weakness. If you will rescind the decree of exile from Publius Cimber, here I am ready to stand guarantee for my brother's good behavior in future."

"Here we all stand, O Caesar," said Cassius softly.

Caesar scowled. His eyes looked more tired than angry. He held a scroll in his right hand—more than likely one last petition pressed on him as he took his place in the Senate, with no time to pass it to one of his attendants. As for the attendants themselves, Brutus could not see them anywhere. That was usual: They would be outside with the litter bearers, waiting for their master's return, gossiping, yawning, peeing against the wall, playing at dice or knucklebones to pass the time. If great decisions were made within the Senate chamber—decisions to affect them and their children—it was of less interest to them than how the dice landed and whether or not there would be something good to eat for dinner.

"Enough!" Caesar's voice, famed for its power, rang out through the pillared hall. "Let it go, Cimber; my mind is fixed. I have given judgement on your brother, the judgement stands—"

Brutus saw the hands dip into the folds of the togas, saw the conspirators press nearer, saw Casca's hand emerge first, the dagger a lightless shape in his hand. He moved forward, his own sword out, Antony's sandals slapping the floor behind him, just as Tillius Cimber grasped at Caesar's robe as any suppliant might, pulling it away, laying the neck bare.

"—and I will not rescind it."

"Then die!" Casca shouted or shrieked. His blade jerked down, shaking.

A clean stroke might have killed Caesar on the spot. As it was, he struck the dictator's neck at the base from the back, where the muscles were thickest and the draperies of the toga glanced off most of the blow. Caesar wheeled, seizing the dagger that was still in Casca's trembling hand.

"Casca!" Caesar's words were the crack of a thunderbolt. "What does this mean?"

"Help!" Casca yowled, lost to terror of his own deed. "Help me, brothers!" It was pathetic, but it was enough. Well or poorly dealt, from a hero's hand or a coward's, the first blow had served its purpose.

Now every conspirator's hand lifted up, swords and daggers raised so that none present in the Senate could mistake what they saw. They closed on Caesar, whose bellows of indignation and gasps of pain and shock were soon devoured by the grunts of men shoving each other roughly as each fought to have his blade too taste the victim's blood.

Brutus sped forward, but the air around him took on the same near-impenetrable quality he recalled from the dream. Every step seemed to fight its way through deep water. By the same token, the conspirators' blades too had become captive in time, pulling back and stabbing in slowly, slowly, with a ghastly grace. And Caesar's face writhed open-mouthed, no sound coming from the distended lips, though every edge that slipped into his flesh drove the eyes a little wider, bared the teeth a little more in an always changing grimace of pain.

Brutus watched his own hand rise like a sleepwalker's to seize Trebonius by the hair and pull the man's head back. His sword floated on air, then dove through. The harsh sound of steel grating against rib bones was muffled by the white wool of the toga. Trebonius' scream shattered the spell.

Time burst back onto its proper course. Cassius and the rest were staring at him where he stood over Trebonius' body, his sword stained with blood. Their arms were crosshatched with the marks of where they had cut one another in their struggle to reach Caesar, and two of their number—Naso and Bucolianus—lay bleeding badly. Most could not believe what their eyes had just told them and stood dumbstruck, their minds seeking an answer.

They had no time to find it. Antony stepped in front of Ligarius. His first swordstroke shattered the arm holding the sword. The man crumpled and a second stroke to the skull finished it. The other senators gasped and fled. Cinna and Galba ran with them.

Casca tried, but Brutus was waiting for him. He took a blow to the upper arm as he raced past. It cut deep, though not enough to stop him. Brutus let him go; he would be found later.

"Finish him," Cassius snarled at the remaining conspirators still ringing Caesar. He gestured curtly with

his sword, a shepherd turning his dogs. "Traitor." His eyes
were on no one but Brutus.

Time did not slow now; it froze, taking Brutus with it.
He dimly saw Antony stepping in to cut down Rubrius
Ruga with a slashing blow that sent blood gouting from
an opened neck. Unlucky Basilus strove to obey Cassius'
command, only to have his flesh mistaken for Caesar's
by the renewed attacks of Tillius Cimber and Albinus.
His sword-arm dangled, meat at his side. With Ruga dead,
Antony marked Aquila for his next man, but Aquila was
a fast learner by other men's mistakes: It only took a
blooding by Antony's blade to make him flee.

And over all, like a veil, like the moonlight seen through
the passage of a ghost, Brutus saw Cassius' sword
descending against him. He could see the tiny nicks and
pittings that marred the edge and found he had the time
to wonder whether a killing blow hurt at all.

Then his own sword pulled back and jabbed in and
up, piercing the thickest part of Cassius' carefully folded
toga, tearing through the tunic, finding no resistance of
bone. Time came unstopped as Cassius' body slammed
into his with the full force of the dead man's charge. Mad
thoughts danced through Brutus' head: Cassius was not
attacking him, he was committing suicide and had chosen
Brutus to help him by holding the sword.

Then in his ear the whisper, a serpent's breath: *"Traitor."*
Cloth dragged against cloth as Cassius slid down the length
of Brutus' body, his sword falling, Brutus' blade pulling
free, blood painting one long smear of red.

Brutus stared at the body sprawled at his feet. He was
still dreamwalking—this was not happening, his mind
could not encompass it. A shout distracted him, snapped
his eyes from Cassius' corpse. Antony was in close combat
with Tillius Cimber. The conspirator was plainly terrified
to have to face one of Roma's finest fighters, but terror
gave him supernatural strength. He was holding his own—
more than that, he was beating Antony back while Caesar,

wounded and bleeding, slumped against the base of Pompey's statue. He was holding off Caecilius and Marcus Spurius with—of all things to tempt the gods to laughter—his pencase.

Then Brutus saw Albinus come from behind the monument.

Antony could not reach him in time, beset by Cimber. Brutus started forward, a warning on his lips. His foot caught under Cassius' shoulder; he fell forward over the body. His thought as he fell was: *O Lady, all this and still Caesar will die!*

Caesar heard his cry, turned his head, saw Albinus, sword in hand. The old man dropped the scroll that he still clutched against all reason and dropped to the floor just as the blade stabbed down. His hand shot out, plunged under Trebonius' corpse. Battle-hardened fingers closed on the dead man's sword, battle-forged reflexes brought it up to jab into Albinus' unprotected belly. One Brutus watched the other gasp, then gurgle as Caesar gave the embedded sword a half-twist and yanked it out, followed by a flow of blood and a stink of entrails.

Caecilius and Spurius gaped at the impossible: a dead man himself dealing death. Caesar's eyes drew them into the abyss of Tartarus. Brutus heard them whimper like puppies before they bolted.

"Brutus! Help me!" Antony's plea fetched him. He clambered up from the floor and joined his sword to Antony's against Cimber. What had been a fight became a murder. Bleeding freely from a host of Antony's slashes, Cimber gathered his toga more closely about him, drew back his sword for a last blow, stabbed out blindly and fell.

There was silence in the Senate.

Antony dropped his sword and rushed to Caesar's side. Brutus stood where he was, over Cimber's body. The Senate house was deserted except for the three left living and the scattered dead. Brutus could hear a distant

tumult—word of the assassination had spilled into the
streets. People were running, shouting, panic was
spreading. Some cried that Caesar was dead, some
shrieked, some cheered, some called out that Antony had
died with him, and Brutus, and Cassius.

But he's not dead, Brutus thought dully. *Not yet. Those
wounds—*

He felt warm wetness seeping against his chest. Fresh
blood welled up, soaking into the white wool. Cimber's
last blow had found a mark.

From somewhere ever farther and farther away, Caesar
was calling his name. He opened his mouth to answer
and collapsed into darkness.

CHAPTER THREE

Traitor . . .

The word and the blood, always together, faithful haunters of his nights, good dream-hounds never leaving the trail of the one they'd marked for their master and their prey.

Traitor . . .

Cassius' disembodied face rising out of the darkness, the darkness deepening from holy black to obscene crimson, rivulets of blood like tears trickling from a death-mask's eyes.

Traitor . . .

A fluttering along the verges of the waxen eyelids. The mask floating on the surface of the scarlet pool as Caesar's spurned diadem had done—how long ago? Dreams knew no time. In dreams Brutus reached down to raise Cassius' dripping death-mask from the blood, held it at arm's length while the word came over and over and over again from the sealed, cool lips:

Traitor . . .

And the eyelids would always open then, exactly then. The eyelids would open and two small serpents, the horned asps of the Lybian desert, would spring from Cassius' empty sockets to sink their fangs into Brutus' helplessly staring eyes. No matter how many times the dream came, no matter that he knew it by heart, when the snakes leaped for him, mouths agape, fangs agleam, he could not look away. The fangs sank deep, and over the sound of his own eyeballs bursting with venom and pain he still heard—would always hear—that one word:

"Traitor!"

Warm arms fell over his chest, slipped beneath his head. Two fingers rested lightly on his lips, holding back the tail-end of his waking scream. "Still?" Portia's voice chased away the demons of the dark. The sweet, familiar scent of her breasts comforted him as he shook, lost to everything but the ebbing terror.

" 'Still'?" he echoed. His fingers clung to her skin as a soldier clings to his sword. "Always. *Always*, Portia. Every night for over three months now."

"I know." She settled him more comfortably against her and gently stroked his hair. "If you would only heed me—"

"Dreams are not sickness." He sat up straight, pulled away from her. At the first hint of the suggestion she had made to him when the dreams first started, he was himself again, all control. "The priests of Aesculapius can't cure a man of dreams."

"It would be better than doing nothing, than suffering this way," Portia persisted. "You haven't had a decent night's sleep for much too long. I'm worried about you. How can you go on living like this? And if you can't—" her voice dropped "—how can I?"

He slung his legs over the side of the bed and sat looking down at the mosaic of nymphs and satyrs at his feet. Someone had told the artist to portray the judgement of King Midas, who oversaw a contest of music between the satyr Marsyas and the god Apollo. No one had told him that for a bedroom he might have chosen a more light-hearted portion of the tale than the moment Apollo flayed the satyr alive for daring to challenge the god.

"Maybe you should go home," he told her.

"If that's your command, I will." He felt the bed shift on its leather webbing. He didn't even have to look behind him to know that his wife had drawn the cover around her like a stola and was drilling his back with her best matron's stare, the one she used to make the servants quail and scamper. It was a look that chilled the whole sleeping chamber, even with the summer weather.

Still not facing her, he replied, "I only want you to be

happy. You've told me more than once that you don't sleep well here."

Her hand grabbed his shoulder so suddenly, wrenched him around so swiftly that he fell back onto the mattress and struck the back of his skull a glancing blow against the headboard. In the dark, Portia loomed over him like a statue of Juno in her most humorless and imposing aspect. He remembered being very small, accompanying his mother to the temple of the great goddess, gazing up at her from the place of an insignificant boy-child. He could not now recall whether he had then been more terrified of Juno's towering size or of the sheer power of all that set her apart as female. The terror was back now, in this darkened room, in this house not his own. He told himself that this was not the goddess, this was his wife Portia, before the old fears could take root.

"I don't sleep well here because *you* don't," she gritted. "And if you want to serve my happiness so earnestly, first find your own."

"I am happy here," he muttered, knowing he lied, knowing she was wise enough to know the same.

"Here in Caesar's house?" she asked. "Or here in Roma?"

"Both."

Her brittle laughter startled a guard who was making the rounds of the house. Brutus heard sandalled feet in the hall outside stop short, then take off at a brisker pace.

"What would my father say if he could hear you now?" she asked. "Spouting more lies than a slave-trader with bad stock. He once told me that of all the young men he knew, you alone seemed to grasp the fact that virtue and duty were more than words to be mouthed for your pedagogue. What's happened to you, my husband?"

Brutus took a long breath and let it out in a slow, steady stream. He saw it ruffle the tendrils of Portia's unbound hair and felt an irrational surge of desire for his wife.

Anything to escape this argument, eh? He was never a better cynic than when taking himself to task.

"All right, I admit it; I lied," he said. "But not in the way you think. You want to know if I'm happy? I don't think I've ever expected to find happiness. From the time I was small, I knew that would be a fool's quest. Happiness flares brightly for a breath, an hour, a day . . . and is gone. As for what it leaves behind—" He shrugged against the mattress; the wool stuffing whispered. "I'm not a very brave soul, Portia; I never sought happiness because I knew I couldn't bear what I'd have to face once it left me."

She bent forward, her hair brushing his cheeks. The scent of almond oil clung to it. "There's a fresh lie to go with all the rest. You'd have better luck passing them off on anyone but me; I know you too well. If you felt it was your duty, you could bear anything, even happiness."

He caught a glimpse of her teeth gleaming in the dark and knew she smiled at him. "There's a challenge I'll never have to face," he said, smiling back. "I've found something even better than happiness."

"What?" Her fingertips traced the stubbly line of his jaw.

"Contentment." He reached up and drew her mouth down to his.

They made love as they always did, with caresses that had lost none of their ability to arouse but all of their spice. It pleasured him in the same way that drinking a familiar wine did. It was the same as the last time, and the time before that, all glow and no spark. He asked himself whether Portia felt the same, for all her gasps and half-smothered cries. He found himself caught up by the realization that when he had made love to that other woman—the gods' own messenger—pure sensation had robbed him of all thought.

They finished and lay side by side, hands touching but not clasped. He knew that she would always be there and she knew the same of him—there was no need to cling. He stared up at the ceiling, marvelling at the way he felt sated and starved at the same time.

"Will you?" Portia whispered.

"Will I what?"

"If I leave this house tomorrow, will you come with me?"

He sighed. "If I could."

"He's commanded you to stay?"

"No, but—" He couldn't find the words. "You don't understand."

"I understand that you almost gave your life for him. Can't your freedom be the reward for that?"

"Portia . . . do you hate me?" He felt her arm twitch away from him stiffly. "I left our home that day intending to kill him, for the sake of Roma. Instead I saved him. I killed many men to do it; I killed my friend, my brother Cassius. Junia's moved to their villa near Cumae; I'll never see the boy again if she can help it. Or her, for that matter."

For a time she did not answer. At last she said, "I don't hate you, my husband. If I did, I wouldn't take the coward's way; I'd tell you."

Knowing she did not hate him, he longed to ask the next question logic demanded: *Do you love me, then?* He did not. He could not. He never had, and in his heart he knew that in spite of all aches and yearnings to hear her answer, he never would. Why? He lacked the philosophy to pursue the matter. Perhaps, he told himself before letting it go, he also lacked the courage.

She does not need to love me. Our pairing holds desire and pleasure, obedience and respect. That's more than sufficient for any marriage, he told himself. His bones protested to the very marrow, knowing otherwise.

He spoke aloud, clearly, to chase away all other thoughts: "I can't leave his house because he needs me."

Portia made a disgusted noise deep in her throat. "For what? He has Antony. He has Octavian." She shuddered.

"Vesta, how I loathe that boy. Colder than the power of a thousand fires to amend. There's no pity in him, no moderation, nothing but where he is now and where he means to take himself. Anything that lies between those two points had better get out of his way or be crushed." Another shiver rippled over her. "I wish he'd stayed in Greece. I wish *I* were in Greece now he's in Roma."

"He's not so bad; he's only young. He still has no idea of who he's supposed to be. If he seems cold, it's only because he's trying to assume a grown man's air of dignity. That can be very difficult, you know."

Brutus voiced words of comfort he didn't mean. The truth was that Portia's reaction to Caesar's nephew was approximately his own. From the moment that young Octavian had arrived in Roma, fetched by the news of the assassination attempt and Caesar's reaction to it, the boy had chilled Brutus worse than an alpine storm.

It was impossible to forget their first encounter. If not, Brutus would have done so gladly. Alas, certain nightmares refuse to be banished easily or at all. He recalled opening his eyes for the first time since the Ides of March. (Later he was told that he had lain unconscious and fever-ridden for over a month under Caesar's roof while Greek physicians alternately conferred, despaired, and tried without success to ban Portia from his bedside.) He blinked against the light while indistinct shapes swam themselves solid.

And there they were: Octavian's eyes, staring down into his own. That thin mouth, small and hard as a frost-killed bud. The pale, frail face of sickness flushing suddenly with the icy rage of a thwarted child. If Brutus had recaptured his voice at the same instant he regained his sight, he might have shrieked for someone to come and shield him from this apparition.

Now he shared Caesar's house with him. They ate together, spoke together, went to the baths together. The boy even smiled at him sometimes and never missed the opportunity to praise him for having been the chief instrument of his beloved uncle's rescue (words which he invariably spoke when Antony was sure to overhear). But Brutus knew what hid behind words and smiles both, and what lurked within Octavian reeked of Avernus.

No matter what his own feelings were, there was Portia to think of. He held her to him, hoping that the united warmth of their bodies would work some arcane magic to drive off Octavian's living specter.

The door exploded in a hailstorm of blows. Brutus and Portia sat up suddenly, cleaving to one another like children lost in a forest. He felt her nails bite into his flesh. "What is it?" he shouted into the dark. "What's wrong?"

"Caesar wants you!" The guard's voice came only slightly muffled by the thickness of the wood between them. "At once!"

"Now what?" Portia mumbled, pulling the cover over herself. "This is a fine hour to be summoning you. Maybe I will go home; it might be the only way you'll get an unbroken rest."

"Hm?" Brutus was only absently heeding her. He shouted for slaves, one of whom fetched light, the other helping him into his tunic and slippers. They were both young boys, with a sulky, half-spoiled look about them.

"I think he's envious of the time you spend with me," Portia persisted. She had no qualms about speaking in front of the slaves. "You know what the soldiers used to sing about him? Every woman's husband and every man's wife. You're no Hyakynthos, but he's no Apollo either. He wants you all to himself."

"*Portia!*" He caught the glimmer of deliberate mischief in her eyes and suddenly his whole air of offended dignity deflated around him. He managed a sheepish smile. The slave-boy attending him curled his full upper lip into a sneer that was there and gone.

"Will you follow me, Master?" The lamp-bearer stood

by the door, his words for Brutus, his contemptuous stare for the woman in the bed.

Impudence! Brutus made it his business to give Portia a kiss so that the pair of them could see it, then left.

He strode through the well-lit, well-guarded halls of Caesar's house. As expected, the boy conducted him to the tablinum, snug and well furnished with all manner of books and the dictator's records. There were so many cupboards and storage chests for the scrolls that rumors already hinted that Caesar intended to move into more spacious quarters, if only to gain some breathing space before the books overwhelmed him.

As it was, there was only one chair and one table in the tablinum, both reserved for Caesar. Therefore, when Brutus' guide opened the door to admit him, the boy remained outside. Caesar was waiting for him—that was to be expected—likewise Antony and Octavian. All three looked up to meet Brutus' eyes.

The fourth man did not look up, did not get up from his shivering huddle of whip-striped flesh, did not do more than crouch before Caesar's table, a high, thin, constant whine of terror trailing from his lips. What hair he had left was so thickly matted with blood that the color was a bad guess. Brutus could see that the soles of the man's feet were crusted and seeping from the marks of burning irons.

"Welcome, my son," said Caesar. There was nothing fatherly in those words. It was no more than a term of affection that Caesar had used more than once, quite casually, when speaking to Brutus even in the days before the assassination attempt. "I apologize for disturbing your rest, but you know how I am: I sleep better when all old, unfinished business is settled." He chuckled softly; Antony and Octavian grinned in unison as if they had been trained to it, like dogs.

"Unfinished—?" Brutus stared at the broken man at his feet, trying to read the riddle.

"You're still half-asleep, my friend," Antony said, coming forward. He showed jackal's teeth. "Let me help rouse you. We'll want you fully awake for this." His hand plunged down to seize the crouching man by the hair and yank his face up. "After so long, eh?" Antony sounded proud, smug.

Brutus stared. What was he supposed to see in this ruin of a human face? It was a blown eggshell, ready to shatter at the slightest touch, destroyed for any purpose except holding more white-eyed terror than a dozen nightmares could contain. He sensed the eyes of Caesar, Antony and Octavian resting heavily on him; he had no idea what they expected him to do or say.

So it fell to Octavian's lot to speak first: "Don't you know him? It's not been all that long a time. We thought he'd escaped us for good, run so far beyond the bounds of Roma that we'd sooner meet under the earth than on it. And all that time, he'd taken refuge with one of his old freedmen, on a farm near Spoletum."

Brutus could only shake his head, his eyes never leaving the captive's face. Somewhere a ghost walked. His glance drifted down. There was an old scar on the upper part of the man's right arm. It looked decidedly out of place, all properly healed among so many fresh hurts. It was the cut of a shortsword, and by its own inexplicable power it called Brutus back with a strength the man's face had lost forever.

"Casca?"

The eyes went wide, the mouth shook, a thread of drool escaping one corner of the lips. As a boy, Brutus had tried to befriend a dog on one of Cato's country estates, but the beast had cowered just like this. It lacked even the will to flee. Cato later explained that the poor creature had belonged formerly to a shepherd who brutalized it past belief, trained it to come whenever called by name even though a beating invariably awaited it. It became so that the unlucky dog was finally terrified of its own self.

So now Casca.

Brutus looked at Caesar, doing his best to shut out awareness of the gleeful expressions Antony and Octavian wore. "What will you do with him?"

"I'd think that's obvious," Caesar replied. He beckoned Brutus nearer and laid his hand on his shoulder. "You almost gave your life for me, but it pleased the gods to favor me by letting you live. Where they take one gift, they often grant another: Wisdom. I'm not a man who needs to learn my lessons twice, certainly not if that means hazarding you a second time. We will do with him what was done with the rest."

Brutus did not need to ask what that meant. By the time he had recovered from his wounds enough to walk abroad to the forum once more, the heads of Caesar's enemies still decorated the rostra. The passage of time had not been kind to them, nor the ministrations of carrion birds, but there they stayed to gawp at passersby. Silent pedagogues, they were nonetheless more than eloquent: Caesar had learned the error of mercy.

"I . . . see." Brutus sucked in his lower lip. "Yet what I *don't* see is why you summoned me here, now, for this."

Antony made exaggerated clucking sounds with his tongue. "And here we thought you'd be pleased! Your orderly soul should rejoice to see the tablets cleared, the sand made smooth, the parchment scraped clean—!"

"Any or all of which could have waited until morning," Brutus said coldly. These days he had less than no patience with Antony's overdone joviality. "He has been captured, and I'd say from the look of him he won't be trying to escape. So why this haste? You're famous for your pranks, Antony, but if you wanted to amuse me, this one isn't working."

Antony held onto his leer with every tooth in his head. "You don't understand, friend," he said, all gaiety. "It's Caesar's pleasure that this last traitor's head be on display before dawn, so that he may finally look nowhere but to the future, and Parthia. Old accounts must be cleared before new are opened!"

"Then call for the executioner!" Brutus snapped.

Octavian's smile was a sliver of thorn. "We have."

The severed head in its leathern bag weighed more than Brutus had imagined it would. Its heaviness made him all the more aware of the burden his own neck bore daily. Tonight it seemed to him that his brains were made of lead, as were his feet. His throat choked on bitter dust when a guard, not recognizing him at first, challenged his passage.

"I'm fulfilling Caesar's orders. He wanted to see this before dawn," he told the man, and opened the bag to let him see what it was Caesar anticipated so eagerly.

The soldier cast a casual glance into the bag. He did not even shudder. A loyal veteran, like all of Caesar's new bodyguard, he had seen worse. Judging from his age, Brutus would not have been surprised to learn that the man had been present when the Egyptians made Caesar a gift of his rival Pompey's head.

"I think he's asleep," the soldier said. "Shall I wake—?"

"I'll do that," Brutus countered.

The soldier shrugged. "Suit yourself." He nodded towards the closed door of Caesar's sleeping chamber.

Brutus opened it as quietly as might be and closed it behind him. He stood with his back to the painted wood, getting his bearings. He had been in this room over a score of times before this, but never in the dark. It astonished him that so small a space could be transformed so radically by the mere exclusion of light. False dawn silvered the open windows on the far wall. He caught sight of the pilum of one of the sentries posted outside, a whole man reduced to the outline of a strong arm holding fast to a heavy spear.

It was more than what they had left of Casca.

Brutus set the bag down between his feet and squatted over it like a peddler come to market. The relic still smelled more of fear-sweat and burned flesh than of rot. It was too freshly severed for that. He reached into the bag and pulled it free. He did not tug it out by the hair—there was too much of Antony in such a gesture—but instead cradled the back of the skull and the raw bottom of the neck.

The eyes had rolled up to bleach the sockets. Looking at it now, Brutus could not think of Casca alive. Forevermore, any passing thought of his onetime ally would be figured as *this*. He hoped he would not have to think of Casca often.

We were his instruments, Casca, he thought. *You and I and all the others: Cassius' instruments. Now he's dead and you are mine.*

He slid one hand up into the neck until he found the knife. Wrenching it out of soft flesh and sinew, he wiped it and his hands on the wadded-up length of cloth he had also brought in the bag. The knife was small by necessity, but the job he had in mind for it only required a blade long enough to cut a sleeping man's throat. It would not do to have his hand slip on the hilt; he worked without allies now, and there would be no Cassius, no Casca, no Trebonius, none other to amend his work if he failed to kill Caesar on the first try.

No one else. No one left.

He set the head down almost reverently atop the folded bag. Brutus gave thanks that Caesar and his dogs had left him alone to see to Casca's death. He hoped that he had paid his slave Alcander enough for having done so distasteful a piece of work. But then, to the slave it was not distasteful at all; it was only another chore to perform for his master. Alcander was strong, capable with a sword, close-mouthed; a little truculent, perhaps, but obedient. When summoned, he had come swiftly to Caesar's house on the pretext that his mistress Portia was urgently needed in her own home and he was to be her escort. He moved with remarkable stealth for a man of his size, enabling him to slip into the garden where his master awaited him with a sword, a bag of coins, and a task.

Brutus hoped that by now Alcander was safely home, Portia with him. He contemplated Casca's empty eyes, longing to pour into them all his own conscious thought. He did not want to imagine what would happen after he did what he should have done all those months ago. His only concern was—had to be—the moment and the task at hand.

He knew now that his dream had been a deception, a vision sent through the ivory gate to lead him astray. Dreams were clever: They could choose words and images from the deepest places of a man's own mind to work their wiles. Dreams knew him better than he knew himself, knew how he honored Roma, reverenced duty, served the ideals of the Republic above all things. As that lout Antony had said, his was an orderly soul. He craved all things in their rightful places.

He did not crave slaughter. He did not crave blood, nor the riot of terror and bloodshed that had followed on the events of the Ides. When the killing madness was on old Marius, when Sulla Felix removed all arguments against his policies by permanently removing all dissenters, each man must have told himself he was only doing his duty, serving his people, restoring Roma. Now Caesar, encouraged by Antony and Octavian, had set his feet irrevocably on the same path. To repay a known enemy with death was in its way logic. To demand the deaths of men simply because there was some slim future chance that they might become enemies . . . that was to court chaos. By all the sacred orderliness of things that the Republic had once created and guarded so carefully, so long, Brutus knew that chaos could only be the instrument of Roma's destruction.

I believed a false dream: I saved the life of chaos' servant, not its enemy. That was my mistake. Brutus tightened his hand around the knife. *It's not too late to correct it.*

He moved towards the bed where Caesar slept. Since the Ides, the dictator had kept to his own room for sleep, no matter what Calpurnia's feelings on the subject might be. In the watery light, Caesar's body lay like a long, low range of hills, a landscape of slumber. He had commanded Brutus to do the work of a common executioner and gone back to finish his night's rest without a second thought. The warmth of summer air called for open windows, but the encroaching dawn made him muffle up his face with the cover to keep the light from his eyes.

Brutus stood over the sleeping man, the knife in one hand, his other hand closing delicately on the cover's edge as if he stood ready to unveil the body of a virgin bride.

His death, then mine. And afterwards it will remain for Antony and Octavian to tear each other to pieces, like wolves. Once they are gone as well there will be no other single man now living great enough to fill Caesar's place. The Republic will return because it must, because Roma can't be governed by the gods alone.

He adjusted his hold on the knife. He would have only one chance to slash that throat into silence. He would not hesitate; for Roma's sake he would not fail.

A jerk and the cover lay at the foot of the bed. A sharp movement, down and across warm flesh and—

—the knife blade bit deeply into black earth. Brutus fell forward into a tangle of violets. Small, strong hands seized his shoulders, turning him over onto his back before he could recapture a breath. Straddling him, pinning him to the earth, the woman of his visitation smiled down on him again.

"Why now?" she asked. Her body was swathed in sheer Egyptian linen, her skin gleaming through it like the moon through summer clouds. "Why slay him now if you saved him then?"

At first he didn't answer, couldn't answer. He had

forgotten the spell of her voice, its power to bewitch. Second sight of her brought a flood of memory, and like a man caught in the flood's full spate he had to fight for breath.

"Never mind," she said, speaking for him. "I know; I know you." Her lips brushed his. It stirred him more than any passionate press of lips to lips. "Why do you play their game, Brutus?"

He had only the strength to echo: "Game?" His head was spinning, swirling the dying stars in the sky above him. He imagined he saw the morning star caught in the net of her hair.

"Antony's. Octavian's. It's their hands that tried to make you into what you're not, yet you blame Caesar. Can't you see he's as much in their hold as you? While you lay sick and helpless, they compacted against you and your father both. You would have turned your knife against the wrong throat tonight."

Abrupt bitter thoughts cleared Brutus' head the way a physician's acrid brew purged the body. "My father . . ." He laughed shortly. "Not according to him. Antony remains his second in the government, Master of the Horse, and Octavian—"

"Did you spare him for reward?" The woman's harsh demand sheared away all her deceptive softness. "If so, I take it back: I don't know you at all."

"No," he replied, rolling his head from side to side against the pillow of flowers. "That's not why I did it. The reason—my choice—they're the same as why I must do now what I failed to do then. For Roma."

"Little mortal man, what do you know of Roma? What do you know of time, of patience, of what lies beyond the fall of the next grain of sand?" Her fingertips traced the bony sockets of his eyes. "You can hardly see from one end of the day to the other. If you could, you'd never—" She paused. A thoughtful look came to her face.

"Never what?" he demanded. "Never kill Caesar?" He

struggled and to his surprise cast her from his body as easily as shaking off raindrops. He sat up, brushing soil and crushed violets from his shoulders. "Well, I never will, if it's not your desire. I see you have the power to stop me."

"Mmm?" She only half-heard his words. Arms wrapped loosely around her knees, she was lost in thoughts all her own. "Stop you? No. How little you understand. If you will kill Caesar, I can't prevent it; only delay. You can go from me now and do it, if that's what you truly intend."

He was suspicious, alert for trickery. "Are you telling me the truth? Or are you just going to wait until I stand at Caesar's bedside and then snatch me away a second time?"

"I swear I haven't lied to you."

"You swear . . . by what?"

"By the Styx." A tremor passed over her skin at the dark binding power of that river's name. Her eyes flashed then, no longer looking inward but catching his in their steady gaze and holding fast. "Listen to me, Brutus. By the same oath I just swore to you, I offer another pledge: Spare Caesar this night and I will let you live long enough to witness the truth of my promises. By the river whose name binds gods and men, I vow to grant you life, long life, a century of years! Take my gift and you may see for yourself that I didn't lie to you that night in your garden, no more than I lie to you here and now."

"A century . . ." Old tales of those to whom the gods granted long life or even immortality whispered their warnings: Aurora's lover Tythonos who lived but aged until she turned his chirring, brittle husk into a grasshopper; the sybil of Cumae whose body dwindled with the immortality Apollo gave her until she was nothing more than a voice rattling within a dried-out gourd, whimpering for the boon of death.

His doubt must have showed in his face, for she laughed indulgently. "Years, yes; years and youth. But no, not youth:

Not even I may restore that. Instead . . ." She pressed her knuckles to her lips in thought. "You will age, Brutus. You are mortal; you must. But your aging will not be as the aging of other men. The effect of five years' passing will be the same as one to you. You will age gradually, untouched by illness or infirmity, body and mind as sound as they are now. I can grant that much, at least."

"All this—for what?" he asked. "My promise not to kill Caesar?" His spine stiffened. A man who had any price but duty was no better than a dockside whore.

"Not to kill Caesar *tonight*," she corrected him. "Take my gift, Brutus; use it. Wait and see the truth of my words: The new Roma will be born, but like all births, there must first be blood."

"Suppose I do take it," he said, feeling his way. "It seems too great a gift for so small a service."

"You don't trust me. Have you marked me for a Greek?" she teased.

"I've marked you for nothing human."

"Ah?" Her brows lifted. "So I'm a monster?"

He waved aside her banter. "Tell me." It was a command clad in all the dignity of his rank. "By the same oath that already holds you, tell me the full price you place on your gift. Leave nothing unsaid."

For an instant he thought he saw her fond, soft look harden with anger. "You make a fine advocate," she said so that he could feel the frost. "Are you wise or only afraid?" Her disdain pierced him, bathed his heart in acid. "Very well, I'll satisfy you. If you accept my gift and come to see that Roma is the worse and not the better for Caesar's life, you have leave to kill him then. I will not take back my gift to you for that. But if you live to see all I told you proved true, then I must have *your* oath to give me a gift in exchange."

"What gift?"

"A death." She said it as calmly as if she were requesting a new pair of earrings.

He scowled. "Octavian and Antony have already tried to make me an executioner."

Her laughter was like the purring of a cat in sunlight. "And is that how you thought of yourself when you were still one of the conspirators? No, no, Brutus; this death is one that even your stern morals would approve. When the time comes for me to ask it of you—if you still live— you'll do it readily enough."

"If I still live?" he repeated. "But I thought—"

"I can only swear by the Styx; I can't immerse you in its waters like Achilles. My gift holds off a natural death, not a violent one. Arrow, sword, spear, poison, dagger, the plunge from the Tarpeian rock, the water's depths, the beasts of land, air or sea, any and all of these can take your life. It will be up to you to prevent them."

She unfolded her arms and slid them around his body. "Do you accept?"

He kissed her first because he wanted to know the taste of a dream, false or true. Then he said, "I do."

She plucked a lone violet from his hair and held it for a moment between her lips. "Then accept this too."

He fell asleep in her embrace, lifted up to the heights with wings of fire, brought back again to earth as gently as the drifting leaves. Her breast pillowed him, smelling of the earth and the sea. Her hair fell over his face, silk and perfume.

He awoke to feel his bed in Caesar's house beneath him, his hands knotted in the cover. He sat up and peered into the gloom like an owl. There was still no more than the pale glimmer of false dawn limning the edges of his window shutters. Where was time? He laid his hands to his face, as if the touch of his own features would tell him whether this too was a dream.

His hands held the rusty smell of blood.

The chamber door slammed open. Soldiers poured into the room, lamp-bearers bobbling in their midst like corks on the Tiber. A noose of swords surrounded him, and behind them rode the fleering face of Antony, the wax mask of Octavian, the sorrowing regard of Caesar who shook his head and murmured, "My son . . . my son . . ."

"What—?" he began.

Octavian stepped between the swords, and slapped him once, hard, across the face. "Traitor," he said, smiling.

CHAPTER FOUR

Brutus sat by the window, his head pillowed on his arms. It was high summer and Roma gasped for a breath of fresh air, a hint of relief from the unrelenting sun. From what he could see between the crossed spears of his guards, the water in the atrium pool looked measurably lower than it had the day before. He glanced up at the compluvium and through that wide opening in the roof saw only cloudless sky, burning blue.

The gods are not pleased with my imprisonment. If a thought could ring with a practiced cynic's bitterness, his did. *Someone should tell Caesar. He might want a drink of water some day.* A dry chuckle crumbled from his lips. *But there: Caesar knew well before I did that the gods' only care for us is as a ready source of laughter.*

He took a deep breath and let it shudder out of his body. The worst thing about remaining Caesar's prisoner was not the certainty of death or the fear for what would become of his family and property after he was gone; it was the boredom. *Like being on the march with Pompey, only this time without even the chance of a battle to decide things one way or the other.* There were days that he woke up wishing that Caesar would listen to Octavian and Antony, give up the whole idea of a trial, and simply execute him out of hand. That was how it would all come about in the end. Why delay the inevitable?

Today was a little different from all those that had gone before, at least. Today Caesar's house rocked with bustle and clamor. Panting slaves raced here and there toting chests and chairs and rolled-up rugs while harried overseers flapped their hands like chickens' wings, trying to herd their underlings into some semblance of order.

"What's going on?" Brutus idly asked the guards. They

didn't respond, although he saw one of them tighten his jaw and heard him mutter a curse under his breath.

You'd like to kill me, wouldn't you? he thought. *You're another of Caesar's most loyal men and you'd enjoy nothing better than having an excuse to get your hands around my neck. You've heard the rumors against me and you've bought every one. I am the monster who would have slain your precious Caesar, that's all you know of me and all you want to know. Are the stories Antony's work or Octavian's? Not that it matters. Whichever one of them's been so busy among the rabble, he's worked all of you like potter's clay.*

A new clatter of slaves passed through the atrium, laden with boxes and bales. Brutus tried craning his neck to follow their flight, but he came up against the unyielding barrier of the guard's spears. He sighed and turned from the window.

His room sweltered and steamed. Windowless except for the lone inlooking square, it transformed itself to a miniature caldarium by day, reluctant to release its captive heat by night. There was a bed, a stool, and the smallest of tables for Brutus' use. No cupboards or chests—he was brought a change of clothes only when his captors decided he might need them—and walls painted a dull leek green merely emphasized what he already knew: This was his prison cell, though it stood under Caesar's eaves, beneath the aegis of the dictator's hospitality.

A scroll awaited him on the table. He sat down to read it, though he had read it over to himself so many times that the words were beginning to lose all sense. It was his only daytime entertainment—that and baiting the guards. When night fell, he was brought no light to read by or even for finding his way to the pisspot, and the overhanging roof tiles edging the impluvium let in little or no brightness from the moon and stars.

The first four nights he had sat up, awake, yearning into the shadows for the otherworldly rescue he was certain must be coming. It did not come. The night held only darkness and her absence. If she had been a dream, she evaded his sleeping hours as well. If she had been a true messenger from the gods, plainly he had served his purpose with her masters. All her talk of long life virtually untouched by age, free of infirmity, had been a test of his gullibility, nothing more. Just as she had transformed the sparrow from stone to flesh, she had given Brutus the illusion of wings, cast him at the sky, and let his own soaring flight bring him crashing headfirst against a wall of glass. On the fifth night he had gone straight to sleep, closing his ears against the imagined sound of divine mirth.

Forgotten by the gods, he seized on the scroll—when it came—as a shipwrecked sailor would cling to a broken spar. If he no longer mattered to the immortals, here was proof that his plight did matter to someone. From so much handling, the scroll was soiled and tattered at the edges. Still Cicero's prim, exact hand stood out in stark relief, each word formed as precisely and to the point as the great orator might have spoken them.

It was a simple message, phrased in Cicero's deceptively simple yet eloquent style: He had heard of the charges against Brutus. He was willing to stand as Brutus' advocate when the case might be brought to trial. He hinted that he would rejoice in an acquittal not just for its own sake, but for the discomfiture such a verdict would bring to others. He was too skilled and circumspect to mention names, but it was no secret that there was small love lost between Cicero and Antony. To this end he was already applying all his resources: Testimony was being taken, evidence gathered. He concluded by informing his client of his faith in a happy outcome and his desire to be remembered always to the good and honorable Portia.

Portia. There was her hand in this letter. Who else but she had been the one to seek out Cicero and plead for the orator's aid? Familiar as he was with Cicero's habits, Brutus knew that for Portia to reach him at this time of

year, she had had to travel at a courier's pace to the great
man's country house in Tusculum.

He set down the scroll. He could not even see his wife's
name written without a grievous pang piercing him to
the heart. Loyal Portia—faithful, honorable Portia who
kept his home as stainless as his reputation and her own.
How had he rewarded her? Man and woman differed in
their desires—the uncounted loves of Jupiter and his sons
stood as testimony to that, the adulteries of goddesses a
short, swift tally next to them—but was desire the sum
of a man? The virtuous man served duty, not desire. Brutus
had taken pleasure without thought, betraying not only
Portia but himself.

The sound of his door being opened brought him back
to the immediate world. Caesar entered without
knocking—his right, under his own roof, but one he
assumed elsewhere as well. He was attended by two guards
with enough flaming hate in their eyes to reduce Brutus
to ashes where he sat.

"This heat—!" Caesar remarked lightly, by way of
greeting. His sinewy hands described the fact that he wore
only a short, white linen tunic. "You will forgive the
informality." That was a command, no matter how
graciously said.

"You're welcome here," Brutus said, motioning Caesar
to the lone stool. Though his mind could not ignore how
ludicrous it was for him to play the host under these
circumstances, his training took over automatically.

Caesar took the seat offered him, his guards falling
into place to either side. He extended his right hand to
one of them, who drew a small scroll from his belt pouch
and slapped it into Caesar's grasp as crisply as if he'd
been drilled to it on the field.

Caesar opened the scroll and let his eyes drift over it.
Brutus stood by, the bulk of the table between them, the
eyes of the guards hot and sharp on his hands. *Do they
think I'm a magician, that I'll conjure a dagger out of*

thin air? If I had that power, I'd have used it on myself long before this. Why has he come? This is the first time he's given any sign that he remembers I'm locked away here. If he wanted to forget my existence, he's been doing a fine job of it . . . up until now. Brutus battled back the uproar of impatient questions struggling to take first place on his lips. If Caesar could wait, so could he.

After what seemed like an hour, Caesar finished his perusal of the scroll and looked up to meet Brutus' eyes. "We are moving house," he said as if they had just interrupted a pleasant conversation about the news of the day. "I've been contemplating a transfer to more spacious quarters for some time. I bought two adjoining houses in this same neighborhood and had them linked. The effect is quite charming, they're ready for immediate occupation, and I've given orders for the move to begin. You may have noticed the noise. I hope it hasn't disturbed you too badly?"

That was enough. That was too much. Guards or no guards, a man had only one death allotted him. "Is that why you're here?" Brutus snapped. "To gossip about houses? To pretend care for my comfort? To waste time that's no longer mine to waste? I'd rather leap into my grave than stand here and play the fool for you. If you have something to say beyond this woman's drivel, say it or get out!"

One of the guards took a step forward, his hand falling to the hilt of his sword. Caesar stopped him with a gesture, the merest tap of a finger to the man's forearm. "Leave us," he said. The guards broke into simultaneous protests, but Caesar only repeated, "Leave us." He did not raise his voice; there was no need.

"Do you think that's wise?" Brutus asked after the guards had left, their reluctance plain to see.

Caesar rested his hands on the table. "You have no weapon, unless you're planning to brain me with the pisspot. It's an unwieldy thing, and if I picked up this stool I'm sitting on, I could smash it out of your hands and stave in your own skull before you had time to bring it down on mine."

Brutus couldn't help but chuckle. "Always the strategist."

Caesar shook his head. "Not always. Not so far as anticipating my enemies. Not from what Casca said."

"Casca—?" So that was why he was here. Brutus' lips pursed. "Even locked up like this, I've heard more than my share about Casca's 'confession.' Even your lowest slave knows all about it, except for one small detail: When did it happen? When you yanked me out of my bed to see him, he didn't look capable of much conversation."

"True, true." Caesar's fingers interlaced over the small scroll. "We didn't speak directly."

"Let me guess: Was it Antony who relayed Casca's words to you or was it Octavian?"

Caesar's eyebrows rose. "I didn't know you were such a cynic, my son."

"Don't call me that." *It means nothing to you.*

"You take your philosophy so seriously, then?" Caesar had misunderstood completely. "Very well; I suppose you have your reasons, though as for myself, men may call me Cynic, Stoic, Epicurean, or claim I believe that beans have souls. Titles are snares for fools. You and the others taught me that."

"Which others?"

"The conspirators. If the idea of a Roman king bothered you so much, you should have killed Antony. That entire travesty at the Lupercalia was his doing, start to end. I never asked him to offer me a king's crown, the gods witness! Least of all before the people. I know them better than he; I could have told him it would be a disaster. But there's no talking to him when he's got an idea for playing out some great scene in public. I swear, he ought to have been a thespian."

"A comedian," Brutus specified. "A bad one." He looked at Caesar more closely. "So you're here to tell me that you never coveted filling old Tarquin's place as king of Roma?"

"Look where it got old Tarquin." Caesar's laugh encouraged Brutus to join in, an unspoken invitation which he declined. Caesar grew abruptly serious and inquired, "Do you believe me?"

"Your explanation's plausible enough." He saw the dictator's face redden slightly when he said that. He wondered what would happen if his words goaded the older man into one of those much-whispered-of bouts of the falling sickness that had plagued him lately. *The guards would probably rush right in and kill me the instant they heard his body hit the floor.* The thought gave him not even the ghost of a misgiving.

"I believe you," he went on. Caesar's angry color ebbed. "I believe you because you're a man of honor, one whose word I trust. I thought you felt the same towards me."

"Your honor's never been in question," Caesar replied.

"Then why am I here? You say you have no designs on a king's crown and I take you at your word. I say that I came into the Senate that day determined to save your life, not take it, and you call me liar, traitor—!"

"I never said any such thing of you," Caesar said quietly.

"In that case you've let Antony and Octavian fill your mouth for you; that's worse!"

"Can you honestly say, knowing me as you do, that I would let any man have that much power over me?" By now Caesar's voice had dropped dangerously low. "I know what you risked, but in light of what Casca said—"

"*When*, in the name of all the gods?" Brutus smacked his fist into his palm, at the end of patience. "When and to whom? To Antony? To Octavian? I saw the marks of torture on Casca's flesh. He was never a brave man, and burning iron will make a stone sing any tune. So they pulled whatever words they liked out of his mouth, came running with them to you, then had him killed before he could take back the smallest lie. Are you blind, that you don't see their malice? To their eyes, I make the third of their triumvirate to rule you, and through you, Roma. They wouldn't be the first to decide that three masters are two too many. Mark my words, I am only the first to go."

The crimson flush of contained rage was back in Caesar's face. Brutus knew the instant after the words left his lips that he had spoken too boldly, too heedlessly, but the heat had conspired with his imprisonment to banish prudence. He'd spoken first and only afterwards realized that Caesar too had come to his present pinnacle of power by the fortuitous death of Crassus and the convenient murder of Pompey, his former fellow triumvirs. Crassus had fallen to the Parthians, but Pompey's death was something Caesar himself had sought actively. If his hands were clean of that blood, it was only because the Egyptians had made him a convenient present of the general's head.

"Be silent!" Caesar barked, rising to his feet, hands splayed on the table. "Will you let it into your thick skull that I'm trying to *help* you? It's been my word alone that's kept you alive these past weeks. As soon as news of your treachery leaked into the streets, the people were crying out for your blood, a fair trial be damned."

"What treachery?" Brutus' voice was flat, beaten. Cassius' death mask was hovering before him, mockery pealing from the sealed lips.

"That you betrayed your fellow conspirators to save my life in the Senate in order to take it afterwards, yourself alone."

An invisible fist drove into Brutus' stomach. He stiffened, silently praying that his expression gave up no secret, said nothing about the fishhooks of ice suddenly birthed in his entrails. "Why would I choose such a course?" he managed to ask.

Caesar gave him a mocking smile. "For the same reason that condemned me to death in Cassius' eyes: To make yourself king of Roma in my stead." His eyes held Brutus a moment longer, then his laughter cascaded through the room, breaking the tension. "*Now* do you see why I've shielded you from the mob? Because from the moment I heard that part of Casca's supposed confession, I knew it was all a farce, a crude fabrication. I agree that Antony makes a fine actor, but he's piss poor as a dramatist." He cupped his chin in thought. "Unless my nephew's the author, in which case I expected better of him."

Brutus goggled at Caesar as if the man had just sprouted wings. "You know it's all a lie, and yet you've still kept me your prisoner?"

"My good fellow, I had no choice," Caesar said evenly. "The people refused to be satisfied with less. You're a fine philosopher and a man of impeccable virtue, but if you ever hope to rise in the world, you'd better learn to read the people. All-seeing Jupiter witness that it's a lesson Antony and Octavian know by heart. The Roman people have more eyes than Argus, more shapes than Chimera, more heads dripping deadlier venom than Hydra and yet, if you persuade them that you're giving them everything they want—whether you are or not—they'll give *you* all you desire."

"And you called me a cynic," Brutus murmured.

"Don't make fun of me, boy," Caesar said. "Not unless you're willing to pay for the joke with your head. I want to save your hide, but not at the price of mine. This rumor of Casca's dying revelation has left me pressed between two boulders. It's not a position I relish. I'd hoped that if I kept you locked up long enough, the people would have the leisure and the sense to recall that kingship is anathema to you, to dismiss the 'confession' for the rubbish it is. Unfortunately, others saw through my scheme. Now there's a sudden uproar for you to be brought to trial. I'll let you guess who it is who's transferred his impatience to the people. Or should I say *their* impatience?"

"So they've forced your hand."

"They believe so." Caesar's expression boded nothing

good for the men heedless enough to dream they could use him. "I have set the trial for two days from tomorrow."

Brutus glanced at the much-read, much-tattered letter lying near Caesar's hand. "I pray my advocate reaches Roma in time. If he thought to have more notice to prepare his case, he'll still be at his country place. A messenger must be sent—"

"If you mean Cicero, forget him." Caesar swept Brutus' scroll to one side with his own. "Antony's been busy. His people have kept watch over your household since you've been kept here. He knew when and where your wife went and he sent messengers of his own after her. They've seen to it that Cicero will stay in Tusculum."

Brutus sighed. "Poor man, he's grown more timid with the years. I hope Antony's thugs haven't used him too roughly."

"Don't waste your time worrying about anyone but yourself," Caesar directed. "If you want to come through the trial a live man, you must put yourself into my hands completely."

"But this is all a sham!" Brutus protested. "You know my nature, my abhorrence of the old kings, all the reasons why Casca's so-called confession is nothing but the most heinous of lies! Why have a trial at all?"

"Because the *people* will have a trial!" Caesar shouted in his face. "Now say once and for all: Are you going to be a sword or a stumbling block?"

Brutus was silent for a time. Then he said, "Tell me what you want me to do."

A storm had broken over the roofs of Roma, Jupiter's thunderbolts shattering the heat, washing the filth from the streets and the sense of oppression from men's souls. The day after the storm dawned clear, with a light breeze blowing from the east like a benediction.

It was the day of Brutus' trial.

He stood in the room that had become his cell, slowly

dressing himself. His tunic was fresh and held the scent of dried rosemary branches, his toga was his best, conveyed to him by one of Portia's favorite handmaidens. The girl had also brought him a letter from his wife.

My husband, it read. *Cicero can not come and I can not discover the reason for it. I can only suspect.*

Yesterday, Caesar visited our home. I treated him with the courtesy his dignity commanded, nothing more. I also offered him an insult or two, not by accident. I spoke to the point about the Forum, turned into a butcher shop by his decree. I told myself that I did so because it was my duty.

Honesty is also duty. The truth is, life is no longer sweet to me without you and I hoped my words would anger him enough to bring us together again, if only as prisoners. Instead he treated me with the calm indulgence so many men reserve for women. To such as he I am mute, I am invisible. I wonder how loudly I must speak, and in what tongue to make him hear?

Caesar told me that you will at last be brought to trial today. As a special mark of favor, he has granted me the privilege of addressing the people on your behalf. He spoke of other matters as well. As he tells me you already know what these are, I will not set them down in writing.

Brutus knew exactly what they were. Caesar had explained these "other matters" to him in detail:

"Whatever else you or I say of Antony he does know that the people relish drama. Seize them by the heartstrings and you have the perfect reins to guide them. I have arranged for your trial to take place as publicly as possible and I've also seen to it that the crowd will be amply seeded with my clients. They're beholden to me and they know how to kindle an outcry from the tinder of a few well-placed whispers. Still, we'll want the flint and steel for the initial spark, eh?" His eyes crinkled; he was enjoying his own way with words.

"For that we will need two things: A man and a woman.

The man will provide testimony refuting the so-called confession of Casca."

"Send to my house for my slave Alcander," Brutus put in. "When I was ordered to kill Casca, my pride wouldn't let me soil my hands on an executioner's sword. I paid the man to do it for me. He could say that Casca took back his words the instant before he lost his head, and he could describe the man and the marks of his torture well enough to make it all sound authentic."

Caesar stroked his chin. "A slave's testimony? Not good." He considered the problem awhile longer, then brightened. "Manumit him at once! There. As a freedman his words will carry more weight."

"Free him just so he can testify on my behalf? It will smell to the heavens of complicity." Brutus shook his head.

"Then *you* shan't be the one to free him, nor shall you do it now." Caesar clasped Brutus' hand in both his own. "Have I ever thanked you properly for the gift of a fine, strong, male slave which you gave me . . . how long ago? Never mind; I have the papers somewhere. They will be produced at the trial, along with the document showing that I gave him his freedom soon after."

"But if anyone in the crowd knows him, they'll also know he still lives under my roof!"

"And did anyone ever think to praise your wife for hiring the man back into your household? At *very* generous wages, I might add." Caesar's grin was not a sight familiar to many, but it was no less brilliant or genuine for all that. "By the way, I am not going to be the one responsible for paying Alcander those wages."

Brutus thought this over. "So Alcander's the man, but—the woman?"

"I thought that was obvious, my son. The woman is your wife."

"Portia—?"

"I'll go to her. She's as soft as any of her sisters, for all of her pose as a stola-clad philosopher."

"That's what you think," Brutus murmured to himself. He remembered how Portia had deliberately given herself a wound, then borne with the pain of it, untreated, to prove to her husband that she could keep a secret. Not that he could tell Caesar that story. The secret Portia ultimately wished to keep was Brutus' initial involvement in Cassius' conspiracy.

"The people are susceptible to a woman's tears. Few ploys work as well with them as an appeal to their natural instincts to sympathize with her plight, to protect her in her weakness. It would be even better if Portia might appear with some small children clinging to her neck, but—ah well! We can't have everything." He chortled in anticipation. Brutus realized that if Antony fancied himself actor and dramatist, Caesar rejoiced in the part of director of the players.

So it was arranged: The "freedman" Alcander would swear to Casca's dying words that recanted his earlier confession and the noble Roman matron Portia, Cato's daughter, would use a display of wild grief and wretchedness to appeal to the mob. The mob might not have the final say over the verdict of a trial, but Caesar would see to it that enough brawny gladiators and ex-gladiators were purchased to make the mob a dangerous creature to cross. Plenty of patricians now living remembered more than a few instances where men of good birth with all of Roman law on their side had still been murdered by commoners of no blood whose only power of oratory was a good, stout cudgel. Truth would have to take refuge under the wings of the Greek pedagogues while plain Roman practicality allowed one lie to undo the harm caused by another.

If Portia agrees, Brutus thought. He finished adjusting the last few folds of his toga and walked to the window. Caesar's house was very quiet. Most of the household goods had already been transferred to the new quarters, most of the household slaves going with them. The kitchen fires were extinguished. A lump of cold, dry bread and a cup of water were all the breakfast Brutus had been offered this morning. There weren't even any olives or honey to make it more palatable.

In the silence, where he could almost hear his own thoughts speak themselves aloud, Brutus pondered the second letter he had received from his wife, the ghost-letter that lay invisibly written between the lines of the actual letter now lying on the table between the half-empty cup of water and the crumbled bread.

She had written of Caesar's visit, she had hinted at Caesar's request for her to appeal to the sentiments of the mob, but nowhere had she said that she would do it.

Truth and honor. Those were the twin gods under whose eyes Cato raised his daughter. If she had come to love her husband as much as she claimed, had she also come to love him more than her father's teachings? Would she set these aside in order to save her husband's life?

He didn't know. He did know that Cato spoke to Portia from the position of greatest power: He was dead.

The dead had an unfair advantage over the living. They stood on the far side of Styx with empty eyes and misty arms extended, pleading eloquently without words. The living were never able to fully enjoy the sweets of life with the eyes of the dead upon them. They feared the angry dead, but more often they pitied the helpless phantoms. Pity was a greater weapon than fear. Though logic shouted out against it, there was hardly a man alive who did not at some time in his life feel that every pleasure he took—from the greatest ecstasy of love to the smallest breath—he somehow also took away from the dead.

Portia was an intelligent woman who would make up her own mind about things, no matter who asked her to do otherwise. If Caesar hadn't recognized that about her, it was a surprise to Brutus: He thought Caesar was more than familiar with such a rarity. He had seen the Egyptian queen Cleopatra when she'd sojourned in Roma at Caesar's invitation. She too was an intelligent woman. Only the blind could help but see how matters stood between her and Caesar.

Perhaps Caesar himself is blind, Brutus thought. *Or else the queen is even more perceptive than anyone knows—smart enough to hide just how smart she is.*

He shrugged to settle his toga more comfortably on his shoulder. The Egyptian queen wasn't his concern now. Portia was. Would she fall in with Caesar's plan?

The door opened and he turned at the sound. Two guards stood waiting. "It's time," said one.

As soon as he stepped out of the door of Caesar's nigh-abandoned house, he was assaulted by his own hunger to gaze up into the open sky. Clouds were blessings, sunlight the food of his soul, the caress of the wind sweeter than the touch of her hands.

Her hands . . .

She was back with him again, the woman of the garden, the lady of the sparrow. He thought he had forgotten her, abandoned all thought of her the way Caesar had abandoned his old house. He was wrong. Every step he took in the free air made him see new beauties in commonplace things he had taken for granted before his imprisonment, and in those beauties he saw her. Every scent of the rainwashed streets—bread and flowers and dung—beat home on him the reality that he had never cast her out of his mind; that perhaps it was beyond his power ever to do that.

He shook himself aware. The guards had brought him into the forum now, in the center of a wedge of other soldiers. He came alert to the armed men surrounding him, and the churning, angry mass of plebeians that snarled and cursed and spat their hatred at him just beyond the dully gleaming tips of the soldiers' javelins. When the guards brought him into the isle of calm where Caesar sat enthroned, waiting, he felt their collective sigh of relief in his bones.

If not for the throngs glutting the Forum, it might have been just another trial. Octavian stood behind his greatuncle's chair, one pale hand resting casually on Caesar's shoulder. *Getting the feel of the purple?* Brutus thought wickedly. Now that he was once more accustomed to a world beyond four walls, he was strangling on his rage against the sickly, slippery stripling.

And what of Antony? There he stood, all meat and ox's eyes, wearing a studied expression of superiority mixed with disgust when he looked at Brutus. Just in case the public didn't know that there was nothing more despicable than a traitor, Antony's contorted, wine-blotched features would remind them.

Caesar stood and the crowd burst into cheers that didn't quell until the dictator raised both arms, imploring silence. Brutus only half-heard his words. Caesar's eloquence was already the stuff of legends. He stretched plain speech like lyre strings over the sounding board of his intentions and plucked them skillfully. The people heard the enchanted music and danced to Caesar's tune.

Brutus did not need to listen closely. He knew what would be said; Caesar had told him. The dictator spoke of the accusation levelled against Brutus in a way that allowed him to interweave recollections of Brutus' previous service to the state, his storied ancestry, and the never-forgotten acts of that day in the Senate. Likewise when he spoke of Casca, it was in terms destined to drag that dead man's life down below the level of the gutter muck.

Brutus lowered his eyes, but managed to observe the effects of Caesar's speech on Octavian. Was the sprat any paler? Was that a cough rising to his lips or just a flood of bile? Brutus wasn't a man given to public laughter, but a knot of it was building in his belly. Even if Caesar's ruse failed, it would be worth his death to have seen that choked look on Octavian's face.

Caesar concluded his oration with a hearty encouragement that justice be done. He did not specify how, even though this was the perfect time for a man of a different mind to call for a traitor's death (mentioning no names). Like the unwritten words in Portia's letter, what Caesar didn't say spoke louder to the people than what he did.

At a sign from the presiding praetor, Antony stepped forward to make his opening address. Brutus wished for a seat. If he was any judge of men, Antony would speak twice as long as he had originally intended, if only to plant in the minds of jurors and spectators alike the words that Caesar *should* have said.

Brutus cast a look at his own advocate, the one who must speak up for him against Antony. He was a junior senator, from a distant branch of Mark Antony's own family. No one had been more startled than he when he received Caesar's command, framed as a request, that he defend Brutus—no one except Antony. If anyone here gathered could look more pasty-faced than Octavian, it was young Lucius Antonius Parvulus. As far as he saw things, whichever way the cat jumped at this trial, its claws would sink deep into his back. Brutus felt sorry for him.

Antony did not plunge into his speech straightaway. Instead he took his place and struck a pose like that of a masked and buskined tragedian about to disgorge himself of a gusty soliloquoy.

That's right, Brutus thought. *Let them feast their eyes on you. Hercules at his finest! But Hercules was a drunk first, and never an orator. Of course you might surprise them . . . and me.*

"My friends—" Antony began. "My fellow citizens of Roma, the Tarpeian Rock awaits the—"

He never had a chance to say more. His allusion to the ancient execution site of all Roman traitors was the last coherent phrase he was to utter at the trial. An uproar from the back of the mob rolled over the heads of the people, gathering strength and volume as it came rushing to the fore, driving all other sounds into obscurity, trampling them into silence. The crowd heaved back and forth, tearing itself apart to make an open path through its core, and through the gap thus gouged out came an open litter borne by eight strong slaves. It was followed by a group of wailing women, the dismal bray of funerary music, and the flame and smoke of torchés. All that was wanted to complete the rites of death was the corpse.

That would be forthcoming. The body that lay atop the litter lived, but the bright stain of blood near its heart shrieked louder than any trumpet that Hades would not need to wait long to claim another client. Swathed in her finest stola, her head and limbs decked with garlands of willow and poppy, the lady Portia gasped out a command and the slaves set down her litter.

Brutus started forward, her name a cry of pain on his lips, but the guards restrained him. With a weak gesture, Portia motioned to the mourners—women of her own household and not hired praeficae—to help her sit up. Propped in their arms, she held out a papyrus scroll and said, "Read, O Caesar, if you would know truth and serve justice."

Horror drained the blood from Caesar's face until he looked a match for Octavian. He waved for one of his guards to fetch him the scroll. It was of an alien, awkward shape, not tightly wrapped. The instant he unrolled it the reason for its unwieldiness became evident.

Brutus groaned aloud as the sacred black dagger of his family, gummed with his wife's blood, fell from the scroll to clatter at Caesar's feet.

Portia sank back against her handmaidens. A shriek of grief shook the heavens. Portia had found the one voice loud enough to make a woman heard.

CHAPTER FIVE

Alcander stood outside the open door of Brutus' tablinum and rapped on the doorpost with his knuckles. His other hand was draped with flowery garlands from wrist to elbow. "Master, we should go now if we're going to get to the temple on time," he said.

Brutus emerged from the shadows of the small room that served him as office and library. There were dark circles under his eyes, though otherwise his appearance showed the careful attentions of a skilled barber. He glanced at the flowers. "Still?" he said. "It's been over a year."

Alcander shrugged. "Yes, but it's not that long since the anniversary of her death. On the day itself you could hardly get near the statue of your ancestor for all the offerings."

Brutus reached out and helped himself to one of the smaller garlands decking Alcander's arm. The white trumpets of flowering jasmine released their fragrance when he crushed them between his fingers. "This didn't come from any common garden."

Another shrug from the freedman. "From some senator's wife, I'd say. It's mostly the women who leave her these. Some of the slavewomen here claim she's appeared to them in dreams, told them their fortunes, promised 'em great things."

"Their freedom, I suppose." Brutus looked up from the crushed flowers.

Alcander's expression remained indifferent. "I don't know. It's not as easy for a freedwoman to make a go of it on her own as it is for, well, someone the likes of me. Though the ones that're pregnant, it's plain enough to tell what omens they come looking for."

A small lift touched only one corner of Brutus' mouth.

This brittle quirk of the lips was as close to a true smile as he ever came, lately. "Aren't you afraid the women will tear you to pieces for removing their offerings from the image?"

"I didn't take these off Lucius Junius Brutus' statue. I haven't even been out of the house this morning. The porter found these all of a heap in the street when he opened the front door, so he sent for me to see to 'em."

"Then they're for me, not Portia?" He contemplated the wealth of bloom Alcander still carried. "Well-wishers' gifts to mark today's ceremonies?"

"I don't know."

"I think you do." The stiff half-smile stayed frozen in place. "You just don't want to say anything to trouble me. You're a good man, Alcander, but I thought you of all people knew me well enough to understand that I'm not afraid of hearing the truth: These flowers too are for her." He sighed. "I think I'll wait until just after the adoption to approach Caesar with my request. Mmmm, yes, just as we're leaving the temple; that will be the best time. He won't be able to turn me down if I ask him before the people. Not unless he's been teaching me wrong."

"What request, Master?" a puzzled Alcander asked.

"To erect a statue of Cato as close to Lucius Junius Brutus' statue as possible."

Alcander frowned. "Cato? Why him?"

"Because he was her father, Alcander."

"Why not just ask to set up an image of her, then?"

"I can just hear what Caesar would say if I asked for that." His voice roughened as he mimicked the dictator: " 'The *people* would not approve.' "

"I'm as much the people as anyone and *I* think it's a fine idea," Alcander grumped.

"You're a loyal man." Brutus patted the ex-slave's shoulder. "But I think I'll play out the game the way I've already chosen: Cato's statue. Caesar won't be able to say no to that, even if he was one of his strongest opponents. He was also a great man, a man of honor, but that's of less moment now than the fact that he sired—" Brutus lost even the weak ghost of that false smile. "In the streets do they still call her the New Lucretia?"

"Yes, Master."

"They would." He walked past Alcander, heading for the atrium. The freedman followed, still bearing the garlands. At the shrine to the household gods, both men paused.

"Shall I lay them here?" Alcander asked, holding up the flowers.

Brutus contemplated the facade of his family's larium, the temple in miniature at which he offered up daily, dutiful prayers long since stripped of any significance but custom. "No," he said at last. "We'll take them to the Tiber."

Alcander made no inquiry, merely gave his former owner a searching look.

"Oh, don't worry about what people will say!" Brutus told him. "No one will say anything if you're the one who tosses them in."

Alcander turned his head slowly back and forth on his massive neck until he only wanted horns to fully resemble a bull brought to the sacrifice. "While you look on? They'll talk."

"Then let them. In fact, if they're bound to talk anyway, I might as well be the one to toss the flowers. He was scarcely more than a boy, if you stop and think about it."

"A young viper," Alcander huffed. "Father Tiber didn't claim his own a moment too soon, far as I'm concerned."

"Father Tiber had help," Brutus said quietly. Even if he kept his eyes wide open, he would sometimes still see that bleak day in the previous year—autumn chilling into winter—when Octavian's body had been found in the river, by the shore of the little island sacred to Aesculapius. In these times the god of healing never enraged his divine colleagues by bringing back life to the dead.

"It was an accident." Alcander spoke with the smugness of a man who knows he is telling an incontrovertible lie.

"Then all the more reason to offer a few flowers to his memory," Brutus countered and marched out the house before the freedman could protest.

He did as he intended, standing on the bridge that linked Aesculapius' temple isle to the rest of Roma. Passersby stopped to gawk, whispering among themselves to confirm his identity. Everyone said Octavian's death was accidental, but no one believed it.

The people are not confused by facts, Brutus thought as he let the last of the garlands fall into the river. *In their eyes, I'm the responsible party—not guilty; they consider the man's death more than justified. I'm the one to praise for it, but softly. Murder is still murder. It doesn't for a breath bother them that there are more than a score of solid Roman citizens who can swear that at the time Octavian took his last swim, I was shut away in my own house, a worse drunkard than even our late friend Mark Antony. Dis take them all.*

Behind him, Alcander cleared his throat loudly. Brutus took his time responding to the sound contrived to prod him into action. Ever since he'd emerged from the haze of wine that had bounded his life for almost nine months after Portia's death, his one small delight in a life no longer delightful was to tease and provoke the loyal freedman.

Almost as if I wanted to drive him away, Brutus thought.

Alcander cleared his throat a second time, more pointedly, and so loudly that the gravelly sound drew the attention of several strollers. Alcander blushed under their curious stares.

"*Now* will you come to the temple?" he growled between gritted teeth. "Before they mistake me for a lunatic and call for help?"

"Don't worry," Brutus told him, smoothing a fold of

his toga. "They probably think you're just another petitioner to Aesculapius."

Alcander's mouth tightened into that expression of disapproval he always seemed to wear these days. "You're going to be late," he said.

"The rites can't start without me," Brutus reminded him. "Whenever I arrive will be the proper time to start."

"Caesar won't be happy if you delay."

"All right, all right, I'm going." As they walked through the streets of Roma, Brutus remarked, "You know, maybe I should decline the honor."

"*Decline—!*" Alcander looked like a man struck by Jupiter's own thunderbolt. "Master, to be named Caesar's son—!"

Named, not acknowledged, Brutus thought. *And why should it mean so much to me? But it does.* Out loud he said, "Alcander, haven't I asked you, time and again, not to call me 'Master'? You're a freedman, made so by Caesar's own hand; act like one!"

The words were like a slap in the face to the man who had stood by his couch all those months while he guzzled cup after cup of unwatered wine, the man who'd held his head for him while he brought the wine up again by the gutsload. The two walked the rest of the way to the temple in silence.

In spite of all Alcander's forebodings and warnings, they were not late. The priest's assistants were just going up the steps bearing the caged doves for the sacrifice when they arrived. At the top of the steps, Caesar stood beaming, backed by his bodyguard and the handful of high-ranking senators who'd been invited to witness this event. He greeted Brutus with a warmth only slightly tempered by the formality of the occasion.

"You're looking well, my son," he said.

"I think you mean I'm looking better than I've been." Brutus managed to scare up a smile that lifted both corners of his mouth.

Caesar's eyes brimmed with regret. "After the rites of adoption are completed and you're a true Julian, I want you to live in my house."

So you can watch over me? So you can see that I don't make a drunken spectacle of myself and soil your dignity? Brutus remained outwardly serene. "I thought we'd agreed that I would maintain my own household and keep my own name, except for official matters."

"If that's still your desire, yes." Caesar looked disappointed. He turned towards the entrance to the temple. "Shall we begin?"

Caesar himself had chosen the site that would host his adoption of Brutus as his son and heir. When Brutus first heard of the dictator's choice, he found it fitting: A temple dedicated to Venus was the perfect place for such a rite. The Julii claimed descent from the goddess herself through Anchises the Trojan, father of Aeneas, ancestor of the twins Romulus and Remus who had founded Roma. It was one of the minor ironies interwoven among the gods' dalliances with mortal lovers that the twins were the offspring of warlike Mars, Venus' divine lover.

The priest performed the sacrifice and gave over the slaughtered doves to the inspection of the *haruspex*. While everyone watched that well-schooled diviner consulting the entrails in search of omens good or bad, Brutus felt a light pressure on his arm.

"Come with me," Caesar whispered.

If any of the witnesses or executors of the sacrifice took exception to the dictator's withdrawal further into the temple building, they said nothing. Even his bodyguards remained where they were. Bemused, Brutus followed.

The temple interior was not dark, despite the fact that the building itself lacked windows. Lamps filled with sweetly scented oils shed soft light over all. The great image of the goddess dominated the interior. Caesar paused at the base of her pedestal and looked up into her carved face.

"When I was young and first learned that Venus was not just a goddess but my ancestress, I used to enjoy every opportunity I got to see one of her images," he told Brutus. "I'd stare at her face until they dragged me away, and even then I'd keep craning my neck to hold onto the last sight of her. Do you know why? I was hoping to spy the family resemblance. When she was portrayed at her best and most beautiful, I was pleased, but when the sculptor's talent fell short, I took it as a personal insult. If her blood was mine, then so was her face, so it had better be pleasing to the eye. At least that was how I saw it." His chuckles diminished by degrees until he was only another old man, shaking his head over the vanished days of his youth.

"Should we go back to the others?" Brutus asked. Here in the shadow of the goddess, he felt strangely vulnerable, even though he knew that the painted eyes fixed on him were only marble.

"Not yet." Caesar clasped Brutus' forearm, holding him to the spot. "They don't need us out there, except at the end, to step out of the temple and gather in the cheers of the people when the priest announces your adoption." The soft light of the oil lamps dug the furrows of age and battle more deeply into his flesh. Brutus could not have looked away if he tried. "There's something I need to tell you."

"What?" Brutus asked, and surprised himself when the word came out as barely more than a whisper.

"Come with me," Caesar repeated.

This time he led Brutus even farther into the temple, to a small door that stood in the shadow of the goddess' chief image. He pushed it open, and pulled Brutus through after him.

Brutus found himself in a little room, windowless, also lit by hanging oil lamps that glittered as if they were made of purest gold, not common bronze. The walls curved in a perfect circle, though the outer shell of the temple gave no sign that its inner precincts held anything but stern, sharp angularities. In the very center of this round chamber stood another statue of the goddess.

This image was not meant to dominate or awe. It was Venus brought down to woman's shape, woman's size, woman's intimate sweetness. Naked, her hair caught up in a fillet, she seemed to step forward eagerly, her face alight with joy to welcome her worshippers as she would her lovers. To see her so, no man would ever dream that she commanded the terrible powers of love and beauty, in their full strength capable of driving him to madness and death. This was the goddess who blessed the first shy, tender touch of lips to lips between Paris and Helen, not she of the all-consuming flame that kindled there and burned Troy to ashes.

"It's beautiful," said Brutus, not really seeing the image. His mind was too preoccupied with puzzled thoughts. *Why has he brought me here to see this? Caesar does nothing without a reason. What's he up to?*

He had his answer soon enough. Caesar's arms were around him, the older man's seamed lips pressed to his own. Brutus' whole body tensed. The old songs of Caesar's legions, at once mocking and proud of their leader, resounded through his head: *Every woman's husband and every man's wife!*

But then Caesar released him from the kiss, held him at arm's length and said, "You *are* my son. Here before the true image of the goddess, our ancestress, I swear it."

"The—the rite—" Brutus stammered. "The rite of adoption's not over yet, so—so—"

Caesar's smile was wide, bathed in delight, brighter than any lamp's weak glow within the small shrine. He clasped Brutus to his chest with a strength unabated by the years, the recurrent bouts of marsh fever, or the periodic attacks of the falling sickness. He looked ready to shout aloud for joy, but when he did speak, it was in a voice at once hushed and tender.

"You are my son," he repeated. "My blood, born to me." His embrace tightened. "I loved your mother. She loved me too, I think."

Brutus, recalling the tale of his mother's shameful, shameless letter to Caesar coming into Cato's hands, gritted his teeth and said nothing.

"It's no accident that you have a reputation for putting your duty before all else," Caesar went on. "Your mother and I might have turned from all other alliances, married, but neither one of us could turn from what we saw as our duty, then. Do you understand, my son?" This time those two final words resonated with affection, were no longer a simple habit of speech. Brutus had imagined this moment many times. He was amazed at how commonplace it felt, how cold.

Caesar released him from his embrace and turned him, unresisting, to look at the statue once more. "I offered this image of the goddess to Venus' temple in the year you were born, in the very month. It was carved by a Roman sculptor's hand, a man whose work was nearly the equal of the great Greeks. I paid for it, and when it was finally placed here I prayed to our mother Venus that the day might come when I could at last stand here before her, in her sight, and claim you for mine."

Brutus tried to speak and found that words would not come. He looked into his father's eyes and there saw all the feelings he had hoped to see, longed to see, prayed to see in those time-vanished moments when he still thought of the gods with his childhood's awe. With so much warmth welling up there to welcome him—*him*, and not some wishful dream-self—why did he feel as if he were running up some ice-encrusted Alpine slope, breathless, frozen from the heart's core out?

Then he felt other eyes upon him. Turning his head from his father's gaze was an effort almost impossible. There was that thickness in the air again, the ponderous weight of time brought to a standstill, tethered by bonds whose unseen ends lay far outside the limits of human reason. From the corner of his eye, Brutus glanced back at Caesar; the man did not stir, did not even flicker an eyelash. All movement had been sucked out of the small, round chamber along with all passage of time.

He felt a hard, cool touch on his cheek. Smooth marble fingers traced the line of his shaven jaw with a caress he had known before. Freed by the touch of those stone fingertips from the heavy air that held Caesar immobile and ignorant of wonders, Brutus could now turn his head with accustomed ease.

My beloved. Venus' image stood with her back to her abandoned pedestal and brought flawless lips to drink Brutus' breath.

At first it was cold—that mouth, that kiss—colder than the icy nest of loss crowding all other feeling from his heart. His teeth grated against stone, his mouth opened to the dainty, darting probe of a stone tongue that bruised the corners of his mouth. But as he stood there, more helplessly locked in the stone's embrace than any noble corpse in its sarcophagus, he sensed the change that came shivering through carved limbs and rock-hard, rock-smooth breasts.

He couldn't tell the precise instant when she became living flesh in his arms. Old myths flittered through his mind like bats, chittering tales of the sculptor Pygmalion who had fallen hopelessly in love with the statue of the perfect woman, the creation of his own hands. Venus had breathed life into her, the sculptor's adored Galatea. Why could the goddess not do as much for her own image?

She was all flesh, with the hot blood racing under the silken skin, by the time she let him go. He stared into her laughing eyes, and that was when he knew.

"You—" He weighed a single wild curl of her hair on his palm, as if it were the anchor-stone that would drag him back into a rational world. "You were never the gods' messenger. You were yourself a god."

"Does that change things so much?" She was Venus newborn, a maiden with the sea's amorous perfume still clinging to breasts and thighs. "You are an educated man, my love. You know the tales. Semele died when she demanded to see her lover Jupiter in his true glory. It was too much for mortal flesh to bear. Men fear to face their gods."

"You lied to me."

"When?" she countered. "When did you ever ask straight out if I were a goddess?"

"I asked you who you were," Brutus maintained. "You wouldn't answer."

She laughed and there were pearls suddenly twisting through her hair. "Perhaps you didn't know the proper way to ask. Perhaps it was forbidden for me to tell you who I was in that manner, straight out, blunt as a peasant's words. And perhaps—" She pressed her cheek to his chest "—perhaps now that my words have saved you from the Furies' wrath, none of this matters at all."

Her arm arced up, sweeping away the temple chamber, wiping all Roma into oblivion. Brutus saw walls and floor and ceiling evaporate around him like sunstruck dew. He clung to the goddess as the two of them hung breathless in a place between worlds, where everything that was not light was music.

He held her to him tightly because he was afraid and because he was even more terrified of admitting his fear. She pressed her living self to him so artfully, with such enchantment, that afterwards he could not recall the moment that he too wore only the skin he'd been born with, or the instant when fear became desire.

All thought was useless, cast aside willingly because it came between him and her. He was beyond everything but pure sensation, lost in a love that filled his soul with laughter. He thought that he would die of so much joy. He prayed that he would die before it ended.

It did end. The goddess in his arms gave an exquisite

shudder and fell back, away, down into a couch of stars and flowers. Her smile stabbed through his eyes with the power of the summer sun.

"You are mine," she declared, the conqueror. "By blood and more than blood."

"Yes," he said, his word little more than a breath.

"So now you see. My hand has been on you from the first. I bought your destiny from the Fates for a price I may not name. You doubted my words, my promises, but keep faith with me from now on and I swear you shall live to see them all fulfilled."

"Faith . . ." He was suddenly shaken. Beyond the goddess' glowing face he thought that he could see a robed and hooded womanly figure, sober faced, straight and strong as a caryatid. "Portia—?" The name choked him with pain. He moved through the shining air of the goddess' own home, his hand outstretched to a dark phantom.

Venus' smile fled, seeing where his eyes wandered. She was up, crouched like a panther, the hot destruction of her stare flashing through space to engulf the hooded figure in a clap of brilliance and blaze, searing it from sight.

"I saved you!" she shouted in his face, her fury driving out even the afterimage of Portia's shade. "I, I alone! Why do you look to her? Let Dis have her! You were never in danger, never, not so long as I held your fate, your soul! I guided her hand when she wrote the list of lies against Antony and Octavian. I held it when she clasped the dagger, turning the lies to truth with her blood. It was my doing—mine and no other that saved you. Any faith you owe, you owe to me!"

Her fury whirled around her like a firestorm. She fed on it, fattened, grew before his eyes until she dwarfed the great image of the goddess in the main temple precinct. She was neither stone nor flesh but flame. A thousand Troys could burn into oblivion from the smallest spark of a word falling from her lips.

Why am I not afraid? The realization stunned Brutus. In the face of the goddess transformed to overwhelming size and splendor he stood more firmly than when she had been no greater and no less than a mortal woman. In that instant he understood that it wasn't Jupiter's unveiled glory that had killed his lover, it was Semele's own fear.

"If you know me," he said, his voice strong and steady, "then you also know there's no need to tell me what I owe and where. I remember the price I promised to pay, once I saw proof that Caesar's life would help the Republic more than Caesar's death. Hear my sworn word! I will honor that promise as fully as I admit my life is yours."

A smile crept slowly across the goddess' burning mouth. "See that you do, my beloved," she said. "See that you do, for I promise you in turn that you won't see me again until the day I come to claim all you've sworn to give."

She opened her arms and let her head fall back as laughter rippled from her body. Her bright hair whipped out in a wind that touched nothing else, the long strands snapping like banners. One lashed out to wrap itself over Brutus' face. He cried out with surprise, clawed it away—

—and stood once more beside his father in the shadow of a statue.

"I think we should go," said Caesar, laying his hand on Brutus' elbow. For him, no time at all had passed. "The people will want to greet you."

"Yes," Brutus replied, never taking his eyes from the face of the goddess. "I think we should go."

CHAPTER SIX

A wind whose voice seemed to carry other voices on its wings swept over the Roman encampment. Brutus stood outside his tent, staring up at the stars, while the campfires of the legions spread themselves out before him like an earthbound galaxy. The wind was cold as an old widow, hurrying down over the invaders with the same speed and lack of pity she had taught her children, the riders of Parthia.

In his hand Brutus cupped an arrowhead. His thumb traced the sharp edge gingerly, pressing it against the fingertip's fleshy ball, tempting it to cut deep enough to draw blood. It had become a ritual with him since coming to this land—a ritual faithfully performed the night before any battle—to test his body's tolerance against some weapon's edge. It was his way of reminding himself what the goddess had and had not promised him. After so many days on the march, so many battles, the gesture had become more habit than trial to see if he could still bear pain.

Alcander's disapproving face formed itself from the leaping flames of the campfires. "Now, now," Brutus murmured into the dark, where only phantoms could hear him. "You didn't think I was going to let the swordblade or the dagger slip on purpose some fine day? If I want to cut my belly open, I'll do it. There'll be no room for doubting whether it was an accident."

I don't care, the wavering image seemed to reply. *I'm still going along to make sure you don't do anything foolish. Foolish . . .*

"And you wading into the forefront of the battle with me was a wise man's choice." Brutus shook his head, contemplating the arrowhead that had been dug out of Alcander's side but had claimed his life anyway. "Did you think that war is the same as a street brawl in Roma? The strength of a man's arm alone doesn't decide who lives or dies, and an arrow doesn't care at all where it drinks."

His ears still echoed with the rumble of the Parthian cavalry charge that had overtaken them when they passed beyond Carrhae. It was as if the spirit of Crassus' overwhelming defeat had risen up from the graves of those slaughtered Romans to claim fresh lives from among their fellow legionaries. Perhaps they felt lonely in the marches of Dis and wanted new companions.

If so, they were to go away still hungering, those poor feckless ghosts of Carrhae. Caesar was no Crassus. He learned his lessons well, especially when he might read them in the fatal errors of others. Too, he had Brutus' counsel to back him, words of advice gleaned from a most unexpected source: Cassius. The man who would have cut Caesar's throat became, after death, the saving of it. For Cassius had ridden with Crassus on that ill-starred Parthian expedition. He had served as the late triumvir's quaestor, no less, had noted well the way in which Crassus' blunders mounted up against them, and had filled many a night in Brutus' company with detailed accounts of all he had witnessed.

In his turn, Brutus told Caesar all that Cassius had told him, and Caesar allowed himself to be instructed. He did not drive his legions to hot pursuit of the Parthians, exhausting man and mount. He did not put his trust in native guides whose loyalty to Roma had already showed itself to be a joke. Above all, he bent his every effort to avoiding a confrontation with the enemy on terrain that favored the Parthian cataphracts, those heavily armed and armored mounted men whose charge could shatter common cavalry. And as for their effect on infantry—!

Are you trying to scare me off? Alcander's floating face smiled into Brutus' eyes. *I haven't come this far to be turned back now. I'm a freedman; you can't order me off. I volunteered, and if I'm part of your units, thank*

Caesar for it! He understands how it stands between us, Caesar does. The ghost's grin grew wider. *Freedom's fine, but fortune's finer. I'll march into the East with you, Master, and fill my hands full of all the riches I can carry! The men who followed Alexander became kings. I'd be satisfied with a good stretch of farmland between the rivers, but if someone offers me a crown, I won't play Caesar, believe me! I'll take it.*

The wind dropped, gulping down Alcander's apparition with it. The Greek freedman had his land now. Carrhae was well behind the legions' march, but even so Crassus' men had managed to summon some few new comrades to their company. Brutus closed his hand tightly over the arrowhead, feeling the edges cut into his palm.

I wonder if there's any trace of your blood left clinging to this relic, Alcander? he thought, uncurling his fingers slowly, gazing down at the twin, thin lines of red oozing up along the arrowhead. *Does it mingle with mine now, another ghost for me to carry?* He closed his fist around the arrowhead and made as if to fling it far from him, out into the night, then thought better of it. Tossing it into the air and catching it again, Brutus strode towards the great command tent where his father waited.

Caesar stood in the midst of his subordinate commanders, a chart unrolled on the table before him. He looked up and smiled when he saw Brutus come in. "Minding your chickens, my son?"

The others—tribunes and legates—laughed, some out of duty, some because they had nothing but scorn for Brutus and his "chickens." That was the name that had been given to the auxiliary cohorts Brutus had raised, trained, outfitted at his own expense, and transported all the way from Rome to the Parthian marches.

"They're bright birds," Brutus replied. "They can mind themselves."

"No squabbling over the pecking order any more?" one legate asked, chuckling over his own joke.

"Not since they've seen the shadow of the hawk," another put in, also enjoying his own wit more than anyone else present.

Brutus let them have their fun. His specially formed cohorts—his "chickens"—had come to claim the first place in his emptied heart.

"Wait and see," he told them. "These are no ordinary fowl. I'm willing to wager that these birds are rare enough to bring back the eagles." There was no hint of levity in Brutus' expression, though his words themselves were playful.

No one spoke of the lost eagles lightly. When Crassus went to his death at Carrhae, taking some twenty thousand soldiers with him, he lost more than men: He lost the silver eagle standards of the legions. The *aquilifer* whose duty it was to carry the eagle for his legion never surrendered it without his life. It represented the power of the legion, and a legion that lost its eagle was disbanded in disgrace.

Crassus lost the eagles of almost seven legions. It was this news that rocked the Senate more than the tally of the dead, for while the slaughter of Roman troops was enough of a catastrophe in itself, this was worse: This was the death of honor.

"The gods grant it," the tribune Gaius replied. Solemn by nature, pious too, he was always the last to enjoy a joke if he ever enjoyed it at all. He was Caesar's distant kin, though Brutus still found it hard to accept the fact that this meant the reedy fellow was his kin too. Gaius was young even to be a tribune—young as Octavian had been young. It would be men like this who would live long enough to watch Brutus age in years but not in seeming. And what would their testimony do to him, in years to come?

Cheer yourself, Brutus thought. *Maybe the goddess lied after all, and your years will settle on you like any man's.*

There were times that he longed to believe that. There

were times that he almost convinced himself that his life was still his own, that he had not given himself up to the goddess, that she had not bound him to her with her oath, unbreakable, taken on the Styx's cold waters.

Caesar laughed to see young Gaius' grave expression. "When you speak of birds and call on the gods, you'd better have an augur ready to interpret the signs. What do you say, my son? Do you think your chickens will perform a dance of good fortune for us?"

"Slaves dance to any tune, if you throw them enough feed," the legate Publius commented lightly.

"My men are not slaves." Brutus surprised himself with the heat of his response.

Publius' plump face reflected only skepticism. "Take that bone to another dog; I won't bite it. When they left my father's estates they were slaves."

"And when I recruited them, that was the end of their slavery," Brutus countered.

Publius snorted. "Just like that? When you put weapons in their hands, that didn't make them any less slaves than Spartacus' cursed crew. The sword doesn't make the soldier. Crassus may have lost the eagles, but he had sense enough to treat slaves the way the gods intended honest men to treat them."

"The cross?" Gnaeus Claudius Rufus had become indebted to Brutus on a number of counts, both since coming to the East and earlier, back in Roma. Now he showed his allegiance, rounding on Publius, matching scorn for scorn. "For every offense beyond sneezing out of turn; that's the way I heard it. There's waste for you! No wonder your family fortunes are so precarious, if that's how your father and his underlings manage good manpower. And no wonder you squeal so loudly over giving up a handful of slaves that most men of means wouldn't blink over."

Publius' face flushed, his jowls trembled. "If we spoke up against the levy, it was with just cause! And if you

and your family didn't, it was only because you've got
your mouth glued so tight to his buttocks—" a jerk of
Publius' beringed thumb in Brutus' direction "—that you
can't get a word out!"

Caesar's eyes narrowed. Silence seemed to radiate from
his person, filling the tent, bringing home to Publius the
full measure of what he'd said in the heat of the moment.
There was no need for the general to speak. Publius was
stammering an apology before Caesar could open his
mouth.

Caesar let him speak, gave him no indication whether
his words were welcome or only serving to burrow himself
deeper into the earth. When Publius at last regained
control of wobbling lips and broken voice, Caesar resumed
outlining the morrow's plan of action as if Brutus' entrance
had never interrupted it.

When he was done, he rolled up the chart and dismissed
his subordinates; all but Brutus. Father and son shared
a roof most nights, though at the beginning of this
campaign it had been Brutus' custom to keep to his own
tent. In those earlier days, his chickens *had* wanted
watching.

"You have an enemy there," Caesar said after the last
of the legates had gone.

Brutus managed a thin smile. "I have a *known* enemy
there; that makes a world of difference."

There was a chest against one wall of Caesar's tent with
a flask of wine, another of water, and two cups beside it.
In all particulars, there was nothing about these to
distinguish them from the same items the common soldiers
used. Caesar poured out a measure of wine, watered it
to Brutus' taste, and offered it. Brutus took the cup and
waited until his father had served himself before taking
a drop. Both men seated themselves on folding stools
beside the table and drank. The wine was thin and sour.
Brutus couldn't help but make a face.

"Terrible, isn't it?" Caesar contemplated the contents

of his own cup with a rueful expression. "I make sure to serve some to any man who enters my tent, After this war is done, they'll be able to swear that Caesar himself suffered along with his men. It's tales like that that make a man's reputation almost as much as what he accomplishes on the field." He took a deep draught of the sour wine, forced himself to swallow, then added, "But you don't need me to teach you the magic of appearances. There you're my master, you and your precious chickens! If I didn't know better, I'd swear that your mother was a second Alcmene; Mercury himself must have disguised himself as me the night you were made."

"My mother didn't need to embrace Mercury for me to inherit a trickster's nature." Brutus set the winecup down; he felt he'd had more than his fill.

"You mean you have it from my blood? You flatter me." Caesar was honestly pleased. "I confess that I do know a trick or two for coaxing Fortuna into a friendlier mood, but you—!"

"You know my reputation: I speak my mind and I speak it plainly. Where's the trickery in that?"

"The subtlest of all: Trick masquerading as truth itself. No, don't scowl at me for saying so." Caesar wagged a finger at Brutus. "Perhaps you've even managed to trick yourself into believing you've had nothing but straight dealings with the Senate."

"They were free to choose," Brutus maintained, that old stubborn look coming over him. "Not one of them *had* to give me slaves."

"Of course not." Caesar was fighting back laughter. "They could have paid the tax instead—never mind that it was cheaper to provide the levy of slaves *and* their furnishings! Oh yes, an easy choice."

"I wasn't the man who called for the tax," Brutus reminded the dictator. "I only provided the alternative after *you* demanded money for the war."

"*Requested*," Caesar corrected him amiably. "It's poor

policy to *demand* anything of the Conscript Fathers of the Senate. It reeks too much of kingship for their liking. You'd be wise to remember that."

Brutus missed the irony of Caesar warning him off matters touching kingship. "Why? I'll never be in your position: Dictator of Roma. I wouldn't want to be."

"Mmmm." Caesar's answer had every meaning and none. Both men sipped their wine without relish, the stillness between them growing.

"Do you think I'm a fool?" Brutus asked suddenly.

"On which count?" Caesar's mouth twitched.

"I'm not asking in jest; I need to know. I could never have raised my cohorts without your help. Even if the senators had given me as many of their able-bodied slaves as I wanted, the regular soldiers would never have accepted them without your influence, your approval. You didn't have to give it. You could have let it all come apart under me before we ever left Roma. Why didn't you?"

"Why . . ." Caesar rested his elbow on the table. "Because I suffer from a fatal malady: I'm curious. I've wanted to see how your plans would turn out from the moment I suspected that you *had* plans touching this war."

Brutus blinked. "The Parthian campaign's been yours from the start! How can you say—?"

"Pardon me, then; you're right. Yes, I've had my eye on Parthia for long before this. King Orodes stands ready to sow discord among us, as he did when Pompey lived. Parthia wants Roma weak, split into factions—so long as there *is* a Parthia." His mouth was set in an expression impossible to interpret as smile or frown. "Still, you do have plans of your own. The war is only one of your tools. Am I another?" Caesar shrugged. "If we can accomplish both our purposes, I don't care where the hand leaves off and the sword begins."

"If any man could hear you call yourself *my* tool, he'd

think that either he or you'd gone crazy." Brutus choked
down the last of his wine, feeling it burn his throat raw.

"Don't try kicking dust in my eyes," Caesar replied. "I
see things as they are. You can blame me all you like for
the funds I—*requested* from the Senate for this campaign,
but you're also the one who prepared the field so that it
would *have* to sprout. How did you do it? Paid whisperers?
A few coins pressed into the proper priestly palms? An
omen purchased here, a portent in the entrails there? I
know how such things can be contrived. By the time I
came before the Senate with my plea, the air of the city
fairly seethed with the passion for war. To speak against
my proposed campaign was not merely to speak against
me, it was to speak against Roma herself! Any opposition
was treason, any man who protested was the lowest traitor."

Brutus hung his head. Revolting as it tasted on the
tongue, Caesar's wine dulled the senses well enough for
him to wish for more. Caesar was right: He *did* see things
as they are. And Brutus remembered them as they had
been. He reached for the wine flagon, wanting to wash
away the memories.

He couldn't. They waited for him at the bottom of his
cup, in the dark lees: A veteran of Carrhae who recounted
the slaughter in a local wineshop was torn to pieces by a
mob who thought his tale of Crassus' errors was meant
to ill-wish Caesar; a senator who called the campaign a
fool's errand was found dead at the doorway to his own
house, a badly scrawled copy of Agave's delirious speech
from *The Bacchae* pinned beneath the body. Rumor said
that when Crassus' head was brought to Orodes, the
Parthian king was watching a performance of that play.
The head was tossed onto the stage and the actor Jason
took it up and recited those very lines, mad Queen Agave's
speech over the severed head of her son King Pentheus.
High and low, all Roma stood ready to avenge the eagles
of Carrhae, the gods help anyone who saw things
otherwise.

"—sleeping?" Caesar's voice intruded on Brutus' thoughts. He became aware of a strong hand on his shoulder, shaking him.

"No, no, I'm awake," he said. "Did you say something?"

"Only an old man's fancy. We fight tomorrow, which means we could as likely die then as another day. I'd hate to reach the shades with such a weight of unanswered questions on me, enough to sink Charon's boat! What madness touched you, to make you dream of bringing slaves into the legions?"

"They are *not* slaves." Brutus slammed fist into palm. "They're free men now, subject to the discipline of the legions like the rest."

"A heavy freedom, that," Caesar remarked drily. "But easier to bear with what awaits them when their twenty-five years' service is done. Your chickens will have citizenship for their prize, if they live long enough to claim it."

"They will live that long, and so will your men, thanks to mine." Brutus spoke with the ardor of a lover defending the virtues of his beloved. "Publius says that the sword doesn't make the soldier, but my men fight with slings, not swords. That's our hope in this campaign, the sling, no matter how foolishly the legions scorn it and the men who wield it. It can outrange Parthian arrows, pierce a cataphract's armor at short range. How else could I raise up skilled slingers in the numbers we need, but from the levies of slaves? No free men would submit to the training required—hard work to master an unfamiliar weapon, and one that ranks low in the legions besides."

"The legionaries do tend to look down on anyone who's not part of the heavy infantry," Caesar admitted.

"Let them." Brutus upended his winecup on the tabletop and rested his eyes on the patterns of the lees. "And let them call me mad for having begun this enterprise. I know that no madness touches me." If he sought a prophetic vision, he found none. "Unless it's madness to save Roma."

"Save her how? And from what? We have peace at home."

Peace . . . Your idea of peace is not mine, Brutus thought, meeting his father's eyes. *Your peace means there's no one left to stand against you and your will. If that means breaking the Senate's back, so be it. But what will happen after you are gone? You see me in your place; I don't. Roma must not be ruled by a single hand. And when I refuse to drape myself in your shadow, a dozen new would-be Caesars will try to tear it from me and from each other. They'll fight among themselves, drowning Roma in blood once more. We'll need no Orodes of Parthia to help us slit our own throats, if—*

He kept his thoughts to himself. He knew how Caesar would greet them: Derision at best. Instead he spoke in a tongue Caesar would understand and welcome. "Wealth," he said. "The wealth of conquest. The wealth of the East for the salvation of Roma."

"A fair answer," Caesar admitted. "Although to tell you the truth, most of the land we've covered isn't worth much except to shepherds."

"It's not this land that will enrich Roma; it's the land that lies beyond. Father—" He seldom called Caesar by that name, and now it stumbled awkwardly from his lips "—we don't need these wastes, but they are the road to richer territories. All we need is to secure the road."

"With slaves?" Caesar seemed to find Brutus' explanation more and more amusing.

"With *freed* slaves. With *trained* slaves. With men born to slavery who will appreciate the gift of freedom, not regard it as their birthright. They won't value it cheaply, and they'll fight to hold onto it—no soldier more fiercely!"

"So I've seen," Caesar remarked. "They *are* surprisingly effective in the field. Your regular troops aren't blind; they've seen how the slaves—*former* slaves—fight. They saw how useful they were in crippling the Parthian archers' attacks." Caesar was not smiling now. The

mounted archers who rode in support of the Parthians'
heavy cavalry were the enemy's most formidable weapon.
Their recurved bows could shoot flight after flight of
arrows, each capable of piercing Roman armor, breaking
the discipline of Caesar's best-trained men. And once
broken out of close formation, the Romans were easy
pickings for the Parthian cataphracts.

"They'll see more of it tomorrow."

"I still don't understand how—" Caesar scratched his
head. "You're no ordinary man, my son. I wish I'd known
you better in your growing. Maybe then I'd be able to
see all this through your eyes."

"You look at me as if I were a visionary," Brutus said,
leaning forward to clasp his hands between his knees.
"You sound as if you expect to hear the Cumaean sybil
speak through my lips. All I am is a practical man; a soldier
must be practical. You've given Roma lands worth a
hundred Parthias, but getting and holding are two different
things. Where will we get the troops to maintain your
conquests? And if we lack the troops, how long can we
hold the territory?"

"So you'd have us hold our lands with slaves?"

"Not all our lands; only what we take here. Every man
who was given to me for my auxiliaries was a slave when
I got him, a slave without any special skill that might let
him earn the price of freedom. But every one of them
knows, from my own lips, that when this campaign ends
they'll own their skins *and* Roman citizenship *and* a
measure of land besides."

"Land? Where? I don't think the senators will surrender
their estates as graciously as their slaves."

"*Here.*" Brutus slapped the table. "What they fight for,
they keep, land and freedom! And they won't be the last.
I want to raise more troops like this. The slaves get no
arms, no training until they're well away from their old
masters, so we never need to face the threat of a second
Spartacus."

"Ahhh. And once they do have weapons to hand and know how to use them, how can they return to Roma? I doubt any of your recruits know their Xenophon." He chuckled.

This time Brutus was able to share Caesar's laughter. "Pedagogues make poor slingers. It's my policy to refuse any man who's read the *Anabasis*. Besides, why would they want to march so far, through hostile territory, when we'll make *this* their new home?"

"You've taken a lesson from Alexander," Caesar said, well pleased. "He too seeded the East with his troops."

"And the East devoured them, year by year," Brutus pointed out. "They were Macedonian Greeks, but how Greek were the children they begot on Persian wives? How Greek were their grandchildren? Alexander only made a good start; we'll see this through. You're right, Father: I *do* have more plans than you know."

"Then keep the telling of them for another time. Now we must sleep. Tomorrow—" Caesar stood, pulled Brutus to his feet, embraced him. "The gods stand with you tomorrow, my son. Alexander's dream shattered because he died too young. Yours must live." He held him at arm's length. "*You* must live."

Brutus clasped his father's forearm warmly. "That's in Fortuna's lap."

The next day brought a hard sun up out of the east. Scouts raced through the camp with word of a large Parthian force approaching. Intelligence quickly spread: Orodes' favorite son, Prince Pacorus, was in command. Caesar had more than one bone to pick with the prince and his father. Crassus' debacle aside, Orodes had done more than a little to promote the civil war between the surviving triumvirs, favoring Pompey, and Pacorus' attempted invasions of Roman-held territory had only been averted by Caesar's arrival in Syria. The prince was a brilliant fighter; the sooner he was gone, the better.

Brutus surveyed the field from horseback. He couldn't help but be pleased with the attitude of his men. Soldiers who had sneered at the news that they were to serve side by side with former slaves now accepted them as worthy comrades, if not equals, and stood ready to defend them. None of their initial reluctance remained. The heat of many battles had melded slave and soldier into a single fighting force. They would not disappoint him today.

A throb of drums filled the air, pounding through the thunder of oncoming cavalry, the jangle of armor on man and mount, the taunts of the Parthian bowmen. Brutus shaded his eyes and sought his father.

Caesar's horse gleamed like the finest white marble in the morning light. Legs clamped tightly to the creature's barrel, there was nothing left of Caesar the dictator, Caesar the would-be king; here he was simply Caesar the general. He had chosen this battleground, resisted all temptation to run the Parthians to earth, let them come to him in their own time, but on his terms. The enemy had the sun to their backs, but Caesar's troops had the high ground to theirs. It was terrain unfavorable to horsemen, yet not so forbidding as to scare off the enemy altogether. Crassus had been thrown from Fortuna's lap by letting others herd him to his doom; Caesar was always the shepherd's hound, never the sheep.

The legions were arrayed so as to thwart any effort of the Parthian archers to surround them. That had been one of Crassus' gravest mistakes, and the enemy had seized full advantage of it. Another had been the foolish assumption that the archers would eventually run out of arrows and be rendered useless. Crassus found out too late that his enemy had come into the field well supported by a baggage train of camels laden with fresh ammunition for the mounted bowmen.

Caesar assumed nothing, trusted no one but his own scouts. (Ariamnes, an Arab chieftain deep in the Parthians' purse, had used his position as native guide to mislead

Crassus' force into the desert where they were so ruthlessly
and efficiently cut down). These men belonged in the
main to the Gaulish auxiliaries, as did most of Caesar's
cavalry with the exception of some Armenian riders. Young
Gaius commanded them, with a special eye to those men
Caesar had named his harpies.

*—which sounds much more impressive than my poor
chickens*, Brutus thought, turning in the saddle to gaze
at Gaius' picked force. *Pacorus is no fool; he's come as
ready to rearm his archers as Suren was at Carrhae. Only
this time, we're ready too.*

The great drums rumbled louder, the clangor of the
brass bells on their frames adding to the din. The spears
and standards of the approaching Parthian cavalry stood
black against the sun. In the midst of metal suns and
moons, Brutus could see the spread silver wings of a
Roman eagle.

He was not alone. A mutter of astonishment well mixed
with snarled curses rose from the Roman ranks. As if
the captive eagle worked some summoning magic, the
vanguard began to move forward to meet it until the
trumpeting of the great *cornuae* from Caesar's post brought
the men up short. Word galloped through the legions:
Move without orders a second time and die as renegades,
not as Romans. Only an ass would rise to such blatant
bait as Pacorus offered; an ass or a traitor. What other
name to put to any soldier who gave the Parthian prince
what he so clearly desired, the breach of legion discipline?

Brutus took a deep breath. The air prickled his throat,
alien. His eyes fixed themselves on Caesar, but Caesar's
eyes never wavered from the Parthian army. The drums
stilled. Somewhere in the van, the prince raised his hand
and brought it down with the finality of an executioner's
sword.

A roar broke from the Parthians, a shout lifted up from
beneath by the renewed beating of the drums. Roman
trumpets blared an answer, shouting Caesar's orders to

his men from brazen throats. Brutus let the air out of his lungs with a sudden rush, only then realizing that he'd been holding his breath against this moment, when the tension broke and battle was joined.

Arrows filled the air almost at once. The Parthian cataphracts advanced in a cacophony of armored man and armored steed, but their slowly mounting trot was outdistanced by the onslaught of the horse-archers. Unarmored, unhelmed, their heralding rain of arrows was their only shield. When they were within range of the Romans, they loosed their shafts, trying to break the close order of Caesar's men and leave them vulnerable to the oncoming cataphracts.

The Roman line held, thick and tight, though men fell in their numbers, shields and mail vests pierced. Still the legions held their ground, closing ranks over the dead. If they spread out they might evade the bowmen, but then the cataphracts would have them at their mercy. Caesar knew this from Crassus, and made sure to pass on the knowledge. Soldiers learned their best lessons from books written in their comrades' blood.

And now Brutus' legions showed their use: Armed with slings—the sole weapon he'd allotted them—the freed slaves set up a rapid fire of shot that was the only thing experience had shown could bring down the heavily armored cavalry of Parthia. Their assault was backed by Caesar's artillery, catapults that assailed cataphract, horse-archer and infantry alike with massive flights of arrows.

The sun climbed the sky, his face scarred by the uncounted feathered shafts raking the heavens. A separate company of Brutus' chickens moved forward, loading their slings with a new missile, a claw made of steel. The centurions commanding the slingers turned to their leader, waiting for his word. The claws, once launched, would not bring down an armored man like stone or lead shot. They served a different purpose. Brutus swept the field, searching for Gaius' cavalry, watching for the right moment.

There they were, on the left flank, rounding the side of the enemy forces, galloping for the baggage train. Their intent was plain. A body of horse-archers took off in pursuit, closing the gap, arrows nocked to the bowstring. Brutus gave commands.

The claws flew, seeding the ground between Gaius' men and their pursuers with metal talons. Again and again the slaves sent volleys of this new missile, dashing along at double pace behind the ranks of legionaries set to shield them. A separate division of horse-archers marked them out, probably imagining that they were the common stone-slingers sent to bring down the cataphracts. They raced their horses straight for the body of slingers and soldiers.

Horses screamed and toppled, pitching their riders off over their heads, rolling on them when horse and rider both fell. On the flank, where Caesar's harpies had almost gained the baggage train, the same disaster unscrolled as Parthian horses plunged the sharp points of the black claws deep into their feet. It was luck alone that decreed which horse picked up a metal thorn—Roman cavalry could become as vulnerable as Parthian if the flow of battle changed—but Fortuna seemed to have taken Caesar from her lap to her bosom in a lover's unbreakable embrace. Romans favored infantry, invested only auxiliary troops in the cavalry; any inadvertent losses they suffered from Brutus' airborne talons were negligible and besides, it wasn't the same as losing Roman lives.

But the Parthians were horsemen; their fortunes in battle clung to the saddle. No matter how impenetrable the armored rider, no matter how swift and keen-eyed the archer on his mount, take down the horse and you took down the man. Parthian warriors were not completely helpless afoot, but matched against trained Roman legions they had little chance.

A new shout went up from the battlefield. Caesar's

harpies had reached the baggage train. In the distance, flames shot up without warning, as if Jupiter himself had sent his thunderbolts to fire the supplies of Roma's enemies. Panicked camels broke free and ran in all directions, their burdens transformed to pyres.

Brutus rode his horse closer, straining to see. The mounted archers whose horses had missed the claws' bloody stab still urged their steeds after young Gaius' company. Bolting camels and donkeys with war-drums still strapped to their backs stumbled and trotted and ran between them, yet they pressed on. A Gaulish rider, tall and broad-chested, waved an empty wineskin at his pursuers, taunting them with words Brutus could not hear. A Parthian arrow split his heart and he fell to the earth beside the burning body of a camel. Then the wall of mounted archers closed around Gaius and his men; Brutus could see no more.

A trumpet call summoned him to action. Following his father's relayed commands, he ordered his centurions to form their troops into wedge formation around the slingers. The horse-archers might have lost any hope of fresh arrows, but they still owned their original supplies. If they regrouped—as it seemed Pacorus was now directing them to do—they might still summon up enough concerted effort to break through the center of Caesar's line and fragment the battle.

Like living arrowheads, the centuries of Brutus' legions moved forward, deeper into the fight. The talon-slingers reverted to launching stone missiles and lead shot against the enemy, taking down armored and unarmored men. Arrows fell from the Parthian side, leaving slaves and soldiers bleeding their lives out on the stony ground.

And now Caesar moved the main body of his legions forward too. Parthian cavalry—heavy and light—who tarried too long found themselves engulfed by Roman infantry. Legionaries had no qualms about hacking open a horse's neck or jabbing up beneath the beast's scale armor trapper. The shrieks of dying horses were more horrible to hear than the screams of dying men.

Brutus leaned forward, his sword drawn. Blood darkened the blade. He could not remain too far behind the lines and still be the man whose first god was duty. To direct his men as he desired, he had to follow them into the clash, had to face the enemy hand-to-hand. A deep slash on his right thigh bled freely, but the Parthian footsoldier who had been lucky enough to claim that stroke ran out of luck the next instant, against the edge of Brutus' sword.

Then a new sound rang out over the clamor of battle. It came from the heart of the fight, from a place of dust and steel and blood. Heads turned at the cry. Brutus wiped dust from his eyes and saw a wonder:

On a mountain made of the Parthian dead, a company of Roman legionaries stood exultant. One among them filled the air with his shout of triumph. Silver wings ablaze, the lost eagle of Carrhae caught the light, the standard's shaft held high in the soldier's hands.

CHAPTER SEVEN

"Babylon's not what it was," said Gnaeus Claudius Rufus, resting his arms on the parapet above one of the city's many gates.

Brutus gazed down at the river, out over the webwork of canals older than many gods. "Everyone says that, every chance they get, everywhere I go, ever since we got here. And not one person who says it has ever been to Babylon before. It doesn't bother me coming from the mouth of a blowhard like Publius, but I thought you respected the truth, Rufus. How can you make such claims?"

"You're too strict with the truth, that's your problem," Rufus replied. "Haven't you heard of the splendors of Babylon, haven't you read the old accounts? The wealth! The glory! The magnificence! Alexander himself—"

Brutus cut in before Rufus could launch himself into full panegyric. "Every city looks more splendid in the histories, and every battle becomes a glorious conquest or a desperate defeat. A wise king who wants to live forever should stop buying swords and start buying historians." He unfolded the palm frond packet in his hand and plucked out a plump fig, bought from a street vendor who smelled of goats and onions. The sweet juice exploded into richness in his mouth. "Do you want one?"

Rufus declined the offer. "Publius got sick from eating those things. Now he's at the mercy of the local doctors."

"Publius got sick because he believed a rumor he heard about Alexander's gold coffin being sunk somewhere out there." Brutus gestured to where the city's surrounding canals were lost in marshland. "Greed smothered the few brains he's got; everyone knows Alexander's entombed in Egypt."

"He told me that he'd heard the tomb in Alexandria's a fake, set up to decoy treasure-hunters from the real

106

thing," Rufus provided. "I guess he was willing to believe any kind of story as long as there was the smell of gold clinging to it."

"I always knew he was an idiot, but even an idiot has the sense to know that the only thing you'll find in a swamp is death: By beast, by drowning, or by disease, take your pick."

"Well, he's not dead yet." Rufus stood tall and stretched the kinks out of his back, arms high overhead. With a yawn he added, "It wouldn't surprise me at all if he pulled through this ague tonight and showed up in Caesar's council tomorrow morning, as much of a pain in the arse as ever."

"More," Brutus said. He ate another fig and wrapped up the rest. The sun of the riverlands beat down on his head. Babylon baked in the heat that drove most sane folk indoors, or to the shelter of any shade handy. Apart from those men assigned to patrol the city, casual passersby were few and far between at this hour. Brutus and Rufus could speak with complete security and no fear at all of being overheard.

"So what are you going to call your city?" Rufus asked. "Libertas?"

"Too obvious. And too likely to turn into a thorn. These men fought hard and well. If they owe us their freedom, we owe them our victory, and the retaking of the eagles. Does a debtor like to be reminded of the sum he once owed after he's paid it back in full?"

"Mmmmhmmm. I see what you mean." Rufus nodded, elbows on the parapet again. Anyone who didn't know the man would take one look at his ruddy face and assume he was about to collapse from sunstroke, but it was merely his normal complexion, an eccentricity of appearance that had earned him his cognomen. "When I first married, my father-in-law made me a very generous loan." He made a rueful face. "One he hasn't stopped mentioning every chance he gets, even though I repaid it years ago. At the time he gave me the money, I could have kissed him. Now I'd take an equal sum to hire a pack of gladiators to kill him." He made it sound like a joke, whatever his true feelings.

"You do see, then. The freed slaves may not have any great love for Roma, but there's no sense in provoking them to hatred."

"Especially now that you've taught them to fight," Rufus remarked lightly.

"Especially now that we need them more than ever," Brutus corrected him. "They were born captive; our ways are the only ways they know, but that doesn't mean they can't turn from them. They're going to live out their lives in a foreign land, surrounded by alien ways. If we drive them to hate Roma, we lose them, and if we lose them, we lose the road."

"Your wonderful golden road!" Rufus grinned. He'd heard much of Brutus' plans for the freed slaves before this. "You've no idea where it's bound to end, but you're setting up guardposts on it."

"I know where it ends the same way you know that Babylon's not what it was. I've read accounts of the riches that Alexander's men encountered in the lands beyond Parthia, and I've heard tell of lands that lie even farther to the east—lands whose trade can only bring prosperity to Roma! But first we must secure the trade route."

"And how big a piece of this prosperity goes right into your purse, eh?" Rufus teased his friend gently.

Brutus shook his head. "I have enough."

"Of course you do."

Brutus gave Rufus a sharp look. People talked; people remembered. No matter how high the principles by which he lived his life these days, there were still plenty of eager tongues ready and willing to bring up his younger days, when his own greed might have rivalled that of Publius.

People change, he thought. *Some do. And cities,*

governments, empires—I used to wring money from the provincials because that was what every Roman did who was in a position to do so. Now I wrack my brain to find the proper name for a city of slaves, searching carefully, so they won't take offense. Is it weakness to change? He pondered the notion. *No,* he concluded. *Only humanity. The gods alone are immutable.*

"Hey! Where are you wandering?" Rufus tapped his forearm. "Have I insulted you? If I did, tell me how."

Again a shake of the head. "I was just thinking about the city. I think I'll call it Alexandria."

"Not Caesarea?" Rufus' nostrils flared with amusement. "Not even Julia? You're not a very dutiful son."

"My father would be the first to commend my choice. If the Conscript Fathers see fit to rename the settlement in his honor, so be it, but for him or me to do it—? We might as well name it Vanitas."

"Yes, but do you know how many Alexandrias there are in this part of the world?"

"That makes it the perfect choice. My men can create their new lives under a name that's established, respected, feared, and that carries no unwelcome reminders of their past."

"Maybe they'll rename it Alexandria Julia some day, just so no one confuses it with the other ones," Rufus suggested. "Or maybe Alexandria Sabina." He winked at Brutus. "That *was* how you expected them to find wives, wasn't it? The old Roman way?"

Brutus regarded him long and steadily. "Do you really want to know? Or are you just jesting?"

"Both. There's a standing wager in the legions: A fortune in spoils and the favor of all the gods to the man who can make you laugh. *Really* laugh, not just those miserly little snickers that sometimes get away from you."

"Well, you lose the wager, Rufus, but if we return to the palace now, I may be able to answer your question."

They left the city walls and descended to street level.

The bulk of temples and other buildings cast slowly increasing shadows to shield the strollers from the blazing sun. Once on their route they stepped into a tavern to let Brutus rest his leg. The sword-stroke had healed clean, but it still pained him. In a way, he hoped the pain would persist, a constant whisper in his flesh that whatever her other gifts, the goddess had not granted him invulnerability. The tavern gave them the chance to dodge the sun and to sample some local beer that tasted thick and bitter. They set out again, and Brutus ate the rest of his figs before they reached the palace gates.

It was still called the palace of Nebuchadrezzar by those who sought it or spoke of it in any way. The man himself was dust, the wondrous hanging gardens he had built to please his Median bride were gone, but his palace still stood and could be called by no other man's name. Alexander the Great had died within those walls, yet even that earth-changing event never changed a single mention of the palace's name.

They found Caesar in one of the rooms he had taken for his personal apartments. It was a source of much commentary that the great general made very sure that he would sleep as far as possible from Alexander's death-chamber while still enjoying the most regal accommodations available. He was seated on a carved chair of Greek design, an open scroll in his hands, his back well protected by a body of eight soldiers. He smiled and rose when Brutus and Rufus came in.

"I was afraid that Apollo had finally claimed his own," he said, greeting them warmly. "Every day at the fiercest hour you always find time to tempt the sun to do what the Parthians couldn't. Now you're dragging Rufus with you. You won't be satisfied until he's redder than a split pomegranate."

Rufus pulled a long face that transformed him into a tragic actor stuck behind a second-quality mask. "We were discussing Publius' health. We didn't think it would be politic to do that anywhere near his hearing; it might upset him. How *is* the poor, dear fellow?"

"How much money do you have riding on his recovery?" Caesar asked dryly. He rerolled his scroll. "The Greek physicians give us every assurance that he'll live. However, I think I'll consult one of the local astrologers for some idea of how *long* he'll survive after I tell him the news."

"What news?"

"That he'll have more than enough time to recuperate from his fever here. He's to be named special overseer of the foundation and furnishing of— *What* did you decide to call that city?" Caesar asked Brutus.

"Alexandria."

Caesar raised one brow. "Not very original. Let it pass; you can come up with better names for the next ones." He held up the scroll. "News from Roma. Our defeat of the Parthians, the recapture of the eagles, and Pacorus' ransom have the Senate and the people so overjoyed that they hardly blinked at my summons for fresh troops . . . and fresh funds."

"And my cities—?"

"Oh, they're as madly in love with the idea as if they'd thought of it themselves."

"Wait until we get back and see if by then they haven't convinced all Roma that it *was* their idea," Rufus murmured in Brutus' ear.

"Let them," Brutus replied. "As long as the plan itself thrives, I don't care who's credited with it."

"The Senate moans about the funds to secure what we've won in Parthia and groans because we haven't annexed the whole territory," Caesar said. "When I return to Roma, I'll do my best to make them see that we've taken the right road. Why scatter guards around an entire city when all you need to protect is a single chest of treasure?"

"Pearls," Rufus put in. "There's your treasure. Pearls strewn from here to the Hindu Kush and beyond, and every pearl named Alexandria."

"He's trying to make me laugh again," Brutus confided in Caesar.

"He'd have better luck winning that bet if he took you to the theatre the next time they perform the *Mercator*. Plautus is bones, but he still makes me laugh."

Brutus bridled. "Did everyone in all the legions know about this bet but me?"

"Well, it wouldn't be much of a bet if the subject knew about it. I could've won it quickly enough, but the men would've put an honest victory down to collusion. You've cost me a fat purse, my son." Caesar tried to look serious. Rufus had less acting ability and sniggered into his hand.

"Too bad," Brutus responded without a hint of humor. "I could have used my share of the money—"

"—for your cities," Caesar finished for him. "Now and always. It's too bad you're such an oracle, my son; it's cost us money enough. The senators are responding to my request for new support just as you predicted: They're most of them opting to pay off the tax in slaves. How many more can you afford to equip and transport here?"

"More than enough to seed a second of my Alexandrias," Brutus answered. "And a third, and possibly a fourth. That is, if you've had news from the east as well as the west?"

"Come with me now and you'll hear for yourself." Caesar led the two men from the room, his bodyguard disposing themselves to shield both father and son. Rufus found himself cut off and had to trot along behind.

They came to the great throne room of the palace where titanic winged bulls with the heads of men stood vigilant over the king's seat. Caesar mounted the flight of steps to the royal dais and took the throne without a second thought. This far from the all-seeing eyes of Roma, no one read any lust for kingship into his actions. Servants with oiled beards and brightly colored robes fetched Brutus a chair. Rufus was left to his own devices, along with the other Roman commanders already waiting. He hovered as near Brutus' place as he could.

Seated at his father's side, Brutus stretched out his wounded leg, grunting involuntarily as a twinge ran through it, then gazed down the length of the hall. The throne room was abustle with crowds of people—Greeks, Romans, Chaldees, Parthians, and some whose looks and dress were beyond his knowledge. Soldiers of the legions stood ready to maintain or restore order at an instant's notice, depending on any shift in the human winds, the hushed voices now blowing through this hall. Whispers and murmurs in half a dozen tongues twined their way up the titantic pillars, washed over the colossal hooves of the man-headed bulls.

Caesar gave a small sign with his right hand and a venerable Chaldee whose lush beard looked too black to be real stepped forward, a gold-sheathed staff of olivewood in his hand. He pounded it on the floor, calling for silence. By little and little, like the retreating wavelets of the ebb tide, the voices of the hall stilled.

A trumpet call tore away the newly made silence. From the far end of the throne room, the crowd parted to give passage to a small parade of Roman soldiers. Led by an army musician, his wolf's-headed *bucina* resting its brazen coil around his shoulders, they made their entrance in perfect order, their hobnailed soles striking thunder from the stone. For cape and helm they wore the skins of wolves and lions, the beasts' heads covering their own, black lips drawn back in one last death-frozen snarl of defiance. In their hands they carried the silver eagles of the legions— Caesar's legions, Brutus' legions, and Crassus' stolen flock, now come home. They passed through the mob like a sword through water, mounted the stairs, and ranged themselves to either side of the throne.

Before the passage they had opened could close, a second group of men followed in their wake. They were Roman soldiers too—that much was plain to see by the uniforms they wore—but their step lacked the crisp cadence of the triumphant *aquilifers*, their garb looked old, worn, weathered and stained, and they carried no arms. Still they kept rank and order, drawing themselves up into three rows of eight. One of their number stepped forward and saluted Caesar.

Caesar returned the salute. "You are Gaius Domitius Niger?" It was not really a question. Caesar made it his business—his survival—to know things. "*Optio* of the first cohort of Marcus Licinius Crassus' second legion?"

The man's heavily scarred face convulsed as if he were fighting demons in his belly. If it had been his dark complexion that gained him the name Niger, it was well-earned: His skin was burned almost as black as a Nubian's. But if the name had come to him because of the color of hair or eyes, all evidence of that was gone: His hair was storm gray, and where his right eye was already milky with the haze of one cataract, the left showed the first invading veils of another. Despite these marks of time, he held himself tall, shoulders well back, and when he spoke his voice revealed him to be a man still in his prime.

"I am Gaius Domitius Niger," he replied, his good eye steady on Caesar's face. "I am no *optio*; I am a slave, taken at Carrhae. As were they." He gestured stiffly to include the uniformed men standing with him. "I have no legion but the dead."

Caesar rose from his seat and descended the stairs. Without a word from the dictator, one of the *aquilifers* came after him, holding the silver eagle high. Facing the man Niger, Caesar announced so that all those crowding the throne room might hear: "No Roman of the legions is any man's slave! No legion of Roma dies while her standard remains in Roman hands!" He extended his hand and the *aquilifer* gave him the eagle, sparkling wings outstretched. He thrust it out before him, so that even Niger could not help but see what gift it was. The *optio's* calloused hands closed on the smooth shaft. Brutus thought he could see copious streaks of tears leaking from the man's eyes, but if that were so, Niger betrayed his discipline no other way.

Caesar remounted the dais, turned his back on the throne, and declared to the hall, "These men—my soldiers!—and all their goods and families are under my protection, according to the terms I have made with King Orodes of Parthia. They are no one's slaves, but free Roman citizens, wrongfully held subject in the city of Merv, in the easternmost reaches of the Parthian lands. Now justice has been done! Recompense will be made!"

A cheer went up from every Roman present, a cheer in which all prudent non-Romans likewise joined, even those present in Parthian dress. As Caesar spoke on, Brutus heard Rufus' voice whisper, "So that's where your new freedmen will get their wives; from the liberated captives of Carrhae. Caesar gives them back their legions—in name, anyway— and their honor. All they have to do is give Caesar's son their daughters. Brilliant! How can they say no, or hold their children too good to nest with Brutus' chickens? The girls were born slaves, and your former slaves are all blooded fighters. There are worse marriages made every day."

"They won't all come back from the east," Brutus murmured. "It's been years, they've built whole new lives in Merv, some have left their bones there. The sons will inherit their dead fathers' freedom, but they'll have no reason to leave their only home or send me their sisters." He shrugged. "That suits me well."

"Why would—? Oh." Rufus patted Brutus on the shoulder. "This time your Alexandria's built for you; it just happens to be named Merv."

"Ssh."

The audience continued. Envoys from Orodes' court presented their lord's compliments and good wishes as hollow as clay cookpots to the man who had defeated and captured the favorite son of the Parthian king. Gifts were brought, some of them true gifts and not just part of Prince Pacorus' ransom. The prince himself had been returned to his father's court as soon as the bulk of the ransom was paid over; Caesar could afford to appear gracious.

Brutus observed all this with only half an eye. His mind was elsewhere, stealing like a shadow from Nebuchadrezzar's palace, out over the walls of Babylon. Once more he sat on his horse on the battlefield, watching the distant baggage train burn, the camels' packs well doused with the oil-flasks of Gaius' riders. He and his horse were the only living creatures to see the leaping flames. The ground was bare and hard, cracked and rocky except where the blood of the dead watered it to life.

Brutus? It was young Gaius, the tribune who had led Caesar's harpies to their glorious doom. He came on foot, the fires behind him twinkling through his eyes, his mouth when he opened it to speak, the marks of lance and arrow slitting his flesh.

No. Brutus pulled back on his horse's bridle. The beast took a few skittering sideways steps, tossing its head angrily, and returned to its original place like steel to the lodestone. *Go away, Gaius. I bear too many ghosts. I have no room for you, too.*

You have no choice, Brutus. The young tribune's face was the color of cream poured over water. *No more.*

Brutus shut his eyes so tightly that small bursts of color, diamond-patterned, swirled behind the lids. *It's hot in the throne room and my father can out-talk a dozen men. My leg hurts. I had too much of that bad beer. The figs were heavy in my stomach. I'm asleep. You're a dream.*

He opened his eyes. He was back in the throne room. Gaius was gone. Rufus was poking him in the back, discreetly, so that no one could tell that Caesar's son had fallen asleep in the midst of his father's audience.

The audience was over. The Parthian envoys were withdrawing, Caesar was smiling, and the level of chatter in the hall was rising slowly but surely. The crowd had done their duty as witnesses. Now they would enjoy a feast of speculation as their due.

"We can go now," Rufus murmured. Caesar was already gone, his bodyguard in close formation around him. If he'd wanted Brutus to attend him he would have given a sign. He hadn't; he had more than enough of other matters to occupy his hours. The *aquilifers* and the bucina player fell in behind him, the delegation of freed legionaries from Merv tagging after. Already their stride had regained a little of the old military precision. *Optio*-that-was Gaius Domitius Niger marched at their head, his failing eyes on the eagle soaring before him.

Brutus and Rufus followed them only part of the way back to Caesar's quarters before dropping out of the procession. "Got any more figs?" Rufus asked.

"All gone."

"Then let's get some more."

Brutus gave the man a quizzical look. "Weren't you the one so certain that Publius fell ill from eating figs?"

"Oh, I don't want to *eat* them; I just want to *get* them." Rufus' teeth were only a little yellow. "The sun's slacked off; the city's coming alive again at this hour. Today's the first time you or I've been able to get away from our thrice-damned duties long enough to explore, enjoy! Let's seize the day while we can."

Brutus was about to reply that *he* didn't think of duty as something to be evaded. He was too good a Stoic for such childish attitudes. Then he felt a phantom's breath stir the newly shaved nape of his neck and heard Gaius' voice say *You have no choice, Brutus. No more. You're led by the nose or the balls or the brain, all the time telling yourself that you've got the master's end of the chain. You don't. One time you thought you had a choice to make, a choice of your own free will.* Mocking laughter scraped the inside of Brutus' skull. *Who chooses now, Brutus? You or the man your duty tells you you ought to be?*

As sudden as a fist to the gut, Brutus knew he wanted beer and wine enough to drown in.

"Let's go." Walking as fast as his convalescing leg would allow, he fled with Rufus into the streets of Babylon.

CHAPTER EIGHT

Rufus' face was ice—white, cold, every line cut deep and eternal, grim beyond the chance of change. At first Brutus thought it was a trick of the light that had robbed his comrade's appearance of its normal animation and flush of color. The little door from which he had emerged gave on darkness, only the hint of a sliver of lamplight within, and the street where Brutus had been told to wait was already deep in twilight. Still, for a man who had gone through that door so red to emerge so white—!

"Rufus?" Brutus tried to lay his hand on the legate's arm. "You were in there so long that—"

The ice mask shattered into a bug-eyed stare of panic. Rufus pulled away from Brutus' touch so fast that he slammed his elbow against the baked brick wall behind him. "Don't touch me!" One hand cupping his injured elbow, Rufus formed the fingers of the other into the trembling sign to ward off the evil eye.

Brutus knit his brows. "Are you well? Were you fool enough to drink one of that accursed dwarf's potions? You idiot, you don't know half the black roots these Chaldees can slip into an honest man's wine!"

"I drank nothing." Rufus' voice grated from his throat. The warding gesture was steadier now. He rubbed his elbow tenderly and backed another step from Brutus.

If Brutus believed him, he gave no sign of it. "It's a ruse they all use, these so-called magi. Slip a man an evil vision in a cup, then sell him a fistful of charms to deflect bad fortune. How much did he take you for?" He cocked his head, scanning what he could of Rufus' hands to see whether his comrade had been mulcted of more than one of his gold rings.

Rufus jerked his whole body against the wall. "Stay where you are," he told Brutus. More than a few people

118

strolling through that narrow street heard him, though the words came out like a dog's low warning growl. They stopped to watch. Not one of them was Roman. Part of their interest was simple curiosity, but more of it was keenness to see the Roman conquerors playing the fool in the streets of Babylon. Knowing this turned Brutus' stomach to stone.

"For the love of all the gods, Rufus, you're making a spectacle of yourself," he gritted, closing in whether the man wanted it or not. "Talk sense. Act sane. If I need to drag you off by the neck and lock you away with the mad, I'll do it, but stop giving these cattle something to gawk at."

Rufus' eyes darted left and right. He couldn't help but see the crowd gathering near. Brown, wrinkled faces split into grins that showed more gum than tooth. Smooth-skinned eunuchs put their plump heads together, whispering with delight. Children clung to their mothers' robes, swinging forward like young monkeys to get a better look at the two fearsome high-ranked Romans, now no better than a pair of street-beggars squabbling over a coin.

Rufus was still afraid—Brutus could see that in the sliver of white rimming his eyes all around—but he recalled himself, his position, how his actions must reflect on the rest of his countrymen, what would happen if word of this scene reached Caesar. He tightened his jaw and glowered at the mob. "Get out of here!" he shouted. "On your way!"

They only laughed. Many pretended not to understand a word of what the Roman said. Still others mouthed his speech back at him soundlessly, capering to the back of the crowd when he started towards them.

Brutus remained unruffled. He took a few silver pieces from his belt pouch, jangled them ostentatiously in his palm, then with a high-arcing toss sent the coins flying over the heads of the first rank, into the place where the crowd stood thickest.

A fight broke out almost immediately. Those who wanted money couldn't tell their rivals from those who only wanted to get out of the way. As the shoves and shouts and the women's little screams multiplied, Brutus calmly laid hold of Rufus' arm and pulled him back through the doorway.

The turmoil outside was cut off the moment the heavy door shut behind them. Inside there was only silence and the smell of frankincense overlaying stale beer and old man's urine. A flame danced from the snout of a clay lamp on a table. Shadows turned heaps of round-bellied pots and piles of indistinguishable objects into a geography of monster-haunted caves and god-stalked mountains.

Brutus strode forward to where a battered metal cup lay beside the lamp. Reflected flame shimmered over the dark lees still puddled in the bottom of the cup. Brutus picked it up and sniffed it suspiciously, then dabbed a fingertip in the muck and laid it to his tongue.

"How do you know I did not poison it between the time your friend left and you made him return?"

Brutus started at the voice, reedy with age, that spoke Greek with a foreign lilt. He knew it. He had heard it before, in the evil hour when Rufus first insisted they enter this squalid place. The legate had gotten it into his head that their exploration of the city would be incomplete without a visit to one of Babylon's famed astrologers. Inquiries at the Ishtar temple steered them here; a priest spoke the name of Na'id-Sin the magus with reverence bordering on fear. They entered the seer's lowly dwelling and found that the great Na'id-Sin was old, feeble, and smelling more of the pisspot than the incense-breathing stars. Brutus could not conceal his skepticism at first sight of the reputed seer, and so he had been banished to the street by the magus' surly slave.

But Rufus stayed to hear his fortune.

A fine fortune to be found in a place like this! Brutus thought. "Well?" he called into the dark. "Did you?"

The shadows stirred and gave up a manling clad in

robes whose richness shimmered even in this poor light, a pearl shining in a sewer. When he walked, the floor echoed, as if he wore the built-up wooden shoes of a tragedian beneath his garments. If he did, even so, the top of his high headdress only just cleared Brutus' shoulder. Any hair he might conceal beneath it was likely to be as white as the scant, poorly curled whiskers straggling across his upper lip and chin.

Brown eyes bright even without the lamp's reflected glow blinked at Brutus. "Do not fear," the dwarf said. "All it holds is wine and a little honey to take off the bite. It is the cup of hospitality, not deceit. I can no longer provide my customers with the finer pressings, and it would not do to pour them a cupful of vinegar. Too often what I tell them is sour enough."

Na'id-Sin stretched out his hand. It trembled with palsy, but he managed to keep it relatively steady until Brutus understood what it was he waited for and handed back the cup. It clattered against the clay lamp when he set it back down on the table. "So you have changed your mind and come to hear my reading after all." He turned his back on the Romans and shuffled into one of the room's more obscure corners where he hunched his small shoulders over some unknown task.

"I'm here because whatever you told poor Rufus scrambled his brains for him," Brutus snapped above the sounds of metal vessels knocking against one another and the thin, high sound of liquid being poured out. "What did you do to him? What did you say?"

"I'm going," Rufus announced before the dwarf could answer.

Brutus whirled to stop him, but the door had already slammed. All that Brutus got was a puff of warm air from the street, the there-and-gone sounds of the world outside. "*What* did you do to him?" Brutus repeated, his rage shaking the small room. He started forward, reaching out for the dwarf. Dry crunchings under his feet released a mixed bouquet of scents and a spray of dust that doubled him over with sneezes.

Na'id-Sin concluded whatever had held his attention in the corner. His fingers snicked and a second lamp—metal and horn, as large as his head—lit up in his hands.

"There is a hook in that beam over the table," he said serenely, holding the light out to Brutus. "Hang it for me, please. Jabal usually does it for me, but he will not be present when I work. His god, like you, has no use for fortune-tellers. I try to explain to Jabal that I do not as a rule read the future, only the past. He refuses to see the difference, and if he will not—after ten years in my service—I doubt I will be able to make you see either."

Brutus took the lamp from the dwarf without comment and hung it from the hook as bidden. Rufus was gone—Rufus who had been his friend had fled from him as if he'd seen a bloody skull where Brutus' face had been. Why? Brutus had to know. If he turned his back on the Chaldean now, he never would.

The light from the horn lamp robbed the little room of all evil shadows. What had been a sinister den of the unknown was now just another wretched mouse-hole burrowed into the clay bricks of Babylon. Brutus saw a rolled-up sleeping mat against one wall, the barley straw poking through the ticking, strong with the reek of mold. It did not look big enough for two men, even when one was Na'id-Sin. The slave Jabal most likely made his bed on the bare earth. A second table shouldered itself into the wall opposite, its surface packed with stacks of clay tablets except for where a lesser pile of scrolls were crammed on end into a cracked pot of Samian ware.

"I would invite you to sit down," the magus said, "but I have only one stool and that is for me." So saying, he reached under the table, dragged it out, and sat down. It was built low to the ground, to accommodate its owner's short legs. Na'id-Sin slapped his hands to his knees and grinned up at Brutus, who loomed above him like a temple pillar. "You see?" he said pertly. "Many things that happen in this world come from one cause while seeming to spring from another. I did not refuse you this seat out of any lack of hospitality, but because I am an old man and you would not be able to use it anyhow. You would squat on it like a frog in a well and you would end by toppling over backward before our conversation was well begun. And *that*, Roman, is what I did to your friend, the noble legate Gnaeus Claudius Rufus." He slapped his knees a second time, as if that concluded everything.

Brutus had other ideas. "You'll give me a better explanation than that or you'll come with me to answer for your doings to Caesar himself. What sorcery of yours turned him from my friend into—"

"—your enemy? He is not that, Roman," the dwarf replied evenly. "He loves you too dearly and owes you too much ever to turn against you. But he does not feel he owes you his life in payment for the honor of being your friend."

"When did I ever ask him for—?"

"How many of them are there now, with cold emptiness where living eyes once gleamed and a handful of ashes for a heart?" The dwarf's voice rose and fell in sing-song cadence, his words transformed into a nasal chant. "Man with a shadow edged in the goddess' holy, all-consuming flame, how many common souls have come too near you, only to feel it pass over their flesh, burning it away? She who shared your bed and died, he who shared his dagger plot and died, all who held to that same death pact with him and died, he who was your father's former heir and died, he who stood second only to your father in power and died, he who gained his freedom at your hands and died, he who—"

Brutus pressed his hands to ears, closing out the litany of deaths. The seer named no names, but did name just enough for there to be no hope of error. He knew. The reader of black stars knew.

In time, Brutus lowered his hands again. Na'id-Sin sat staring at him like a plump owl. "So the man who values duty fears truth?"

"No. No, I—" Every indrawn breath made his chest ache. "How much did you tell Rufus?"

"Only enough. He asked me how high your star would climb and I told him first how hot it flamed. You see, it is as I said: I do not read the future. I used to, but it is an art requiring more strength than I have left me, these days. So to put him off, I let him gaze with me into your past."

"And he saw . . . her?" The image of the goddess in all her guises smiled down at Brutus from the horn lamp.

"She did not choose to be seen. But I, who served her Ishtar mask, still saw her. Your friend did not. All that the vision let him see was the deaths."

"I didn't kill them." Brutus' fists clenched. "Not Portia, not Antony, not Cassius, not Octavian, none of them!"

"Does the dagger kill or does the hand that holds it?" With a grunt, the dwarf got up and shuffled over to a shelf set within easy reach for him. It held a white clay bowl, a bottle of blue glass, and a thin silver wand, its length twined with a golden serpent. Holding all of these objects awkwardly, Na'id-Sin returned to lay them out on the table. "You have not answered my question," he said, looking up at Brutus.

"It has no answer." If he spoke with enough assurance behind his words, they would have to be true.

"Did you think you could join with an immortal and be unchanged? These gods of ours are hungry. They are kin to the old gods who were not satisfied with any feast but the flesh of children. But the old gods are dead. Their world has been tamed. The gods who now reign will accept a sheep, a bull, a pig, a dove, a pinch of incense if nothing better is offered. And what will the next gods demand? Or will they only request?"

"When we asked at the Ishtar temple for a reputable

fortune-teller, the priest sent us here," Brutus said. "He said you had once served there with him. Now I see why you left. You're a blasphemer."

"Truth is often twinned with blasphemy."

Brutus made a sound of disgust. "And charlatans often pose as wise men. You've cost me a friend, but you've made an enemy."

"You?" The dwarf didn't sound at all afraid. "Then you share the company of your betters. The gods also fear the truth. They dislike hearing that immortality clings to life by such a slender thread as man's worship." He unstoppered the bottle and poured a thin golden stream of oil into the white bowl. Unhurried, he recorked the bottle and put it back in its place on the shelf before returning to the table, taking up the wand, and raising his eyes to Brutus expectantly.

"What?" Brutus snapped at the unasked question in the dwarf's eyes. "Are you offering me the same trash you foisted on Rufus? A vision? Truth?" He spoke those last few words with enough scorn to penetrate the densest sensibility and leave behind no doubt as to his meaning.

Na'id-Sin ignored Brutus' mockery. He held the serpent wand between the thumb and forefinger of his right hand. The stubby fingers showed wrinkles, age spots, and places where lighter skin spoke of heavy rings once worn, now gone. The only adornment left was a clear emerald set in silver that bulked huge on the dwarf's forefinger. The wand trembled as the hand trembled, the serpent becoming a blur of gold over the surface of the oil.

Suddenly the wand was still, immobile, held in a hand grown smooth and spotless, decked with many rings. Brutus' eyes widened, flew from the transformed hand to the yet-old face of the magus. The Roman ran his tongue over his teeth as if searching for the drug-bought illusion contained in the one unwise taste of lees he'd had.

The eyes could be tricked easily, he reasoned; the other senses less so. He would not prove as ripe a mark as Rufus, he *would* not! He reached out his own hand and saw how it shook. Still he forced it forward to touch Na'id-Sin's, to feel for himself whether the magus' skin were young. The dwarf did not withdraw his hand, only waited patiently for Brutus to do what he would. Brutus' fingertips met skin that was sleek and plump with youth, scraped themselves over the golden prongs holding rubies and pearls firm in their settings.

As he rested his hand on the dwarf's, the serpent wand began to quiver. One by one the rings vanished. Brutus' third finger, that had rested atop an especially brilliant pearl, fell without warning onto a whorl of gnarled and flaccid skin covering a gemless knuckle swollen with the bone-ache.

"I would ask if you believe my powers now," the dwarf said amiably, "but I see it would be a wasted question; the answer is in your face. It is my belief that the gods allow us only so many times that our mouths—or even our hearts—may call out for answers. When our allotted questions are spent, our lives are done. Only then do we find the last answer. However—" He shook his hand—a deliberate move this time, and not the palsy—and cast off Brutus' touch. "Do you wish to risk one of your questions here? I can promise you that you'll have a more satisfactory answer than if you put it to one of your gods."

Brutus realized that his breathing was rapid and shallow, as if he feared the very air surrounding the magus, didn't dare to draw it too deeply into his lungs. "Am I—?" he began. "*Am* I the death of any who come too near me?"

Na'id-Sin shook his head. "That is the wrong question. The answer is already given."

"No," Brutus said, feeling cold. "No, it can't be so. Not all of them have died. Not all—" His pulse pounded so hard in his throat that he thought it would choke him. "Why would she do such a thing to me? Why, if she rules love, would she turn me into an instrument of death?"

Again that dismissive shake of the head. "A false

assumption yields a false answer. Who *rules* love? For that matter what is—?" Na'id-Sin chuckled, a sound of laughter that shook itself into a wheezy cough. When he recovered himself he said, "I am not one of those visionaries who claim to read the will of the gods. My scrolls and tablets are all mortal. Ask otherwise, but know that this is the last question you may ask of me."

"Show me—" Brutus paused, his mind working wildly. He had seen the magus' hand transform, he *had*, he knew it was neither drugs nor madness that changed old flesh to young. He believed in the dwarf's words as he believed in his powers, because he could not deny them by any evidence of the rational mind. "Show me how I may end the deaths—*if* I may end them?"

This time the dwarf did not shake his head. He stared at Brutus steadily, eyes narrowing to glittering slits while a smile slowly uncurled the corners of his lips like the tendrils of a vine. "Yes," he said. "Well asked, fairly asked. By the oath I took when I left her service, I may not turn from giving you your answer, no matter what that gift will bring to me."

"Her service?"

"Have I not said already that your goddess and I are old friends? Or perhaps *friends* is not the word to suit our relationship."

"Lovers?" Brutus stopped himself before he could blurt out an astonished *You?*

"Why not me?" the magus replied just as if Brutus had spoken the word aloud. He was not angry. "You are one of those men who likes to think that love accompanies all his couplings—if not on his side, at least on the woman's. And so she who is the sower of fire, the world's hunger, the enchantress who takes naked wants and makes them bring forth flowers to cover their claws . . . for you she must be love." Na'id-Sin laid down the serpent wand. "I will give you what you ask, but you must give me time. Your question begs the future. As I have told you, to read what will be demands much of me. I must wait for Jabal to return and help me make my preparations."

"When shall I come back for my answer?" Brutus asked, with only a fleeting thought of never coming back at all.

"Come tonight, if you do not fear the streets. Come after you have dined, so that later you will not tell yourself my visions were only the product of your hungry gut." Grizzled brows rose. "Of course, you can come tomorrow morning if you prefer the city by daylight—?"

"I'll come tonight."

The dwarf nodded. "Good."

As Brutus was leaving Na'id-Sin's dwelling, the door opened before he could lay a hand to it and a tall, lightly muscled man with olive skin and pitchy hair came in. He wore a simple robe, unbleached, undyed, though his belt was bright blue and lavishly fringed.

Na'id-Sin clapped his hands together and exclaimed, "There you are, Jabal! Not before time. Come in, come in. There is nothing afoot at the moment to irk your god. However, I do have a few errands for you to do."

"More witchery," Jabal grumbled.

The dwarf took his slave's testiness with good humor. "How else do I put bread in your mouth but through witchery? Never fear, when I see your god I shall tell him to hold you blameless."

Brutus heard master and slave bickering over a list of supplies as the door closed behind him.

He did not know how he managed to find his way back to the palace. The streets around him transformed themselves into the streets of a dream city, where wide ways became suddenly narrow and well-known routes abruptly doubled back into unknown territories. Nevertheless, he ultimately found himself in the palace of Nebuchadrezzar, in his own rooms. He summoned a servant and ordered some bread, a few olives, and wine. He ate the olives, nibbled at the bread, and didn't touch the wine.

I wonder whether this counts as dining? he asked himself, and knew the answer. The magus had said that visions of the future cost him much; the preparations to receive them must be complex, requiring more than the little time it took a man to eat a handful of olives and a mouthful of bread. He left his room and wandered through the halls. He thought he smelled roasted meat coming from somewhere, but as he was following that scent his nose was assaulted by another—more pungent, less pleasing. Since he felt neither hungry nor sociable, he decided to follow the second clew of odors and wound up outside the room that had been given to the ailing Publius.

The door was ajar, letting the sour-sweet smell of sickness escape. Brutus peered through the crack, pushing it open wider by degrees. The room was furnished with a brightly painted bed, a pair of tables, a large chest, a chair, a stool, and a number of bronze lamps. Only one of these was lit. It burned cheerily on the table beside the sick man's bed, the flame dancing over the belly of a green glass bottle and a silver cup.

Brutus stole into the room as quietly as he could. Publius lay with his hands atop his considerable stomach, his scant hair plastered to his brow with sweat. His eyes were closed, but even at a distance Brutus could see the rise and fall of breath in the bulky body beneath the coverlet. As he came nearer, he noticed that the sickness had pared away a little of the legate's flesh and colored the remainder like tallow.

"Publius?" he whispered.

The purple eyelids fluttered. Dry lips parted with an audible rasp. Brutus tossed aside the little water remaining in the cup and poured out a fresh measure, then held it to the sick man's mouth. Publius threw one arm over Brutus' neck to help himself sit up, then drank and sank back, weary but satisfied.

"So you've come to say goodbye?" was his greeting.

"I came to see how you were faring," Brutus replied. "The word I had was that you'd recover."

"Huh. So there is worse news than knowing you're going to die." Publius' speech was as dry as his lips had been. "And do I have you to thank for my posting? Sent off to herd your thrice-cursed chickens off into the middle of nowhere? I'd rather wring their necks."

"Then you might as well cut your own purse open while you're at it," Brutus snapped. Despite the lingering signs of sickness, Publius sounded ripe for an argument, and Brutus was happy to seize on any distraction to keep his mind from thoughts of the waiting magus. "You refuse to see my first Alexandria as anything but your exile from Roma. Meanwhile the Senate teems with men greedy for a foreign governorship where they can grow rich!"

"Your *first* Alexandria?" Publius snickered. "It cheers me to learn that I'm not the only one who'll suffer. I know where this golden city of yours will be established, Brutus, and if I could grow rich on rock and desolation, I'd set myself up in Babylon as the greatest magus of all time!"

Brutus shook his head. "You're hopeless."

"Is that a diagnosis? I'd rather be dead and buried in Roma than buried alive in Parthia."

"Oh, you'll live, Publius! I can see that better than any doctor. You've already recovered your stupidity. But maybe you'll learn, given time." He started from the sickroom.

"Call *me* stupid?" Publius shouted after him. "At least I've got more sense than some people I could mention, hunting lions that aren't there just so the people can see him as Alexander and all the Assyrian kings rolled into one!"

Brutus paused in the doorway. "What are you babbling about?"

"Where have you been all afternoon? They turned the palace on end searching for you. I got the whole story from the slave who tends me. A man from the northern marshes came into Caesar's presence with news of a lion, maned and raging. He said that only the great conqueror could hunt and slay such a royal beast, saving his people." Publius snorted. "He was only angling for money. Lions have too much sense to linger in these blasted lands—even my slave knows that! But Caesar liked the idea of sallying forth in a scene out of one of those old carvings on the walls. I don't think he even knows how to shoot a bow well enough to bring down a rabbit, let alone a lion, but—"

"He knows," Brutus said. He had stood to weapons' practice with his father times enough to understand that Caesar's soldiering went beyond sitting astride a horse and giving orders. If there was a weapon in use in the Roman legions, Caesar was familiar with it at first hand. "The gods grant you the power of true vision, Publius. Let there be no lions."

The sick man shrugged. "You don't need to worry about that. It was all done on the spur of the moment, and when they couldn't find you, they set out straightaway. I doubt they'll be back until after nightfall. The slave said that the hunting party left well supplied with torches. I think that Caesar has a taste for the dramatic. If you can't come home in triumph with a lion's skin wrapped around your shoulders like Hercules, at least give the people a torchlight parade!"

He burst into laughter that soon turned into racking coughs. Brutus left him without another word.

The sun was well down and night lay over the city. Brutus left the palace and made his way back to Na'id-Sin's place at the double. He didn't even take a moment to look up and see the brilliance of the stars.

He was not afraid of the streets. He had his sword with him, and he passed a number of Roman patrols. He reflected that this city had probably never been safer by night than since the conquest. The usual predators were still holed up in their lairs until they could gauge their chances of evading the soldiers' attention. Then they'd return to their old business of pouncing on lone passers-by after dark.

He found Na'id-Sin's door and knocked, expecting Jabal to admit him. There was no response from within. He knocked a second time; still nothing.

I'm a fool. The thought struck him bluntly. *The slave is never there when the master works his magic—the dwarf said so! And no magus would leave his dabblings untended just to answer the door.* His practical mind assured that this was only so that the client would be sure to discover the sorcerer in some impressive, sinister pose when he entered. His spirit whispered that Na'id-Sin had no need for cheap theatrics. He had already shown Brutus his power simply, effectively, impressive beyond any effect of colored smoke or flashing sparks.

Brutus opened the door of the magus' house and went in.

The horn lamp still burned over the table. A bowl glittered gold in its light—not the simple white clay vessel Brutus had seen earlier, but true gold, hammered with a pattern of serpents. Stretched out between the table and the door lay the body of Na'id-Sin.

Brutus hurried forward to kneel beside the little man. The dwarf lay on his stomach, face to the earth. Brutus felt for a throb of life under the jaw, at the wrists, at the springing of the throat.

Nothing.

He turned the body over gently. The dwarf's elaborate headdress fell away, releasing a cascade of jet-black hair wildly at odds with the whiteness of his beard.

"No one knows how old he truly was," came a weary voice from the shadows. "Not even I."

Brutus was instantly on guard, hand to his sword. He thought he knew that voice. "Jabal?"

"Here I am." The magus' slave moved from his place

in the darkened corner, the slightest of motions that broke his illusion of invisibility.

"What happened here?"

The slave shrugged. "He performed the necessary rites and he died of them. I do not know how old he was, but I do know he was old. Or so I believe. So I want to believe. It will be easier for me to sleep nights if I can believe he was only a poor, weak old man with a poor, weak old man's heart, and that the vision he conjured was too strong for him to behold without paying for it. Otherwise—" He shrugged again.

"What was the vision?" Brutus asked, slowly rising from his knees and glancing nervously towards the tabletop.

Jabal squatted in his corner, hands linked between splayed knees. "I do not know. I do not want to know. The Lord forbids me to pollute myself with witchcraft." He refused to look up from the ground. "My master told me that you had asked for a vision that would tell you how you might end the deaths. He did not tell me which deaths, but to my mind if a Roman were sick of death, it was a great thing, a prodigy! So for that reason, I elected to remain under his roof while he worked. Maybe the Lord destroyed him on my account."

"Lord? You mean your master killed himself?" Brutus was perplexed by the slave's peculiar way of expressing himself.

"My master is not my Lord." Jabal shook his head. "Look in the bowl, Roman. See if anything remains of the vision— if a vision came at all. You paid for it."

Brutus took a step nearer the table. He looked into the bowl. It was filled with dark red blood, the smell too familiar, too strong for his mind to offer the comforting lie that it might be wine. He saw the horn lantern's glowing reflection on the surface, his own face, and—

"Portia!"

She stood in a place of mists and ghostly flowers. At the sound of his voice she raised her eyes to his and opened

her mouth, but it filled with blood. Blood flowed from
her lips as water from a fountain, flooding everything
away. He plunged his hands deep into the crimson sea
as she vanished from him. He covered his weeping face
with bloody hands, calling and calling her name.

CHAPTER NINE

"Brutus!"

He blinked his eyes at the summons, feeling the lashes stick together.

"Brutus!"

Strong hands clamped themselves to his shoulders, shaking him. The taste of salt was in his mouth, and the coppery smell of blood in his nostrils.

"Brutus— Ah, curse you, a dead man! Now what have you done?"

The hands spun him around. His eyes were still partways gummed shut by the blood streaking his hands, but he could see a face emerging from the blur of his vision. Rufus' jaw was like the edge of a newly sharpened sword, still humming from the whetstone. His ruddy skin was splotched with white as Brutus' arms to the elbows were a patchwork of red. Still stunned by what he had seen in the golden bowl, Brutus hadn't even heard the man come in.

"Damn." Rufus spoke with a soldier's economy, his eyes fixed on the little corpse. "You've killed him. If we weren't screwed before—"

Brutus shook his head weakly. "I didn't—"

"He did not kill him." Na'id-Sin's slave stepped forward boldly. "I am his witness. The magus was old and he died of a shock his age could not bear."

"Who the fuck are you?" Rufus snapped.

"He's Jabal, this man's slave." Brutus had at last regained his voice. "Don't you remember, Rufus? When we first came here—"

"Ten thousand years ago," Rufus muttered. "Before the end of the world." His hand closed on Brutus' right elbow with only a little hesitation at the sight of the blood still trickling down. "Come on. We've got to get you out of here."

135

"Why? Where? Is something—?" A different light kindled itself in Brutus' eyes. "You're no longer afraid of me. Rufus, what's—?"

"We're going back to Roma," the man said sharply. "Now, tonight, as quickly as possible. And we're praying that your arrival alone will be enough to hold the Senate stunned until the legions loyal to you and your family can reach the city. If not—" Rufus didn't even bother to shrug. "—we're dead."

"But why?" Brutus demanded. "Why must we go back? There's so much work yet to be done here, the city, my men, the returning captives—"

"Unless you are there, in Roma's heart at the very moment the news breaks, ready to defend everything you've worked for here, all will be lost: The slaves, the city, the peace with Parthia, *all.*"

Cold dread rose from the pit of Brutus' belly. "What news?"

"He's dead," Rufus said. "Caesar's dead."

He thought that a lake of ice had spread itself beneath his feet, then cracked wide and plunged him into the abyss. "No." He shook his head, as if his denial would be enough to unsay Rufus' ill-starred words, restore some small measure of sanity to his world. "He can't be. It's a lie. How could—?"

"Do not waste precious time on questions, Master," Jabal said easily, cupping his hand under Brutus' other elbow. "Heed him now, ask later."

Brutus turned an inquiring look to the slave. "Master?" Shock had robbed him for the moment of strength and will.

Jabal only showed his teeth in silence, as if taking his own advice to reserve questions and answers both for a better time. Between the slave and Rufus, Brutus found himself hustled out of the dead magus' lair and into the streets of Babylon.

The streets were packed, but not with the native city-dwellers. The moment Brutus emerged into the freshness of the night air, he was struck full in the face with the familiar scents of leather and mail and sweaty wool that clung to the trained men of the legion. A cluster of helmets closed around him, a forest of spears began to move forward, sweeping him and his companions along.

They rushed through the streets like a flood, pouring out through one of the city gates to where a modest river-going craft awaited them with the patience of a draft ox. Brutus was carried aboard and dragged below by Rufus and Jabal. The darkness around him creaked and stank, the air tickled his nose with the dust of long-vanished shipments of grain. His heart slammed in unreasoning panic, only one explanation for this absurd flight bursting from his mind:

Treachery! I'm being herded off to die! He could think of no one immediate cause for it, but the slave Jabal was a man of wisdom: Sometimes there is no room for questions. Whether this plot was the work of men still true to Antony or Octavian, whether it had been merely the purchase of the disgruntled Publius, whether it had surged up from diehards in the legions who still resented his "chickens" in their midst, he didn't know. It didn't matter. He began to struggle, scuffling with the two men in the dark, trying to reach his dagger.

"Damn you, stop that! Have you gone insane?" Rufus was an exasperated voice and a thread of fear-sweat out of the blackness of the hold.

Jabal was less: Just a sigh of resignation. Brutus felt the slave's grip on his left elbow drop. He had only a breath to take before a fist smashed into the side of his head and a deeper night fell on him.

It was a darkness free of dreams or visions. For that, he was grateful. He floated on the bosom of oblivion, cast adrift from all thought. In a place without men or gods, he felt himself rise above the world's harried breath, serenity wrapped around him like a sleeping dove's wings. He did not know how long he clung to nothingness; he wished he might remain there forever.

Splinters and pinpricks of light intervened, invaded his peace. A cool breeze tickled his cheek, the moon's yellow curve slipped beneath his eyelids. Wooden planks lay warm beneath him, still holding fast to a dying measure of the day's heat. He raised his hands before his face. There was only the light of moon and stars to see by, but it was enough for him to tell that someone had washed them clean of blood. He started to sit up and moaned, half his face throbbing.

"Wine?" Rufus sat on a low stool beside him, leaning down. The little rivercraft's mast was at his back, two leather packs at his feet. He leaned forward with a cup. Brutus took it and drank. "It's good you're awake," Rufus went on. "We land soon. An unconscious man can't ride."

"Ride?" Brutus passed his tongue over his lips, chasing the last taste of the grape.

"To the sea," Rufus replied. "As fast as we can. Faster. If we outdistance the couriers, we'll make our own arrangements for passage—though I doubt we'll get there before they do. They were given the pick of the mounts, and we've lost time on the river. It was simpler to take ship downstream, even if it is the wrong direction; we'll have to circle around."

Brutus swallowed the sensation of floundering in a heavy sea, forced himself to be calm or at least appear calm. "You have me at a disadvantage, Rufus," he said, dominating the fear shaking his liver loose inside him. "We're not children; tell me plainly why I've been carried off, where, and on whose authority."

"I told you: Caesar's dead. You've got to reach Roma and secure your gains here, your hold there." He eyed Brutus closely, then added, "You don't believe me."

"Why should I?"

"I think you called me your friend, once."

"I still would. You're the one who chose otherwise." The words had the savor of ashes. Of all men, Brutus knew how readily friendship could turn to enmity. Portia's face was not the only one that came to him with a gift of blood. There were nights when he still saw Cassius' death mask in the shadows. *What I did, I did for Roma,* he told himself, pleading before an invisible tribunal, letting each nobly shining word weight down one pan of the scales of judgment. But the cold laughter of a host of phantom cynics poured itself into the other pan, sending his words flying away like thistledown.

"Would you rather keep me as your friend or as your ally?" Rufus snapped.

"If you see a difference between the two, I don't."

"Your friends die readily; your allies have some hope of survival."

Brutus spat. "That magus' false visions again—" He tried to sound skeptical; he was no great actor, so he failed, and Rufus noticed.

"What did he show you, Brutus? How strong a seeing was it? Strong enough to kill him, I know. The Judaean said so." He leaned back against the mast. "What will you do with him?"

"Who?" Feeling battered and tired, Brutus would have paid a helmetful of gold for an answer; instead all he got were more questions.

"The magus' slave. The one who struck you belowdecks. You know: Jabal. I thought I'd consult you before I had him killed. He *claims* that I haven't the right to harm him without your consent, says his master gave him to you for a present. He's got a glib tongue, I'll give him that, even if what he says is past belief."

"It's true," Brutus said abruptly. Not even he could explain what possessed him, to make him blurt out such a lie.

"Is it?" Rufus looked doubtful, but didn't press the matter. "Then his punishment will be left in your hands, just as he said. May you have joy of the gift."

"Joy . . ." Brutus stood up and leaned against the mast, gazing over the side of the boat to the shore slipping by. His own sigh mingled with the breeze filling the sail. "Where is he?"

"Below. I had him bound and beaten—nothing he won't recover from easily enough—just on account. If you can credit it, the man insisted on cleaning you up where you lay before taking his punishment. He's either devoted, crazy, or up to something, the gods know what. No matter: If he *is* your slave now, we can't have him striking his master. Though to be truthful, he did me a favor, laying you out cold. What evil spirit got under your skin? If you'd drawn your blade, you might have killed me."

Brutus glanced down. His dagger was still where he always carried it. That was a fortunate sign: If he were a prisoner, Rufus would never have allowed him to keep any weapon. But if not, then was what Rufus had said—?

—true? No. Impossible. He thrust the thought away.

"And if I *had* killed you, I suppose that would've gone to prove *a posteriori* that you still were my friend, no matter by what other name you call yourself." Brutus managed a weak laugh.

Rufus let it go its way without joining in. Instead he spoke a word to one of the several legionaries on deck. The man made a crisp gesture of acknowledgement and disappeared down the hatchway. He came back soon enough, preceded by the Judaean slave.

"Your property, returned to you before witnesses," Rufus said. "What's your pleasure be done with him when we make shore?"

Brutus only gave Rufus a quizzing look.

"He can't come with us," Rufus continued. "I don't know whether there will be enough horses for us all, or even if this man can ride—"

"I can ride," Jabal said, his speech a little thick from swelling lips. "I may be Judaean, but I was raised in Nabataean lands where they teach their sons to sit horses well enough. You didn't beat that knowledge out of me."

"Be quiet." Rufus didn't bother raising his voice. He was one who expected slaves to obey the way he expected water to run downhill.

"There will be enough horses," Jabal persisted. If he had been water, he would have been just as contrary to Rufus' expectations. "You do not want me separated from my master. I am his eyewitness, even if I am no more than a slave. My word will be enough to clear him of any suspicion in the magus' death. It is not as if the little man was a dead Roman."

"I can answer for myself in the matter of Na'id-Sin's death," Brutus responded, biting off the words.

"If we are stopped on the road for it, you have no time to waste on giving answers, Master," Jabal returned almost cheerfully. "Questioning would delay you; it might even keep you here, when it is worth your life to be away. Time has become everything for you."

Brutus cast up his hands in exasperation. "So I keep hearing! Why should I believe it from your lips *or* his?" He gestured at Rufus.

"You equate my word with a slave's?" The Roman bridled.

"You forget, Rufus: I'm not a man who sees slaves as others do," Brutus jibed. "It's not a popular way of thinking, and there are more than enough men eager to see it brought to a short, sharp end. False rumors can be as deadly as daggers, in the right hands."

"Meaning mine?" Rufus countered. "So instead of a quick knife through the ribs in some dark corner of the palace, I had to spread the lie of Caesar's death and carry you this far from Babylon before I could kill you?" His laugh was desert-dry, and it was no sooner heard than gone. "False rumors lack proof," he said. "I do not."

Rufus stood and faced Brutus. One hand, thickly calloused from the sword, seized him by the wrist while the other pressed something small and round and hard

into his palm. Then Rufus released his grasp, leaving
Brutus staring at moonlight on a ring: Caesar's most
treasured ring.

The truth broke his heart's last shielding doubt as if it
were no more than the froth of new-poured wine. He
made the first libation to his father's spirit of tears.

CHAPTER TEN

The slave Jabal climbed up the hillside through the straggling lines of grape vines, complaining bitterly to himself in his native tongue. From his vantage point before the villa, Brutus watched the Judaean's progress with a mixture of amusement and fondness. He knew that he was in for a tongue-lashing once the man gained the house, only to find that the errant master he'd been seeking all morning through the fields had doubled back on his tracks and was waiting for him. Outwitting Jabal was difficult, but evading him was somewhat easier. These days, with the Parthian campaign only a glorious memory, Brutus took his triumphs where he could.

"There you are, Jabal," he said, coming forward to greet him, the picture of innocence. "They told me in the house that you were looking for me. I was in the gardens—I don't know how you could have missed me—unless it was when I was stooped down, inspecting the roots of that new rose that's come from Parthia—"

Jabal shouldered past him, grumbling, as if Brutus were one of the farm's placid oxen blocking his way. Chastened and puzzled, Brutus fell into step behind Jabal as the Judaean marched into the villa, taking no notice of his supposed master. The slave neither stopped nor slowed his pace until he reached the formal gardens at the villa's heart. Here too his sandalled feet never slackened their brisk pace except for the moment they brought him to a particularly sunny corner where the earth was newly turned and a lushly flowering rose bush drenched the air with sweetness.

Jabal's expression was anything but sweet. He merely stood, arms folded, eyes steady, as if he were an animal trainer and the rose bush a dangerous beast likely to spring at him if his gaze wavered for an instant. Brutus came up behind him, at a loss to interpret his slave's behavior. The two men stood there for some time, one guarding silence, the other bewilderment.

In the end it was Brutus who spoke first. "Jabal, what are you doing?"

"Contemplating a miracle," the slave replied. "In addition to your other powers, it would seem you can also fly. What next? Water from a rock? My former master could crack pigeons' eggs and pour out salt, but this—!" He made an exaggerated gesture of astonishment.

"Mercury guide me, because you've lost me," Brutus said. "Miracles . . ."

"You're a philosopher," Jabal stated. "A man of reason. How else do you explain no print of hand or foot or knee in the dirt around the Parthian rose?"

"Taken." Brutus bowed his head in mock surrender. "Fairly taken, Jabal. There's no hiding anything from you."

"But from the Egyptian queen? She's at least as tenacious as I am, and she means to see you face to face. Not when it suits you to come out of your earth, either! The consul Gnaeus Claudius Rufus sends word that she's brought a fine gift to enrich the temple of Venus Genetrix and the shave-skulled priests she's dragged here from Alexandria are insisting that it be installed and dedicated on the ides, not three days from now! You can guess where they found *that* oracle, and it wasn't in the entrails of any dove. The queen of queens is tired of waiting for you. If you do not appear at the ceremony, it will count against you as a mark of disrespect not only to Queen Cleopatra but also to your late father."

"Clever . . ." Brutus rolled the word over his tongue and found it stung like a burr. "I remember when he brought her to Roma that first time. It was—" He shut his eyes. It had been in the year of the assassination conspiracy. *Cassius' conspiracy*, he thought, pushing his own aborted role in it ever farther away. "I did not see her then, but I heard of the stir she made whenever her litter passed the streets."

"She has not lost her touch for spectacle," Jabal said in a manner guaranteed to convey his disapproval. "Or for playing any man she meets like her father Auletes played his silly flute. High or low, she soon brings them over to her side. If you will not go to Roma for any other reason, go to pick out a good, stout wall to keep at your back when she makes her move."

"She can't touch me," Brutus said, hoping he sounded more resolute than he felt.

The slave snorted. "She has touched you already. Or why have you come into the country to hide from her?"

"I have not come to—!"

"The weather in Roma is pleasant, your overseer here does better work without you breathing down his neck, and there isn't the whisper of sickness in the city to drive you out." Jabal ticked off one fact after another on fingers grown soft from over ten years in easy service. "Moreover, the consul sends to let you know that important news from the Parthian trade cities is expected any day now. If it is good, you ought to be there to rub the Conscript Fathers' august noses in it."

"Jabal! You're speaking of the Senate of Roma, and I will not tolerate—"

"And if it is bad—" the Judaean went on, indifferent to his master's indignation "—then you should still be there to pick out an even thicker wall to set at your back. The senators might not care for the foreign queen, but if pacting with her means bringing you down, they'll dance to any tune she pipes."

Brutus made a face like a froward child. "You have all the answers."

"I used to," Jabal countered. "While the great library still stood." He stroked the thick beard he had grown since arriving in Roma with Brutus so many years past. "I am feeling fatalistic today. I think that when I set eyes on the queen of queens I will take her to task for having allowed that marvel to go up in smoke. Then she will order one of her slaves to kill me for my insolence and we shall all be happier."

"Why not charge me with the same crime?" Brutus asked, good humor restored by the slave's outlandish suggestion. "My father had as much of a hand in it as she. Oh, not directly, but his presence in Egypt was the primal cause for the civil uproar that destroyed the Alexandrian library. Then *I* could have you executed for insubordination and we'd not only all be happier, we'd save *you* the trouble of going all the way to Roma to die."

If Brutus wanted to wait for Jabal's laughter, he had an infinite wait ahead of him. The Judaean grouched out some unintelligible words in Greek and stalked out of the garden. Brutus caught up with him in the villa atrium, giving orders to lower ranking slaves for travel preparations. Some hastened off to see to the packing, one headed for the stables to ready horses. A boy was dispatched to ride ahead into the city so that Brutus' house might be ready to welcome him when he came, and so that a proper guard might be sent out from the city to intercept him and escort him home in a style befitting his station.

The thought of rallying this escort made Jabal grumble even louder. "The way you ride, we could make Roma before tomorrow's sun sets, if we started now," he said. "But no, Roma's Pontifex Maximus must have his pageantry! Which means sending some poor soul out to ferret through the lowest taverns in the city, searching for that corps of winebags you support as your guard of honor!"

"They're all veterans of the Parthian campaign, and loyal men to me as they were loyal to Caesar," Brutus said quietly. "They were there to stand with me when I brought the Senate word of Caesar's death. They were the mouth whose words convinced the Conscript Fathers to grant me Caesar's title of dictator, so that the gains of the Parthian treaty would be properly implemented and maintained."

"The mouth? More like the sword at their throats," Jabal commented. "Why don't you just pension them off with a tavern apiece?"

"Soldiers drink when they've got nothing better to do. Or do you think I'd do better to keep a bodyguard of philosophers?"

Jabal's upper lip curled. "You are still handy with a sword, Master, and so am I, yet sometimes we honor ourselves with the name philosopher. You could do worse. At least a philosopher truly understands what he fights for."

"And you think that is an advantage?" Brutus teased.

"You would save on the vintner's bill, at any rate."

"I suppose it wouldn't hurt to ride into the city as you say, without fanfare." Brutus grew more and more thoughtful. "It's not far, and if I arrive privately, Queen Cleopatra doesn't need to know I'm there at all. Not until the moment she ascends the temple steps and sees me waiting for her."

"When I was a boy in the Judaean hills, I saw a fox grin just like that, O my Master," Jabal remarked. But he was grinning too.

No matter how crowded the streets of Roma were on an ordinary day, that tumult was like the peace of Brutus' favorite country villa when compared to this day's bustle and clamor. Everyone wanted to see the Egyptian queen, and Queen Cleopatra wanted to be seen by everyone.

From his hiding place behind one of the great marble pillars of his newly enriched temple of Venus Genetrix, Brutus had a clear view of the wide way her procession would follow. Many of the same senators who had shaken their heads and looked dour over Caesar's infatuation with the foreign woman now had given her not only their permission but their outright encouragement to enter

the sacred precincts of Roma in all the state she cared
to keep.

She must have bribed them heavily, Brutus thought.
*With gold or promises or common cause. I don't think
she can have slept with all of them. No, not she; she reserves
that for the highest.* He felt his neck go cold as if from a
passing breeze, though the day was warm and still.

Brutus stole back into the temple itself. He kept to
the wall, his toga drawn partways over his head, a mouse
passing unnoticed. The place was swarming with
Egyptians. Some were dark-skinned, some fair, with
Macedonian bloodlines almost the equal of their queen's.
A chatter of Greek echoed through the main chamber
where a glittering statue of the queen herself stood facing
the vacant pedestal where her gift, Caesar's image, would
stand.

From the sanctuary of shadows, Brutus contemplated
the statue, his father's doting gift to his mistress. He
compressed his lips in disapproval, a hard eye taking in
the precious overleaf transforming the Egyptian queen
into a golden incarnation of Venus. She held a baby in
her arms, her child by Caesar. Like all males of his line
he was named Ptolemy, but the queen called him
Caesarion, in case any man might be in danger of forgetting
whose son he was. The baby was now a boy of some
fourteen years, yet there he remained, frozen in time and
gold. The sculptor's art had made him over into the god
of love, Venus' child with his deadly bow and arrow. To
any right-thinking Roman this image must look like
sacrilege. To Brutus—

Do not waste your anger against the Egyptian. Was
that a whisper in his ear or only an alien thought invading
his mind? *Your love and faith move me deeply, but I am
more than able to call in all debts owed me.*

"Lady . . ." He lifted his eyes, but all they saw was the
mockery of Caesar's gift, Queen Cleopatra with her infant
son at her breast, playing at Venus and Cupid. When

Brutus ordered the glorification of this temple sacred to Venus Genetrix, divine foundress of the Julian house, he had tried to have the impious image removed.

He failed. Caesar was dead, and in the manner of the dead he had acquired new love among the living; love tempered with a healthy measure of fear. A powerful man makes a powerful ghost. No one would touch an image that had been Caesar's pleasure to erect, not even when the man requesting its removal was the new dictator. As Jabal had said, Brutus was known to be a man of reason. The only trouble with such a reputation was that it garnered him more respect than fear, and fear got things done more often than respect. But no one really *feared* Brutus, and so the statue of the Macedonian and her brat stayed.

You might have made them learn to fear you, came that selfsame purl of words on the outermost boundary between the imagined and the real. *To fear and to obey you, even in this, in the teeth of your father's angry ghost.* He thought he saw a flash of light blink from the gilded statue, though no wayward sunbeam could have entered at the angle needful to strike such a spark. *They offered you your father's office as they offered it to him, for life! Why did you let it go?*

There was a humming in Brutus' ears, a murmuring voice incessantly demanding *Why? Why? Why?* until the words became a thousand tiny hammers that beat against the golden face of Cleopatra, denting and smoothing and remodeling the shining mask into the placid countenance of a long-horned Egyptian cow. A crown surmounted by the sun's own blazing disc sprang from her brow, and before Brutus' astonished eyes her bared breasts began to flow with milk. The trickle became a stream, the stream a flood that inundated the temple, turning all it touched to unstained whiteness.

Whiteness was everywhere, glorious, dazzling, blinding. Brutus clapped his cupped hands to his eyes, and still the shining penetrated even that self-imposed darkness, an inescapable brilliance to mark the birth of gods, the death of stars. Breath rushed into his lungs and leaped out again in a cry of anguish that was a plea for mercy.

The sound rose up, plunged down, and reverberated through the temple, until at last it shattered into the hundred different noises of a Roman street. Somewhere a cow lowed loudly. Brutus opened his eyes and blinked into the sunlight of another day, a day some nine years past.

He stood behind the great altar that rose before the temple of Venus Genetrix. From this vantage he watched as the great sacrificial procession approached. The streets teemed with citizens, men of rank, and plain riffraff. When Roma's dictator-for-life and Pontifex Maximus called for a ceremony, it was always a thing worth seeing.

A wink of sunlight caught itself in the net of gold embroidery worked so richly into Brutus' toga. The triumphal purple he had worn at all public events since his return to Roma and his utter conquest of the Senate stood out in brilliant contrast to the plain robes of the attendants beside him. He held out his hands to the fire already kindled on the altar and saw his fingers sparkle with more than a dozen rings. His father's glimmered brightest of all.

He stole a glance over one shoulder. The temple doors were open wide, so that the chief image of the goddess might look out and bear witness to the honor being done her. *Has time turned back?* he wondered. *Is this mere memory, or another of her gifts, a chance to undo what is already done?* His memory of that day was perfect: He could not forget it if he tried. *There's only one way to find out.* He drew a fat gold ring from the first finger of his right hand. It was a favorite of his, an understated masterwork of the goldsmith's art, simple yet elegant, worth a fortune, a gift from some fawning Parthian noble whose name and place were too minor to demand remembrance.

After Caesar's ring, it was the one adornment Brutus cherished most, took off least.

Brutus cast the pearl ring into the flames and thought, *We'll see.*

More, came the voice. *You may see even more than this, if only you will act other—*

"Hush." He spoke the word as little more than a whisper, though he thought he caught sight of one of the attendants giving him a peculiar look. He glowered, and the man quickly looked away. The sacrifice was approaching, a rarity, a pure white bull garlanded with Parthian roses bright as blood. Brutus had ordered it so, spared no effort or expense in locating such a unique animal. This must be an offering few would forget. He drew the folds of his triumphal toga over his head and waited.

He performed his part of the ceremony flawlessly, as befit the man of virtue who took his duties as Pontifex Maximus to heart. Every aspect of the sacrifice was seen to with the precision the gods demanded, from the consecrated meal sprinkled over the beast's head to the deathstroke that spilled its blood. Brutus observed the altar flames consuming the goddess' portion, looked sideways to where a body of senators stood waiting, their hands fettered with the cages of a score of snowy doves, a lesser sacrifice to Venus. He smiled.

Now I could motion them nearer, make the sacrifice, say nothing, leave all things in place as they are at this instant.

You could. The voice caressed his ears like the soft, warm wind of a summer's evening. *You should. Think of all it would mean!*

Dictator for life. The most powerful man in Roma. The most feared. The senators jump aside at even the hint of my shadow crossing their paths.

Yes! the whisper urged. *Yes!*

He raised his hand as if to beckon the first man forward, then instead turned the gesture to one that demanded a

halt, that commanded silence. He stepped down from
the altar of Venus, feeling the goggling eyes of the senators
upon him. The air reeked with smoke, burning flesh, newly
shed blood, the sweat of so many people. The faces of
the crowd spread out below him looked like a net of frog
spawn bubbling the surface of a pond.

He heard the words pour from his mouth, the carefully
phrased speech by which he conjured up great Roma's
spirit and his father's shade to stand before the Senate
and the people, witness to the rightness of what he did
this day. He reminded them of how no man save one
had ever ruled as dictator for more than a single year.
He spoke of how his father had been the one man great
enough to receive the dictatorship for life, how he would
never dream of setting himself on the same level as Caius
Julius Caesar, how to do so would be almost tantamount
to sacrilege, an offense the gods could not ignore or forbear
to punish. Roma herself would feel their wrath, and he
was a man who had never failed to place Roma first in
all things. He did not know whether the words he uttered
were the same as those he'd spoken at this same event,
nine years gone, but his heart knew that it didn't matter.

As he spoke, he began to divest himself of his triumphal
robes. Silent as a shadow, Jabal glided out of the throng
ranged on the temple steps, bearing a plain toga not half
so white as the bull so recently sacrificed. The Judaean
was accompanied by a pair of Brutus' servants, and
together the three contrived to regarb their master even
as the heavy folds of castoff purple and gold puddled to
his feet. It was a dance long practiced, with an eye to
this day's doings, and it was nimbly executed. Brutus
uttered the final words of his speech, commending the
rule of Roma to the Conscript Fathers, just as Jabal and
the others stepped away to leave him robed in white,
reborn a common citizen.

Common? the voice in his ear mocked. *Never that.*

Never that, Brutus agreed inwardly as he raised his

arms to accept the cheers of the throng, to gather in the stunned expressions of the senators. *Dictator for life, when my life's no longer common? When age refuses to embrace me as swiftly as other men? To take such an office is well for men who have no need to throw dust in the public eye. Blame your promised gift to me if you blame anything for what I've done here today.*

The voice was silent, but the presence of the goddess hung about him like a stormcloud. From the open doors of the temple behind him, he could feel the angry eyes of the great image boring into the back of his neck. He was suddenly stricken cold with fear.

He closed his eyes and his thoughts were transformed into prayers that sought to placate and cajole the goddess. *I will still have power*, he pleaded. *I will still be Pontifex Maximus of Roma. I will still be a force for Roma's benefit, still be able to oversee the founding and strengthening of the new Alexandrias. Besides, I haven't forgotten what my father's fate almost was for having accepted the life dictatorship, against all precedent. To rule with so much power smacks of kingship. We Romans aren't famous for letting our kings live.*

But he lived! the voice protested. *He lived to fulfill his office to the last. Only death took the dictatorship from him.*

Then I have gone him one better, Brutus thought as the sounds of the crowd faded from his ears. *My father's office outlived him, but I have outlived the office. I am free of it.*

He opened his eyes. He was back inside the temple of Venus Genetrix. Cleopatra's statue was unchanged. He looked at his hands. The pearl ring was gone.

A hubbub from just outside the temple jerked Brutus' attention fully into the present. He heard the jingle of the sistrum, the shrill piping of the double flute, the rumble of approaching drums. The Egyptian priests all flew to the doorway, two of their number pausing only long enough to kindle the incense-laden braziers surrounding the vacant pedestal. Their voices united in a chant whose words eluded Brutus. It might have been Greek, transformed past recognition by their accents and the distortions of music. Then again, it might have been Egyptian. It was said that the queen alone of all her royal house took pains to learn the language of the land she ruled.

Alone in the temple, Brutus stepped away from the wall, uncovered his head, took his place between two of the smoking braziers. He almost gagged on the thick, sweet reek of burning gums, but he stood firm. When the formalities outside the temple were done and the procession entered, he would be the first thing they would see. Clad in the plainest toga he owned, head bare of any crown, he would be a more striking apparition for his simplicity than the queen for all her gorgeous display.

What was it that Jabal had said when he counselled Brutus on how best to greet the Egyptian? *You will be the cold, crisp, slap in the face that echoes over all the hills of Roma.*

Brutus fidgeted for a moment with the lay of his toga, then commanded himself to be still. A breath of scented smoke wafted over him. He thought he heard laughter too musical to belong to any mortal woman. He waited.

"Clever?" Brutus pretended to be surprised by the queen's choice of words. "That isn't something too often said about the members of my family. Even the name means—"

"You need not translate." Cleopatra reclined on a couch covered in Coan silk the color of unwatered wine. "My Latin is at least as good as my Greek. But so what if your *cognomen* implies a certain . . . slowness of mind? You and I both know how much and how little a name truly means."

"Mmmm." Brutus looked into his winecup; it was empty.

Before he could speak, a honey-skinned slave had refilled it for him from a golden vessel set with turquoise and rubies, each the size of his thumb-joint. He heard the sound of someone clucking his tongue behind him. He didn't even need to turn around to see the look of distaste on Jabal's face; he could picture it readily enough. The Judaean had a Spartan's innate mistrust for any flaunting shows of wealth. And if Brutus were free to tell himself the truth, he would admit that the degree of luxury in the queen's house troubled him as well as his slave.

"Yes, that little byplay of yours in the temple was more than clever of you," Cleopatra persisted. "It was brilliant. When I show myself to my people it is often as the goddess Hathor made flesh. But you—! You revealed yourself as more than any mere divinity. You were the living spirit of reproof, the chaste ghost of the old Republic and all its simple values, its unadorned virtues. And you won."

"I didn't think we were at war, great queen," Brutus replied. "Egypt is under the protection of Roma."

"I am Egypt." She said it as if it were a truth every schoolboy knew. "Stand against me and you stand against my kingdom."

Brutus said nothing. With the years he had learned the uses of silence. When the Conscript Fathers raised yet another howl against his policies, he kept quiet, letting his adherents shout them down with reports of increased trade coming through to Roma in safety via the pearl-strand cities, Brutus' many Alexandrias. Profit spoke louder than rhetoric. More than one senator had turned his hand to clandestine trade, pacting as a silent partner with the growing merchant interests. With the cash-or-slaves levy now deeply in place, only those most conservative members of the Senate still decried Brutus' measures as criminal. There were not too many of that stripe left.

He thought there were very few.

He leaned forward to sample a platter of artfully sliced fish, still keeping himself to himself. In honor of her guest, the queen of queens had used restraint when ordering the dishes for this dinner, even if she had shown none regarding the manner of its presentation. The food was good, honest fare, prepared with artistry but not artifice. Having heard tales of Queen Cleopatra's lavish banquets with their uncountable exotic dishes, Brutus wondered whether this almost painfully plain meal served forth on gemmed gold plates was a joke at his expense.

"Tell me," the queen said, finally compelled to break the silence. "Tell me, was that the only time you tried your hand at drama, or do you treat your people to other spectacles? Besides the triumph they accorded you for Parthia, I mean."

"That was my father's triumph." He saw the way her eyes widened and flashed briefly with anger when he called Caesar *father*. He remembered the boy who had stood at the queen's side when the procession entered the temple—a proud boy, dressed sumptuously in the old Egyptian style to give the people a sight to remember. His eyes too had shown that same carefully banked rage when he saw Brutus, heard the senators and Roman priests hail him, understood who he was. Young Ptolemy called Caesarion had been well schooled by his royal mother, and he was old enough to recognize his rival.

I was wrong. We are at war after all, great queen, Brutus thought, setting the ambition of mother and son in the balance against his own aspirations. *But I have more at stake in being Caesar's son than your son ever could. Be careful of the child: His desires are not yours, as you could see for yourself if you weren't his mother. You want the power of Roma to shore up the land of Egypt. He wants the power of Roma to serve himself. And I—* Brutus lifted the winecup to his lips, paused, set it down untouched. *If I think for a moment that you'll try to suborn Roma, you or your brat, then yes, I will stand against you. To the death.*

"Is something wrong?" Cleopatra gestured at the cup.

"Have your slave taste it, if you are afraid." She spoke lightly.

"Jabal is not my taster," Brutus replied.

"Then what? You keep him near enough. I have sent all my attendants away, except the few who must be here to serve us. I wished to speak with you privately."

"You may trust Jabal's discretion."

The queen took the measure of her guest and his slave the way a general might contemplate the ranks of an enemy army. "You make it sound as if he saved your life, at the very least. Yet if that were so, why is he still your slave?"

"I've tried to make a freedman of him. He has declined the gift. He's a Judaean, and he tells me that according to the rules his people have concerning slaves, if the slave prefers to remain in his master's service after he's been offered his freedom, he must have a hole drilled through his earlobe against the doorpost of the master's house."

Jabal took one step forward and turned his head slightly. A plain bronze ring adorned his right ear. His smile was insufferable.

Auletes' daughter frowned. "Since he is your slave, dismiss him. I have things to say to you that are no concern of his." She clapped her hands, commanding the attention of her own slaves, and with a wave of her hand sent them scampering from the triclinium. She regarded Brutus expectantly.

Before he could act or even speak, he heard the quick, retreating slap of Jabal's sandals as the Judaean left the room. Privately he cursed the slave, partly for anticipating a command that had not been given, but more for having abandoned him to a solitary audience with Cleopatra.

He did not want to be alone with this woman. He knew this as surely as he knew his own name. Jabal had been right: Brutus had hidden himself away in his villa to avoid this very moment.

Looking at her now, across the low table, in the intimate setting of the triclinium, he saw that she was by no means beautiful. Yet there was something about her, some indefinable power to attract, to enchant, to undo even a man such as Caesar. It was that unknown, unnamed strength of hers that scared Brutus. Oh, she was educated enough—a woman of native intelligence well-trained would frighten many men—but such creatures were nothing new to him. Portia too had been schooled as well as clever.

Portia . . . The magus' last vision was never far from Brutus' mind. He had puzzled over it long and hard, trying to understand its message. He had asked for a way to end the deaths that seemed to dog him, and he had been given sight of his dead wife's face against a backdrop of blood.

"I *said* that you may feel free to call him back, if you must." The queen's voice sounded an uncharacteristically harsh note in Brutus' ear, jarring him aware. "In fact I would prefer it if you did, since he seems to have taken your tongue with him."

"I ask your pardon," Brutus said, realizing that he had wandered among his own thoughts, shutting himself off from whatever Cleopatra had been saying to him. "What can you say to me, great queen, that you fear to say before a slave? If you expect me to bury your words, I can tell you now that I won't. I serve Roma, freely and openly. Even if you are afraid of how the Conscript Fathers will react to whatever business you have with me—"

She stiffened at the implication. "If I feared the Senate of Roma, I would not risk the journey here. Only petty kings who cling to their thrones by Roma's grace tremble before those old men. Egypt loves me. I am their goddess." She spoke boldly, without a liar's desperation. Either she believed her own words (*Blasphemy!* thought Brutus) or she felt strong enough to dare him to deny them.

"Is that what you wanted to tell me?" Brutus asked. All at once he was calm and unafraid. The Roma he loved, the Republic he had given so much to preserve, both were built on a foundation of centuries of piety. Within his own house, every man was his family's chief priest, keeper of the rites honoring lares and penates, exemplum of order holding back barbarism and chaos. One woman— no matter her hidden power, no matter if she called herself queen or goddess—could not stand against so much. Her own vanity would bring her down. "You are no longer on Egyptian soil. Here we recognize the difference between actors and gods."

To his surprise, she laughed at him. "So that was the price you paid for the enchantment!" She rolled onto her back and stretched like a lioness. Her breasts shook with rich gusts of mirth.

"What are you talking about?" he demanded, sitting up straight on his couch. "What enchantment?"

"The spell of youth you bought from—Oh, who knows where? Perhaps you travelled down to Cumae and paid the sybil's price. Perhaps you dealt with one of those Parthian magi—though my priests assure me that the Parthians' only magic is illusion. Perhaps you even travelled into my realm to consult a true magician. Wherever you got the charm, the price is plain: To own it you gave up everything human about you. You are incapable of telling jest from truth. If you could have seen your own face when you reproved me for calling myself a goddess—!" She laughed at him once more. "You have become nothing more than a deathly serious, square-hewn block of duty and *dignitas*. So much dull solemnity in so young a shell!"

His fingers dug into the flesh of his knees, his teeth clenched to control any improvident reaction to her mockery. "The queen flatters me. I am not as young as—"

Cleopatra turned over onto her belly suddenly, brightly ringed hands slamming against the table before her. Plates jumped and chinked, platters and serving vessels rattled. "Have I no eyes?" she cried. "Or must I have no mind, because I am a woman? I know when you were born.

You were a youth *years* out of your childhood toga the day that I was born! I have lived thirty-nine years, you more than fifty, yet look at you! We might as well have been born in the same year, you and I." Her face contorted as if she saw a leper sharing her table. "I only *call* myself more than mortal. You—" There was envy mixed with her revulsion. "What *are* you?"

Brutus rose to his feet, never taking his eyes from her. "What will you gain if you know that answer?" he asked. "Even supposing that I know it myself."

The lioness' tensely coiled body slowly relaxed under his steady gaze. "Then you admit it?"

"As the queen says, she has eyes . . . and a perceptive mind."

Cleopatra's fingers curled, kneading the Coan silk under her hand. "How—?" she asked. The word shivered on her breath. "Tell me. I can meet any price you ask, double it. To live forever—"

"—is a curse," Brutus said. "The queen is too wise not to know that."

"So you can die?"

"No man is immortal. No man would want to be."

A trace of humor stole back to her lips. "That is because no man has a woman's imagination. He sees eternity as tedium, not opportunity."

"Maybe," Brutus conceded. "Still, I won't live forever."

"No, but while you live, age shuns you. I doubt I am the only one to see that, though I think I am the only one who has had the courage to confront you with it."

Brutus recalled certain looks he'd caught on the faces of senators old enough to have known him since before Cassius' conspiracy. He'd only glimpsed their expressions in passing, when they had no way of knowing that the dictator's eye was on them. What had he seen? Nothing so simple as fear. Their taut nerves sang like bowstrings when he passed too near them, as if he housed a greater evil than his reforms. Their eyes held awe tinged with hate.

He inclined his head slightly towards her. "You were speaking of a woman's imagination—?"

To his surprise, she took no offense at that. "Ah. Very well, deny whatever you like. If I owned a gift like yours, I too might be as jealous of it." She rested a finger on her lower lip. "I think that you have made a better bargain than neverending life. When I die, my people will entomb me provided with enough riches and servants for a true eternity of joy and comfort. But to reach it, I must pass through the house of age. Even I, the queen of queens, must see these hands wither into claws, this skin crumple from silk to papyrus! There are times I believe it would be better to leave this life before I feel the years close their shackles on my neck. Death is still my slave, Roman, and I know how to command slaves."

"Death is every mortal's slave," Brutus said. "And every mortal's master. When I was young, I often wondered how a slave could survive his lot in life. Why go on, your whole existence subject to another's will, when true escape was always so easy, so near at hand? Then one day I realized the way of it: Even a slave wants to live, and the slave who forgets his master's presence lives best. The man who turns his mind away from the inescapable can escape. Your life is very sweet, great queen, and you sweeten it more with every new ambition for your kingdom. If old age is the price you must pay to see your plans unfold exactly as you dreamed them, you'll pay it. You'll pay it."

"So you are his son," she said, as if this were some oracle's revelation. "You have his wisdom—though many would call it mere cunning. But these also are only words. Keep your secrets. If I need the answers that badly, I too can travel to Cumae." She sat up gracefully, her actions alone transforming the couch into a royal throne. "Let us speak honestly, then, because we can. Let us speak of immediate practicalities touching our two realms and leave the rest to the gods. As you say, let us survive by forgetting our masters while we can. We know each other, Marcus Brutus. You want certain things for your land just as I want certain things for mine. Before I leave Roma I mean to make you see that our differing desires can become one." Her sharp-nosed face was shining with the eagerness of a marriage-ready maiden.

"Go on."

Jabal walked beside the litter that carried the dictator back to his own house. "You were closeted with the queen of queens for a long time," the Judaean remarked.

"So I was," Brutus replied casually. "You should have stayed."

"I was commanded to leave."

"I am still your master, by your own choice, and I never gave that command."

"That again." Jabal heaved a sigh that sounded contrived. "What would I do if I were a freedman? My first master trained me in many tongues and many letters, and what came of that? He died old and poor in Babylon, of the same sort of sickness that finished your father Caesar. Lion hunting! More men have caught their deaths from the marsh fever's claws than from the lion's talons. My second master, Na'id-Sin, had more use for my back than my brains. As long as I stay in your service, I am assured that you will always find use for my true talents. If I must strike out on my own, who knows what I might have to do to survive? I do not have the wish or the skill to become a tradesman. My wife would starve."

"You could always become a pedagogue," Brutus suggested, still smug in his enjoyment of the way this evening's business had concluded.

"I, who once knew the wonders of the great library of Alexandria! I, to beat the backsides of a pack of snotty Roman brats to try to make learning penetrate their skulls! No, thank you." A brief silence descended after Jabal's indignant outburst. The slave himself broke it to ask, "So what did you speak of with the queen?"

"Oh, what you might expect." Brutus waved his hand languidly. "Our deepest desires."

Jabal snorted. "I know you too well to rise to that bait. Her physicians still know more of her body than you do. All of your desires center on Roma. You might as well dedicate your manhood to the unholy Cybele for all the use you get out of it."

"Now it's my turn to tell *you* 'No, thank you'!" Brutus shuddered visibly at the thought of the great Asiatic mother-goddess' priests and their rites of self-mutilation. "How could you think that I would ever want to—?"

"What! You took me seriously?" Jabal was startled. "You are a wise man, Master, but you seem to have trouble recognizing a joke."

"You're not the first one to tell me that," Brutus replied. "Not even the first one tonight."

"Do you know what you need?" Jabal adopted a friendly tone so different from his usual brusqueness that Brutus leaned over the side of his litter to pay close heed. "You need a wife. If a man lacks a sense of humor, he is in constant danger of death, strangling on his own self-importance. A good woman lets the fresh air into her house and the stale air out of her man. I know that my own wife—"

"I had a wife," Brutus said, looking straight ahead, avoiding Jabal's eyes. "I won't have another."

"Then at least take a mistress! Do your gods insist you give up the joys of the marriage bed when your wife dies?" He shook his head and answered his own question: "No. I have lived here long enough to know that much. My Lord has given us countless rules to govern love and lust, marriage and desire, but even so the heart of His commandments urges us to find happiness, to raise up children—"

"Your god also urges you to mutilate your sons."

The slave bridled. "It is the mark of the covenant; it sets us apart."

"Then accept that my life, too, is a thing apart," Brutus said. "Leave it to me to lead it."

"Lead it? Drive it over a cliff for all I care!" Jabal didn't like being closed out of an argument with his master. The two men had often enjoyed protracted discussions of philosophy and faith in the years since Brutus' return to Roma.

When they reached the dictator's house, the porter took Jabal aside and whispered something in his ear. Jabal shook his head and grinned. The porter uttered a low curse and several coins went from the small pouch at his belt into Jabal's hand.

"What was that all about?" Brutus asked as they entered the atrium with its tranquil pool.

"Perdix is not a very good judge of character," Jabal replied. "He thought that you and the queen would certainly—"

"You rogue!" Brutus didn't know whether to laugh or scowl. "After all your talk of my taking a mistress, you bet against my sleeping with the Egyptian queen?"

Jabal turned up his palms, one still cradling the coins. "What I counsel and what I know are two different things."

"And Perdix paid the wager on your word alone?"

"He trusts me. He knows I am honest," Jabal stated. "Also, your chief laundress is his wife. If she finds evidence that I have lied, I will pay back the—"

Brutus covered his face with his hands. "I didn't need to know that."

"Then you should not have asked," the Judaean pointed out reasonably enough. "You know, apart from how well I know you and your inclinations, it was still a safe bet for me to make. The queen of queens once shared your father's bed. Perdix is a Thracian. I do not think they are so particular about family matters as you Romans, and

Perdix is stupid even for a Thracian. He assumes that everyone else follows the rules of his people."

"The queen herself would've seen no problem in taking me to her bed," Brutus said. "She wed two of her own brothers, the custom of the Egyptian royal house. To sleep with her lover's son would have been nothing."

"It *was* nothing," Jabal reminded him.

"At least this way she's safe," Brutus murmured.

"What? Not that again. Master, why is it that you are the most rational of men in everything but this? Do you really believe you live under a curse?"

"A curse that doesn't touch me," Brutus said softly. His answer called up another one of those disgusted snorts Jabal favored.

"*I* am still alive!"

"So is Rufus. But he declared himself my ally, not my friend, long ago. And you are my slave." Brutus looked up through the compluvium at the stars.

"And she is your opponent, first to last. Even if she had become your lover, it would have only been the opening move of a game of hounds-and-jackals to her. There never was any danger of your so-called curse touching that one!"

Brutus nodded and went to his bed.

Chapter Eleven

Brutus swam up out of sleep into the sounds of feet running, voices shouting, fists pounding on doors. He released his dreams reluctantly, so sad to leave the warmth and peace and mellow light of the quiet places behind his eyes. It was rare these days that he dreamed at all, and rarer when the dreams were pleasant. In this one, he had been walking through the olive grove at his favorite villa, the one nearest Roma. A woman was with him, Roman by her dress, her face a smudge of color behind the ivory smoke of her veil. Her grip on his hand was as firm as her step. He couldn't say whether she led the way through the dusty green trees or if he did. He knew it didn't matter.

Then the noise, the commotion that shook away the olive trees and the sunwarmed hillside and the woman. He reached out, trying to cling to her hand a moment longer, striving to pull himself back down into the comfort of sleep. Her fingers turned to water in his hand, trickling away.

He awoke to the pungent smell of smoke. Jabal was at his bedside, holding out a tunic as if it were a shield. "Put this on, get dressed, come!" the Judaean barked.

Brutus struggled into his clothing, still fuddled. The smoky smell was stronger. "What is it?" He bent over, fumbling with the fastenings of his sandals. Something glimmered at the edge of his sight. His fingertips closed around the pearl ring.

"What are you gawking at?" Jabal demanded.

"I—" Brutus blinked at the same jewel he'd cast into the altar flames. Absently he slipped it back into its wonted place on his finger. "Nothing," he muttered. His sleeping chamber was on the second floor, with windows that looked out into the street as well as down into the garden.

He lurched across the floor and stiff-armed the shutters open, expecting to see all Roma ablaze.

Instead he saw only the walls of his neighbors and heard only the street traffic noises of a typical day's awakening. To the west, towards the nearest curve of the Tiber, he picked out a thread of smoke climbing the sky. A chirruping flock of sparrows crossed his sight, circling once before landing in the garden.

He turned form the window and leaned back against the frame. "What do you mean, waking me like this, making me think the Gauls are on us, scaring me out of my skin? Damn you, Jabal, are you crazy? Why—?"

"The horses are waiting." Jabal bit off the words. "Your things are packed. The consul Gnaeus Claudius Rufus is below, in your tablinum. He wants a few words with you before you go."

"Where do you think I'm going?"

"I could not tell you." The Judaean's jaw was set tight. "It was no idea of mine for you to flee the city over a trifle. Your friend—your *ally* the noble consul—has other ideas."

"Rufus wants me to leave Roma? In the name of the gods, why?" Brutus started for the door. He hesitated only to confirm Jabal's earlier information that he would find him in the tablinum.

The tablinum was empty. Rufus was in the garden, the nail-studded soles of his sandals crunching out a sharp, nervous rhythm from the gravel paths. Brutus came racing out to meet him so quickly that the two men almost collided. Before Brutus could say a word, Rufus spoke:

"She's dead, Brutus. Found dead this morning, before dawn, with the poisoned goblet still in her hand. That's her pyre you smell, loaded down with enough spices to choke all three of Cerberus' throats. The true Egyptians in her suite are horrified—they'd pickle her properly if anyone gave them a say in it—but the boy said—"

The rest of his words degenerated into a meaningless

series of clucks and squeaks and gurgles. Brutus saw the consul's lips moving, heard sounds emerge, and could not understand them any more than he could read the message of a butterfly's flight. Yet still the core of the matter managed to seep through the stone wall of refusal, finally making contact with Brutus' brain in a way that could not be denied: Queen Cleopatra, called Thea Philopater, was dead.

He could not believe it. The philosophers he studied and loved often claimed that the senses were liars, so why must he believe Rufus' words? No. He couldn't. Dead? The queen of queens, now flame and burning meat? All of her powers as woman and lady of Egypt and self-styled goddess, nothing more than ash and smoke? Her image flashed across his sight, wiping Rufus' haggard face away. Eyes bright, hair dark beneath the fallen petals of her rose wreath, she was more real dead than the consul was alive. The vitality of the woman would not be driven away into the shades of Tartarus so easily, merely because it was no longer convenient for her heart to go on beating.

Even as he wondered at the depth of his own feeling, he knew he had felt this all-consuming denial before, when he learned of his father's death. Then too the news had come suddenly, without warning.

Then too it had been Rufus who had brought him word. *He caught a chill in the marshes while hunting the lion and it became a fever. The physicians say they never saw the like, it overcame him so quickly. But he'd had the marsh fever before, when he was younger—everyone in Roma knows that much—and he's had recurring spells of it over the years, burning and freezing and shaking like a branch in a gale. Only this time, it shook the life out of him.*

"What words do you have to ease my mind now, Rufus?" Brutus mumbled.

"What?" The consul was taken aback.

Brutus blinked. He was unaware that he'd turned

thoughts into words spoken out loud. "I'm sorry," he said. "I've only just woken up. What was it you were telling me?"

"I was saying that it mightn't be a bad idea if you went back to your villa—not the one you left, one of the farther ones. News of the queen's death is tearing through the streets, even though her priests *claim* they kept it quiet. I had more trouble than I care to tell you, getting here. You know the little Isis temple? That's where they're burning her body—brought it there before dawn with the quietest of funeral processions *I've* ever heard of. No musicians playing and no professional mourners wailing until they reached the temple steps, yet here comes half of Roma's riffraff to gawk and clog the streets and toss rumors around like a juggler's fireballs."

"What rumors?" Brutus asked, though he could guess.

"Different ones," Rufus hedged. "Variations on one tune, mostly."

"That I killed her." There was no need for the pretense of a question.

To Brutus' surprise, Rufus shook his head. "That you wanted to kill someone else and that she prevented it. And for *that* she had to die."

"In Jupiter's name, who would I want to kill that she—?"

"You aren't his only son," Rufus said softly. "They also say that you didn't put aside your ambitions when you put aside the title of dictator; that for all your protestations otherwise, you intend to turn your chair into a throne and that when you do—*when*, not *if*—you want no potential rivals of Caesar's blood at your back."

Brutus could feel his eyes growing wider and wider with each incredible statement Rufus offered. "Are those the rumors? That I would try to kill young Ptolemy because he's—because the gossips claim he's my half-brother? And for what? So that I could make myself king of Roma unchallenged? I, a king?" He flung his hands up in disgust.

"Maybe you can claim you've seen the limits of human stupidity, Rufus, but after this, I'll never say it's possible!"

Jabal glided into the garden, wearing the calm demeanor of a true philosopher around him like a cloak. "People believe what suits their previous opinions," he said. "Forgive me, Master, but I could not help overhearing. People also prefer to believe that no one can be any better than they. If a man appears to be richer, or more powerful, they put it down to Fortuna and the stars. If he seems to be smarter or more virtuous, they cherish the thought of one day seeing him revealed as a fraud, just as stupid and vicious as themselves. They feel cheated when this does not happen and they caper with joy when it does."

"Jabal is right," said Rufus. "How many Romans do you think would turn down a crown if it were offered to them? Honestly, now. And how many would be the first to stick a dagger through the heart of any who got in their way? Even if that stumbling block were only a fourteen-year-old boy."

"I am not like them!" Brutus snarled.

"That is why they hate you most of all," Jabal responded. "That is also why they will grab hold of any story, true or false, that paints you in their colors."

"I still don't see why I ought to leave the city."

"I was there, Brutus," Rufus said. "I was at the lighting of the queen's pyre. Her brat gave the funeral oration, in the best style of a good Roman boy of high birth. He was even dressed the part, in all simplicity, unlike his late mother's habit of ladling out Eastern splendor whenever she stuck that beak of hers outdoors."

"Speak no ill of the dead," Brutus said with piety that was pure reflex.

"You should have seen him," Rufus went on. "Not much to look at, at that awkward age, but more than one of the spectators started chirring about how he was his father's living image. Then the lad announced that for the kindness and reverence that the good people of Roma had always showed his mother, and for the sincere love she had for them, he would turn over a certain sum of money to the Vestal Virgins to finance a great series of gladiatorial games in her honor."

Brutus moaned.

"*And* with a free disbursal of wine included," Rufus pressed. He spat. "Most of that mob would sell their own mothers for a decent set of games, and all of them would do it for a skinful of wine."

"Besides, a funeral is a very emotional rite," Jabal put in. "This is especially true when the spectators have no personal loss connected with the event. They can enjoy a good, cleansing, sympathetic cry and go home no worse for it. And when they see a child left motherless—!"

"Fourteen is no longer a child," Brutus said.

"It is young enough. And I think this Ptolemy has the talent to be as young or as old as suits him for the moment. If the boy inherited only half the shrewdness of his parents, he is formidable."

"You're right again, Jabal." Rufus was nodding and looking anything but sanguine. "Octavian was the same, may the gods assuage his spirit."

"Octavian . . ." Brutus had not heard that name spoken in his presence for years. "They say I killed him, too. And he was only Caesar's grand-nephew."

Rufus didn't bother to deny it. "Whoever did it, you're all the safer with him gone. Too bad the same can't be said for little Ptolemy. I tell you, Brutus, you should have seen how he worked that crowd!"

"I intend to," Brutus replied, turning his back on the consul and heading for the house.

"Where are you going?" Rufus blurted, hurrying to catch up to him.

"I'm going back to my room and I'm going to dress in something fit to be seen in in public."

"You can't be serious! You mean after all I've told you, you're going *towards* the gates of Avernus?"

"Through them. The pyre's still burning; I can smell it till here. It would be rude of me, as Pontifex Maximus, not to make an appearance at the funeral of one of Roma's most gracious allies."

Rufus grabbed his shoulders and spun him around. "You're going nowhere but straight to your villa until this has blown itself out!"

Brutus uttered a low, exasperated sound from deep in his throat and shrugged off the consul's grip. "Rufus, you're a fool," he said.

"Oh, *that's* right. The populace ready to take you apart just to see the pretty colors and I'm the fool. Well, maybe I am. I'm still your friend, after all these years, so that's enough claim to idiocy for one man."

Brutus raised one eyebrow, truly startled. "I thought the dwarf scared you clear off calling yourself my friend."

One corner of Rufus' mouth curved up in a sardonic smile. "If I'm at a dinner party and someone warns me off a tasty-looking dish on the chance it might be poisoned, I have two choices: I can avoid it altogether, and perhaps deprive myself of a real treat if my well-meaning informant was wrong; on the other hand, I can have someone else taste it for me and if he suffers no ill effects, I'm free to feast."

"In other words, Master," Jabal remarked drily, "I have been the noble consul's official taster. Since I am still alive after so many years in your company, it must be safe for him."

"But you're my slave."

"And do you not also count me as your friend?"

Brutus smiled and laid one hand on the Judaean's shoulder. "You know I do."

"*Quod erat demonstrandum,*" Jabal concluded.

Rufus made a noise like an angry cat. "You two would mince philosophy fine while the city burned down around your ears! Look: Call me friend, call me ally, call me fool if you like, but don't be one yourself. Get away now, give the smoke time to clear, let the people find something else to divert themselves with, then come back. I tell you what, I'll furnish the money for an even grander set of games to celebrate your return. That'll fix everything."

"You're forgetting the free wine." Brutus kept a straight face, but his eyes glimmered with mischief.

"Free wine as well, at no one's expense but my own. And a free feed, while I'm at it. That should make the vermin happy. At least they can't holler for your blood when they've got their mouths full. Now will you listen to reason and *go*?"

Brutus' solemn mask lasted only three breaths longer before it began to shiver and crack around the edges, at last disintegrating amid peals of helpless laughter. Rufus stared as if he'd witnessed his friend turn into a werewolf. When Brutus did manage to regain some control over his own mirth, he said, "Save your money, Rufus; save your wine too. Either we'll drink it together or you can pour it out at my funeral as a libation to the dead. Whichever happens, it's all in Fortuna's lap. I can only do what I know must be done, and that does *not* include fleeing the city over—what did you call it, Jabal?"

"A trifle," the Judaean provided.

"Just so. What's more, you might as well know that I would never *flee* Roma for any reason. My duty is to her life, and I'd be a very poor Stoic not to embrace my duty."

"Wonderful," Rufus grumbled to an unseen audience hidden among the roof tiles. "He takes advice from slaves. He hasn't had a woman in his bed for years, but he embraces his *duty*."

"Do not blame me for that," Jabal said. "I keep telling him to take a wife, but he—" The slave looked around. "Where is he?"

Brutus had disappeared into the house. The two men exchanged a look and went after him.

Brutus stood on the roof of the temple of Mercury and looked down on the mob choking the streets near the little Isis temple. For a funeral that was supposed to be as quiet and as private as possible—if one believed the words of the Egyptian delegation—Queen Cleopatra's obsequies had grown in scope and grandeur with astonishing rapidity.

Even more astonishing was the tone of order surrounding them, in spite of the seemingly unpremeditated arrivals of one highborn Roman after another, each armed with a fine speech in praise of the late queen's countless virtues. It was amazing how well timed each arrival was. No sooner did one senator finish saying his piece and descend the temple steps but another just happened to appear, ready to add his words to the invisible mountain of praise heaped up over the queen's burning corpse. Not a single speaker was interrupted by the tumult attending the arrival of his successor, not a single newcomer had to bide longer than five breaths before his predecessor ceded his place.

"It's a miracle that they haven't blown out the flames entirely, with all that wind," Brutus murmured to himself. He watched as the current speaker seemingly plucked a flowery figure of speech from thin air, for he had brought no scroll with him to prompt his words. Antony too had enjoyed a reputation as an orator who needed no prepared speech. He could twist the hearts of a crowd like so many strands of copper wire, the power of his words enhanced by the illusion of spontaneity. The truth was that he prepared his remarks beforehand, the same as other men, but took the time and trouble to learn them by heart. He should have been a tragedian.

Instead he was as dead as Octavian, as dead as Cleopatra, as dead as so many others who—

Brutus banished such thoughts. *Rufus no longer thinks of me as accursed; why should I? Now is not the time to fall into that pit. There's no rational cause for it, it's no reasonable assumption.* So he told himself, most severely.

He focussed all of his mind on the scene below, to derive strength of reason from the growing display of irrational behavior at his feet. The people were howling, tears and snot running down their faces. He could see the shiny trails streaking their skin, though he could not quite make out the face of the speaker well enough to put a name to him. He was young—that much Brutus could tell from the way he held himself, and from the thick, black wealth of his hair—but beyond that, he was only another man.

Brutus came down from the temple roof. Inside the temple itself, a portion of his honor guard stood waiting. According to his orders, as conveyed by Jabal, they had come singly or by twos, secretly, their uniforms hidden under drab cloaks, their helmets ignominiously crammed into leather bags such as travellers used. There were only eight of them. A man of his stature needed attendants but refused to come into the midst of the crowd with too many men. No one must be able to claim that Brutus feared the people of Roma. The two strongest, aided by Jabal, had brought javelins for all their comrades to carry. The crowds were too fascinated by the goings-on at the Isis temple to pay much attention to men wrestling long, heavy, clattering, cloth-wrapped bundles through the streets. Bringing the javelins had been awkward, but necessary: If the guard came only for show, it had better give the people a sight striking enough to sate their eyes and cow their hearts at the same time. Ever blessed with foresight, Jabal produced a clutch of red-dyed feathers and tied a bunch to each javelin with gaily colored ribbons.

When Brutus emerged from the temple of Mercury in the midst of his men, it seemed like some conjuror's splendid trick of making great things materialize out of nothingness. By now the crowd around the Isis temple was thick enough to have oozed back into the surrounding streets, so he didn't lack an audience. Staring straight ahead, eyes fixed between the heads of the two men preceding him, Brutus still managed to catch sideways glimpses of the people's reactions to his sudden presence in their midst. He heard more than one harsh cry for his blood strangle itself into uneasy silence, saw more than one face once red with anger go white with fear.

The crowd melted away before him like frost before flame. Here and there he spied a look of hate, a glare of loathing among the ashen faces. *They don't need to love me,* he thought. *In fact, they are safer hating me. If what Rufus once feared is true—* He could not hold back a short, raspy laugh at his own foolishness. There was no curse attending him! Death was the world's way, and if those who loved him—or even those who drew too near to him died, what did that mean? Not a thing more than rank coincidence. His friends didn't earn death for their affection any more than his enemies won immortality for their hatred.

A thought fluttered up inside his skull like an errant moth: *Whom are you trying to persuade?*

Something soft struck his cheek, tickled his face. He clapped a hand to his jaw and saw that he had captured a rose petal. More were falling all around him. Somewhere in the crowd he owned allies as well as foes. He walked over the sweet-smelling tatters of blossom and ordered himself not to think about any time but the present, any place but this.

The most recent speaker was still at his post at the top of the steps leading up to the Isis temple. He was sweating heavily from the heat of the pyre. It was a windless day; the smoke of Cleopatra's burning climbed the heavens. At this close range, Brutus could see the man's face perfectly. The sight pierced him like a dagger blade.

"Cassius . . ."

Almost as soon as the name left his lips, he was in a panic to know whether anyone had heard him, whether any man in the crowd had noticed how his voice shook forming it. He tightened his jaw, willing away the weakness. This was no ghost he saw; it was only Cassius' son, his own nephew, Junia's boy. A man, now. Brutus didn't think it possible for the child to have grown so much, so fast. To him it seemed like only yesterday that he had witnessed the lad having his first shave, assuming a man's toga, putting off the *bulla* from around his neck.

You should still wear that charm, lad, Brutus thought. *It's not children who have most to fear from the evil eye.*

He stared at young Cassius until he became aware of the silence that had settled over the whole crowd. The only sounds to reach him were the crackle of the queen's pyre, a cough or a sneeze from the mob's heart, a lone whisper slipping away like water from a cracked jug, the creak of leather on leather and the muffled ring of metal on metal when one of his guards shifted weight. For a moment he imagined that he and everyone massed around him were nothing more than a seer's conjured vision, frozen immobile, trapped beneath the shining surface of a golden bowl full of water or blood.

Then young Cassius spoke, and the bowl shattered. "Hail, Pontifex. Have you come to tell us we break the law?" There were equal parts of mockery and challenge in his voice.

"There is no law that bans honoring the dead," Brutus replied. He motioned for his guards to step away from him and mounted the temple steps.

Young Cassius and some of the dead queen's entourage tried to position themselves so that Brutus could not gain the topmost step where the pyre itself burned and where all other speakers had stood. If he contented himself with a place one step down, he would appear diminished in the eyes of the crowd; he knew this. He did not try to shoulder past them, or even to reach the highest step left open to him. Instead he paused less than halfway up the flight and turned, one hand reaching into his toga.

"People of Roma!" he cried, drawing out a small scroll and holding it to his chest. "I have not come to interfere with these final rites for Queen Cleopatra Thea Philopater.

I have rather come to add my own poor measure of praise for one whose love of Roma was almost as great as yours!"

The crowd began to stir. Brutus' strange words set them on edge. They were not prepared to hear him speak of the dead queen as a friend of Roma. The senators and highborn men who had come before had used such words, but mostly they had limited their remarks to thinly veiled hints at Brutus' guilt and ambition, leaving the woman little more than the victim's role. Brutus was certain that were the queen alive, she would be furious to hear herself so demeaned.

He held his tongue; his teachers had always stressed the importance of a man's words, but he had learned for himself the greater value of a man's silences. He eyed the crowd, gauging the effect his opening remarks were having. Those towards the back of the mob heard rumors from the front that Brutus had *something* in his hand, but they couldn't see what it was. An angry buzz spread through the press. The people were hungry to know, and they were prepared to hate any who stood between them and the satisfaction of their curiosity. This instantly included anyone who barred Brutus from standing where they might all see him.

He heard with satisfaction the shuffle of feet from behind him. *They are making room for me now,* he thought. He tightened his grasp on the scroll in his hand. It was only a copy of one of Aristophanes' plays—Brutus cherished a secret fondness for comedy—but no one in the audience could know that. Jabal had thrust it into his hands as they left the house.

"What do I need this for?" Brutus had demanded.

"If you come before them empty-handed, they will believe your presence at the queen's funeral was not planned."

"They'd be right."

"Never let the people know they are right," Jabal had said, straight-faced. "They are usually right for all the wrong reasons. You know that you go to the Isis temple on the spur of the moment because you are innocent of the queen's death and want them to realize this. They will assume you have come there out of panic fear, nothing else. Take the scroll. Call it your speech, carefully prepared. Call it a letter from the queen's own hand, giving you the guardianship of her son. Call it anything you like, so long as it saves your skin."

Brutus' mouth had twitched in a half-smile. "And if someone should ask to read the queen's letter?"

Jabal had taken the query seriously. "Put him off until tomorrow. I can have it written by then."

Brutus remembered how loudly he had laughed at his slave's—his *friend's* willingness to dabble in forgery for his sake. "When all this is over, I'm going to give you your freedom, like it or not," he'd told Jabal. "*And* your whole family too."

"Thank you, but I think Cyma and the children would rather have a holiday than hunger. You are an easier master than independence, and I have gotten out of the habit of any work but philosophy."

"You know that when I die, you won't have any choice about it: You'll be free then, like it or not."

Jabal gave him a tight, crooked smile. "I can wait. Now as I was saying, if you truly wish to show me some gratitude—"

So Brutus had promised the Judaean slave and his family a seaside holiday without knowing whether any of them would live to set eyes on the ocean again after this day.

A swell of sound from the crowd brought Brutus back to the present. He gave a quick glance behind him and saw that young Cassius and the rest had indeed cleared a place for him. He mounted the temple steps slowly. He knew what he needed to say to turn the mob's anger from him: A few remarks to evoke his father's refusal of a crown, a few more to recall that Brutus who had driven out the last king of Roma, and most of the harm wrought by Cleopatra's death would be undone. He reached the top of the steps, turned, and raised his arms.

"*Murderer!*"

The impact from behind almost pitched him down the steps headfirst. It was pure luck that sent him lurching sideways against one of the temple priests. The scroll fell from his hands, went rolling away. His thoughts scattered: *Who—? What has—? If someone picks up that scroll and sees what it truly— Why don't my guards—?*

His guards did not come running to his rescue. They stood where he had left them below, their faces frozen and unreadable beneath their helms. He pushed himself away from the scowling priest and turned his head to see what manner of assault against him could go unchallenged by his most loyal men.

Small fists pounded his arm, his back. "Assassin! Dog! Set eat your liver raw!" Cleopatra's son pummelled him with more fury than strength, his voice rising, breaking, his words coming out choked by sobs. "I curse you, I curse you, I curse you ten thousand times to the black lands! You killed my mother! You—!"

Brutus sensed the humor of the crowd change even as he held up one arm to keep the boy at bay. A child's pure grief and rage at the man he named his mother's murderer would do more to sway these people than a dozen skillfully polished speeches. The Egyptian priests were coming forward now to remove their young lord, to remind him belatedly of Pharaoh's dignity. Despite their chiding whispers, Brutus could see the pleasure in their eyes. In one short, hot outburst, the boy had done more than twenty senators to undercut their enemy.

And as the priests drew young Ptolemy Caesarion away, Brutus caught sight of a similar glint of satisfaction in the boy's own expression.

Why, you cunning little bastard!

At that moment, Brutus couldn't say whether his anger outweighed his begrudging admiration for the boy. His mind was too taken up with the problem of salvaging the situation. He saw Jabal slip through the crowd to gather up the fallen scroll and breathed a little easier, then raised his arms a second time for silence.

He got none. The crowd was slipping away from him, irate faces twisting into masks of hate, grumbles rising into shouts, complaints, and accusations against him. If they dared, they would swarm up the steps and tear him limb from limb. It had been known to happen. All it wanted was one unlucky word, one badly judged action, one spark.

"People of Roma—!" He tried to make himself heard over the swell of mob noise and found that he was shouting like a fish seller. He saw his guardsmen change position, stringing themselves across the bottom of the temple steps, javelins lowering by degrees from upright to battle-ready, the little draggled bunches of red-dyed feathers coming loose, blowing away on the wind.

The wind had come up out of nowhere. It blew from the dead queen's pyre, casting a gritty pall of smoke over the temple steps. Brutus coughed and wiped his stinging eyes. The sweetness of the scented gums that Cleopatra's priests had larded onto her body made his head spin. He gathered his breath for one last, desperate cry: *"People of Roma!"*

And suddenly, silence. The smoke was gone without the lightest breath of a breeze to shift it, the cloying smell of incense vanished along with it. In its place there were only flowers.

Flowers! A hecatomb of flowers, an avalanche of blossoms that spilled down the temple steps, a storm of bright petals swirling from the cloudless sky. Brutus looked down and saw that his feet were covered in blooms and that more were falling from his upflung hands. He looked to either side and saw stark fear in the eyes of Roman senators and Egyptian priests. Even young Cassius had gone white, and still the flowers fell.

The people swayed this way and that under the perfumed rain, like cattle caught in the open fields in a storm. Then one man among them looked up into the sky and bawled something—a word, a name—that Brutus could not hear. Others near the man looked to where he pointed, his other hand making the sign against the evil eye.

Brutus too looked. At first his eyes were dazzled by the sun. Then he thought he saw a cloud, white as a dove's breast, shaped into the semblance of a more than human beauty.

The goddess smiled and stretched out one cloudy hand over the crowd before she melted into a fresh miracle of falling flowers above the Isis temple. And as the shower of petals laved him, Brutus wondered whether he was the only one there to whom their perfume smelled like the embrace of a woman.

Chapter Twelve

As matters fell out following the Egyptian queen's funeral, more than a year had to pass before Brutus could redeem his word to Jabal and the Judaean's family concerning a seaside holiday. It was only when he handed over the documents of manumission that the former slave insisted on what he called his rights.

"But you're a freedman now!" Brutus protested. "Free and still in my service, you and Cyma both, so don't come complaining that I've left you to starve. You can travel to the shore any time you like!"

"That's the poorest excuse I ever heard for a man not keeping his promise," Jabal grumped. He continued to grump until Brutus knew himself defeated. They went south with the rest of the nobles who fled the heat and fevers of Roman summer for the delights of Pompeii.

Now Brutus stood on the edge of the foam-flecked sands and filled his lungs with the scent of the sea. Above him, stars and a crescent moon gave the only light—he had forbidden Jabal to bring a lantern. Lately, his only hope of tranquility was found in solitude and darkness. Solitude was impossible; Jabal always saw to that. Brutus was resigned to having the Judaean hovering over him like a motherly hawk (or, as he had told the man more than once when at the end of his patience, like a vulture). It had been bad enough when they were still in Roma, but he had hoped that Jabal's vigilance would slacken once they reached the sea. It had not.

Now he heard the Judaean clear his throat loudly enough to alert half the sleepers in Pompeii. He sighed. "Yes, Jabal, what is it?"

"Master, it is not my place to command your comings and goings, but do you not think that—well, that perhaps

183

you have been gone from the banquet a little *too* long? The others may be worried."

"Worried!" Brutus sent laughter flying away over the silvered sea. "Why should they worry? Nothing can harm me—even the scruffiest street beggar knows that. There are certain advantages to being a god."

Behind him, he heard Jabal shift uneasily from foot to foot. The Judaean never did know how to respond when his master spoke of such things. *As if he'll never be quite sure whether or not I'm joking,* Brutus thought. *And yet he of all men* should *know.* Not for the first time, Brutus felt an isolation of the spirit that was nothing like the solitude he desired. To be alone with one's thoughts could be either prize or condemnation. Suddenly the summer night was very cold.

"Shall I return to the villa and tell your host that you will follow?" Jabal said at last.

"My 'host,' Jabal, is my nephew. Why have I never heard you speak of him so? It's not as if I have so numerous a family."

The freedman came nearer so that Brutus could see the stern set of his features. "It is not my place to speak of the noble senator in such familiar terms."

Brutus' patience snapped. "Then what *is* your place? To hint and mutter and eye young Cassius in a way that as good as shouts *Watch your back near this one, Master?"*

"It is not my place to teach you common sense either," Jabal replied evenly.

"Well, if I'm not to trust him, why are you chivvying me back to his villa? To his very dining table? Do you imagine that he's ignorant of how poisons work?"

"You are not his only guest tonight, or I would have done everything in my power to keep you from under his roof," Jabal said, still unruffled. "He is not the sort to deal with you in front of witnesses, particularly since one of his guests is the noble Gnaeus Claudius Rufus."

"And another is the noble Rufus' new wife, Caecelia

Albina." Brutus chuckled good-naturedly. "There's a pair—the red and the white. He never takes his eyes off her, the old fool. Young Cassius could lean across the table and stab me in plain sight; Rufus wouldn't bother looking my way unless Albina complained about my body having fallen over some dish she wanted to sample."

"Very funny," said Jabal in a way guaranteed to convey the fact that it was not. "At least he *has* a wife."

"That again!" Brutus rolled his eyes in mock exasperation. "Is that your greatest ambition, Jabal? To see me married?"

"You claim you want no part of being a god." These were not easy words for the Judaean to pronounce, but he forced himself to go on. "Then be a man like other men! Love, marry, have children, grow old—!" He stopped, bowed his head, lowered his voice. "Your pardon, Master. I did not mean to say—"

"Never mind, Jabal." Brutus turned his back on the freedman. "You're right; we should be going back. My head's clearer now, but for awhile I imagined that it would split itself in two if I had to listen to one more scrap of silly gossip."

They climbed the path from the shore that led to the outer garden gate of young Cassius' villa. From the triclinium came the sound of pipes and cymbals, song and conversation. Young Cassius was a generous host: Women as well as men reclined on couches ringing his dining tables. Slaves moved gracefully among the guests, wiping fingers on soft cloths, pouring wine.

Rufus had already consumed more than his fair share of the fine Pompeïan vintages. He was holding forth in his old battlefield voice, reducing all other diners' chat to whispers or silence. Brutus resumed his place in time to hear Rufus finish his reminiscences of Babylon and the dwarf magus, Na'id-Sin.

"—and it was what he saw in that last vision o' his that killed him," the former consul concluded, slapping his hand down on the table. "Yep, killed him dead as that

plate o' squid. Deader. All o' which goes t' show that—"
he dropped his voice dramatically "—mere mortal men
was never 'tended t' go stickin' our noses into the doin's
o'—" a monumental belch erupted in the midst of his
words "—o' th' gods."

Every face turned to stare at Brutus. He expected as
much, yet for all that his hand still shook slightly as he
made himself pick up his goblet and drink. "Excellent,"
he said, setting it down once more. He stretched himself
into a more comfortable position on the purple-draped
couch. "If I didn't know better, I'd say these grapes were
grown at Delphi; they bring our friend Rufus such wild
visions."

The diners all laughed dutifully, except for Rufus and
his wife. The former consul gave Brutus a wounded look;
Albina did laugh, but not out of any urgency to please.

"Why go so far afield?" she asked lightly. "Cumae's
nearer. Perhaps the sybil's become a vintner. These days
the people only trust visions they can pour into a cup."

"You know that's not true," young Cassius drawled.
"Reverence for the gods of Roma has returned. The
temples flourish with offerings, piety and the simple values
get more than lip-service now. Just this morning I received
a letter with word that they've closed the great temple
of Cybele and chased her eunuch priests past the city
walls. The building itself will be rededicated, newly
adorned, and consecrated to Venus, with its treasury
liberally applied to that end."

"Such is the will of the people." Lucius Licinius Calvus
uttered a burp to rival Rufus', completely shattering the
solemnity of his tone.

"The people's *true* will demanded that the temple be
consecrated to my uncle." Young Cassius inclined his head
in Brutus' direction. "So the letter said. They'd have had
it their way, too, if not for some dried-up old breadcrusts
in the Senate."

"When I return to Roma, remind me to commend those

men," Brutus said, an edge to his words. "They saved me the trouble of undoing a great sacrilege."

"That's not how the people see it," young Cassius said, signalling a slave for more wine. "Especially not the people who were present at Queen Cleopatra's funeral. Was it only a year ago? It seems like ages. I'm not protesting the way things are, but it strikes me that it ought not take longer than a year for a man to climb Olympus."

"That's enough!" Brutus thrust himself upright, glowering at his nephew.

"I'm only jesting, Uncle." Young Cassius wore a face as bland as a plate of milk. "I thought you would be happy to hear that the people are coming back to the old ways. Wasn't that your plan? To win back the Republic? Every Roman master of his own small farm, an end to the great estates, the cities clean of landless men dependent on the government for bread, nobility transformed into a matter of virtue, not property?" He spoke without apparent guile, yet Brutus sensed a phantom barb or two beneath the surface, a sting there and gone too quickly for a man to point out its presence with any certainty. "We were fools to oppose you, I see that now. You had only Roma's future at heart."

And your future, Cassius? Brutus mused. He knew the rumors: Even the beloved of the gods must have an heir. Roman gossips inevitably brought up one name when they discussed the matter. Who better to stand as Brutus' picked heir than this young man, his sister's son, blood of his blood?

Blood . . . No wonder Jabal's so eager for me to marry, to sire sons. Well, Jabal, both you and young Cassius will have to wait. I'm not yet ready to give either of you satisfaction.

"Those Eastern cults—" The aged Servius Sulpicius Paulus shook his head slowly. "Pernicious things, all riot and wailing and wild carrying on, just the sort of rubbish to appeal to the rabble. No *dignity* to them. No restraint.

Nothing for the mind, just the emotions, and then only the loudest, the most disorderly, all whipped up into a frenzy that'd make a Bacchante blush!" He levelled a hard stare at Brutus. "If calling you a god is what it takes to bring the mob back to their senses, then I'll be first to do it, as loud as my voice will let me. Curse it all, what harm can it do?"

"Hubris . . ." Brutus lowered his eyes. "The gods will be the first to punish me for it."

"Oh. I forgot. You believe in all that. Well, don't fret over it." The older man waved away all of Brutus' misgivings. "You're not the one calling yourself a god; you're safe enough."

"If I don't deny what others call me, I consent. Do you think the gods are so easily gulled?"

Paulus clung to his convictions. "What the gods accept as true doesn't matter any more than what the people accept as true. They're grateful for worship, and if naming you one of them brings the people back to their temples and away from those Eastern abominations, ha—! They'll share their temples with you and welcome!"

Brutus stood up, a sour taste in his mouth that had nothing to do with the wine. "If I were to call myself a king, the people would want me dead. Yet if I call myself a god, they allow—no, they clamor for it! Am I the only one here who sees this as madness?"

Old Paulus snorted. "When you've lived as long as I have, you'll stop looking for the people to behave rationally."

"What makes you think he hasn't lived that long?" young Cassius murmured.

Brutus left the triclinium without another word. He strode past the half-conscious porter and was well down the road before Jabal caught up with him.

"It is not my place to say this," the Judaean stated, "but I think you might have waited for someone to summon your litter. The bearers are in a turmoil. Two of them had gotten more than a little friendly with our host's kitchen girls, so when the porter went off shouting for them to assemble and go after you, you can guess how they were found. They were still trying to pull on their clothing when I left, and their comrades are not helping matters. They are pummeling them without mercy, convinced that you intend to whip them all for inattention once we all reach home."

"Don't they know me better than that?"

"Which 'you' would that be?" Jabal inquired, the question tart as vinegar. "The mortal man, the—*being* they would make of you, or something in between? I have heard the stories: Your gods' reported malice is only exceeded by their capriciousness. If I were still your slave, I would not know what to expect of you either."

Brutus held up his cupped hands as if to catch a drink of rainwater. "I never asked for wonders." The ghosts of flower petals danced over his empty palms. "I could have handled the crowd on my own."

"So you did."

"Is that what you believe?" Brutus flashed the freedman a penetrating look. "You were there with all the rest, you saw what happened, and you still refuse to admit you saw a goddess?"

Jabal shrugged. "How can I admit to seeing something that I know does not exist? I am already an exile from my homeland, but never from my faith. While the great library at Alexandria still stood, a man might read of many such supposed 'miracles.' Illusions, every one."

"Then your god never shows himself to his favorites? Never performs marvels?"

"I do not number *true* miracles among what I name illusions."

Brutus' mouth flirted with a smile. "A very convenient way of looking at things. I think that if I had been born a Judaean like yourself, I might have known more peace of mind."

"Oh yes!" Jabal didn't bother keeping the sarcasm out of his voice. "We enjoy extraordinary peace of mind! All that ever troubles us is wondering which nation will fall on our necks next."

Brutus only half heard him. "The people of Roma thronged the temples of Isis, of Cybele, of any foreign cult whose worship offered to bring them closer to the god. Their own gods were remembered, but only out of habit. There was no—no faith, no passion. I doubt if even a tenth of them expected anything to come of it, but they sacrificed anyway, to be on the safe side. Now they say that I have shown them that the old gods of Roma aren't so distant and unapproachable after all, that they may still reveal themselves to us, stir our spirits, touch our lives, even touch our—" He shivered. "They can't know what it's really like. They can't see the price. All they can see are the flowers falling from heaven."

"The price, Master?" Jabal laid his hand on Brutus' shoulder and spoke as if to a nightmare-ridden child.

To his own surprise, Brutus found himself pouring out the full tale of his doings with the goddess, from that long-ago night in the garden to the apparition at the Isis temple. He left out nothing, speaking on even while he saw successive looks of pity, unease, fear, and sometimes revulsion cross the Judaean's features. As he neared the end of the telling he said, "I don't even know what she will ask of me. What if it's something so vile that—?"

"That is possible." The freedman offered him no more comfort. "More than possible. And if it proves to be so—?"

Brutus' expression hardened. "I will not do anything that betrays Roma or myself."

"From what you've told me, this—Venus as you name her—wants Roma's health as deeply as you do. I cannot say whether she might feel as protective towards you."

"But she loves me!" Brutus' vehemence startled even

himself. More softly he added, "If not, why save me? Why choose me? Why—?"

"I am no magus, Master. I have no answers." Jabal patted him on the back. "Maybe the lady was right: Maybe you ought to go to Cumae."

The peasant edged his way along the narrow track that led up to the mouth of the cavern. There was only space enough for men to walk it in single file, and so Brutus, his freedman, and his two guards strung themselves out behind their guide.

At Brutus' back the sun was setting, touching the buildings of the acropolis with flame. If he turned, he could just see the first lights being kindled in people's houses. The trees rooted to the gentle slope above him were filled with the whir of wings, daybirds seeking their nests, nightbirds awakening.

"You know—you know that you mayn't find nothing, Master," the peasant said, stumbling over his own words. "You won't be holding me to blame if there's not nothing to see?"

"We will not hold you to blame," Jabal answered for Brutus. "Nor will you hold us to pay you for nothing."

"Oh, that's fair, yeh, fair enough." The man stank of goats. He had a strange way of cocking his head every few moments, as if he alone heard a voice that called his name. In one hand he held a small lamp made of pinched clay, fueled with burning fat that smelled as if he'd mixed olive oil with melted tallow.

They were almost to the cave mouth when Jabal called a halt. Taking the peasant's crude lamp, he used its flame to kindle the wicks of two fine horn-sided lanterns. One he kept, one he handed over to Brutus. The two guards would bear no lights. They expected no trouble, but they kept their hands free just in case. All of these precautions left Brutus feeling like a small boy with an overprotective nursemaid. He held his lantern high as they entered the cavern.

At first it looked as if the peasant had been as great a prophet as the sybil: There truly was nothing to see. The cavern mouth was one end of a fairly short tunnel which widened into a high-ceiled stone chamber, its walls thick with smudge but otherwise unremarkable. The dust of dead leaves, blown in from the outer world, lay deep underfoot. Brutus raised his lantern. By its light he noted what might have been the pawprints of some small animal, but no other disturbance to the dust.

"Let's go back," he said, letting his lantern come down slowly at his side.

"Oh, you mustn't let this be all you see here, Master! No, no, no!" The little peasant's hand closed on Brutus' arm, his thick black fingernails digging into the skin. "See, it's not by *this* road she comes. So my mother would say. This is the *men's* road here, it's t'other that's more travelled, only I don't know where to find the entry for it. Ha!" Fragments of brown tooth showed in a nervous grin. "How would I? Man and all."

"I find it difficult to believe that *if* the Cumaean sybil still sits, no man has come seeking her in—" Jabal stooped, sifted a handful of the cavern dust through his fingers "—centuries."

The peasant's head was jerking sideways with frightening rapidity, his smile flickering like a poorly trimmed lampwick. "No, Master, no wonder, no wonder there at all! See now, firstways I already told you, I don't know will we find her or—or anything in here! This is only what my mother told me for true, and she claimed she'd come often enough, once for each of us nine, to find out would the birth go well. I never did come myself—what for? My life's a straight road, don't need no woman to tell me a future I already know. What'd I have to pay her for her words anyhow, even did I need 'em? But my mother said she's here, the sybil, the one who sold the books to that king. Could be it was all lies, or just a tale to tell us kids, but could be—could be—"

"Lead us," said Brutus.

The little man obeyed, conducting them across the cavern floor to where the mouth of another passageway awaited. Their shadows leaped and capered on the walls. By lanternlight Brutus saw that here too many torches had trailed smoky fingers over raw rock for uncounted years.

The second passageway was considerably longer than the first and led downward. Although it didn't seem to shrink in size, Brutus still couldn't cast off the feeling that the earth was slowly closing her fist around him. When a small breeze passed over the short hairs of his arm, he had to restrain himself from rushing forward to see whether it heralded more open spaces ahead. It did; his spirit soared as he stepped into the second chamber of the so-called sybil's cavern.

It was not just relief he felt, but sheer elation, for the first sight to greet his eyes was a heavy bronze tripod. It stood before a chair that looked as it if had sprouted from the cavern floor. The interwoven bodies of carved serpents formed its back, and its arms were supported by winged figures that were beast and bird, sea-creature and woman all at once. The tripod itself was decorated with grotesque faces, leering, tongues lolling, an eternal mockery of any mortal foolish enough to seek knowledge of the future. Behind the tripod and the chair was an altar of white marble, plain and unadorned except for the lingering stains of blood, all brown.

All brown . . . all old . . . Brutus' exaltation plummeted as he came nearer, saw the unmistakable signs of long disuse touching chair and tripod and altar. Jabal was walking along the rear wall of the chamber, holding his lantern first high, then low, seeking his own sort of answers. The peasant scurried to squat against the rocks in the shadow of the altar, head tilted to one side, listening to his voices.

Brutus approached the tripod and looked within. It

held only ashes, white and cold, to the depth of a man's forearm. His breath stirred them into little puffs of faintly scented dust. The two guards leaned in over his shoulder, the lantern's glow turning their faces into stone and shadow.

"Nothing." Brutus straightened his spine, gave his back to the tripod. "If there ever *was* any true oracle here."

"True enough, I would say," Jabal commented, continuing his circuit of the room.

"And yet— Remember what we found when we first came to Cumae: A dozen would-be oracles at lowest count, some in temples, some at roadside shrines, a few just half-crazy beggarwomen in the streets. Every one of them swore she was the only true Cumaean sybil."

"Yes, except for that last poor girl who claimed she was the pythia of Delphi." Jabal ran his hand over a place where a metal torch holder was riveted to the stone. "And still I tell you that whoever held that throne was not just another of the false oracles. Those keep to the town, where pickings are plentiful. This place is secret. It was by the greatest good fortune that we came here."

"I heard what you were seeking, Master, word came 'round, and so I came," the peasant piped up from his place against the wall. "Yeh, soon as I heard you wanted the real sybil—well, where she was, once—not my fault if now—" His head jerked and he fell silent.

There was another opening in the rock to the left of the tripod. Brutus and Jabal chose to investigate its secrets at the same moment. Two lanterns probed the darkness. This passageway too appeared to slant downwards. There was a strong wind blowing out of that rocky throat, and a strange smell—

Brutus sniffed. The odor was there all right, but it didn't seem to come riding up on that wind from below. He wrinkled his nose and gave Jabal a questioning look. "What *is* that smell? Where's it coming from?"

The Judaean was equally puzzled. "Oily . . . something more than tallow . . ." He took a sniff at his lantern, then

shook his head. "Not that. Not coming from down there."
He glanced back to where the peasant still huddled, hugging
knees to chest, eyes wide, head moving in more and more
rapid spasms. "Do you think it could be hi—?"

The spear spat from the black tunnel that had brought
them into the chamber, piercing one of the guards from
spine to breastbone. He fell forward with a choking
sound. His comrade wheeled, sword out but no shield
to protect him. A second spear flew, missing him by a
handspan.

Brutus stooped to gape at the spent missile. His eyes
flew from the spear to the tunnel. "What—?"

With a cry that sounded like pigs being slaughtered,
the peasant sprang for him, a short, bronze-bladed knife
in his fist. Brutus was knocked from his feet, his lantern
flying, as if Phaethon had traded the sun's chariot for
the moon's. It spun wildly across the cavern, its horn sides
smashing when it fell. The freed flame caught on
something dark that gleamed as it seeped over the rocky
floor. In the now leaping light, Brutus thought he saw
yet another mouth leading from the sybil's hall. It was
low and narrow, a space easily concealed by the body of
one determined man, however small. Then the bite of
the peasant's blade took his senses from everything but
survival.

The little man was ill-made, but he was stronger than
he looked. He straddled Brutus' waist, knees dug in deeply
against his quarry's sides. Brutus tried to pitch him off
and couldn't. Flat on his back, he was dimly aware of
the sound of other voices filling the chamber, sandalled
feet pounding over rock.

"Traitor!" It was Jabal's voice. "Your own uncle—!"

"Who killed my own *father*!" Young Cassius' voice
boomed out in the enclosed space. "He's the traitor here!"

Jabal spewed out a string of words beyond Brutus'
understanding—curses in his own tongue, most likely.
There were other oaths filling the air, cries of pain, gasps,

screams. Another shattering sound and the light was diminished, though the fire from Brutus' ruined lantern was still spreading, devouring the black streamlet from the once-hidden cave mouth.

Brutus tried to roll the peasant off him, but it was no good. Head bobbing at a furious rate, the man was also able to hold Brutus' sword arm immobile. Similarly, Brutus restrained the other's knife-hand, but not so well. The blade darted in and out, slashing and stabbing, mostly missing the mark, once or twice striking home.

Brutus gritted his teeth and rocked his body to the other side, where the dark liquid continued to flow and the flames followed. He bent his knee, got one foot braced on the cavern floor, and pushed with all his strength. The peasant did not give up his grip, but the shove carried him onto his back, Brutus' weight holding him down, just as the fuel trickled into the filthy tangle of his hair and the fire leaped after. The peasant's head became a torch, thrashing against the stone as leaves of fire closed over his face. Brutus scrambled away, drawing his dagger. His sword was somewhere, buried in the leaves.

The fire had spread, ringing the tripod, licking over the bodies of fallen men. It gave light, but not enough to lend a man accurate sight. It turned faces to smears of brightness and shadow, gaping holes where mouths must be. In such a fight, ears served better than eyes. Brutus strained to pick out Jabal's voice from the tumult, or that of Quintus, his surviving guard.

If he still survives . . . Brutus staggered against the wall. From here, the fight looked like a single beast, many headed, many limbed, with steel fangs that flashed in the light and were gone. The beast was howling for his blood. It was a clever beast; it spoke with the voice of his nephew.

"Idiots! You'll slash each other to bits before you find him! You! Bar the entry; he mustn't escape. You! Where's that torch, the one you put out before we—? Well, relight it! How can you expect to kill what you can't—?"

A shriek ripped young Cassius' throat. Dumbly Brutus leaned towards the sound. He felt lightheaded. The fingers clutching his dagger stuck together and the blade dripped blood, though he had yet to strike a blow in this battle. A deep breath shot his ribs through with pain. His throat was burning. He knew that something important must be happening, but there was too much smoke, too much fog, and the stone beneath his feet was shifting like river ice breaking up in the spring.

The ice cracked, then split wide open. He tumbled forward into the cool dark.

CHAPTER THIRTEEN

He returned to a world almost as dark as the deepest sleep without dreams. There was cloth underneath him, but stone beneath the cloth. He flexed his fingers and felt pain. Something was binding his right arm, though when he lifted it, it moved freely. His eyes adjusted to the gloom. Somewhere in the distance was a cool gray glow, light enough for him to see that what he had mistaken for bonds were only bandages. He sat up slowly, letting his breath out in little gasps around a dozen different sites of pain.

He was in a cavern, another room hollowed from the rock. It was smaller than the sybil's chamber, though the ceiling was higher. When Brutus looked up, he saw a sliver of daylight far overhead.

Then he heard a low moan and alien words spoken in a familiar voice. "Jabal?" The unknown words stopped. "Jabal, are you here?"

"Here I am." The answer trembled on the air.

"Where?" Brutus cast his eyes all around the cavern, saw nothing. "*Where* are you?"

"Here. In the light."

Though his wounds protested, he got to his feet and limped towards the pale glow. His left leg was heavily padded and bandaged at the thigh; putting weight on it was agony. Still he forced himself on.

The light bled down from another cave that lay just beyond an in-curving in the wall of Brutus' own. Here the roof was higher still, pierced in many places with slits that let in the light and air of the outer world. Brutus gauged the light and guessed that it must be dawn. But which day's dawning? That he could not say.

"Master . . ."

Jabal lay bathed in the daylight on a pallet stuffed with

straw and moss and flowers. These leaked freely through many small rents in the cloth covering, their mingled fragrances muting the smell of blood. Brutus hobbled to the Judaean's side and lowered himself carefully, to spare both his own pain and Jabal's. The freedman's bandages were smeared with bright scarlet. One eye was gone, and a dagger's stroke had mangled his face still more. A finely turned and figured black clay bowl rested on the ground beside him, along with a matching beaker and several folded cloths.

Brutus saw that the bowl was full of bloodied water. He picked up the beaker and shook it, heard it slosh, poured off the dirty water and poured in fresh. He tried to make his hand become as gentle as a woman's as he dipped a cloth into the water and did his best to cleanse the freedman's face.

"No." Jabal's hand closed on Brutus'. "Leave off, Master. Useless . . . useless . . . You should have listened to me. Stay safe. You said it yourself: Her gift . . . life. You will not . . . but you can be killed. Fool to come—"

"Ssh. Don't talk. I'm going to find whoever's been looking after us. They can send for help from my villa." He tried to rise, by Jabal never slackened his grip. Brutus could not move.

"Safe now." A smile pulled up only one corner of the Judaean's mouth; the other had been slashed open. His back teeth showed to the gums. "Killed . . . the bastard."

"Young Cassius? You?"

"Spear . . . fell. Not much good in close, but . . . the one that missed Quintus . . . poor Quintus." A dribble of tears leaked from Jabal's remaining eye. "All that . . . for what? We have come to it at last, Master. All we need . . . to get past the shadows."

"Quintus," Brutus repeated. "Quintus too is dead, then. And the others? The ones with young Cassius?"

Jabal did not answer. He still lived—Brutus could see the shallow rise and fall of his chest—but he was too weak for speech. Gently Brutus disengaged the Judaean's hand and stood up. There was only one passageway leading from this rocky cell. He hesitated, wondering if he ought to leave Jabal alone, whether he should stay at his friend's side and wait. *Someone* had bound their wounds, *someone* had brought the cloths, the bowl, the beaker full of water. Someone would have to come back.

He went to the entry and peered into the dark. He could see nothing, nor feel any draft of air. He couldn't know whether this tunnel would lead him to help or only take him to a place where other tunnels branched off, other caverns loomed. He might become lost, wander forever, and Jabal would die—

Jabal will die in any case. The thought was hard and bitter as an olive pit. For all its hardness and bitterness it was no less true. He had seen battlefields enough to know a dead man in the making. He went back to the pallet.

The Judaean opened his eye almost as soon as Brutus settled himself back down beside him. "Did you see it, Master?" he asked. His voice had grown stronger, his breath more even.

"See what?"

"The world. The world beyond the cave. The true world."

"The true—?"

A ripple of laughter welled up out of the freedman's chest, catching only a little over the ruined mouth. "And you call yourself a philosopher! I wish that I had known you when you were a boy. I would have taught you properly. To think a man of your stature does not know his Plato!" The laughter ebbed back into silence.

Brutus laid his hand on Jabal's brow; it burned. "The cave," he repeated. He knew what his friend meant now: Plato's cave, a mind-toy of the Greek philosopher that turned all earthly things into mere shadows of their real selves, shadows cast against a cavern wall. Men were the cave dwellers who clamored after the shadows, thinking them the real things, the things worth hunting, worth having, worth holding until death. They lived and died for the sake of shadows.

But should one man crawl out of the cave into the light, see the true nature of things and not just the shadow, go back into the cave again to tell his fellows what he had seen—

"—they would kill him." It had been years since Brutus had read Plato. He didn't know whether he was remembering the philosopher's conclusion to the tale or whether his own experience of men had written him a more fitting ending. "Yes," he said, gazing down at Jabal, though the freedman now gave no sign that he could hear. "Yes, they would kill him."

"They have killed him," said a voice behind him, and a small hand dropped like ice on his shoulder. "As they might have killed you."

Startled, Brutus instinctively turned quickly towards the voice, but a searing pain across his ribs pulled him back short. The small hand tightened, cold fingertips numbing his flesh. "I am not your enemy." The voice was lilting, female. It came from beneath a heavy veil, white as the foam of a waterfall, white as the fine wool stola falling to her feet. "Come with me."

Slowly Brutus stood up; he was not much taller than the veiled speaker. "I'm not leaving Jabal. Dead or alive, he comes with me or I don't go."

"He will be brought." She gestured, and four other figures, veiled like herself, emerged from the mouth of the tunnel Brutus had chosen not to explore. They brought two poles and a cloth sling which became Jabal's litter. The Judaean panted and groaned when they moved him, pallet and all. The guttering spark of life still burned.

"Now will you come with me?"

Brutus nodded and followed the woman. Neither she nor the others carried light, yet when they entered the darkness of the tunnel it didn't seem to make any difference to her. Brutus had to feel his way, stumbling over irregularities in the floor; she glided on gracefully ahead of him, as at home in the pitchy black as if she were a bat, the floating edges of her veil become great, snowy wings.

The tunnel seemed to go on for far longer than any Brutus had yet seen since entering these caverns. It switched back on itself, ascended, dropped, widened briefly only to narrow once more. Sometimes a fresh sliver of daylight winked down, taunting Brutus with hints of a world left behind.

Perhaps I'm in Avernus, he thought. *Jabal is dying, but maybe I'm already dead. One shore of the sea looks much like the other. Am I bidding him a good voyage or welcoming him home?* By the faint light from above, he cast a furtive glance at the veiled figures walking before him and behind him. *Certainly these move as silently as the spirits of the dead.*

The tunnel blossomed out into the trumpet of a stone flower, a vast cavern where torches flared in metal brackets and a pool of water the color of milky emeralds cast back countless eyes of fire. Beyond the pool was a small altar, little sister to the one Brutus had seen in the sybil's chamber. This one shone, stainless white, a shallow golden bowl chained in place at its side.

The woman led Brutus around the verge of the pool, up to the altar. She picked up the bowl and held it out to him. He took it, not knowing what service she wanted of him. She knelt beside the pool and cupped green water in her hands, poured it into the bowl. Then she took it from him and with a nod of her head indicated that he too should add a measure of water from the pool.

He did as she wished; he saw no harm in it. She passed the chained bowl back to him and with a gesture urged him to pour out the water as a libation on the altar stone.

He poured out water; the altar was washed in milk.

Brutus.

She was there, the goddess, as simply and miraculously as the milk dripping from the altar. His name rang out inside his head, then turned itself to sounds spoken by human lips as Venus appeared at his side, between himself and the veiled woman.

"Brutus . . ."

He didn't know whether to laugh or to curse all she'd done to him or to take her in his arms. She smelled of the seafoam that had given her birth, and there was a wreath of myrtle in her hair, pale pink flowers starring the glossy leaves. He reached out his arms to her as naturally as drawing breath.

She stepped away from him, bare feet kissing the stone. "This is not the hour," she said.

"Then when—?"

"When? Maybe soon. Maybe never." Her words turned from caresses to claws drawn over his skin. "You have been untrue to me, Brutus. You have sworn yourself to me, and I have given you all that I promised in return for your devotion. Say if I have not! Youth clings to you. You live on, but escape the marks of time. Don't you owe me something more than words of gratitude for such a gift?"

"Lady—" Brutus' hands were raised in supplication. "Lady, you said you would ask a service of me, but until now, you've asked nothing. How have I betrayed you?"

"Oh, what a man you are!" She pronounced it as an insult. "Like all men, you come into my temple to ask a favor, you leave a sacrifice as a bribe, I grant what you desire and we're quit. You want merchants, not gods!"

"But—but what is it you want of me?" Brutus was still weak from loss of blood. The image of the goddess wavered before his eyes, as if seen through water. He remembered the words of the dwarf, Na'id-Sin, who had spoken of the lessening hungers of the gods. *You were wrong, poor man. This one is still hungry enough to swallow the world.*

"I want you to live. *That* is what I want. Yet if I take my eyes from you, you run to court death. How many times? How close have you come to the lip of Avernus?"

"In truth—" Brutus lowered his hands, bowed his head. "In truth, I thought that I'd come there now."

Her laughter spread dove's wings and swept through the cavern, scattering light, making the stones glow like a thousand rainbows. "Could I be here, if that were so? How can I exist without living flesh to worship me, heed me, hear my call? Only the flesh knows love, Brutus."

"Then where am I now? And who are these?" He spread his hands to indicate the white-veiled figures. Their numbers had increased in the time he had spent talking to the goddess, creeping out of the darkness, standing all around the cavern in the torchlight. The one who had brought him here moved unobtrusively away from man and goddess, back to the place where Jabal lay.

For a moment, Venus looked like a mischievous child. "They are those who disagree with me. They are the rebels whose spirits cling to love long after the flesh has burned from the bones. The Lord and Lady of Avernus don't know what to do with them, and so they have most graciously given them over to me. As I shall give one of their number to you." A fresh peal of laughter sparkled diamond-bright from the iridescent stone.

"To me? But—" He started forward when a guttural groan of pain from Jabal yanked him back. He rushed to kneel at the Judaean's side, took Jabal's hand in his. It was cold, but still held life. Brutus lifted his eyes to the goddess.

"You say that I court death?" he cried out to her across the emerald pool. "Why would I bother, when death follows me like a dog? Any I love, any I count as friends die! What use are years without age if I must live them out alone? You gave me a curse, not a blessing!"

"A curse?" The goddess' smile vanished, her face becoming a cold, closed, unreadable thing, the face of a statue. Flowers dropped from her hair, withered from pink to brown at her feet. "*A curse?*" The warm welcome of her breasts hardened, sweetly blushing softness turning to stone the color of ashes. *A curse?* Her mouth no longer moved, yet the words thundered all around Brutus, making his bones quake.

What do you know of any curse, Brutus, that you imagine yourself important enough to be its victim? Those you love die? Death steals your friends? I can name your "curse" easily! It is life. It is being born mortal.

"Noooo!" The anguish of all his losses pulled that word from Brutus' lips. "Too many, there are too many who know me and die for this to be anything but—"

Your enemies die too. Remember that, when making up your tally! Is that a curse also? The image of the goddess grew before Brutus' eyes. The green pool swirled with yellow stars. One by one as they had come, the veiled figures began to drift back into the hidden recesses of the cavern.

"Then *prove* I'm not accursed!" Brutus cried. "Show me, give me a sign, let me know beyond any doubt that the deaths—friend and enemy—don't fall on my head!"

The carved face of the goddess seemed to soften. *Proof?* A fountain bubbled up in the center of the pool, a spring of softly chuckling water. *What proof will satisfy you, my lover?* The warm shades of life flowed back into rock-hard breasts and frozen limbs. The goddess took a step towards Brutus.

"Not that." He held up one hand, and Venus was stone where she stood. "Heal him," he said, resting that same hand on Jabal's chest. "Restore my friend to life."

No answer came from the hardened lips, no words of consent or refusal echoed through the cavern or came to touch Brutus' mind.

"*Heal him!*" Brutus shouted at the image. He forced his protesting body to leave Jabal, to run up to the statue and clasp its chill hands. "Give him back his life and take—"

The marble hands slipped from his grasp, fluttered themselves from stone to feathers. The image shrank, shone, transformed before his eyes into the living body of a dove that swooped around him once before flying away, indifferent, free.

Brutus returned to Jabal's pallet and sank down, defeated. "So I am accursed."

The same small hand whose touch had startled him so badly earlier now ventured to stroke his arm. Out of all the press of white-veiled figures, she alone remained with the two wounded men in the now deserted cavern. "Men ask many things of the gods," she said. "If the gods choose not to answer, what does it mean? That the sacrifice was lacking? That the petitioner is unworthy? That the gods have no answer to give? Neither one thing nor the other."

"Perhaps your gods are wiser than you think." Jabal's voice had become an old, old man's. "They give you no answers because they know that you will only return with more silly questions." His laugh became a cough that brought up blood.

"Master," he said when he was again able to speak. "Master, if you will promise me to look after my family, to make—to make my death easier for them to bear, then *I* will give you an answer."

Tears were flowing from Brutus' eyes. "You never had to ask me for that, Jabal. You know I'll take care of them. Lie still. You don't need to give me anything."

"But I want to. Better a gift from me than from—Ah, may I be forgiven, but I have seen such things here! If I did not know how to tell truth from illusion I might think— My eyes are not my own, I have a fever, it affects the eyes. The visions—" He sighed. "My people were once prophets, Master. My family, my blood-kin bred visionaries who—"

Another spate of coughing shook him. "If I had owned their gifts, we would never have needed to come seeking your Cumaean sybil. I might have told you everything you needed to hear, all your answers. Instead, it is only now, lying here, that words have come into my mind . . . such very strange words . . ."

His voice dwindled to a small, faint piping, but his hand shot out to squeeze Brutus' arm in a raptor's hold. "The dove falls to the eagle's talons, but the child of the eagle fears to fall to the child of the dove." He took a deep breath that broke into a series of short, sharp intakes of air.

When he could speak again, he tilted his head as if only then hearing his own most recently uttered words. He looked cheated, puzzled, and angry to be so. "And that—is prophecy? Were those the words that wanted to be born so badly? Nothing but nonsense. Oh Master, I am no seer after all. I am only—"

Brutus saw the Judaean's hand fall lifeless.

CHAPTER FOURTEEN

All of the tears he shed for Jabal, all of the sobs that shook his battle-weary body, at last had to subside. Brutus looked up from the corpse of his friend. The sole remaining white-veiled woman sat on her heels, calm and still, her hands folded on her knees.

"You're still here," Brutus said. No matter how hard he strained his eyes, he could see nothing of the face behind the thickness of the veil. And yet the cloth seemed to have been woven of spiderweb, so lightly did it float around her.

"I am here to serve you, my lord." There was something odd about her voice, as if its pitch and tone were false, intended to conceal its true sound.

"The goddess' gift. Yes, I remember." He shook his head. "I want no more of her gifts. She couldn't give me what I asked for, so why must I settle for anything else?" He stared straight through the veil to where he supposed the woman's eyes must be. "Go away, sorry spirit. Go back to your sisters."

The veiled woman rose in one slow, elegant motion. "I have no sisters and I can't go back. By the goddess' will, I'm no longer one of them. When I gave my life for the sake of love, I surrendered my will to her, and my destiny even after death." A tiny sigh rippled the folds of her veil. "I thought—she thought you would be pleased with our gift."

"Well." Brutus rocked back on his hams, hands on knees. "If you're telling me the truth, I'd better make the best of it. Do you know the way out of here?"

"I do."

"Then guide me. And help me with Jabal's body." He got onto one knee and slung the dead man's arm over his neck, then looked at her expectantly.

208

The woman never moved. "We must leave him here," she said. "The way out is too long, and you're still too weak to carry him unaided."

"I won't be unaided if you give me a hand," Brutus snapped.

She shook her head. "We must leave him here," she repeated. "Even if I help you, he'll slow us. You've been gone from the waking world too long. Overstay here below and you may never return."

"What makes you think that frightens me?" Brutus slowly lowered the Judaean's body again and sat back down on the cold rock, breathing hard. "It wouldn't be so bad to die. Yes, if I were dead, let Venus ask any service of me she liked: It wouldn't matter. I'd be beyond her hold at last."

"Don't be so quick to envy the dead, Brutus."

"I've heard that more than once. Is there any truth to what you're saying?" he demanded. "Or are you just Venus' echo? For all I know, you're no spirit and never were. If the goddess could remake me into her tool, why not others? How do I know you're not simply a living woman to whom Venus has promised half the world? And all for leading a poor fool like me down the path she wants me to go."

The woman said nothing. Her hands vanished up underneath her veil. They emerged an instant later. Brutus found himself unable to resist as she reached across Jabal's body to seize his hand. Something small and round and damp dropped into his cupped fingers before she let him go. He stared into his palm and saw the golden glint of an *aureus*, its stamped surface bearing tooth marks near the edge.

(He remembered: The party that had followed his own passage into manhood, the great Cato very drunk, giving him a gold coin like this and insisting that he bite it to test its purity.

"That's the way, boy! Never trust anyone's word but

your own, and always trust more than your poor senses!"

Although the coin was more ready money than the young Brutus had ever had in his hands in his life so far, he never spent it. He carried it with him always, a memorial token of that day, until at last another day came when he gave it away freely, out of a shattered heart.

He remembered: Standing beside the bier where Portia lay, her eyes shut, her death-wound covered over. The dead required passage money if their spirits ever hoped to reach the other world. Any coin would do, even a lowly bronze *as*. The ferryman of Hades didn't care how much he was paid for his service, so long as he was paid something.

Brutus opened his dead wife's mouth and placed Cato's gold *aureus* under her tongue.)

"It can't be." He turned the coin over in his hand, then looked up. The woman's veil was gone.

"My lord." Portia bowed her head. "Husband."

Afterwards, the thing that stayed most tenaciously in his mind was the fact that no matter how long the road back to the outer world, he felt neither hunger nor thirst until he left that path behind him and stepped back into daylight. Only then did the pangs hit him so hard that he almost doubled over from the hollow ache. A single deep breath of the world's air and his throat became like sun-parched soil, ready to crumble at a touch and blow away.

Portia took one look at him, holding onto the side of the cavern mouth, and hurried him into the shade of some nearby bay trees. "I'll bring food and water," she said, and picked up the hem of her stola so that she wouldn't trip over it as she ran down the slope.

Brutus watched her go with the same bedazzled detachment of a dreamer uncertain of whether he is still waiting to awake. He closed his eyes, revelling in the feel of the breeze against his skin, air that didn't smell of stone.

The sun was not far above the horizon. He hoped that they had emerged near the spot where he and the others had first entered the caverns. With luck, Pompeii would be near, and he might see Apollo end the day's journey from the gardens of his own villa.

A hubbub of many voices roused him from pleasant reveries. Portia was coming, her stainless white stola now smeared with dust and sweat, a gourd of water in her hands. Behind her came a whole suite of yammering farm laborers—slave or free, there was no knowing—along with women who still smelled of cooking food and woodsmoke, a dirty tousle of children, and a trio of mongrel dogs for good measure. The cookwomen carried baskets full of food, the men brought a pair of dusty donkeys, the children came apparently because the whole affair wasn't noisy enough and the dogs agreed to help correct this.

"Ahhhh, that *is* him, sure enough!" one of the men exclaimed when they came within sight of Brutus under the bay trees. "Remember the time Postumus fell ill with the belly-gripe? Well, maybe it was nigh ten years gone, but *I* recall it. I've got reason: That's when the master needed *me* to drive him and the family back to Roma in the big *raeda*. I got to see the dictator's self give a fine speech before I came back home again, *I* know what he looks like. Yes, that's him or his ghost," he finished, smug as a cat.

"Don't say such ill-omened stuff!" One of the cookwomen gave the man a cuff on the ear that knocked all the satisfaction out of him. "Ghost, is it? Idiot! Even if he's not him, to call a man dead before his time—!" She took another swing at the offender, but this time he dodged it.

Portia knelt beside Brutus and passed him the gourd. "Slowly, slowly," she cautioned as he put it to his lips and tried to drain it in a single pull. "It's ice cold, from a good well. You'll give yourself cramps. Here." She took a piece of thick brown bread from one of the cookwomen and put it into his hands. "Nibble on this—*nibble!* Just a little; see how it sits with you. If you can stomach it, I'll give you an apple and some cheese."

"I thought that Venus gave me back my wife, not my mother." Brutus wiped his mouth and gazed into Portia's eyes. He imagined that his joy in being alive and safe— better than safe, reunited with his better self!—was so great that his whole face must be a lesser sun. His joy was overwhelming; he thought he would burst with it.

The smile she gave back to him was gentle, the same as everything else about her. "I found a big estate nearby. The master is staying in his town villa now, but his people will help us. After we get you back home, I'll have them come with me and bring out the bodies of your—"

All of Brutus' happiness blinked away like a snuffed candleflame. "How do you know there are more dead than Jabal?"

"She said there would be. When she summoned us out of the shades, she told us what would happen in the sybil's cave."

"What *would* happen?" He had to be sure of her words. "You mean she knew . . . before?"

"The goddess? Of course she knew." Portia saw nothing extraordinary in this. "She said that she would look after you herself, but that when it was over there might be other wounded. They would be our charge. When the fighting was done, we all saw the bodies and she told us whose they were and which we should leave behind. Only one of your men was still alive then. Why do you look at me like that? What have I done wrong?"

"Not you." He took some more water into his mouth, rolled it around, spat it out. "She knew we were there, Quintus and Fabius and Jabal and I. She knew, and she could've done something to save us. She didn't."

Portia pressed his hand to her breast. "You're safe."

"*Us,* curse it! She could've saved *us!*" He shouted in her face so loudly that the waiting women backed off hastily and one of the stolid donkeys shied and almost bolted. Without being asked, the peasant rabble removed themselves to a safe distance downslope from the unfathomable doings of the highborn.

Brutus forced his voice down to a more measured tone. "She could have saved all of us, not just me. She could've warned us. Instead she let us follow that lousy traitor into young Cassius' trap, let my men be killed, let Jabal—" His voice caught. He yanked his hand away from Portia's tender hold and covered his eyes. "Ah, gods."

"The others were only men to her," Portia said scarcely louder than a whisper. "One of them didn't even acknowledge her existence. But you . . . she loves you."

Brutus' breathing was harsh, his hands still pressed to his eyes as he replied, "I've seen the gifts of her love. I think—" He let his hands fall into his lap and gazed at his dead wife's face. "I think I've known it long enough. I want no more of it."

Portia shook her head the way a nursemaid might over the antics of an incorrigible child. "So you say. No more of her gifts, of her love? I know otherwise. I've known it from the moment I first saw you in her arms."

"Saw—?" Brutus gaped.

"In the garden. In our—our old house. I couldn't sleep for worrying about what might become of you the next day, when you went to kill Caesar. I sat in my bed, staring into the darkness. Then I decided that I might feel better if I had a little fresh air. I was only going to toss a blanket over me for a cloak when I heard a silvery voice whisper in my ear *Come out, if you must, but come secretly. Cover your head, hide your face, let no one see you.*"

"And you—you heeded this . . . *voice?*" Brutus took a big bite of the bread, regarded Portia skeptically. "Now I don't know who you really are. My wife wasn't one to follow midnight fancies or to mistake the tail end of dreams for truth."

His attitude didn't seem to wound her feelings at all.

"You can believe I'm anyone you please. I'm still Portia; not the legend they've made of me, only Portia, who loved—who loves you. I was alone, frightened, in the dark. Even legends can know fear. Yes, I listened to the voice. It didn't sound like anything out of a dream. It was solid enough."

"A voice, *solid?*" He knew he was chopping words fine. She said she'd been frightened; he too was suddenly afraid, reluctant to hear what this woman might tell him.

She dismissed his flimsy attempt to distract her from her story. "You know what I mean. The voice was *real*. I did what it said. I passed through my own house like a thief, stole from pillar to pillar in the peristyle, hugged shadows. I saw you there in the garden, my husband. I saw you and her together, and all you did, and all she showed you."

He found that he could no longer look into her eyes. "Portia, I didn't want you to—"

She caught his breath on her fingertips, stopping his words. "Wed to you all those years, and you think I never knew you? Oh, but I did! More than anything I knew that no matter how dearly you loved me, your first love was always elsewhere."

"Not always," he protested. "No, not that. It was only when she came to me that night, and with a goddess' powers to deceive, to lead me wherever she wanted me to go— If she'd been an ordinary woman, I would never have—"

"She never had the power to take your will, my love, even though she is a goddess." Her hands cradled his face, made him look at her so that he could see her smile. "And even being a goddess, she still couldn't hope to claim first place in your heart. That's always been reserved for duty, for Roma. That's what I've always known." She stood up and gave him her hands. "It's time we went home."

The simple words were a line thrown to a drowning man. Brutus' head spun with the effort of trying to understand the whims and demands of gods and goddesses. One of his old masters of philosophy taught that the deities of Rome were merely helpful devices for sorting out the bewildering array of elements that made a universe, like the many compartments in a doctor's pillbox. (Of course the fellow was a Greek, and accounted glib even by others of his kind and calling.) Brutus had had enough of powers and mysteries. All that he desired was peace.

Na'id-Sin's last vision came back to him, the answer to all the deaths that had dogged him since he first embraced the goddess' service that lost night. ("Show me how I may end the deaths—*if* I may end them?") The answer wore the face of the woman he now saw standing before him.

He stood up and took her hands.

There was peace, but only after war.

When Brutus came riding into Pompeii on donkey-back, word tore through the town like wildfire, and the word was *miracle*. Brutus himself was at a loss to understand why the mere sight of him—wounded, yes, but not badly enough to merit such a public uproar—was enough to send a town of Pompeii's sophistication into frenzy.

Only when Rufus came galloping through the surrounding mob did he learn the reason. The former consul rode a fine white horse and had no qualms about using the animal's hooves to cut a way through the shouting press to Brutus' side. Brutus saw the man's face go from white to its normal red and then to white again, as if in the grip of some terrible illness. Rufus had squeezed himself into his old armor somehow and wore his sword in plain sight.

Without bothering to dismount, he leaned forward and demanded, "So you're not dead?" It was an odd sort of welcome.

Brutus tried to turn it into a jest. "Not nearly dead

enough to have caused all this." He gestured at the gabbling people surrounding them. Portia waited a short distance off, seated demurely on her own donkey, her veil back in place. "This display of the people's love for me is very gratifying, Rufus, but I was only gone—"

"When you left, the moon was near the full. She's almost there again. Damn it, where have you *been*?"

"Near the full . . ." He couldn't believe it. He darted desperate glances all around him for Portia, hoping she'd heard, praying she'd have some explanation. She was too far from him for either. He pressed his lips together. "Was there no word? No one to say where I'd gone? I left with Fabius and Quintus, two of my guardsmen, and Jabal. Jabal knew where we were headed; he must've told his wife. Didn't Cyma say—?"

"She was the first one I sought out. She'd vanished from your villa, along with his children. One of your servants said she'd heard you'd gone seeking an oracle. Around here that means just one thing: the sybil. I sent men to inquire after you at all her so-called lairs—you'd never believe how many there are in these parts, all set up to fleece the faithful. Cunning wretches." He shook his head. "Those trails went cold fast. A day after people first remarked on your absence we thought we had a clue. You know Sulpicius Senex, the pup who's just been named quaestor? Hardly enough fuzz on his cheeks for one scrape of the razor, but carries himself like a granddad."

"I think so." A few possible faces to match to that name tumbled through Brutus' mind.

"Well, he and some friends of his came back from a country excursion and claimed they'd seen you and your men taking the southern shore road. We sent messengers that route, but no luck, which is about what Senex and his friends had."

"How do you mean?"

"Just that more than one of them got too deeply into the wine, turned clumsy, and had a spill down a slope that was more rocks than soil. They were all pretty badly cut up. Senex may have to grow a beard to hide some of his scars, Jupiter help him."

Brutus didn't respond. Everything around him melted away—the crowd, Rufus, even Portia. He was back in the sybil's cave, fighting for his life amid fire and shadows. He took a few deep breaths then said, "I think you'd better help us get through this crowd to my nephew's house, Rufus. You know how close young Cassius and I have become. He must be very worried."

"Funny you should mention young Cassius—" Rufus began.

Of course once the truth of things came out, there could be no mercy for the surviving conspirators. Sulpicius Senex and the rest made a full confession. Senex spoke well and freely, unashamed of what he'd done. In his eyes, he'd defended the ancestral rights being eroded by the radical seeds Brutus had planted and still nourished. The others were less eager to incriminate themselves. Then Brutus himself was brought forward to confront them. They took one look into his eyes, blanched, and babbled out the whole story so rapidly that it came out as gibberish and needed to be repeated several times for the sake of recording the evidence.

When their words had been taken down and they were led off, Rufus turned to Brutus. "How did you do that?"

Brutus shrugged. "Murderers can't approach their victims' bodies; the old wounds open up and bleed afresh. Maybe they were afraid I'd do the same."

The conspirators were brought back to Roma in chains and condemned by the very senators who would have praised their plot to the skies if the former dictator had had the courtesy to stay dead.

But Brutus was no longer spoken of in the streets of Roma as merely the former dictator of Roma. On plebeian lips he was never mentioned as anything less than divine. His name was uttered in tones of deepest awe even by those members of the aristocracy who had long hated him for the complex threadwork of laws that made slaveholding and large estates less and less profitable. He was no longer a man.

He did not age. He could not die. He brought back the souls of the dead.

There were still more than enough people living in Roma who had known Portia well enough to testify that Brutus' new woman was indeed his dead wife. They called him another Orpheus, although a sensible Roman Orpheus who'd had more common sense than to panic and disobey Hades' orders. *He* hadn't even thought of looking back, like that fool Greek musician! Every man who recounted the story took personal pride in the outcome and every woman sighed over how delicious it all was.

As for Portia herself, while the streets of the city roared and seethed with crowds demanding the conspirators' blood, she calmly opened the doors of her new home to welcome back friends from another lifetime.

"The only thing that troubles me is they never stay long," she told her husband that night as they lay together. "They send word asking if they can call on me, they come, they embrace me, and then they sit there staring at me like owls until I ask them if anything's wrong. Then they rise up in a flutter, chatter something about another visit yet to make, and fly away. They only come once; they never come back."

Brutus kissed her cheek. "You can't say that about Albina."

"Rufus' wife? She's a sweet girl, but we don't speak the same language. She's nowhere near my age."

"Nor Rufus' age either." Brutus chuckled. "If it doesn't bother him, it shouldn't bother you. Don't you want friends?"

She returned his kiss. "I have you."

He said nothing, but held her to him all the more tightly. These days he never slept apart from her. He would never say so, but he was haunted by the fear of one day waking up and finding that she had been a dream.

If it was a dream, it was one well steeped in blood. The conspirators were sentenced to be thrown from the Tarpeian rock, although public outcry railed against such leniency. Brutus stood by in the midst of his newly augmented bodyguard while the sentence was carried out. The shattered corpses were beheaded for good measure, the heads set out on display on the Forum rostra.

Young Cassius' body too was brought up from Pompeii and shared his friends' fate posthumously. It was all that the executioner's slaves could do to fight off the mob that wanted to tear the corpse to shreds. By the time young Cassius' head reached the Forum, it was only a ball of meat and bone, barely recognizable as human.

Rufus was the one who brought Brutus and Portia the news of Junia's suicide. Brutus did not attend his sister's funeral, though Portia did. It was the last death Brutus could name as a curse.

That night, he dreamed that he was back in the sybil's cave.

There were torches flaring in the shining brackets on the wall and nothing at all left of the stale smell of long uninhabited places. An incense-laden flame burned in the tripod. A purple cushion rested on the carved throne, its rich material cradling the water gourd that had first quenched Brutus' thirst when he'd returned to the upper world.

In his dream, Brutus approached the throne and its strange burden. He picked up the gourd and held it to his ear. A faint buzzing came from it. He concentrated on making sense of the sound, shaking the gourd once or twice in his efforts. Finally he was rewarded: The buzz became the hoarse, reedy voice of a crone.

Who disturbs my endless waking? The sharp, querulous demand startled him so badly that he dropped the gourd. The voice spoke again, this time loudly enough so that he didn't need to press the gourd to his ear. *I know you. You are the promised one, the one to end this ageless captivity. Oh, may you be blessed! Please, wait no longer, I beg of you. Set me free, my lord!*

He knew then, in the way a dreamer simply owns all knowledge in his dream, that he had found the true Cumaean sybil. He knelt before the throne. "How can I set you free? You asked Apollo for the gift of prophecy and the gift of eternal life—he gave you both—but you forgot to ask him for the gift of youth as well. Men say you're little more than a voice and the shrivelled husk of a body, no bigger than a grasshopper's shed shell."

So I am. I can not deny it. Child of the eagle, will you look on me and save me?

"How can I restore what the years have taken? How can I undo the work of the gods? How can I set you free when your captivity is something you chose for yourself?"

Questions, questions, questions! Have you too come here only to take what few answers I own, to give me nothing in return but more questions? I hold too many questions now!

The gourd buzzed and vibrated as furiously as a wasps' nest. A thin keening rose up from it, the sound building on itself, doubling and redoubling into an ominous roar that shook the torches in their brackets and blew out the tripod flame. A crack like a thunderbolt echoed through the cavern and the gourd split open like a riven eggshell.

Brutus woke with a scream, streams of cold sweat bathing his body.

CHAPTER FIFTEEN

Brutus never spoke of what he had seen in his dream to anyone, not even to Portia. He never had that dream again, yet he was never able to forget it. It lay over him more snugly than his own skin. Once he came close to speaking about it to Rufus, more than five years after the fact. The two old friends were having a private dinner party in Rufus' house. Good wine still had the same effect on Brutus as on other men, no matter who called him a god.

"Rufus, what frightens you?" Brutus asked. His tongue was loosened and his mind was wandering down strange paths, led on its wanton way by an excellent measure of Chian.

"My wife." Rufus still had a robust laugh.

"I'm serious."

"You think I'm not?"

Brutus threw a handful of almonds at him. "If I speak first, will you *try* to give me a sensible answer?"

"I'm too old to be sensible. But go ahead."

"Well, that's it, you've said it for me: Old. The thought of aging, that's what scares me more than anything."

"Which is why you've elected not to do it, I suppose." Rufus could be mordant when he liked. "Haven't shared the secret trick with me yet. And you call yourself my friend!"

"It's not a secret that's mine to share or a gift I can control. That's my whole point: I *can't* control it. And since I can't control it, what's to prevent it from someday just—taking wing?"

"Of all the fool—! Look Brutus, I was there in the Senate the day they tried to kill Caesar. I saw you almost die saving your father's life from Cassius and that lot. I served with you in battle against the Parthians. Pfaugh, forget

221

all the rest of it, *I saw you come back from the dead!* Yet despite going through all that, how much have you aged? Five gray hairs, maybe six. A crease or two between your eyebrows and the start of a fold under your chin. And that's *all*, so stop babbling about how you can't 'control' age. You don't need to control a thing if you've already scared it clean away! You'll never know age, so why fear it?"

"Who's more likely to be afraid before a battle?" Brutus muttered. "Old veterans or green recruits?"

"That example won't help your argument. I've known plenty of veterans who shat themselves before every fight, and just as many new men who stayed cool as ice through their first blooding. If you mean you fear age because you don't know what to expect of it, you're all hollow. You *do* know. You've seen other men grow old, though not one of them—" his eyes twinkled "—who's done it half so handsomely as me."

"Albina tells Portia that you're a fake, Rufus." Brutus couldn't help but be lured away from solemn thoughts by his friend's jolly nature. The wine didn't hinder his good humor either. "You only pretend to be an old man by day, but she claims that when it's dark you shed your disguise and become a man of thirty."

"There goes *my* secret." Rufus feigned a heavy sigh. "So now are you afraid of age because you *do* know it or because you *don't*?"

Brutus' indulgent smile slowly turned over on itself. "Because I do. Too well. I've seen it. Not the way others have, in the faces of old men and women, but in the face of the thing itself: Old age. I've seen it plain, without the little scraps of life that trim its claws and soften its fangs. What I've seen is age without honors, without comforts, without another heart to share its burdens, without the faces of grandchildren to distract—" He bit his tongue. "I'm sorry, Rufus. I didn't mean to mention—"

"That's all right." The former consul's jovial dismissal sounded as false as his earlier sigh. "Albina says she doesn't mind the situation if I don't. She says she's just as content not to have children, says she's got more time to spend with me this way. She says that there are plenty of other couples who're more than happy childless, you and Portia for one. She says—she says—" He drank off a full goblet of unwatered wine and said nothing further. Brutus joined him in his guarded silence, and the tale of his dream remained untold.

It was at the next Ludi Florales, when the streets of Roma were breathless with blossoms and the brightly colored gowns of women, that Rufus brought the news to Brutus' home:

"What do you think? I'm going to be a father!" He had to shout to make himself heard over the din of musicians filling the palace with melody and song.

"What?" Brutus cupped his ear and leaned across the banquet table.

Portia had heard well enough for the two of them. "A baby! Oh, Albina!" She rose from her couch and dashed around the table to embrace Rufus' wife. No longer quite so young, Albina had become Portia's nearest friend, perhaps the only one still willing to treat her as just another woman. Brutus knew that, like him, Portia never seemed to show the traces of the years. This was much whispered of among the ladies who gained status by calling themselves Portia's friends. Not all the whispers were of unmixed awe; many were pure envy. Only Albina remained kind and constant.

Brutus watched as his wife bubbled over with the shared joy of Albina's pregnancy. They sat on the same couch now, Portia heaping garlands of flowers into Albina's lap, laying her hand on the younger woman's still-flat belly, whispering and giggling like a girl. His heart gave a curious lurch. He distracted himself by turning to the guest on the couch to his left—a crabbed old senator whose name

Brutus never *could* recall—and plunging into a long discussion of the unrest in Judaea. Since there was pretty much always unrest in Judaea, it was a topic that never ran dry.

Throughout Albina's pregnancy, Brutus behaved as if the whole situation didn't exist. Portia's giddy reports on her friend's progress were met with either disinterested silence or a quick change of subject. Dinners that included Rufus and his wife never failed to conflict with other meetings that demanded Brutus' presence. He was a busy man, a man of untold influence in the government; Rufus must understand that the welfare of Roma came before all else. After all, it was a true friend's duty and privilege to understand such things.

When the birth came, it was well omened, falling during the rites of the Bona Dea, protectress of women. Albina and her son both survived it, and on the ninth day following the birth Portia said her first harsh word to Brutus since their return from the sybil's cavern:

"*Why* won't you come with me, you mule? We've both been invited to the naming and we both must go!"

"That's hardly a logical conclusion." Brutus pretended great absorption in the scroll presently open before him on the *tablinum* table. "Just because we were both invited doesn't necessarily mean—"

"I say it does." Portia's hand splayed itself over the parchment, making it impossible for Brutus to continue with the charade of reading. "Do you think you've been fooling me, Brutus, with the way you've been acting about this child? You can't. The thought of it's eating you up inside with envy, the same way it's done from the first."

"Where did you find the thread to spin out *that* fable?" He tried to laugh off what she said. "Why can't you accept the plain truth of the matter? I am simply too busy with more important affairs to attend—"

"Now who's spinning fables?" Her gaze was steady, admitting no contradiction. "You do envy Rufus and

Albina. For all the power and advantage you and I enjoy, they now have the one thing that can never be ours."

"I begrudge them their son?" Brutus snorted. "When have I ever said so? How can you claim—?"

Her eyelashes brushed her cheeks. When she spoke, her voice held too much pity for his comfort. "You forget how well I know you, even better now than I did before I died."

He winced. He didn't like it at all when she spoke of her death. He said so.

She pursed her lips. "I'm only saying what's true. You never used to think that the truth was your enemy. I *did* die. Being dead opens your eyes to many things you never saw before. Life—life's a thousand distractions every breath. The dead have time to learn more things than the living know exist."

"Nonsense." And again, more gruffly: "That's nonsense."

"You think so? Many disagree with you, my husband. That's why I can hardly leave this house, except well escorted. I'm besieged at every turn by people who beg me to share my knowledge, to show them the road I walked, the pathway back from death."

"They do?" Brutus was honestly surprised. "No one's ever bothered me with such requests."

"You? You're a god. People don't badger gods when they want something really important. They petition, they supplicate, they bribe, but they never badger. Gods get to keep their secrets. I'm merely the god's bride; I am more approachable."

"I wish you'd have told me about this sooner. I'll put a stop to it at once."

"No you don't." Portia wagged a finger in his face. "You're trying to evade me again, to slip away from what's really important: We are *both* going to the naming ceremony for Rufus and Albina's son."

Brutus shook his head decisively. "I've already sent a generous gift for the child, but I *can't* go. I've just received certain vital messages. The situation in Judaea is growing worse all the time."

"That's your tame excuse for everything, lately. The situation in Judaea is *always* worse; it's never been known to grow better, not since Pompey took the land. I doubt it ever will. If Judaea falls apart because you spend an afternoon honoring your friends, it was never meant to endure in the first place!"

Brutus rolled up his scroll, secured it with a green silk cord and slipped it into the leather bucket on the tabletop. "How long has it been since the last time I told you that you should've been born a man?"

"Not long enough for me to have forgotten the insult."

As Portia had promised him, the situation in Judaea survived his inattention for one afternoon. Brutus himself survived the festivities at Rufus' house with less success. He began by drinking as much strong wine as he could find as early as he could find it. He remembered almost nothing of what happened after that, except that the baby looked as red as he expected someone named Gnaeus Claudius Rufus the Younger must look. It was also rather puny and squally and smelly. He couldn't understand for the life of him why he fell into disgrace with his wife for saying so, out loud and before every witness at the party. By Apollo, hadn't *she* been the one to remind him that truth was not his enemy?

Portia refused to see it that way. He retired to his tablinum to ponder the peculiarities of women, even those who had enjoyed the seasoning effects of death. There were times he thought that Aristotle had been right about the whole female sex, Portia included, but that was only when his head throbbed the worst. That night he chose to let Portia sleep alone for the first time since her return. Still the philosopher, even at a depth of so much wine, he concluded that it would be better if *he* chose what she had already decided.

He was still dealing with the physical aftermath of Young Rufus' naming feast when Portia came scratching at his tablinum door the next day. When she saw him, her face contorted itself into a war of expressions—anger and sympathy waging a losing fight against the poorly suppressed urge to laugh out loud.

Do I look that bedraggled? he wondered.

Victory went to the laughter as Portia threw her arms around his neck.

I suppose I must, he thought ruefully.

"Did I make such a great fool of myself?" he asked in a small voice.

"Beyond a doubt." She kissed him. "I've just come back from Albina's."

"Oh." He was positive that he didn't want to hear the details.

"Ah, take that look off your face! You were under sentence of death, but I persuaded her to forgive you for my sake."

"Just . . . like that?"

"Well, she did make me swear to recognize that I owed her a life for a life." Portia laughed. "She does love a good joke!"

"And Rufus?"

"Which—? Oh, you mean the ooooold man?" She turned her hands into arthritic claws and made her voice go all quavery. "He never asked for your execution. By the time I got there, he'd already gotten Albina all primed to forgive you. The trouble was she couldn't give in to *him*—he's only her husband—but when I arrived, she had her excuse. It was fine if she conceded to *me*. Everything fell out neatly."

Brutus sucked in his lower lip and looked at his wife askance. "I hope that's just another one of those jokes Albina loves so much. A matron's duty to her husband—"

"Lectures on matronly duty? To me? You *don't* want

to live, do you?" Portia made a disgusted noise and left him to his scrolls.

He sat at his reading table, his head still pounding like Parthian drums. That same morning a messenger had come with correspondence from the east: There was trouble in Judaea.

In the year that King Herod the Great sent the former dictator of Roma the regal gift of a pure white camel, decked with trappings of purple silk and gold, the ex-consul Gnaeus Claudius Rufus died in his sleep. While slaves crowded the wharf at Ostia, arguing whether the beast were painted or came by its color naturally, Brutus stood with Portia, Albina, and Young Rufus watching fire devour the body of his last true friend.

He died in peace, Brutus reflected while the smoke of Rufus' burning smeared the springtime sky. The thought brought its own revelation: *He died because his heart stopped beating, not because it blocked some spear or sword or dagger meant for me. This is a death that touches me, but one that I've done nothing to bring about. So they were right, all those who swore I wasn't accursed. The proof of it lies there, amid the flames.*

He glanced at Albina. Rufus' widow had aged visibly in the years since the birth of her son. Seen side by side with Portia, it was the ex-consul's relict who now looked like the elder of the pair. As for the boy himself, he was staring into the fire with the fierce, focussed gaze of a seer demanding visions.

He loved his father very much. Brutus could understand that well. He too had loved the man. *If he stares hard enough, long enough, the boy hopes to summon the power to make Rufus rise from the blaze like the phoenix. So he believes.* He tried to recall being so young—barely ten years old—and having such adamant faith. He patted the boy's shoulder and tried not to feel offended when Young Rufus moved away.

When all the rites were done and the dead had been dispatched with every honor, Brutus and Portia went home. She didn't address a single word to him until they were under their own roof, and not immediately even then. Acting as if he weren't there, she walked straight to the gardens at the back of the palace, not even pausing to shed her palla. Instead she settled the light mantle's silk drape more securely over her head as she stood beside the central fountain. Infant tritons and nereids played among jets of cool water spouting from the mouths of marble dolphins. She scooped a palmful of water from the basin and pressed it to her reddened eyes, letting it trickle down her cheeks.

Brutus came up behind her and embraced her. They stood so for a time, with only the sound of the plashing water to keep them company. "We'll help Albina, of course," he finally said, resting his chin on her shoulder. "Young Rufus will have everything he could ever need."

She turned to face him. "He needs a father."

"What are you asking me to do? Take Rufus' place? Even if I knew what that entailed, Albina would never hear of it. She'd rather keep the boy to herself."

"For now," Portia said. She stepped out of the circle of his arms to gaze into the water once more. "Do you know that when she first woke up and found Rufus dead beside her, she kept it a secret, even from the servants? She got up, tossed on a cloak, and hurried here, to me, to beg me to bring him back to her. 'You know the path,' she said. 'You can lead him home again. You swore to me ten years ago, a life for a life!'"

"When did you ever——?" Brutus was nearly speechless with astonishment when Portia refreshed his memory. "You said she was *joking.*"

"I thought she was. Do you think I would've sworn the oath I did if I'd thought she was serious?"

"You swore——? Oh, Portia!"

She shrugged off a folly that was past mending. "In

any case, I convinced her that it would be foolish to call
in such a debt. The gods don't give up their prerogatives
graciously, and they might very well visit some terrible
punishment on her house if she pressed the issue. So
she agreed to accept what had happened and went home
to begin the arrangements for his funeral."

"Why didn't you just tell her that you *couldn't* do what
she demanded?"

Portia took a drink of water from cupped hands and
said, "Because I would be lying."

Brutus took her in his arms and kissed her. He did it
because he didn't know whether what she said was more
nonsense, or desperation, or another joke-that-might-not-
be. Her mouth was cool and wet, tasting of moss. They
went back into the palace and made love, quietly and
urgently as two slaves who fear discovery and punishment.
He put everything from his mind except the warmth and
the scent and the comfort of her body. It was easier to
do that than to ponder the true implication of what she'd
told him. He was so successful in his efforts to put the
whole subject out of his mind that he didn't think about
it again until he had to. That was in the year that the
white camel died.

The keeper of the menagerie said that the camel had
died from eating dirt. Brutus came home to pass this
intelligence on to his wife who in turn remarked that
being the royal gift of Herod of Judaea didn't automatically
include a guarantee of common sense in an animal. The
two of them were still laughing about that when one of
Albina's slaves came to them with a letter for Portia.

She unrolled the letter and read it. The blood left her
face. Brutus caught her when her legs buckled or she
would have fallen. She dropped the scroll, began to weep,
ran from the room. So it was that Brutus had no one
with him to help ease the blow when he picked up the
papyrus and read that Young Rufus was as dead as the
white camel. He had tried to climb the garden plum tree

and his foot slipped, leaving him sprawled snap-necked on the grass amid a storm of falling blossoms.

Brutus dashed after Portia, but couldn't find her anywhere in their living quarters. The palace was too big for his liking, yet he'd had no choice about living there. The Senate told him that he embodied the dignity of Roma, and Roma must present a properly impressive face to foreign ambassadors. For once he agreed in principle with the Senate.

Now the palace loomed as boundless and as chill as a mountain sky. He ordered servants to help him search the echoing strings of rooms for Portia. They scattered like rabbits in the shadow of the hawk, only to come creeping back into his presence one by one to report that they had not found the lady.

"Master, perhaps she's not here?" one maiden suggested. "I can ask the porter if he's seen her go out."

Brutus gave himself a sound thump in the head, one he felt he richly merited. *Of course the porter! Why did I assume she'd stayed, just because her litter's still here and the bearers weren't summoned? She's decided she couldn't wait for the litter to be fetched and made ready; she knows Albina must be insane with grief and needs her. Portia's run off afoot to comfort her friend.*

Somewhat eased in his mind, Brutus gave calm orders for someone to bring him a horse. He rode well attended through the streets of Roma to Albina's house.

Portia wasn't there, nor Albina, nor the corpse of the child. Professional mourners keened around an empty bier in the atrium under the stern eye of Albina's old mother. Brutus silently admired this steel-haired matron who carried herself with a queen's grace. He could tell without exchanging a single word with her that here was a lady who held duty to Roma as sacred as he did himself.

It was so. The first sentence out of her mouth was a blazing excoriation of any Roman who let his wife run

wild through the streets like a harlot, whether that man
had once been dictator or not!

"—coming here with her hair loose and her tongue
hanging out like a dog's! And what does my daughter do,
to my shame? Grabs the child's body from its proper place
and presses it into that wench's arms, gabbling all sorts
of nonsense." She shook her head. "I'm not to blame.
There was never any lunacy in *my* family. Her father's
aunt, now— In any case, the two of them are gone."

Brutus thought his heart had frozen; it was no more
than a lump of ice in his chest. "Where?"

The old woman looked at him narrowly. "How would I
know?" she snapped. "If I'd had any idea they were going
to rush away like that, I would've done what it took to stop
them, I can tell you that much! As it was, they were out the
door before I could stir hand or foot. I'm little better than
a common cripple, suffering the tortures of Tartarus with
this ache in my bones, not that Albina ever cared." Her
mouth compressed itself into a straight line, a smile of grim
satisfaction. "She'll learn. Old age is a punishment. I can't
say I'll be sorry when it's my time to—"

Brutus hurried from the house, remounted his horse,
ordered the men attending him to question everyone they
could find in the streets. Two apparent madwomen, one
carrying the body of a dead child, couldn't pass through
the streets of Roma unnoticed. The guards obeyed, and
soon a trail was discovered.

It led from the fine house Gnaeus Claudius Rufus
had built for his family down into one of the worst
neighborhoods marring the city. Narrow streets and
many-storied buildings sheltered lives that were as dirty
and noisy as they were brief. The congestion was only
a little less atrocious than the stink. Here and there a
pile of half-cleared rubble marked the spot where a
careless landlord had built cheaply only to have the
cramped and dreary rooms of his *insula* come tumbling
down.

In these quarters it became a bit more difficult to follow the trail. Not only were the mad and the dead more commonplace sights, but the people who lived in these warrens were less willing to aid interlopers. Brutus' guard might shout and rail and threaten all they liked, they were still talking to stones. "Do you realize who that is?" the men demanded indignantly, gesturing at Brutus on his horse. It didn't matter; the people didn't care. They regarded Brutus with no interest whatsoever. His horse, on the other hand—well, their eyes lit up as they took the measure of the beast. A horse could be stolen and sold.

Brutus held up an *aureus* so that everyone might see how the sunlight glinted off the golden coin. "This will be for the man who leads me where I wish!" Immediately the human stones came to life as a score of voices erupted with offers of help; a minor scuffle broke out. The victor was a broad-backed man who claimed to be a blacksmith, though he smelled more of the wineshop than the forge. He led Brutus through the streets and even turned bold enough to guide his horse by the bridle.

"In there," he said at last, gesturing to the open doorway in an *insula* that looked like many others. "That's where I saw 'em go in."

"What is this place?" Brutus asked.

"Daria's house, though it beats me why them poor ladies'd want to come here. Daria an' her girls—"

Brutus didn't care to hear about Daria and her girls. He dropped from his horse and plunged into the house, the guards trooping after. It was dark inside, and the walls gave off the smell of cheap perfume, stale wine, and old piss. He ran into Albina so unexpectedly that he knocked her against a wall.

"Where is she?" he demanded, seizing her by the shoulders. "Where's my wife?"

Albina looked at him, tiny teeth showing in a dog's senseless smile. "On the road. Come. She'll be returning soon."

She took his hand and led him into the courtyard. A few blades of sallow grass poked their heads up between the shattered tiles ringing a dry fountain. Portia sat with her back to the basin, the child's corpse laid across her knees, her eyes as empty as his.

"Portia—" Brutus started forward; Albina made no move to stop him. He knelt before his wife, gently taking up the small body and laying it to one side. "Portia?" Her flesh was cold to the touch. When he tried to lift her hand, it wouldn't budge. He whirled furiously on Albina. "What's happened to her?"

The dog's smile was still fixed on the matron's face. "I told you: She's on the road. She'll be returning soon, bringing him back with her by the hand. She told me so before she left."

"You mad bitch, what road? The Avernan path? She's walked it twice already, there and back. Do you think it's no more than a stroll down a country lane? What've you forced her to? The gods—"

"The gods too keep their promises, and punish oath-breakers rightly," the woman replied, calmly replacing the body of her son in Portia's lap. "A life for a life: She herself swore to it."

"It was a *jest*, you stupid—"

"It was a jest *then*." Albina sank cross-legged to the ground. "We'll wait for her together."

The guards asked their master whether they ought to place the madwoman under arrest. Brutus shook his head. "Not yet. What good will it do?" He too sat on the damp, broken tiles and waited.

They all waited—Brutus, the guardsmen, the mother. The light of the open sky above them waned. The sounds of music and laughter drifted into the courtyard from the apartments where Daria and her girls served their clients. Once Brutus caught sight of two "women" spying down from an upper window. Despite the heavy layer of powdered chalk whitening their faces and the inexpert application of antimony outlining their eyes, it was clear they were but children. One of them had a chest almost as flat as a boy's; she might have had eleven years, perhaps not even that.

So it was that Brutus understood why Portia had come here when she needed to take the nearest path to the place of the dead.

Time passed. The guards stirred and muttered. Albina sat on the chill ground as straight and smiling as if she were once more in her own home, seated on plump cushions, the hostess of a fine dinner party. Nothing could move her or steal that terrifying smile from her face. Brutus tilted his head back and saw Venus' own star shine out against the darkening heavens.

Then the child's hand moved.

It was only a twitch of the fingers, but it was enough. Albina gave a hoarse cry and swept up her son's body.

An eagle and its prey, Jupiter and Ganymede, Brutus thought, his mind wandering to the strangest reflections, stunned by the miracle before him. At his back the guards gasped and chattered like African apes. In Albina's arms the boy opened his eyes and began to wail as if he were still an infant at the breast. The guards set up a shout, and the noise brought whores and customers alike to the windows. When they caught word of what had happened, they too raised their voices in wonder and praise.

Brutus crept on hands and knees to Portia's side. Her face was slack, her eyes still empty, though he thought he saw a shimmer of life in their depths. "Come back," he murmured in her ear. "Come back to me, my wife; come back and see the marvel that you've done, my only love."

Her head turned at the sound of his voice. She tried to smile. "Your only—?" The breath gusted from her lungs in a rush that smelled of ashes and in his arms her body crumpled into dust.

❖   ❖   ❖

On the day that the priests of Aesculapius gave Albina their final verdict—that the gods might allow a boy with a snapped spine to live, but never to walk again—Brutus left Roma. He took ship at Ostia, bidding farewell to a crowd that held not a single soul he'd ever called friend. The plebs cheered him loudly, the patricians offered a more circumspect farewell.

No one asked him why he had chosen to go. He was a man whose word had once been law, whose influence was still a potent if subtle force within Roma. He was more than that, he was a demigod. If a demigod elected to proceed from the funeral rites for the divine Portia to begin immediate preparations for a long sea voyage, who would chide him for it?

If anyone had had the courage to question him, Brutus had an answer ready: "I am going to Judaea. There is great unrest in the land." And he knew that once he said that, he would have to laugh until he cried, so perhaps it was better that no one asked him after all.

Chapter Sixteen

Brutus walked along the battlements of Herod's palace in Jerusalem and did his best to blot out the thin, nasal droning in his ear. The nerve-scraping voice belonged to a Roman lady of uncertain age made even less certain by the amount of cosmetics she wore. She simpered and fluttered at his side, blathering on about how she had come to Judaea only because her husband had insisted.

As if I even once expressed any interest in why this magpie's here! he thought. *The truth is, I'd be a happier man if she were anywhere else, as long as it's far away from me.*

But he knew he would never say such things out loud. Though he had passed so many years of retirement in Judaea—self-imposed exile was closer to the truth—he had not managed to adopt the more lax attitudes of the East. He was still too dearly wed to duty, even the duty of putting up with bores because they were Roman citizens far from home. He sighed, nodded absently at her words, and periodically remarked, "Oh, really?"

"Yes, oh my goodness, yes," she assured him. "*Dear Fortunatus!* He simply can't exist without me. He practically got down on his knees and begged me to make the journey with him. He said, 'Larentia, my darling, I'd gladly trade a king's ransom in purple for the privilege of seeing your precious smile when I wake up each morning!' Didn't you say just that, sweetmeat?" She peeked over one shoulder and batted her eyelashes at the fat, fiftyish man who ambled along a step or two behind them.

"Um," he replied. It was the wittiest thing Brutus had heard the fellow say since King Herod himself had introduced them at dinner that evening.

That was no introduction, it was a death-sentence. A slow death, too. I do believe that the king wants to punish

237

me for some offense or other, Brutus thought, trying not to breathe too deeply. The lady Larentia wore a scented oil that was a painful misalliance of myrrh and orange blossoms. *I wonder what it was? The rumors I've heard must be true: There's a demon lodged in Herod's brain. If I weren't who I am, he might've had me killed years ago and I'd go to my death not knowing how I'd sinned against him! Come to think of it, it's not beyond him to arrange my murder anyhow, if that demon gets the proper hold on his mind.*

Brutus glanced at his companions. Larentia was yammering about how rich her Fortunatus was and how much richer he would be when they returned to Roma. "He's *such* a brilliant businessman!" she chirped. "He said to me, 'Larentia, my heart, the gods scattered those sea-snails over the Middle Sea for a reason, and the reason's so I can turn 'em into purple, turn the purple to gold, and turn the gold to pearls that'll make you even lovelier than you are!' Isn't that just what you said, my dear?"

Fortunatus opened his mouth, but all that emerged was a belch. He looked sheepish.

I wish I knew what I've done to deserve this, Brutus thought. *I almost wish I still held the dictator's office: that oily creature Herod would never dare put me in this position then. No, what I* really *wish is that I knew how I could pay back him for this appalling night. Scorpions. Yes, I do think it'll have to be something with scorpions.*

Unaware of Brutus' musings, Larentia's jaws kept up their relentless pace. "What a shame that my wonderful Fortunatus is only an *equite*. I'm just a woman, but even I can tell you that the Senate of Roma would be the better for it if a few more seats were filled by men of business like him. *They* know how to run things."

"Larentia!" A strained look knotted the fat man's jowls and his sallow cheeks turned the rich color of the regal purple dye that was his fortune.

For an instant it seemed as if Fortunatus had done

the impossible: Larentia stopped talking. Unfortunately, it was at best a temporary miracle. She soon got the bit back between her teeth and was off again, this time pawing his arm. Judging from the simpering look on her face, she must have thought she was being coy and charming, but her touch only sent chill prickles coursing over Brutus' skin.

"Oh, but my lord, you don't for a moment think that I meant *you* don't know how to run things? Why, when I heard that you were in Jerusalem I got my hands on just as much gold as it took to obtain an invitation to the palace—those eunuchs are a greedy horror, every one of them—solely for the purpose of meeting you! I can't tell you how deeply I admire you and all you've done for Roma. My dearest Fortunatus is especially grateful. Why, if it weren't for your string of Parthian trade cities, he'd never have such a wonderful piece of the Cathay trade and silk would cost the earth! No, no, no, all that I'm saying is that if a man of his talents and abilities were made a senator, things could only be *better*. Better than they already are. And they're just marvelous now, really."

"You hold me in too much esteem," Brutus murmured. "I hardly run anything at all, these days, unless you count my association with the legions. Even that's mostly ceremonial, a nominal honor done an old soldier." He spoke quickly, doing his best to belittle himself. It was his one hope of a painless, polite escape. Bone-pickers like the lady Larentia never lingered too long over an already meatless kill. "I can't take the credit for Roma's present good fortune. My influence over matters there has dwindled with time and distance."

"Tchah! You're too modest. And you have no idea how sorely you're missed back home. Why are you wasting yourself in this backwater? I know why my darling Fortunatus is here—he's tireless in the pursuit of profit, Roma would simply *blossom* under the care of such a man—but why you?"

Brutus had been asked that question many times over the years, by many souls besides Fortunatus' prattling wife. By now he had his answer pat: "I first came to help the local authorities settle some disturbances. When those were seen to, I simply stayed on. Some flatter me by claiming that Judaea enjoys increased tranquility by my mere presence. I wouldn't know about that, but I do know that this is a very strategic place for anyone who wishes to keep a close eye—but a discreet one!—on the situation in Parthia. The Conscript Fathers understand that I am of more use to the state here, and thus they graciously arranged matters so that I could give up my office as Pontifex Maximus. Once that was taken care of, there was nothing left to demand my return to Roma. Besides, the climate here is better for my health."

"You don't mean to live here *forever*, do you?" Larentia rolled her eyes and tightened her grip on his arm.

"Perhaps I do."

It was an innocent answer, but the woman reacted as if he'd just declared his intention to devour newborn infants raw, on the advice of his physician. "Oh, how *can* you say that? How can you turn your back on Roma? The marvels you've accomplished are nothing next to all the great things you could yet do, especially if you elevated the proper men to help you: *Practical* men. *Down-to-earth* men. *Special* men." Each adjective was accompanied by a squeeze of the arm, for emphasis.

"Special . . ." Brutus sighed and rested his eyes on Fortunatus, who was still red in the face and puffing like a porpoise in distress. Gently he disengaged his arm from Larentia's clutches and said, "You're right, lady, I can't deny it. I can honestly say that I've never met a man quite like your husband. When I return to Roma I'll see about following your suggestion for his advancement."

"You *will*?" Larentia's squeal of delight was marginally more irritating than all her previous wheedlings. "Oh my. Oh goodness. You know, when we were first presented to you, I thought that there was the greatest thrill of my life, to have actually seen you face-to-face. I thought, 'Won't my friends just die of envy when I go home and tell them I spoke to the divine Marcus Junius Brutus.' Oh, and that you actually spoke back to me," she hastened to add. "And now *this*! The gods will bless you for it. Well, I suppose they have to bless you anyway, you being one of them and all. Fortunatus! Fortunatus, my jewel, I insist, I absolutely *insist* that you found a temple dedicated to the divine Marcus Junius Brutus the very instant we get home!"

"Yes, dear," Fortunatus replied, breathing somewhat easier.

Brutus gritted his teeth. He felt deeply ashamed of himself for what he'd promised this poor, silly woman. *When I return to Roma, I'll see about following your suggestion.'* The deceitful words echoed in his mind, mocking him. *I never intend to return. Now all this talk of temples! Bad enough that there's already one of them standing in Roma. The last news from home described it to me and I wanted to sink into the earth. Portia and I, images on a plinth, incense clouds billowing up around us—ugh! But there was no preventing it. I was here when they planned it, built it, dedicated it. And here I stay. No, one travesty's enough. I mustn't allow another.*

"Perhaps it would be more appropriate if you left doing that until after your appointment to the Senate was confirmed," he suggested to Fortunatus. And then, before Larentia could butt in, "That would please me most."

"Whatever you like, lord, anything, anything, your pleasure above all." Fortunatus bobbed his head like a wind-tossed apple ready to snap from the stem. Then, in an undertone, "Do you think that maybe . . . I know how my lovely wife thinks I'm a new Croesus, but the expense of building a whole temple is rather more than I . . . You always did have the reputation for praising the old virtues and . . . I don't have any use for those young

ne'er-do-wells who call a man tightfisted just because he's
not a heedless spendthrift like . . . You know, there's quite
a sane, sensible, *economic* method we might use to—"

"Fortunatus, you are *not* suggesting that we take back
our offer!" Larentia looked ready to pitch her once-beloved
spouse off the battlements.

"No, no, my dove, not at all, it's only that—" Fortunatus
took up his start-and-stop conversation with Brutus again.
"It's just a thought I had . . . Not something we'll do if
you've any objections, even the . . . Well, as it happens,
when we first arrived in Jerusalem we were taken to see
the temple of Venus here and . . . Very modest little place,
hardly more than a shrine, really, but still a pretty thing
and . . . You see, our guide took special pride in showing
us how they've set aside one corner of the place to honor
you, so rather than build a whole temple to you back
home, seeing as how there's already one standing, and
plenty of lovely temples sacred to your divine ancestress
Venus as well, with all that spare room in some of them . . .
It would be very nice, and I'd spare no expense when it
came to the image . . ."

"Where?" Brutus dug his fingers into the plump flesh
of Fortunatus' arms. "Where is this shrine, this Venus
temple, the one your guide showed you? Where?"

The merchant's blobby lips trembled. "Wh—wh—
wh—?" was all he could manage. Brutus' abrupt, almost
ferocious interest struck him speechless.

"Merciful Juno, where *should* it be?" Larentia shoved
herself between the two men, sheltering Fortunatus in
her arms like a baby. "It's where it's always been, that's
where! Have you been living in Judaea all these years
and only now come to Jerusalem? Is that why you've
no idea of where the one and only temple to Venus
stands? Or do you just enjoy frightening my innocent
darling?" Her painted lips made her look even more
like a bloody-mouthed Hyrcanian tiger guarding her kill.
Brutus looked into her eyes and knew that, reputed

demigod or not, he would be very wise to be wary of this woman.

Fortunatus moaned, in agonies over what his wife's too-ready tongue might have stirred up. "Larentia, please, the divine Marcus Junius Brutus didn't mean to—"

"No, Fortunatus, the lady Larentia stands within her rights." Brutus offered his hand, a gesture intended to make peace, but Larentia took up a more defensive posture, drawing her mate even farther from Brutus' reach. "I shouldn't have spoken to you that way; I apologize."

Larentia gave a skeptical sniff and held her ground.

"You speak the truth, lady," he told her. "I *have* been to Jerusalem many times over the years. I even own a small villa in the hills. I've found that if we wish to safeguard Roma's interests in this land, we must keep a close and constant eye on the doings of this city. Unfortunately that's the very reason why I don't know the city itself so well: I'm never here except on the most vital business, and that invariably keeps me chained to either the palace or the Junia fortress or once in a while the outer court of Herod's great temple."

His confession and apology worked a wonderful change in Larentia. She released her protective hold on her husband and was once more transformed back into her chatty, flighty, fawning self.

"Oh dear, you *don't* say!" she gushed. "What a dreadful, dreadful shame! Fortunatus, we simply *have* to correct this state of affairs. I'll tell you what, tomorrow I'm going to send you the very man who guided us through Jerusalem. He's a treasure, an absolute treasure—a Nabatean, but he hardly cheats you at all. He'll be more than happy to bring you to the Venus temple, if that's where you want to go, and afterwards he'll make sure you see all the other sights. There's a tomb he showed us that's *so* impressive. Now who did he say was buried there? King Somebody."

She was running through a list of all possible occupants

of the memorable tomb when a messenger from the king joined them. Brutus had never been so grateful to Herod as at that moment, even to the point of dismissing his previous plans involving scorpions.

The lord of Judaea (by the grace, courtesy, and military backing of Roma) received Brutus in his bedchamber. Like all things touching Herod, the room was constructed on the epic scale, all splendid marble, porphyry, gold, silver, silks and scents. The king himself lay on a bed whose furnishings alone would have fed five of the city's poorest families for a year. The body of the bed itself was fragrant cedarwood, enhanced with gems, ivory, and gold.

Like wrapping a weeping sore in scarlet, Brutus thought dispassionately. Though gorgeously dressed and artfully adorned, the aging King Herod was the smashed shell of a man. Puffy eyes set above gray and purple sags watched Brutus with malicious interest. A gnarled, arthritic hand weighed down at every joint with thick gold rings beckoned him to approach.

Brutus stepped forward, offering the king the most perfunctory of salutes.

Herod smiled and made an elaborate gesture of greeting. "How did you enjoy the evening air, my brother?" he inquired. He spoke fluently, but with a slight accent.

"Pleasant enough, though there was a little too much of it at times," Brutus replied with a lightness he didn't entirely feel.

"Ahhh, Lucius Fortunatus Murex and his redoubtable wife." Herod nodded. "I thought it would please you, to be in the company of your countrymen."

"Whether I'm here in Judaea or off to the east, I'm surrounded by my countrymen. The legions of Roma are more than enough company for me."

"And you have their loyalty." The king's color darkened and a dangerous note came into his voice. "It is a wonderful thing to have, loyalty."

Brutus refrained from comment. Since his arrival on

Judaean shores years past, he had heard nothing of Herod but tales about the king's ruthless attitude towards traitors. It didn't matter who they were or where they lurked, whether they were his closest kindred or his dearest love, he wiped them out quickly and without remorse, one and all. He had even executed the wife of his heart, the beautiful Hasmonean princess Mariame, along with two of their sons.

Her blood strengthened his claim to the throne of the Maccabees, Brutus thought, *but that didn't stop him from spilling it. People still talk about how madly he loved her. There's more madness in this man than love.*

He felt the king's eye on him. Even though he knew he was in no real danger, Brutus couldn't shake off the feeling of dread that settled over him whenever he was in the presence of this man. *Madness,* he thought again. *Madness coupled with cunning. I can almost feel him weighing me in the balance every time he looks at me, calculating whether I'm far enough removed from Roma and my old power for him to risk killing me some day. It wouldn't matter to him whether or not he had a reason to contrive my death, so long as he was assured he could get away with it. And if someone else were to come slinking to the king's ear and offer him that reason—!* He smiled at the king to conceal his unease.

As suddenly as it had come, Herod's black look vanished. He returned Brutus' smile. Lamplight glimmered on the richly oiled curls of his beard. "I ask your pardon if you found their company tedious. I will do whatever is necessary to make it up to you, to redeem my reputation for hospitality. You only have to ask and it will be done."

"There *is* something—"

"Name it."

"My time with Fortunatus and his wife wasn't entirely wasted. They brought me some information and I'm more than grateful for it."

"Information—?" The king's bushy eyebrows came

together in a frown. His hands tightened into white-knuckled fists. The servants attending him shrank visibly at such storm warnings, and Brutus observed these changes with concern.

Now I've done it. Why did I have to use that word? I've stolen his chief treasure. Nothing dares to happen in Judaea unless King Herod knows of it, through his spies. Knowledge is his armor, may the gods save the poor fellow who points out the chink in it!

"I've made it sound more momentous than it is," Brutus said smoothly. "That's what comes of spending half your life making speeches. Orators should never be allowed to have normal conversations. They told me that there's a temple to Venus here, although they couldn't tell me where. I've taken a fancy to see it, that's all, to honor the divine foundress of my house."

"Is that all?" The king relaxed, Brutus and the servants along with him. "I know the place well. I will bring you there myself, tomorrow morning."

But when the next day dawned, King Herod was unable to fulfill his word. The palace rang and shook with the sounds of inhuman shrieks, shuddersome howlings. Herod's sister, the princess Salome, presented herself to Brutus.

"My royal brother, the king, is unwell," she said, her kohl-rimmed eyes filled with such studied innocence that only a fool would ever turn his back on her. "Sometimes he is served improperly watered wine, and it makes his head ache the next day. A minor ailment, but his physicians agree that he should not leave the palace until it subsides. The effects of the sun—"

Another shriek echoed from somewhere not too far away. "I wouldn't call that minor pain," Brutus remarked.

The princess was the mother of grown children, but her laugh retained the silvery notes of girlhood. "Oh, that's not my royal brother; that's the slave who didn't properly mind the watering of his wine." Another laugh. "Lord, I only jest. We are not barbarians. That's my hairdresser, Zimra; she's in childbirth. I myself will accompany you to the temple of Venus, in hopes that you will ask the goddess to give her an easy delivery."

"You're free to ask her yourself. The goddess will be much more impressed by a petition from a princess than from an old warhorse like me," Brutus said, trying to be gallant.

"That is impossible," Salome replied. "I must not be seen even entering the temple, or the priests will be scandalized. Next thing you know, they'll be inciting the people to riot. The only temple any of us may enter without causing an incident is my brother's. Sometimes it's very tiresome, but I do it to keep the peace."

"You're as wise as you're beautiful, Princess," Brutus said. Salome thanked him prettily, but her eyes glittered as coldly as her brother's. The same mouths that had told Brutus of the fate of Queen Mariame and her sons had also let him know of Princess Salome's role in it all. Herod listened to his sister, especially when she whispered of Mariame's conspiracy to kill the king and bring one of her boys to the throne. He listened to Salome and he killed his only love, though a few simple questions asked in the right places would have told him that the sole place Mariame's conspiracy existed was on his sister's lips.

That's no woman's voice, Brutus thought as he and his guards left the palace, their every step haunted by more shrieks, more howls. *Not even a woman in childbirth.* But he was so thankful to pass out of the palace gate that he chose to leave its mysteries in shadow.

Herod can keep his demons, he concluded. *I only hope that when they finally take him off, I'll be able to help exert enough of Roma's authority to keep the peace here while his heirs fight for the throne. Or should there be a throne? This is a turbulent realm. If we kept a more direct rule over these people, maybe we'd be spared their constant feuds. More than half are over their religion. Apollo*

*witness, I loved Jabal like a brother, but I never could
understand his beliefs. One god! One god to rule over all
the rest, yes, like Roma rules over all of our domains,
but one god alone? What would he rule? How would he
rule? Juno protects the births of the same boy-babies that
Mars destroys in war. How could one god rule two realms
so opposed to one another—and so many other things
besides!—without flying into a thousand pieces?*

As he got into the litter than had been prepared for
him, he decided to leave the Judaeans' god to the Judaeans.
*I have other fields to plow. A shrine to me, in Venus'
temple? I won't allow it. I couldn't prevent them raising
a temple to me in Roma, but I can put an end to this
nonsense here. If I leave it unchecked, I'm as impious as
the men who set up my image. One god or many, no man
was meant to call himself divine.*

The temple to Venus was as modest and as pretty as
Fortunatus had described it. It stood in one of the more
fashionable quarters of Jerusalem, well distanced from
Herod's temple. It appeared to be deserted. No priest
came out to welcome Brutus and the rest, not even when
one of the princess' own guards climbed the steps and
bellowed their presence into the sanctuary. Brutus
overheard him reporting his failure to the princess in
the abject, fearful tone so many people used when dealing
with one of Herod's blood.

At a command from Salome, the bearers drew the
princess' litter even with his so that the two might confer.
"You heard him? No one's there."

"Then it looks as if Zimra will have to do without Venus'
intervention," Brutus said.

"Who?" she answered a little absently.

"Your hairdresser. The one in childbirth."

"Oh. Oh!" Salome gave a charming peal of laughter.
"Yes, I suppose she must make do. At least now you have
seen where the temple stands. You can come back here
whenever you like. Let us return to the palace."

"I think I'll stay," Brutus said. "I see the door is open. The priest must be coming back soon." He stepped out his litter and motioned for his guards to start up the temple steps ahead of him.

"As you wish, Lord." Salome shrugged.

Brutus stood at the top of the steps watching the two litters and the princess' armed escort move away down the street. Only when they were well out of sight did he instruct his own men to wait for him in the shadow of the peristyle. Then he went inside alone.

He knew she would be waiting for him. He'd known it since he had seen the open temple door, since Salome's guard had failed to turn up any living soul on the premises. *Priests don't leave their temples open and unguarded,* he thought, listening to the echo of his footsteps. *Not even for a little time. Not in a city where thieves don't care whether they steal from a man or a god.*

Inside the temple it was cool, and a dim gray light bathed everything. Brutus saw the image of the goddess first— a provincial effort that made Venus look as if someone had nailed a pole to her backbone. He walked around it slowly, waiting for it to move or speak. It did neither.

"I'm here," he told it, and felt like a fool when no answer came. The stone lips with their thin and flaking coat of red paint stayed stone. He looked around and saw no costly offerings to the goddess, nothing to tempt a thief. This temple wasn't just modest, it was poor. There was no harm in leaving the great door open if there was nothing inside worth stealing. Maybe the priest would return soon.

Then he saw the second statue in the northwest corner of the sanctuary, the corner closest to Roma. It was a naked man, somewhat lanky but well muscled, neither young nor old. Its face was his own.

He opened his mouth to utter a curse, but it came out as a growl. "When I find out who's responsible for this— *display*—I'll crucify him! And as for the so-called priests who permitted this sacrilege, I'll—"

"Oh, come now, you mustn't blame the priests," the statue said. "They were against it from the first. As for the donor, he hails from one of your own trade-route cities, one of the first freed slaves to settle there. I came to him in a dream and told him how the image must be made. He obeyed me; a pious man. The priests were more difficult, almost as narrow-minded as you. They saw it as sacrilege. For them I had to send a whole week of nightly whispers and dire warnings."

The goddess stepped out of the marble shell of Brutus' statue. "I don't know why you're complaining," she said, putting her arms around his neck. "At least your image looks better than mine."

He tried to embrace her, only to find himself holding air. She had disappeared from his arms, though the temple sanctuary thrilled with her laughter.

Soon, my beloved, came her voice. It was everywhere, filling the chamber, singing through his veins. *Sooner than you know. The time has come. For all the years I've given you, for all the power to turn Roma from her downward path, I've come at last to tell you what you owe.*

"How may I—? How may I serve you?" He didn't want her to hear the fear that closed sharp claws around his throat. This was the moment he'd been dreading for these many years. He'd rehearsed it in his mind a thousand times, given it the best and the worst endings he could imagine, tried to bury it, failed. He stared at her statue because he had to fix his eyes on something or he knew he'd run away. He also knew that running away was useless. "What do you want from me?"

A nothing. A trifle. The stiff image of the goddess glowed with all the colors of dawn. *A life. A woman.*

"A life . . ." His mouth filled with dust. "Who—?"

The face of the statue began to change. He saw how Venus' features lost their formal beauty, melted into the soft face of a young woman barely come of age. The marble eyes darkened with life. Stiff yellow-painted ringlets tumbled over the statue's shoulders, becoming a gently curling fall of hair the color of a raven's wing.

A life, the goddess repeated. *A life, and all your desires, now and always, sealed. So much, Brutus, for so little. One life . . . hers . . . Mariame's.*

CHAPTER SEVENTEEN

It was a small hill-country town like many others. The people went about their business without giving the Roman troops a second glance, or so it seemed. The truth of things was more subtle.

As the soldiers marched past the well, the women either left their clay jugs where they lay and vanished into the houses, or else stood their ground, cold eyes seeing nothing even though they looked right at the men. Men who were wide awake and attentive pretended to doze, observing the invaders from beneath lowered eyelids. Children whispered in delicious fear, alternately tugging one another out of the way or shoving one of their number closer to the foreign soldiers. One boy, perhaps eight years old, was bold enough to make an ugly face at the centurion before retreating to receive the admiration of his friends. Then a group of some five older women made it their business to herd the little ones back into the nearest houses, gently shooing those who wanted to be gone, yanking and slapping those who didn't.

Maybe they believe that if they ignore us, we'll vanish, Brutus thought, seeing the last of the children dragged indoors. He reined in his horse and signalled for a halt. While he and his personal guardsman dismounted, the centurion gave the other men the order to take water and rest. The few women remaining by the well scattered at the approach of the legionaries. More doors slammed, far and near.

He had come to this town at the head of a single century. Even so, eighty men was likely a larger body of Roman troops than these folk had seen in their lives. The town was isolated, insignificant, of value only to the people whose families had made it home for generations. War and unrest came to them as rumor, not reality. Brutus passed the horse's reins to his guardsman and strolled around the open space in the middle of town, examining each tight-shut door with an interest that surprised even himself.

Where is she? he wondered, pausing in the shade of the grape vine that overhung one drab house's door. The grapes were small and black, raisins on the vine. He plucked one, ate it, and made a face at the sourness that filled his mouth. *I suppose I'll have to ask. I want to get this over and done with.*

"Galo!" At the sound of his name, the guardsman signalled for two footsoldiers to come mind the horses, then sped to Brutus' side. Tall and broad-chested, with a head of thick yellow hair, everything about him testified to his Gaulish blood, the blood that had given him his name. Utterly devoted, he was the nearest thing to a friend that Brutus had, these days.

"I'm here, lord," Galo said, massive white teeth flashing. "What do you wish?"

Brutus lowered his voice. "There's a woman in this town, a young woman I need to see. Her name is Mariame. She's living in the house of the priest, Zachariah. I need you to find out where he lives and arrange for us to lodge there."

Galo saluted crisply. In all the time he had served Brutus, it never once occurred to him to question his lord, his idol. This time was no different. Where another man might have asked for some few details—*Who is this woman? How is she important to you?*—or at least given him a searching look, Galo only set himself to fulfilling his lord's desire.

The guardsman cast his eyes over the small, huddled houses of the town. By and large they were alike in their poverty, though here and there were a few that stood out from the rest. Subtle marks such as slightly greater size, or uncracked walls marked them as the homes of men marginally better off than their neighbors. Galo headed for one of the largest and least cracked only to return crestfallen.

"The priest lives *there*," he said, pointing to one of the smaller houses. He made it sound like an indictment. He was used to a world where priests were rich, or at least decently housed. "It doesn't look big enough to lodge a mouse."

"Never mind. Go and tell the priest that Roma needs his cooperation and aid."

Brutus watched Galo go off a second time. *Roma . . . Sometimes I speak as if I were still Dictator. They've made me a legate of the legions here, but as for that—* He made a face. *It's a title that can stand comfortably with or without me behind it. What I told that clapperjaw Larentia about nominal honors wasn't wholly a lie. I command a legion, but these men aren't really mine. One decimation of the ranks might wipe out every legionary truly loyal to me. The rest don't care who commands them. It's not like it was when my father was alive. His soldiers were proud to call themselves Caesar's men. It's not even the same as when I raised up my "chickens."* He sighed. *I can imagine what the Conscript Fathers said when they made the arrangements. "If Brutus wants to play soldiers, let him play. Give him his personal guard, give him a legion, if that's what he wants! Just as long as he keeps the game far from home."*

He broke off his revery: Galo was coming back, an elderly Judaean trailing after him.

The priest Zachariah spoke neither Latin nor Greek, but he'd understood *Roma* well enough. The old man's ignorance was no great stumbling block: Brutus had become fluent in Aramaic during his years of self-chosen exile. *I wonder what Jabal would say if he could hear me now?* he mused. *Probably criticize my accent. Forgive me, old friend: To this day I've been unable to find your family. The gods alone know—* He banished the thought and concentrated on winning the priest's confidence.

It was such an easy task, so readily accomplished, that it left him with a queasy feeling. The words poured out of his mouth as slick and fast as a drunkard's vomit and Zachariah smiled and bowed and went to rouse the whole town with news of the honor being done them. As for Brutus himself, he and three of his men must spend this night under Zachariah's own roof, the old man wouldn't hear of anything less.

Brutus relayed the priest's invitation to the centurion, and the centurion passed down word to the men. They were to wait where they were until called for by those householders who would give them hospitality. They were to move quickly, keep the peace, not drink too much, and be ready to leave with the dawn. The centurion himself would remain with them until the last man had his billet, then he would join the divine Marcus Junius Brutus and his guard at the priest's house. Any offenses committed against the townsfolk would bring down the wrath of the divine Marcus Junius Brutus himself, let the men know this and fear!

"—more, you bastards even *wink* at one of the local girlies, it'll be me you answer to, and after what I'll do t'you for that, you'll be praying it was *only* the wrath of the divine Marcus Junius Brutus come down on your thick skulls, do-I-make-myself-clear?" he concluded.

Brutus shuddered with distaste. He'd spoken to the centurion a minimum of once every three days about not calling him "the divine Marcus Junius Brutus" in front of the men. It did no good at all. *Talk of thick skulls, that man owns one that's solid bone straight through,* he thought. He didn't know whether he was more fed up with the centurion or with himself. He and Galo went back to their horses and led them the short distance to Zachariah's house.

The priest's wife was waiting in her doorway to welcome Brutus and Galo, a basin of water for washing already in her hands. Zachariah had brought word of the guests to his own home first; she was ready for them. She was not as old as her husband, but still well advanced in years. The few strands of hair that had escaped her headcovering were a rich brown heavily barred with gray and her mouth and eyes had been pinched by the hand of laughter.

She didn't know quite what to do with the horses. "We have none of our own," she said. "Not even a donkey. We have nowhere to stable them. Oh—" She was genuinely distressed.

"Galo, take the horses." The woman's grateful look made Brutus smile.

While Galo went to find shelter for the horses, she conducted Brutus into her home as graciously as if he and all the other unlooked-for mouths in his train were heaven's own blessing on the town. She showed him the room where he, Galo and the centurion would be able to leave their gear and sleep the night. As she led him out again he realized that she had given the visitors her own sleeping chamber, the only one in the house. Tonight she and her aged husband would very probably have worse lodging than the horses. He decided not to speak of it or do anything to amend the situation until later; he would not shame her. She was so very, very glad that he had come!

"My husband told me that you're going to take a personal hand in settling the rebellion," she said, bringing him out at the back of the house. Here a bench stood in the shade of a flourishing gourd vine. She urged him to sit and offered him bread, salt, a few olives, and some very bad local wine. "It's so dreadful! We usually don't learn about such upheavals until they're decided one way or another, but this—! It seemed to arise overnight and spread like spilled oil."

"Bad news always seems to travel fastest," Brutus said.

She settled herself onto the bench a decent distance from her guest, nodding her head in agreement. She moved slowly, but not with the painful slowness that spoke of old, aching bones. "It seems as if we closed our eyes in peace and opened them to war. The roads run with blood. Travel is impossible without an armed escort. Families are torn apart. It's just so—so—" Without warning, she began to cry.

She was only at the other end of the bench from him. He wanted to offer her the simple human comfort of two arms to hold her while she wept. He knew he didn't dare. If he touched her, that would make her human, with a heart that could be touched, torn, broken, and a face he would remember.

You will find the woman Mariame in the house of Zachariah the priest. That was what the goddess had told him. This one was too old to be the one he sought and looked nothing like the vision of his quarry's face. She looked old enough to be Mariame's mother. If he was about to kill this woman's child, he couldn't think of her as human. He needed no more sad ghosts.

"Elisheba?" A voice trembled just inside the shade of the house. A young woman came out into the dappled light filtering between the broad leaves of the gourd vine. She hugged the old woman to her bosom, speaking softly and so rapidly that most of her words eluded Brutus' ear.

Her words didn't matter; he had seen her face. It looked much less impressive when seen this way, and not as part of the goddess' vision. It was a very ordinary face, with no claim to beauty besides the gloss of youth and health. There had been times on the road to this place, this moment, when Brutus had lost himself in thought, trying to puzzle out why Venus had named this woman as her chosen sacrifice. He couldn't find a single logical reason, not for all his philosophy.

If she were beautiful, too beautiful for any mortal woman, it would all make sense then. The gods are jealous, and the goddesses—! Troy knows how deadly their jealousies can be. But she's not beautiful. She's hardly pretty. In a few years she'll marry, have children, fade, age quickly— He bit his lip. She would do none of those things. She would only die.

Zachariah's wife soon recovered herself. She apologized to her guest and covered over most of the awkwardness of her outburst by introducing him to her cousin, Mariame. "I beg you to pardon me, Majesty, but you see, the rebellion is more to us than unhappy tidings. My dearest cousin— She came to us because she was afraid. She lives too close to the fighting and her husband's gone. A friend of his, a merchant, needed an extra pair of hands along for a journey to the coast, and like—" her voice was rising in anger "—like a foolish boy half his age he turned his back on his trade, his bride, and her—"

"He went to help a friend," Mariame said quietly. "A friend who promised him enough money in payment so that we could buy a donkey of our own. There was no work for him at home, except sometimes a coffin. He used to say that if more rich men died, he'd be rich too, only then who'd make *his* coffin when—?" She struggled to turn the rough sound that welled up in her throat into laughter. "I'm sorry, Majesty. I talk too much and I forget that not every man is as patient as my husband."

By the next dawn, everything was arranged. When the Romans marched away, the townsfolk were actually smiling, and not merely because they were glad to see them go. Zachariah had brought word to his people of Brutus' benevolence. Would any other man of his stature condescend to help a poor woman like Mariame so readily? Everyone knew that Elisheba's cousin had lost all knowledge of her husband since the troubles. The former dictator (May he be blessed!) would send word through the Roman forces to discover whether the men were dead or living. If dead, well, there was unrest in the land and these things happened. If living, he would have him brought to Jerusalem and reunite him with his bride.

For Mariame was going to Jerusalem under Brutus' protection, that was the big news. He had even offered to let her name an escort of townsmen, if she felt uneasy as a woman alone among his soldiers. She'd refused the offer: The Roman troops had behaved impeccably that night. Besides, she told her cousin Elisheba, if the Roman meant her any shame, who could have stopped him from doing what he liked then and there? He had no need to conceal his evil wishes, if he had any. The town could not stand against a century of Roma. No, he was a good man. She said it so that he could hear. She too blessed his name.

He'd meant to have her die on the road south. It would be an easy death to cover over. She was little more than a girl, and the road was hard, and death often awaited the young and the weak who ventured into the wild world. The countryside itself might provide him with the means to do it and the excuse to leave him clean of it—a cliff, a venomous snake, a wild beast. Failing that, there was always the rebellion. So many ways—

It was on the road south that she told him she was going to have a child. He brought her to Jerusalem unharmed and gave her a safe place to stay in his villa. She'd never seen so much magnificence, though to Brutus' eye the place was serviceable, if a little rustic. She walked through the rooms as if treading on glass. She didn't draw an easy breath until he suggested that she help some of the kitchen women with their tasks. Then he rode away into the city, straight to the temple of Venus, alone.

Her image was the only one there. Before he'd ridden north, Brutus had demanded the removal of his own statue from the sanctuary. The priest was eager to point out to his unexpected guest how faithfully he'd discharged the order of the divine Marcus Junius—

"Get out," Brutus commanded.

"Yes, lord, at once. But first I'll bring you fresh incense so that you may make an offering—"

"*Get out.*" The priest was gone.

Brutus stood before the goddess' statue and glared up into the painted eyes. "A life, you said. *A life.* That was all you asked and all I promised. She's with child! When would I have learned that? Too late? Never?"

A low humming like the wrathful sound of awakening bees filled the temple. The image of the goddess neither changed nor stirred, but her voice came to him from the heart of that angry buzz. *What difference must it make that you've learned it at all? I will have her life; it was promised to me.*

"*Her* life. Hers alone!"

Brutus, have a care. I am not one of your crabbed philosophers. Don't chop logic with me or you'll be the one to suffer for it.

"Do you think that scares me? Suffering and I are old friends. It's hardly left my side since the night you first came to me. I've lost so much—"

You mewl like an infant. The voice was contemptuous, aloof. *Put all you've gained against your losses and see which way the balance tips. You have wealth, power, dominion. Men call you a god!*

"And does that make me one? I was content to be a man! I won't become less than that, not even for you."

When have I ever asked that of you? The voice changed tone, now softer, more insinuating, though the air still thrummed with the angry buzz. *You have power,* it repeated. *I gave it to you, now use it in my service. It needn't be your hand that takes her life; only your word. You will be free of the blood.*

"Why?" he asked. "Why must I take her life by my hand or by my word? You owe me that much explanation."

There was a touch of condescending humor in the goddess' voice. *You're confused, Brutus. I've given you too much already. I've spoiled you because I love you, but you must remember what is right, what is just. When you speak of debts, speak first of what you owe me.*

"What I owe you? Yes, let's speak of that, in the name

of justice. I never asked for wealth or power, and I swear by the same Styx that binds you, I never wanted to be called a god. Every time I hear men speak of 'the divine Marcus Junius Brutus' I want to sink into the earth. I am a *man*."

Oh, you are far more than a man, my love, and I've given you far more than you can guess. But if you will not fulfill your promise to me for the sake of my other gifts, you must at least do so for this: I have given you the health of Roma. I have loaned you the power to save what you have always loved best in this world.

Brutus shook his head. "What do you know of Roma? If I've given myself to her, it's because I understand the sacrifices she asks. She doesn't want me to be a god, just to make her an offering of the best that I can bring her as a man. I give her my honor, my devotion, my virtue for all its flaws. I give these willingly. If I give her blood, there's a reason for it that a man can fathom. Lady, who was it took my friends from me, my father, my wife? Was it Roma or was it you?"

It was life, Brutus. Will you turn your back on life, then? You've lived long, and you'll live longer. I've promised you a hundred years, and I am bound by the Styx oath to fulfill my promise. But how binding is my oath if you refuse to keep your part of the bargain? Shall we see? Are you ready to leave this life?

He wanted to answer her defiantly, to show himself to her as a man with no fear of death. He called up all the words of the philosophers who had taught him the Stoic way of acceptance, of serenity. If she would kill him, he would prove to her that life had no hold on him before he died.

But the temple around him blew away on the breath of life, and all the sweetest portions of existence danced around him. Fiery sunsets, the smell of the sea, long midnight arguments over some small point of philosophy, spring in the hills of Tusculum, the soaring words of

Aeschuylus, the warm joys of love, a star, the thousand small rubies of a pomegranate, Chian wine, the antics of children—

"No." He sank to his knees like a woman at her husband's bier and covered his face. "One life. *One!* Or take mine."

For a time the only sound within the temple was that fierce humming. It closed in on Brutus, wrapped him in a skin that crawled with unnumbered tiny fires. It crept into his head and threatened to burst out through his eyes.

And then it stopped.

Brutus . . .

A cool breeze caressed his skin. He raised his head and saw that the sanctuary had been restored around him. He could even hear the tumult of the Jerusalem streets outside, muted by the closed temple door. He looked up at the statue. The pedestal was empty. As he watched, the remaining stone puddled down into a shining pool of whiteness. It rose on edge, the disc of the full moon, its surface a perfect mirror and in it—

—in it age.

He gasped to see the hideously ancient creature trapped in the bright revelation of the moon's disc. Bent and wrinkled, a purple-patched scalp rimmed by a few pathetic tufts of hair, it huddled on its knees, cringing from the blows of each succeeding moment. The smell of the sea couldn't penetrate a nose congested by yellow snot, the words of Aeschuylus and the stimulation of philosophy alike escaped a mind that had withered like a fig. Chian wine and the pomegranate's jeweled fruit tasted alike to the dulled tongue, while the brightest star was nothing but a blur glimpsed through milk-shrouded eyes. How to enjoy the Tuscan spring when it lay the eternity of six months away? And as for children, as for love—

A man entered the cavern of the Cumaean sybil, but all he found there was a gourd. When he picked it up, a small voice from inside it begged him, "Let me die!" But to do this, he had to open the gourd, and what he found inside it was his own body, seamed and scarred and dried to a husk like a grasshopper's castoff shell by all the years the goddess' boon had kept at bay. He saw flesh sag, joints turn into protruding knobs of bone, muscles lose their hold and set limbs shivering. Worst of all, he felt the keen fire of his mind dwindle and die to an ember encrusted with ash. When he tried to call for help, all he could do was whimper, "Let me die, but not like this! For like this, I am not alive!"

He sobbed, and the creature in the mirror opened a toothless mouth to ape him. The sob became a wail of purest terror. He collapsed full length on the temple floor and offered the goddess everything, anything, all!

The priest must have heard his despairing cries, for the temple door opened and sunlight washed over Brutus' body. He sat up and looked at his hands. They were the strong, capable hands of a man in his prime. The priest was looking at him strangely, but only as one might regard a potential madman, not a horror. That was how he knew that he was himself again.

He gave the priest a generous gift more for the sake of silence than piety and went back home to see about a death.

CHAPTER EIGHTEEN

"Lord, is something troubling you?" Galo hovered anxiously at Brutus' elbow as he strode through the small olive grove belonging to his villa.

"Nothing, Galo, I'm only thinking about things, nothing important, this and that. I needed a little solitude, but—walk with me. I might change my mind and want the sound of another human voice."

"Yes, lord," the Gaulish guardsman said, falling into step beside him.

The two men ambled up the hillside path that wound its way beneath the trees. "When do you think we'll get some good of these, lord?" Galo ventured to ask, stopping to rub a leathery leaf between thumb and forefinger.

"I didn't plant these to get any good out of them. Otherwise I would've planted more. There are too few to yield us enough oil for this household's needs."

The big Gaul was puzzled. "Then why have them planted at all?"

Brutus' lips curved slightly. He too fondled the edge of one tough leaf. "Because I like their shape. Because I like the color of their leaves, green when one breeze blows, silver with the next. If I were a better philosopher, I'd read a lesson in that. But I'm unworthy of the name. Philosophy should mold a man's life, imbue it with the essence of reason and virtue. For me it's become words and wind. I've debased it to the paint on a harlot's face."

"My lord, what you say—!" Galo was visibly alarmed.

"Hm?" Brutus turned his eyes from the olive leaf to the man. "Oh. I'm sorry, Galo; I didn't mean to upset you. It's a mistake for me to voice my thoughts—what trifles!—but it's a mistake I can't seem to stop making. Pay no attention to me. I am an old man. Old men say many things."

Now the guardsman was staring at Brutus with the hard look of a peasant who has been tricked once at market and won't be tricked again. "If you're an old man, then I'm an ox."

"Better keep clear of the goad, then." Brutus plucked the olive leaf and twirled it by its stem. "Do you know how old I am, Galo? A little more than eighty. I swear this to you in the face of the sun and by whatever gods you choose to name. You can ask your comrades to confirm what I say, or if you like I can have you read some of the accounts of the Parthian campaign. I'm mentioned there by name."

Galo's lower lip stuck out. "I can't read, lord. Your oath's good enough for me. But if you are as old as that, then why don't you look—?"

Brutus only shook his head and stroked his cheek with the olive leaf. "When I say I planted these trees, I mean just that: I *planted* them. I came out into this little plot five years ago and put them into the ground with my own two hands. That was the year you came into my service. They've blossomed once since then, this very year, but it'll be another fifteen years at least before they bear anything like a worthwhile crop. You're a man of, what? Thirty years?"

"Twenty-nine, lord."

"Then if the gods show you mercy, you'll live to see that harvest. But here's the thing that elates and terrifies me all at once, Galo: So will I. And on that day I will not look that much older than you."

The Gaul whistled low between his teeth. "My lord, I believe you. I hear what the other men call you. Will you—? If I serve you well, will you give me your blessing? It would be a great thing to have the blessing of a god given face to face."

The olive leaf dropped from Brutus' hand and spun to the ground. "Galo, are you a virtuous man?"

"I—I think so. I'm not sure what you mean by it, but

I'm honest. I'm brave. I'll always be loyal to you, my lord. Is that what you mean by virtuous?"

"There are philosophers who don't know what that word means, though they wouldn't have the virtue to admit it. You are honest, Galo; that's good enough. Very well, answer me honestly then: If you knew that my blessing would give you the same gift of long, almost ageless life that's mine, what would you be willing to give me for it?"

"Anything, lord," Galo answered readily.

"Now tell me this: What if my price for that blessing were the same as what the Great Mother Cybele asks of her priests?"

Galo turned pale. He had been in Brutus' service only five years, but he had come to the East before that. It was impossible for him not to know that the priests of Cybele castrated themselves for the goddess. Each postulant danced himself into a frenzy fueled by drugs and wine, and when its pitch was highest he slashed away his manhood. If he survived the shock and loss of blood, he put on women's clothing and became the beloved servant of the goddess.

Brutus weighed the Gaul's terrified silence for some time before offering him even a single word to set his mind at ease. "Now you've seen the danger of letting your tongue outrace your better judgement. Don't be afraid, Galo. If I give you my blessing, I'll give it freely, and as a man. As for the gift of life, it's not mine to give. Even if it were, I don't know whether I would give it to any other man. There's more of curse than blessing in it."

"I don't see how," the guardsman responded, breathing more naturally. "I think it'd be a wonderful thing to live so long and stay so young."

"But I must die at last. All men must. Because I've had so much longer to enjoy the sweets of life, the parting will be that much more painful for me. When I'm gone, all will be over for me; there will be nothing left of me from where Apollo rises to where he sets."

"You can't say that, lord!" Galo protested. "Your name will stand, your images, your laws, the cities you've founded—!"

"Stones," Brutus said. "Words. But of me, of my flesh and blood and face, nothing."

"My lord . . . has no son?" Brutus didn't answer. "No children?"

Brutus laid his hand on the trunk of the nearest olive tree. "I could have had my servants plant these. I did it myself instead. I thought that it must be all the same, one way of giving new life or another. I deluded myself, but not forever." He looked at the trunk under his hand and sighed. "No, Galo, I have no children."

The Gaul turned his gaze away. Brutus recognized what the poor, loyal fellow must be feeling and pitied him for it. *You don't know what to make of me, do you? You want to escape, you want to come back and find me restored to being the divine Marcus Junius Brutus, you want this conversation to have been an ivory-gate dream. You would run off, but you're more afraid of me now than when you thought I was a god. It's been my ill luck to have that effect on many men. Ah well! I'd better save what's left of you if you're going to serve my needs.*

He slapped a wide, meaningless grin on his face and adopted a cheerful voice. "Come, you've wasted enough time hearing out an old man's ramblings. Let's go back to the house. It's almost time to eat. I don't know about you, but I could devour a whole farmyard full of roasted chickens, beaks and all." He clapped Galo on the back and steered him down the slope to the villa.

The farther behind that they left the olive grove, the more Galo recovered his lost self-possession. Brutus soothed him skillfully, speaking of simple pleasures and daily matters, the doings of the legions as they beat back the rebellion and the trivial domestic problems that had cropped up at the villa. "And that little Syrian girl of yours, the one who's my best cook, I hear she's got a temper. How do things stand between you?"

Galo gave a heartfelt sigh. "You heard right about the temper, lord. She wasn't at all pleased to hear that we'd be going off to Egypt. She hasn't stopped yelling at me since the news came down, always shouting, 'Why are you going *there?*' "

"She'll get over it when you bring her back some pretty bauble from Alexandria."

"She's not that sort of girl, lord. She wants answers more than trinkets. I wanted to give her an answer but—" he spread his hands, at a loss "—what answer *could* I give? There's rebellion here, not in Egypt, yet away we go!"

"You're a good soldier, Galo. Were you trained to question or to obey?"

The big Gaul's face flushed. "If you suspect my loyalty, lord—" He scowled. "This is all her fault. One smart clip on the ear'd cure her of questions *and* temper, I'll wager."

"Let the girl be, and don't blame her for her concern. She's fond of you, she wants to know whether you're going into danger, it's natural. And as for your loyalty, I'd sooner question whether the sun will rise in the east tomorrow." He patted Galo's shoulder, a companionable gesture which he had never bestowed too freely. "The rebellion here is well in hand. Roma needs us elsewhere, that elsewhere being Egypt. And since it is a matter that concerns the king himself—"

"The king!"

"Ptolemy Philopator Philometor." Brutus mouthed the name as if it were a lump of wormy meat. He would *not* call Egypt's king by his other name, Caesarion. His eyes narrowed, recalling how the cunning brat had almost destroyed him at Queen Cleopatra's funeral rites. Since then, the boy had retreated to his own realm where nothing further was heard of him. In fact, he had become a model client-king, doing everything in his power to help Roma share in Egypt's bounty.

Brutus knew it wasn't reasonable to carry the old grudge with him down the years. His logical mind coaxed him from it, saying, *The boy was very young, untried, malleable. He was most likely Young Cassius' tool, controlled either directly or through the Egyptian priests' love of gold. You know these Egyptians! Ptolemy hasn't given you a single problem since that day and oh, the crises he might have provoked! What would the price of grain be if he fixed matters so that Egypt withheld her harvest? Even though the senators sell off their estates piecemeal to the new farmers, the change goes too slowly. There are many Romans who continue to wait for their share of land; the city still throngs with the landless poor. It would riot with them if they lost their cheap bread. Yes, were he willing to risk the consequences, Ptolemy's had the power to twist your sack for years; he hasn't used it. Proof enough that even if he's not loyal he is at least a dependable prude. Weigh the years of peace against that one solitary day! When will you see the king that is instead of the boy that was?*

Brutus knew that all this was true. Still he tasted a spoonful of bile at the thought of a meeting now. The fact that Ptolemy had shown himself to be a trustworthy ally over the years didn't make him any more likeable.

Well, they would meet. Brutus had no other choice but to travel down to Egypt, to the great palace at Alexandria. The king had written to him in his own hand. To Ptolemy's credit, he had forborne to name Brutus *brother*—a mark of informed self-interest if not outright wisdom. The letter was full of hints at conspiracies and traitors in Ptolemy's own court, voices that whispered darkly against the kindly hand of Roma. A rebellion in Judaea was an inconvenience next to the havoc a rebellion in Egypt might bring. It was in the best interests of the

Senate and the People of Roma for Brutus to attend to this threat personally. If Brutus closed his eyes, he could still see the meticulously inked characters of the king's letter:

There is no man alive who so embodies Roma as you. You have put off the Dictator's mantle, but you can never put off the shadow of so much power. You have denied your godhood, yet even here in Alexandria, merchant-travellers speak of your temple with awe. If there is a nest of rats in Egypt's granary, dread of your power and your wrath will dig it out into the open before the vermin have the chance to breed.

Come with all speed, I beg of you, but not with all display. The same whisperers who pact against holy Roma hint that she is weak, that her best men are afraid to show their noses on foreign soil without a half-dozen legions at their backs. They say that once, Roma's name alone was enough to shield her sons. Arrive with an escort of more than a century and they will gain courage and adherents, seeing their words proved true. Arrive with more than a single legion and you might as well hand them Egypt.

If you love Roma, save Egypt.

It was prettily phrased, artfully presented. The king's messenger was no ordinary servant, but one of his lesser nobles, though he had arrived in Brutus' presence modestly escorted. *An example for me to follow in turn?* Brutus mused. *Yes, if I were a complete fool. I'd sooner trust my arm in the crocodile's mouth than my life in Ptolemy's court.*

Still, he would go. Ptolemy's aristocratic messenger informed him that the king had dispatched similar letters to the provincial governor and to the Senate itself. In these—so the lordling claimed—his king reminded them that this was the first time he had ever called upon Roma for aid. The governor and the Conscript Fathers would never dream of dictating the divine Marcus Junius Brutus' course of action, but ignoring Ptolemy's plea would leave him looking at best like a clod, at worst like a coward. *I don't trust the whelp, but I don't fear him. He'll see me in Alexandria, though not as ill-escorted as he'd like. Two centuries to get me there, and word sent ahead for me to be able to draw upon the locally garrisoned troops, if need be. What is a legate of Roma without his legion? I will come to you, Ptolemy, as you request, but not because you request it.* A rueful smile twisted his mouth. *I will come because it suits my own purposes.*

He gave the big Gaul another pat on the back. "Galo," he said, "how would your little Syrian like it if you didn't have to go to Egypt?"

Mariame's face stayed with him for the whole journey to Alexandria. It floated before his eyes by day and haunted his dreams by night. It gazed at him with nothing but gratitude and affection, and it scored his spirit worse than all the scorpion-tipped whips of the Furies.

She'd come out in front of the villa with the servants to wish him safety in his travels. Her hands were floury—she must have been making bread when word of his departure reached the kitchens. There was even a small streak of flour on her right cheek. That was the face he saw in front of him every day of the trip, bright-eyed, trusting, touched with that little white smudge.

At night it was worse. At least the daylight apparition kept silence. In his dream she offered him a blessing for the journey and a promise to keep him in her prayers. And then she shyly asked him if perhaps she should go back to her cousin's house. There had been no word of her husband, she shouldn't overstay, Brutus had done so much for her already—

He heard himself reply with words of comfort, telling her that she would have news of her missing husband soon, that he would set more men to the task. He even dispatched a messenger then and there with the appropriate orders. She thanked him a thousand times, then reached into the neck of her robe and pulled up a necklace of painted clay beads. The midpoint of the strand was a lump of crudely carved turquoise, a treasure to one such as she. She grabbed his hand and closed it around the necklace, begging him not to shame her by refusing such a humble gift.

"It will bring you luck."

"If it's supposed to bring me so much luck, why can't it bring a single night without dreams?" he muttered more than once on the road.

The dreams stopped when Brutus' party reached Alexandria. It might have been exhaustion catching up with him at last, it might have been the confusion of seeing all his followers properly settled in. Whatever it was, it was welcome.

Although there were more than enough subordinates to see to the disposition of the two centuries accompanying Brutus, he took almost proprietary pride in reviewing the arrangements made for his troops' comfort. It was also a useful ploy for postponing his first interview with Ptolemy.

He had taken the king's advice about the size of his escort, up to a point. To arrive with one hundred sixty men at your back might look like the act of a fearful man, but once Ptolemy's people saw the size of the baggage train, the whole matter put on a different face. Richly laden camels bawled and bellowed under the weight of gifts from Roma's representative to Egypt's king. Sturdy donkeys skittered over the city pavement, their panniers bulging with a fortune in lesser presents for the highborn of the court. Add to this the lesser army of servants, men and women both, whose job it was to see to the soldiers' needs on the road—with all of their gear besides—and it became a wonder that the divine Marcus Junius Brutus hadn't brought more soldiers. Someone had to guard the gifts, the beasts, the common people, and the baggage.

Brutus concerned himself solely with the welfare of his soldiers. The pack animals and the camp followers were turned over to the care of Ptolemy's palace staff without a second look or thought. Only when he was satisfied with the legionaries' welcome did he allow an obviously impatient major domo of the palace to lead him to his own quarters.

Brutus, attended by eight of his personal guard, was given a huge, lofty-ceiled suite of rooms cooled by breezes wafting off the Middle Sea. Ptolemy's servant took especial pride in mentioning that the bed itself had been slept in by Caesar. He called him the divine Gaius Julius Caesar until he took in the full dose of poison in Brutus' look. Making every obeisance, he cleared out of the rooms, leaving the scent of rose oil behind him.

Brutus lay down on the bed that might have been his father's. He doubted it. The Egyptians were never fonder of stories than when they hoped to gain something from their audience for the tale. Without bothering to remove his clothing, he slept and didn't dream.

He woke up the next morning to the sun on the sea and the curious hook of a thought: *I wonder how many days it is now that she's dead?*

From that moment on, his day became a slowly accumulating lump of questions like that one. He gathered them up singly, in the same idle, lightsome way Persephone had gone along the earth happily picking flowers until the lord of Hades sprang on her and swept her into shadow. Persephone's nosegay was scattered over the grass, but Brutus held tight to his ever-growing bouquet of queer thoughts until by sundown he had enough to weave into a garland only he could see.

I wonder how Galo did it? Was it with a dagger or a rock or just his hands? I wonder if he did it there in the villa or took her somewhere farther off? How would he manage to lure her away? Would she go with him so readily? What could he say to make her come quietly?

*Maybe tell her a lie, that some word had come from her
husband? I wonder if her husband ever will return? What
will they tell him when he comes looking for her? I wonder
when Galo did it? I wonder how many days it is now
that she's dead?*

The unseen flowers twined their blossoms around his
neck in a slowly tightening noose. He could feel their
petals tickling his ears as he walked into the banquet hall
where King Ptolemy waited to greet him.

"Hail, Marcus Junius Brutus!" The king rose from his
couch, an elegant affair crafted of gold, strown with purple,
glowing with pearls. Two score and more elegantly dressed
diners—Egyptian nobility, Roman aristocrats, a scattering
of ambassadors from lands near and far—all followed
the king's example, rose from their places, and did Brutus
honor.

He was conducted to the only other couch occupying
the high dais, its head almost touching that of the king's.
Before he could recline or even sit, Ptolemy embraced
him before the whole assembly. The sly-eyed boy had
grown into a lean, handsome man in his prime. His grip
on Brutus' arms was firm and strong; it was said that he
hunted, wrestled, and followed a self-imposed training
regimen that would make an old Roman proud. Brutus
gazed into his eyes and saw the ghosts of his father and
Egypt's queen, there beyond hope of denial. When his
face was at rest it showed more of Cleopatra's blood, her
serenity, her calculation. When he smiled, he became
another Caesar.

It soon became apparent to Brutus that Ptolemy had
inherited their sire's knack for bringing off theatrical
gestures. He made a grand show of taking a heavy necklace
of lapis and gold from his neck and presenting it to his
most honored guest. The others present made the
appropriate noises of appreciation, little cries that gained
in volume when the king then placed the treasure around
Brutus' neck with his own hands. "Hail, brother," he

whispered in Brutus' ear as he fastened it. "Wear it in health. Papyrus is a great remedy for many ills."

Brutus had no idea what to make of that odd utterance. Well, if Ptolemy had grown up to be as mad as Herod, though not even half that monster's age, it was no affair of his until it involved Roma. He made a speech of thanks that was short but eloquent, if he did say so himself, and took his place for the banquet.

Brutus left the hall as early as good manners allowed and went directly back to his rooms. All of the lamps had been lit by the palace servants and a fresh complement of his guards were stationed unobtrusively but strategically throughout the suite and outside. The air smelled faintly and not unpleasantly of incense. He lay down on his bed, stared up at stars painted on the ceiling, and asked himself where he had really been from the time he'd left these rooms until now.

Was there a banquet? If there was music, I never heard it. If there was food, it tasted like air and filled my belly the same way. Wine? I must have had several cups of it—I remember drinking to the health of half a dozen people whose names I can't remember and couldn't pronounce—but my head's as clear as mountain water. And if King Ptolemy said a half-dozen words to me or a hundred thousand, they're gone.

He got up and walked to the window, hoping the sea breeze would blow his thoughts into some more tractable form. The light of the Pharos offered ships the good news of safe harbor, but here on dry land Brutus wandered in darkness. In the end he decided that he would try to sleep. If he were lucky, there would be no dreams this night either.

When he removed the necklace, Ptolemy's gift, it was the first chance he had to really see the three thick gold plaques set between the lapis strands. Each of the two smaller ones bore the figure of a kneeling goddess. The images looked as if they were doing worship but—

Why would a goddess worship a stand of papyrus reeds?
Brutus asked himself as he weighed the gift in his hands.
He was not entirely surprised to feel that while the center
plaque was larger than the two flanking it, it was noticeably
lighter. After that it didn't take him long to learn the trick
of opening it and finding the carefully folded scrap of
papyrus within.

He read its message. "No," he said aloud to the empty
room. "I don't trust him. Alone? He must think I'm—"
He read the message again. The hour named had passed,
but the day named had not yet come. Brutus would have
all of tomorrow to decide. The message spoke of the
consequences that might result from his decision. He
crumpled it up and fed it to the lantern nearest his bed.
"I won't go," he said, speaking out loud to force himself
to attend, to remember. "These are lies, impossibilities,
a trap—" He finished undressing and went to bed,
determined to give the matter no more thought, this night
or ever.

He dreamed of Mariamē. Before dawn came, he had
made his decision.

Chapter Nineteen

In the morning Brutus awoke to a commotion of voices and the sound of men fighting. Feet scuffled and slid across the floor amid the sounds of grunts and muffled oaths. He sat up in bed and grabbed his dagger. Since coming to the court of Ptolemy he'd never let it stray far out of reach.

Then he heard the shout: "Curse it, Naso, what're you doing? You *know* me! Let me go!"

Brutus' eyes opened even wider. He flung himself out of bed and came racing from his sleeping chamber, naked, barefoot, the dagger in his hand trembling. He found three of his guards of the night before in a knot, their spears cast aside, their arms locked around a tall man who cursed their mothers and tried to shake them off like raindrops. His thick yellow hair looked even brighter in the Egyptian sunlight drenching the room.

"I don't care if I do know you, Galo, we're under orders!" the one called Naso returned, panting with the effort of keeping the larger man's arms pinned to his sides. "It's only 'cause I *do* know you that we haven't yet split your skull, but don't push me! Now you get out of here while you can, else we'll call the rest of the fellows and lay you out pretty."

"But I've got to see the legate! I've got news he'll want to hear!"

"Think you're the first one's come here with—*oof!*—that story?" Naso and the other two did their best to hang onto their prize, but it was hard work. "Ever since we come here there's been a damn parade up to his door! And every last one of 'em says he's got news the legate'll want to hear *right now*. It's all we can do to see 'em off. What're you doing here anyhow? You're not even s'posed to be here. Last I saw you, you was crowing over how we had to go on the march and you didn't."

277

"That's—" Galo was breathing hard, still trying to get free of the guards. "That's all changed."

"Obviously." Brutus made sure to speak loudly enough to be heard over the sounds of the struggle. The guards heard him, saw him, dropped their holds on Galo and saluted. The big Gaul, dishevelled from his recent tussle, saluted as crisply as if he had just stepped forward for inspection.

"Return to your posts," Brutus told his men. "Come with me, Galo." He led him back into the bedroom where he motioned for him to take a chair. "What are you doing here?" he asked coldly, putting on his loincloth.

The guard was taken aback by this frosty reception. He hesitated a moment before replying, "L—Lord, I thought that you should know—that you would be happy to know—"

"The *logical* thought would have been that some news can wait," Brutus interrupted. He opened the ornate cedarwood chest by the wall and took out a light linen tunic, a lifeline if the day turned too hot for the sea breezes to counter. "I didn't come down here with the intention of leaving my bones with Alexander's. I would've been back in Jerusalem soon. There was no need for you to follow me. If you're expecting a reward for it—"

"Reward?" Galo echoed. He sounded startled and resentful at once. "That's never been your way. If a good soldier does his duty, it's only what's expected; that's how we're trained when we come into your service. A word of praise, that's all I look for and all I thought to have."

"And you couldn't wait to have it." Brutus turned his back on the man as he slipped the tunic on over his head. He couldn't bear to look at him; he knew he would see him as a monster, and that his revulsion would show plainly in his eyes. *A monster of my own making,* he thought. *He's not to blame; he only obeyed my orders. But I still can't look at him without feeling ill.*

"Keep it, then, if even a word costs you so dear!" His

ferocity snapped Brutus around to face him, like it or not. The Gaul was on his feet, fists bunched. "I thought the reason you set me the test was to take my measure fast. I can see why you did it so: It takes years before one man knows how well he can rely on another, but it takes decades before he sees through to that man's spirit."

"Test?" Brutus barely moved his lips around the word. Galo didn't hear; he couldn't have heard. He went on as if Brutus had said nothing. "Any soldier can obey orders. Where's the—the *virtue* in that? But for things that require more from a man than blind obedience, you've got to have someone tried by fire. You have to *know* him, right to the heart. We don't give up who we really are so easily; I know I don't. But if you need a man like that—loyal, reliable, not a sheep—and you don't have decades to find him, well, you do what you must."

He set his lips in a scowl, but his eyes were sorrowful. "I thought it would bring you joy to know that you've found that man in me."

Brutus could hear the sound of his own breath, the throb of his own blood. Every object in the room had suddenly become brighter, sharper, etched with a clean acid light. "You didn't kill her," he said.

Galo shook his head. "Lord, you know already that I'm no philosopher. I told you what I am. I don't fear much of anything—except maybe the sky coming down on my head—and I'm honest, and I can tell what's right to do from what's wrong. If that's virtue—" He shrugged. "What had that little woman done to want killing? Nothing I could see, and believe me, from the moment you told me to do the job I asked around! She won't help in the kitchen at all when they're cooking pork, but that's just part and parcel of her religion. That was when I knew the truth of things."

"Truth . . ." Mariame's face arose before Brutus' eyes, then rippled back into the face of the goddess before trickling away.

"That you were testing me." Galo looked proud of himself. "To see if I'd be a hound or a hawk. You've got plenty of hounds. You've only got to whistle and they run to obey you, no matter what you command. But a good hawk knows better."

"So she's still alive."

"Alive and well. You can see for yourself if you won't take my word."

"You mean she's *here?*"

"Don't worry for her sake, lord, she's fine." Galo misconstrued Brutus' reaction. "It was an easy journey, and besides, she wanted to come. She's more than fond of you, beyond plain gratitude for all your favors."

"How did you—? When—?"

"We rode in your train, back behind the camels, with the cooks and such. My girl packed us up pretty—we didn't take one morsel of bread out of the soldiers' mouths—and Mariame put in her hand at mealtimes to help out."

Brutus had the dizzying feeling that one weight had been lifted from his shoulders only to be replaced by another so heavy it would bend him in half, snap him in two. Still, he had to know: "Why didn't you come to me sooner? Before we reached Alexandria?"

Galo snorted. "My lord, you think I didn't try? First of all, you had almost two days' march on us when we set out after you. By the time we caught the tail-end of the baggage train we wanted a few more days' easy pace. When I tried to get up forward to see you, I ran into a solid wall. You had more spears surrounding you than an artichoke. Yes, most of them knew me, but they were like those fellows out there." He jerked his thumb towards the outer rooms where Naso and the rest were posted. "They had their sacred *orders*. Pack of hounds. I wanted to make you glad with my news, and I didn't think you'd rejoice to hear I'd died like a fool. I fell back to wait for the proper time."

Brutus began to pace the length of the room, shaking his head slowly, like a stunned plow-ox. "You shouldn't have brought her with you, Galo," he said. "Not all this way. You shouldn't have done it. You should have turned back and waited for me in Jerusalem. Do you know she's pregnant? You should never have come."

"I knew," Galo replied. "I couldn't help but know; she told me. The fact is, my little Syrian told me first, back home, when I was asking around about Mariame. You know these women; it's the talk of the kitchen. That's what tied it up neat for me. Kill a woman who's innocent of any wrong? You couldn't order that and be who you are, lord, not in a hundred years. But when that same woman's with child—! Not in a thousand. What man would? I know there's some who'll do such things if the girl's an embarrassment or the baby's an inconvenience, but I can't call such creatures *men*. You told me yourself how you feel about them, about children, that day in the olive grove." He grinned. "Anyway, once Mariame found out I was going after you to Alexandria, it would've taken a whole legion to hold her back."

"I've heard that some women go a little crazy when they're carrying a child," Brutus said. He sounded beaten down. "I thought she was more practical. If she wanted to thank me, she could have stayed at home and—"

"She didn't come for your sake, my lord," Galo said. "It's her husband; he's been found."

"In *Alexandria?*" This surpassed belief.

Galo was no spinner of wild tales. The Gaul had a pragmatic streak in him as thick as a stone wall. "He's being *brought* to Alexandria. That's what the message said. And from here he's to be put on a fast ship back to Judaea. The way of it's this, Lord: He and his merchant friend found themselves cut off by the rebellion in one of those minor seacoast cities—more of a pimple than a port—and there they stayed until our troops cleaned out the roads. First safe word through was one of your own messengers, from those you sent out seeking news of Mariame's husband."

"Yes . . ." Brutus had put more than words behind the promise he'd made to Mariame, Zachariah, and Elisheba. It was bad enough that he would take Mariame's life; he couldn't add a further measure of deliberate deceit to his account. He'd used his connections to send many agents out to hunt up word of the young woman's husband. He'd never expected any of them to succeed. "But if he was in Judaea, why send him here?"

"There were still pockets of trouble between him and Jerusalem. It would've cost more in men and money to bring him safely by the overland route, and he was almost in Egypt where he sat, so it was cheaper to ship him to Alexandria, then load him onto the first fast ship headed north."

"You make him sound like a bale of trade-goods."

The big Gaul spread his hands, palms upward. "It wasn't my decision. No more than when she insisted on coming with me after you so she could be here to greet her man. She's an odd one. Extraordinary odd."

"Galo, if you want to be as wise as you're virtuous, never assume there's such a thing as an ordinary woman," Brutus said meaningly as his thoughts spun.

This is what comes of trying to smear another man with blood you've shed. Or will shed, must shed. He shames me, Galo does. Straight as a road, no evil in him, so ready to think only the best of me, even now. My good hound who thinks he's a hawk. If he treats other men with so much goodwill, then may the gods shield him, else he'll die young.

Galo's voice broke in. "Lord, will you be coming to see Mariame? I know it'd make her happy if—"

"When I can," he said. *Only when I must,* he thought. He pursed his lips. "I'm glad you've come after all, Galo. I think I'll need my hawk to fly for me tonight."

"Lord—?"

"There's something I must show you and much you

must hear. Wait." Brutus fetched the necklace, Ptolemy's gift, and let the Gaul see it. He told the man most of what he'd read in Ptolemy's message, though he couldn't show him the papyrus scrap itself. That, the lampflame had already devoured.

Galo had that mistrustful peasant's look about him again. "I've seen pike dead for a week that smelled prettier than this. He says you're to come alone?"

"In effect. I may bring two attendants—more would be too conspicuous—and he'll do the same. But they're to remain behind in the house where the temple warden and his wife live. It's only when I enter into the temple itself that he wants me to be alone. For the sake of secrecy and security, he claimed."

"Mmmm." Galo rubbed his chin. "And these two attendants, can they carry arms?"

"So I assume. There'd be no question of my going at all if he'd insisted we come defenseless."

"That's a little better, but still— How can it be anything but an ambush?"

"If this were a game of knucklebones, that's how I'd wager."

All the worship Galo had for Brutus didn't stop him from rolling his eyes and demanding, "Then why go at all?" as if trying to reason with a stubborn child.

"Because sometimes the bones roll out counter to the most seasoned gambler's experience. Ptolemy's a greased lamprey and there's no love between us, but if he thinks it would profit him to play my steadfast helper, he might even outdo you in a show of loyalty." He tried not to smile at the Gaul's look of pure outrage. With a dismissive shake of the head he added, "Forgive me; I jest."

Galo didn't look ready to share in the joke. "Then I pray the gods you also jested when you said you'd meet him under those terms."

"I have no choice: He has a gift for me that he'll only give if I comply."

"That must be some gift."

"Better to call it bait. Still, it's a bait I must nibble, on the slim chance of the king's sincerity . . . this once." Brutus' lips twitched at the corners. "Twenty letters, two signet rings, and a list of names. To you it's worthless, except for the rings—their owners can afford the best—but to me it's priceless. When Ptolemy bid me come here in order to end a conspiracy, he lied."

Galo regarded his lord askance, one eyebrow lifted. "You don't look too surprised by *that*."

"Most of these Eastern kings are crookeder than a viper's track. It's how they hold onto their thrones. As for Ptolemy himself—" He shrugged. "I haven't put faith in him since he was fourteen years old. However, that's not what I meant when I said he lied. There is a conspiracy afoot, yes, only it's not here and it's not against Ptolemy's rule or Roma's hand in Egypt. It's against me."

The Gaul's jaw dropped. "You, lord?" He looked as if the unlikely chance of the sky falling on his head had come to pass.

Brutus nodded. "In Roma. I could say it began because I've been gone too long, but that wouldn't be true. Their conspiracy was born well before I left. You've heard of Young Cassius' plot?"

Galo turned his head to one side and spat eloquently. "I only hope your Hades has a fit place to stick a traitor like him."

"Please, it's enough for me to know you've heard of it. I don't like to think of him suffering now for what he tried to do to me. All debts are paid with death. I remember him as a baby, I saw him become a man."

The guard looked as if he'd rather spit on Young Cassius' memory again. "I wasn't yet born when it happened but yes, I heard."

"He and his men were only a very small piece of the greater scheme. When they failed so dismally, when I seemed to come back from the dead, the surviving

conspirators went into hiding. The men who first made
the compact against me are now either dead or so old
they're no longer a threat, but they've managed to pass
down their hate to their sons and grandsons."

"Why do they hate you so?"

"I took my power and changed their world. I tore their
toys out of their hands before they were done playing.
They were comfortable the old way. They could buy slaves
and the slaves would till their land for no wages and as
little as they cared to feed them. With what they saved
from slave labor and what they earned from crops they
could acquire more land, more slaves."

Brutus dangled Ptolemy's necklace from his fingertips,
letting the gold plaques catch lozenges of sunlight. "Poor
farmers have only their families to help them till the land.
If one year's crop fails, the family starves. A man can't
watch his babies die, so he borrows money from a rich
neighbor to tide them over, but what happens if the next
crop fails and the debt comes due? Or what if the man
himself dies with the debt unpaid? The land goes to the
neighbor and sometimes, too often, the man and his family
do too. That's how it was."

"How it *is*, lord," Galo said softly.

"Yes, you're right." He tossed the necklace into the air
and caught it one-handed. The lapis beads rattled like a
sistrum. "That's still the way of things, but it's not so bad as
it used to be, if you'll believe that. When I was Dictator, I
made it less and less comfortable for the patricians to keep
to the old ways. If you can't come against a man with a sword,
come at him with a tax law; you'll draw more blood. Owning
huge, slave-run estates became more trouble than profit.
Little by little, my laws have been bringing them down,
breaking them up, giving land back to men with none. Well,
not *giving*, but I also set laws in place that assure a fair price."

"Lord . . ." Galo looked physically pained by what he
wished to ask. "Lord, you're not Dictator any more. Why
don't they just do away with your laws?"

Brutus managed a wry smile, there and gone. "The outer strands of a spider's web are sometimes torn protecting the inner ones, the inner ones are what snare the spider's meat. I saw to it that before I stepped down, I left behind a web of lesser laws as a shieldwall around those that *must* survive."

"I don't like spiders." The guard made a face. "And I don't understand law."

"Then understand hate. Hate's found the true secret of longevity. Given enough time, a determined man may unravel the most complex spiderweb." He tossed the necklace into the air again, only this time he missed his catch. The precious gift clattered to the floor. "I didn't think they had set themselves to the task again, so soon after Young Cassius died. The harm they may have done already—"

He kicked the necklace the length of the room. "Even if hate lives a hundred years, it can still meet its death in an instant. By the admissions of their own written words, these men are seeking my life: That will be enough to cost them their own. With those letters, that list of names, the evidence of those rings, I can finally put an end to those who'd put their desires above Roma's future." His jaw set firm. "This time, there will be no survivors."

"A proscription, lord?" Galo had heard of those. For the first time, Brutus saw himself reflected in the guardsman's eyes as less than an idol.

"Yes, a proscription," he replied evenly. "They want my life, Galo, but that's not the reason I must take theirs first. No matter how long I've lived, I'm not immortal. I'll leave no son behind me to continue my work. The gods witness, I've thought of adopting an heir. But where to find him? A thousand men will swear they share my vision when all they really want to share is my estate. How to choose the one who's truly ready to follow in the path I've prepared?"

Brutus strode to the window and leaned out to drink the breeze. "If I can't yet name my heir, that's unfortunate for me, but if I can't name all my enemies, *that* is dangerous for Roma. Unless I get that list, I might not eradicate them all and then, when I die at last, the remnants of the conspiracy will send out a thousand shoots, like weeds, and destroy all the good I've done. This mustn't be." He looked back at Galo. "That's why I'm going to meet with Ptolemy."

"On his terms?" The Gaul's eyes widened in alarm.

"Well . . . *he'll* think so." A slow grin softened the tension from Brutus' face. "I haven't spent so many years observing the ways of Eastern kings without picking up some of their more convenient customs." His forefinger traced the winding path of a serpent in the air.

The Isis temple was even smaller than the one in Roma and the warden and his wife looked as if they'd been born in the days of the Titans. Swathed in shapeless linen garments that hid almost everything but their eyes, they were mummies who'd come partways unwrapped and were awaiting the embalmer's return.

Still, they move spryly enough, for mummies, Brutus thought as he watched the warden lead away the horses.

The old man was back shortly, bowing low to the honored Roman guests, ushering them into his house. Brutus, Galo and a third man, a seasoned soldier called Flaccus, were not the first callers. Two of Ptolemy's servants squatted against the wall inside, clay cups in their hands. The warden's wife refilled these for them from an amphora that seemed to have sprouted from under her arm. When she poured, a sour, yeasty smell filled the room. The Egyptians only glanced up when the Roman party entered, then went back to drinking while the warden shared all the hospitality of his home with his new guests. This consisted of bread, salt, and the thin beer his wife poured with such a generous hand.

While the Romans took a ceremonial mouthful of their host's fare, the old man chattered about the history of the temple that was his shelter and his livelihood. As far off as it was from all other habitation, despite the fact that it was reachable by a sand-swept way that hardly merited the name of road, this holy place had seen the faces of the great, Roman and Greek as well as Egyptian. So the old man claimed.

"Once I saw the great Gaius Julius Caesar come here with the queen herself to honor the goddess," he said. "Ah, with what splendor they came! I can tell you the story, if you like."

"Thank you, but I'd rather you took me to the temple first," Brutus said kindly. He nodded towards Ptolemy's servants. "I don't want to keep him waiting."

"Pardon! Pardon, great one!" The warden was on his feet, bowing frantically. "I am old, I wander in my mind. So few of the living come this way these days that— Ah! My wife says that I am worse than a flea. When I see a likely ear I jump on and catch hold. Please, this way." He started for the door, then stopped and added, "Your men— You know that they are to remain with us? When he arrived here, his majesty Ptolemy Caesarion condescended to tell this unworthy servant that you would understand and agree to—"

"Yes, yes. I'll come alone with you. Is the temple itself far from this house?"

"Oh no, lord! Once, many years since, I was performing a rite before the goddess when I heard my dear wife scream. You see, I am not just the warden of this temple, I am also its only priest. It would not do to turn our backs on the goddess, eh, Lord?" He covered his mouth with one sleeve when he smiled, perhaps to cover teeth that were either missing or rotten. "At any rate, I did hear her scream and I came running—I could run in those days, lord—and I found that a cobra had gotten into the house. Praise Isis, who gave me the strength to kill it!

From that day to this I have been thankful that the temple stands so near to my humble dwelling."

"Fortunate indeed." Brutus glanced at Ptolemy's servants. They were young, reedy men. Either Galo or Flaccus alone could break their necks with a flick of the fingers. The daggers they carried looked more like showpieces than instruments of death. He winked at his own escort and lightly said, "Stay out of trouble."

Galo saluted, then said, "With your permission." He pulled a small set of reed pipes from his belt. "I've got this to keep me occupied, sir."

Brutus nodded, apparently satisfied. "Well, don't pipe your throat too dry, then drink up all this good woman's beer. If I come back to find you drunk, you'll have a whipping for it when we return to the garrison." This said, he went with the old man. The clear, meandering music of Galo's pipes followed them into the night.

He made some excuse for passing by the stables before going on to the temple. In the past the temple complex must have been spacious and imposing, but now the only structures left in any decent repair were the temple itself, the warden's blocky house, and the stables. These were even bigger and better maintained than the house, which seemed odd to Brutus. However, he had no time to waste pondering the living arrangements of two husks like the warden and his wife. He was more intent on counting horses. There were six of them, plus a white-muzzled donkey. Three belonged to the Roman party, three must be Ptolemy's, and the donkey was such a miserable scrap of hide and hoof that he had to be temple property.

So Ptolemy's kept his side of the agreement, Brutus mused. *Or else he's contrived to make it look so.*

Galo's tune crept into the stables, made the horses prick up their ears. His piping wasn't good, but it was loud. He played a camp song of the legions, one of scores the men sang about this woman or that and what they intended to do with her when they were free.

Out among the sands, four centuries of the legions would recognize the signal and begin to move into their positions around the temple complex. Two were made of Brutus' men, brought with him from Jerusalem, the other two were commandeered from the garrison at Alexandria. It had been done on the shortest of notice, but it had been done.

The divine Marcus Junius Brutus orders and the legions fly to obey, he thought somewhat ruefully. *The demigod commands more influence than the legate or the former Dictator. Pray the gods I find the same measure of obedience awaiting me when I return to Roma!*

He glanced at the priest, waiting patiently for him just outside the stables. Had the old man heard the sound of so many sandalled feet approaching? Most likely not, judging from his bland smile.

Age has dulled his hearing, Brutus thought. *That's just as well. If Ptolemy's decided to deal honestly with me in this, the old man need never know how many uninvited guests his temple nearly welcomed this night. And as for Ptolemy himself, if the Egyptian fox has chosen not to change the color of his pelt—if we two are playing the same game after all and he's got troops of his own lying in wait—it won't be hard for Roman soldiers to teach them and their kinglet better wisdom.*

Satisfied, he patted his horse's neck and turned to the priest. "Thank you. All's well here. We can go on."

The old man pushed open the smaller portal set into the great door of the Isis temple. The dry air that rushed out carried the smells of incense, honey, and beeswax. Brutus crossed the threshold, his left hand clenched around the gold and lapis necklace that had brought him Ptolemy's message. His right hand rested on the dagger at his belt, but it could as easily draw the sword he carried at his left side. He had come to this meeting in the uniform of a common legionary, plain but useful. A light mail shirt shielded his chest; to wear heavier armor would be to seem afraid of Ptolemy. He wasn't afraid: His real armor bided within shouting distance, over three hundred swords strong.

Ptolemy was waiting for him before the image of the goddess. The old man almost did himself an injury from all the bowings and scrapings and obeisances he performed as he withdrew from their presence. The Egyptian king waited until the fellow was gone, with the door shut behind him, before breaking into laughter.

"There goes my best and truest servant," he said. He gave Brutus a pert smile. "So you've come."

"I had to come," Brutus replied. He gave him back the necklace. "Where are the letters? The list? The—?"

Ptolemy held up his hand in a regal gesture that silently bid Brutus wait. "You will have them, my brother." If he noticed how Brutus winced at that word, he gave no sign. "They are here, hidden at the goddess' very feet." He swept his hand toward the image.

The statue of Isis dominated the interior of her temple. She stood in smooth black stone, gloriously crowned, her breasts bare, the ankh in her grasp. Some vanished hand had carved the thousand pleats of her skirt with a lover's attention, but she was the only treasure left in this place. The towering wall paintings had faded from their first brilliance; in places the plaster was separating from the rock beneath. Gilded wall brackets stood empty while the light came from footed torches made of simple iron, unadorned. If there had been stars painted in gold on the sooty temple ceiling they had long since winked out.

Brutus approached the image carefully, showing her the same detached politeness he reserved for all foreign gods. Ptolemy walked at his side, stepping ahead of him abruptly when they reached the pedestal. Brutus went instantly on guard, but the king laughed and showed him that the only reason he'd gone ahead was so that he might work the catch for him that opened the hidden door. The front of the pedestal swung out, revealing a jumble of small scrolls, several folded pieces of papyrus, and a little leather bag.

"Here," Ptolemy said, scooping them out with both hands and passing them all to Brutus in an awkward bundle. "This one is the list." He tugged out one of the papyri and set it on top of the pile in Brutus' arms.

It was hard to carry so many things at once. Brutus set aside everything but the list, heaping the bag, the scrolls, and the other papyri between his feet. His eyes travelled down the roll of names; there were only a few surprises. He sighed. Sons would die for the sake of their fathers' stubbornness, but for Roma's sake he would do what he must.

"Thank you," he told Ptolemy. "You've done a great service; it won't be forgotten. Shall we ride back to Alexandria together, or do you think it would be wiser for us to return separately?"

"I think you should not be in such a hurry to return to the city," the king replied.

"Your Majesty, you don't understand: Speed is everything now. Your court—any royal court—is a bad place to keep secrets. It won't take long before this meeting is common news, not only here, but in Roma herself. I must get back first, lay hold of the conspirators before they realize it's over. If I don't, if even one escapes, all we've accomplished tonight will be wasted."

"Calm yourself, my brother. I promise you that will not be so." Ptolemy gave him a lazy smile. "I do not want to detain you any longer than needful. I only meant that we have used the goddess' holy place for our business and given her not even a word of thanks. It would be impious, would it not, to turn our backs upon our benefactress without offering her so much as the smallest sacrifice?"

Brutus was frantic to be gone, but he had to agree with Ptolemy. It wouldn't take any time at all to throw a pinch of incense into a brazier. "Will you summon the priest or shall I?"

Ptolemy rested one hand on his bosom. "There is no need. I am high priest as well as king; men call me the beloved of Isis. I can perform the sacrifice. However—" he looked at the door "—it might be more gracious to let him assist me." He went to the portal and called out a name.

Hurrying feet came crunching over the sand. The warden and his wife burst into the temple, followed by the king's servants. The old man held a stranger before him, his shortsword to the captive's neck. Ptolemy's men dragged a second prisoner between them, but Brutus barely noticed any of these. His attention was fixed on the two figures who stepped through the portal after the rest, dignified, serene, fresh faces that had come out of nowhere.

He's brought more men with him after all. The fox wears the same fur. So I expected. He felt no fear, only the calm of a well-armed lion hunter finally facing the beast he was prepared to meet. He let the papyrus in his hand drop unheeded to the floor with the rest and drew his sword, at the same time calling for Flaccus and Galo. He shouted their names loudly enough to summon his centuries as well.

In the short silence that followed, a disturbing thought fluttered at the edge of his mind: *If Ptolemy's brought more men here than agreed, why only two?* Their shaved skulls gleamed in the torchlight and they kept their arms folded under cloaks the color of moonlit sand. If they carried weapons, they seemed in no haste to draw them against their master's enemy. They smiled, and Brutus felt the hairs of his nape prickle with sudden cold.

A woman's exclamation of despair jerked his eyes back to the servants' captive. Now Brutus saw her clearly, knew her, though the rough handling she'd received from the king's men had sent her hair tumbling loose across her face.

"Mariame!"

She looked up at him piteously. "Save him," she cried. "Oh please, save him!" She strained impotently against the hands holding her, lunged towards the man in the temple warden's clutches.

He looked like a hundred other Judaeans, with black beard and hair both already going gray, skin browned and wrinkled by the sun. Brutus had never seen him before this, but Mariame's anguish proclaimed who he must be.

Her husband, but . . . how—? Where are my men? What's become of Galo? Why didn't he—? He shouted for his troops again. None came.

"Save your breath," said Ptolemy. He beckoned the two cloaked men. Each took one step forward, shrugging his cape from his shoulders, revealing hands closed firmly around the brazen serpent staff of the true Egyptian magus. The twin serpents' eyes glowed green, and a soothing hum rose from their metal bodies. With the precision of trained legionaries, the magi raised these high in their right hands, an elegant salute to the image of the goddess.

"How many men did you bring with you, my brother?" Ptolemy purred. "A century? A cohort? A legion? It doesn't matter. They can be of no use to you now."

"What have you done to them?" Brutus' teeth clenched.

"I? I am only king and priest, Ptolemy Caesarion, beloved of Isis. But these men—" He gestured to the shave-skulled pair. "They are magicians, *real* magicians, disciples of the goddess, true masters of the old powers. You have no idea the trouble I went to before I could find the genuine article. Alexandria crawls with charlatans, though there are a few less infesting the city now." He wore a wolf's smile. "If a man claims to be a magus, don't you think that at the very least he ought to be able to walk naked through a snakepit and survive?"

"So you found your magi, you've had them kill my men, and now you'll have them kill me." With death confronting him, Brutus felt no dread, only the dull ache of rage against Cleopatra's cursed pup.

"Don't be stupid," Ptolemy replied. "If they could kill you, why would I bother coming all the way out here to have them do it? I don't like leaving sweet Alexandria any more than need be. Alas, the same discipline that gives them their art also forbids them from taking life. Your precious legionaries aren't dead, but they're as good as statues until sunrise."

Blithe as a young faun, Ptolemy drew half a dozen priceless jewels from his fingers and pressed them into the magi's hands. "You are more than worth your price."

The taller of the two bowed low. "Majesty, our spells could not command such strength elsewhere. This is holy ground, consecrated to Isis. Your praise should be for her, not us."

"Fine, I'll cover this temple in gold leaf as soon as I get the opportunity," Ptolemy quipped. "But first things first. We have benefited mightily from the goddess' goodwill. We must repay her kindness at once." He eyed Mariame and her husband in a way that froze Brutus' liver.

The magi too seemed taken aback. "Majesty, what do you intend? You will not spill their blood in this place? We cannot allow it. We will use the powers Isis has granted us to prevent the desecration of her shrine."

Ptolemy laughed. "Do they *look* like sacrificial beasts to you? I never heard wise men ask such foolish questions. Haven't you yourselves called me the beloved of Isis? Then there's no need for such as *you* to teach me how to treat the goddess. Go, go away, you make me tired. Take your pick of the horses and ride back to Alexandria. You are no longer wanted here."

The magi exchanged a doubtful look, yet still they bowed again to the king and left the temple. Ptolemy jerked his head at the warden's wife. "See to it that they're truly gone." The old woman scampered off and was swiftly back to announce that the two magicians were well away. The king was content.

Ptolemy's eyes slued back to Brutus, resting on the sword he still held ready in his hand. "Isn't that getting rather heavy for you, my brother? Let it fall," he directed. "Your dagger too. That is—" he looked meaningly at Mariame "—unless you want to see how she bleeds before you watch how she dies?"

Brutus cursed Ptolemy aloud as he'd seldom cursed any man. He cursed him to the grave and down into Avernus, but he complied. His sword and his dagger dropped atop the scattered scrolls, the folded papyri.

Ptolemy laughed. The old man and his wife joined in his triumphal merriment. They were no longer in the least bent with age, and their ample robes were liberally streaked with blood. The warden's wife had a laugh as deep and rolling as the sea. She tore away one layer of her encumbering veils and Brutus saw strongly muscled arms covered with hair. A young man leered at him through the painted false face of aged femininity.

The man who had been the temple warden's wife was holding a large leather bag. Until now he had carried it slung over one shoulder, hidden beneath his robes. He loosed the drawstrings and turned it upside-down at Brutus' feet. Something heavy struck the temple floor.

So it was that Brutus learned what had become of Galo.

CHAPTER TWENTY

Ptolemy of Egypt, fifteenth king of that name, called Caesarion, prepared himself to offer sacrifice. Attended by two of his servants, the frail-seeming young men of the palace, he stood above the kneeling victim and tried to keep a solemn face. It was too much to ask of one whose whims had been coddled since infancy. He had to smile, had to gloat over all that he had gained.

On the goddess' pedestal, between her sandalled feet, Galo's severed head mimicked the king's wide, inhuman grin. Ptolemy paused in his preparations to stroke the dead man's golden hair.

"A handsome fellow; such a pity that he had to die," he said, his voice oozing false regret. "But what else could we do? My magi cast their spell as I ordered, so that no one within the walls of any temple building would be affected by it. I'd be in a sorry state if my good servants were left rooted to the spot along with your skulking troops. This unlucky man and his companion simply had to be immobilized by other means."

"I wish your pet magicians could see this," Brutus spat. "Desecrating the goddess' temple with Galo's blood— A fine piece of work for the *beloved* of Isis!"

Ptolemy shrugged. "I have no further use for Isis but the invocation of her name, when it suits me. In my heart, I serve the greater goddess, the one who offers her true worshippers more than just a painted smile." He smirked at Brutus. "You have done poorly for yourself, elder brother. So many chances, so many gifts, and now—? Lost. Thrown away. She told me that she gave you every opportunity. Now she's given the opportunity to me."

Brutus stood beside Mariame's husband, both of them held fast by the men who'd played the parts of warden and wife. He had to look at Ptolemy, he could hardly bear to look at Galo. He knew from experience that his captor was stronger than he; it was fruitless to try squirming out of the man's grip. The only weapons left to him were silence and words. "Why did she come to you?" he asked.

"The question should be why she didn't come to me sooner. But I was too young to be of much service to her, at first, and you *are* the elder brother. Precedence, you know." He looked down at Mariame. She was on her knees, her eyes on the ground, her hands tied behind her back. Ptolemy sighed. "Such a small favor for such a great prize. You might have been a god. Think what that might have meant for the rest of the family!"

Brutus bit his tongue. He felt his face grow hot, though that sensation might have come solely from one of the many footed torches in the sanctuary. Once Brutus was taken, Ptolemy had ordered his servants to kindle more; he was not a man who felt at ease in darkness.

His silence irritated the king. "Do you know what you shall be, Brutus, since you'll never be a god? Meat. Carrion in the desert. After I have made this sacrifice, I am going to cut your throat myself."

"So she's raised the price of godhood," Brutus replied, keeping up an outward semblance of calm.

Ptolemy scowled. "She will not make me a god. That was never promised. But she will give me the power to own this world and the years to enjoy it! All of Roma's lands, all of Egypt's old empire, the Parthian realm, the lands beyond to north and east and south, they will all know a single ruler. And when at last I go to meet Anubis, my body will lie in a tomb that is a city and my name will be live on for ten thousand generations."

"Anubis," Brutus repeated. He knew the gods of the Egyptians; he was not at all surprised to hear Ptolemy, his blood pure Greek and Roman, invoke the native deity. Ptolemy himself had already declared his faith in pragmatism above piety. "The one who wears a jackal's head. Yes, that's truly the proper beast to greet you when you die."

The king's eyes became burning slits. "I'll give you jackals of your own, elder brother. I see now it would be wrong for me to kill you. There are some certain . . . ladies who take a close interest in the lives of kin-slayers." He was one of many who feared to name the Furies outright, when to name was often to summon. "But if you were bound to horseback, with only the *smallest* of dagger cuts to sever the tendons behind your knees, and if that horse were to be sent galloping off into the wasteland—" Satisfied with the plan, he gestured for the palace servants to attend him.

One had been occupied with kindling fire in a low, widemouthed brazier to the goddess' right, the other with the preparation of several ritual objects—a cup, a handful of incense, a dagger—laid out on a stone table to the left of the image. A vagrant desert wind soughed through the open temple door nearby, blowing a strand of hair into his eyes. The servant put down the dagger and pushed it back into place, then presented himself to his master.

"It is neither good nor wise for the impious to attend a sacrifice," Ptolemy intoned. "Who is more impious than the man who turns his back on the wishes of the gods?" He gave Brutus a look half pity, half mockery. "I am sorry, elder brother. At first I thought that if you were to witness the sacrifice, you might know the error of your ways. We might even have let you make expiation by offering the goddess another life." He nodded at Mariame's husband. "But you are a cynic, a man without beliefs. I do not dare to run the risk of having your skeptical nature mar the sacredness of this rite. So goodbye." He turned to the two palace servants. "You have heard my pleasure; see to it."

Filled with their own self-importance, the palace servants elbowed the false temple warden aside and took charge of Brutus themselves. Brutus felt the one man's

iron grasp replaced by hands that clasped his wrists and
elbows with no more strength than a woman's. Surly over
his displacement, the warden fell into step behind them
as they steered Brutus toward the door.

*They're barely any threat, without weapons in their
hands,* Brutus thought. *Ptolemy must have selected them
on purpose, just because they* look *as soft as they are.*
He recalled thinking how Galo could have snapped their
necks so very easily. Galo must have thought the same
thing, though he was never one to let down his guard
entirely. Still, he and Flaccus both were probably only
keeping half an eye on the palace men, after Brutus left
the house. They must have been completely unprepared
when the "old" man—to say nothing of his wife!—were
the ones who pounced on them, taking their lives between
one eyeblink and the next.

Surprise has killed more men than strength, Brutus
thought, and to think became to act.

He tore his arms free of the servants' hands with a
swift, sweeping gesture that sent both of them staggering.
He didn't wait to see whether they stood or fell; the prime
danger was the warden. Brutus' eyes darted to the right,
his hands shot out and closed on the iron stem of the
standing torch. He swung it like a staff, catching the warden
squarely in the side and back with its flaming head.

The loose robes of the man's disguise went up in a
screeching blaze. He raced around in mad circles, arms
flailing, face boiling up black.

Out of the corner of his eye, Brutus thought he saw
the "wife" transfixed by what he'd done. He had no time
to waste in dealing with that one; he still had the palace
servants to bring down. They too were aghast, but they
recovered swiftly, drawing their blades. His own was gone.

The dagger on the stone table glinted. He snatched it
up and sprang for the nearest man. Hot blood ran down
his hand to the wrist. He twisted the blade once before
pulling it free.

He heard the sounds of a fight somewhere behind him. A body fell; the air reeked of burned meat. More screams dinned in his ears. A dull blow at his shoulder turned him. Brutus saw the surviving servant staring in disgust and disbelief at the bent blade in his hand. Ptolemy had proved himself to have too good an eye for deceit. Neither his servants nor their daggers must look like threats, the better to lull Brutus' men into a false sense of security. So the blades were cheap bronze, which bent back on itself even against Brutus' light steel mail.

The dagger of sacrifice was iron. The man died quickly.

Free, Brutus stood panting, seeking new foes. A voice hailed him in Aramaic. It was Mariame's husband. The man was standing over the fallen body of the false warden's "wife." He held another of the footed iron torches. "Thank you, *rebbe*," he said merrily, giving Brutus the name of *teacher* for the short, hard lesson on how to save himself. He had passed it on in less than fatal form; the body at his feet still lived and didn't burn. He had only taken advantage of his captor's momentary shock to stun him.

It would have been cause for celebration, except for the little knife that Ptolemy still had.

Brutus saw the glimmer of bronze. It was another of those flimsy palace blades, carried for utility or show, not battle. But it was just long enough to pierce a woman's throat. Ptolemy held Mariame's head up by the hair and made his wishes plain. Mariame's husband and Brutus dropped their weapons and froze where they stood.

Ptolemy began to speak.

Brutus thought at first that he had lost his mind, next that it must be Ptolemy who was mad; the words were a wild babble, sheer gibberish to him. Then the image on the pedestal began to shimmer with light. Smooth black stone paled to the shades of soft, living flesh. The hand that held the ankh began to move, the life-symbol itself become a blur of gold like a star.

Ptolemy had invoked the goddess.

She held out her hands in a gesture of blessing. Even crowned with Isis' diadem, Venus wore her true self so brightly that not even a blind man might mistake her. "So you have agreed to serve me at last, Brutus," were the first words from her lips.

"*What?*" Ptolemy looked like a rabid dog aching to bite. He let go of Mariame's hair. "He agreed to nothing! *I* am the one who called you here!"

She looked him the way a fastidious matron might regard an insect. "Little one, they called your royal grandfather Auletes the Fluteplayer, but I don't dance to your tunes."

"But you promised me—" Ptolemy sounded like a whiny child.

"I promised you nothing. I *offered*. You should have secured my oath on it. I keep my promises." She turned her face to Brutus. "The day is late: Will you keep yours?"

Brutus felt himself being drawn forward, to the foot of the statue where poor frightened Mariame still knelt and wept. His dagger was suddenly back in his hand; he knew he hadn't picked it up, yet there it was. With each step he took, the dagger grew until by the time he reached the bound woman it had become a sword, silvery, all moonfire, with a cruel black edge like the path to Avernus itself. Figures of gods and men danced along the blade; the otherworldly steel whispered and sang of hunger.

"It is not fair!" Ptolemy's enraged cry overwhelmed the voice of the sword. "He had so many chances, and he refused them! Goddess, in my father's name, I demand justice!"

"Your father?" The goddess smiled and held out the glowing star.

Queen Cleopatra of Egypt lived, young and charming. She had learned that men will do much more for a woman who has charm than for one who has mere beauty. She also knew that the world was commanded by men, but that men too might be commanded. It was not so hard, if you had the wisdom to see the way of it: You had only to

*give them what they cherished most and they would be
yours.*

Men cherished sons.

*She had taken Caesar to her bed many times, but each
new moon still brought her disappointment. He was an
old man; sometimes with age the seed lost its worth. Soon
he would turn from Egypt. She had no more time to waste
on old men.*

*There was a fine, strong young man in Caesar's legions
whose resemblance to the conqueror was so great that
his comrades teased him about it relentlessly. He thought
his looks were a curse until the night when the queen
had him brought secretly to her rooms and told him that
she loved him for the sake of that very curse. He lay with
her many times, and when the moon had run through
her monthly course twice, the queen sent him a gift. His
tentmates found him dead the next morning.*

Ptolemy sank to his knees, grinding his fists into his
eyes, howling his denial of the vision. Venus frowned at
the noise, and it choked itself off in Ptolemy's throat. His
eyes rolled back in his head and he collapsed unconscious
on the floor.

During that brief moment of divine distraction,
Mariame's husband darted forward to embrace her. He
grabbed Ptolemy's fallen knife and used it to cut the young
woman's bonds. Together they stood at Brutus' side before
the goddess. Fear lingered in Mariame's eyes, but Brutus
could see her absorbing strength from her husband by
the moment. Both of them regarded him uncertainly, their
gaze on the sword.

"Why do you hesitate?" Venus asked. "You know the
price of refusal. There can be no more chances. What
must I say to make you see? What must I do? What more
do you want of me? Haven't I given you enough?"

Brutus had no answer to give. He sought one in the
faces of Mariame and her husband, in the recollection
of what would become of him if he thwarted the goddess

this final time, in the thought of all the other deaths he had been more than willing to order, and the deaths he would order now, if he survived this confrontation, the conspirators who would have to die, for Roma's sake. Roma needed him—young and strong and at his best—now more than ever. Was one more death too great a price to pay, for her sake? Were two? Were three?

Last of all he sought his answer in the dead face of Galo, his head between the feet of the goddess.

I know I am honest, the head whispered.

"And I," Brutus murmured. "Above all, to myself." He faced the living image. "Your gifts," he said. "Take them back."

"Have you gone mad?" Small blue lightnings flashed and crackled through the glowing golden star in her hand. She seemed to grow before his eyes, grow to a size that the temple couldn't possibly contain. And yet the walls still stood, the ceiling didn't shatter. Venus with all her powers upon her was a wonder great enough to house a hundred contradictions.

"I'm sane," Brutus replied. "I know it. Perhaps I'm more certain of my sanity because I've only now regained it. Take back your gifts, Lady. Take my life if you will. All this time, all these years I thought that what I did, I did for Roma. At last I've found the honesty to know that I did all I did for myself."

"So you would have killed your father? You would have let Roma slide into the decay I showed you?"

"If I spared his life, it wasn't for Roma; it was to have his love. I see now that it was my own glory as Roma's preserver that I sought. And as for Roma, decay is patient as a vulture. This sword you've given me is strong, but not even this last deadly gift of yours is strong enough to cut the Fates' thread." He bowed his head before her in submission. "But it is strong enough to cut mine. I will not kill this woman or her child. Do what you will."

The stone walls of the temple trembled with the

goddess' silent wrath. Chunks of plaster came loose from their places, the painted faces of the gods tumbled to the floor and smashed into flakes and powder. Venus raised the star. It blazed up as if its flames would envelop all the earth. Brutus could feel the hair of his head crisp and singe from the heat. He heard Mariame cry out and saw her bury her face against her husband's shoulder.

Then the fire was gone. Venus stood empty-handed on her pedestal. Just below her breasts, a gold and turquoise scarab pin fastened her pleated skirts. She cupped it in her palms and said, "If she lives, her child will live. If her child lives, I will die."

The scarab spread its wings at her touch and took flight. Her skirts came undone and fell to her feet. She rested her hands tenderly on the swelling mound of her belly and said, "If I die, Brutus, your son dies."

Brutus felt cold sweat trickle down the hilt of the sword. That it was still in his hands was a miracle. He tried to speak, but his lips were leather. He passed his tongue over them and spoke: "My son?"

The goddess nodded. "He's waited so long to be born, my love! He was made between us on that first night, and he has grown since then until now he is a man— more than a man."

"A man?" Brutus looked up at the great belly of the goddess, the swelling womb that overshadowed him and left him feeling small. "But why so long a wait? Why couldn't he be born like other men, Lady, as an infant?"

"Because he is not like other men. The part of him that's mortal might have seen the light years ago, but the part of him that's mine is bound to wait until a fitting place opens for him in this world. If she lives to bring forth her son—" Venus pointed at Mariame "—that place will be gone."

"Why, then—?" He stopped, took a breath, tried a second time. "Lady, you are great, you are strong. I've read the poets who sing of how you are both desired and

feared by men and gods. Why must it be my hand that
does this? Why not—why not your own?"

Venus' melancholy voice filled the sanctuary. "Because
that power has not been given to me and I have no way
to take it, nor does any god. Our hands are tied by the
Fates, bound helpless with the threads of every mortal
life. The rope stretches only so far, but it never breaks."

The goddess' eyes filled with tears that traced bright
galaxies of sorrow down her cheeks. "Oh my love, is this
so much to ask? My chosen sacrifice has always been
the dove, the dove has always been the eagle's lawful prey.
Do this for me and our son will live, he will be a god, he
will take Roma for his portion and never let her fall! He
will govern a greater realm than Roma ever knew . . . or
he will never be. My love . . . my love . . ."

Her words caressed his skin and called up all the ghosts
of old desires; he raised the sword. He stepped toward
the Judaean couple like a man in a trance. Mariame's
husband turned so that he became her shield. She clung
to him in despair, but found the courage to look at Brutus
over his shoulder and say in a small, trembling voice,
"Don't hurt him. Let him go."

Brutus let the sword drop to his side, slide from his
fingers to the floor. He sought the goddess' face and said,
"*There* is love, Lady. There is the true gift, given unasked,
unselfishly. And there is my choice, too. I would rather
never see my son born at all than see him born less than
man."

He turned his back on the goddess and walked unseeing
from the temple. He thought he heard a cry behind him
even more horrifying than the screams of the burning
man, but he didn't look back. He walked swiftly back to
the stable, mounted his horse, and rode for Alexandria.
If Mariame and her husband would find the means to
see themselves back to the city or not, it was no more of
his concern; he was done with them. He hoped they had
the sense to get far away before Ptolemy and his one

living servant recovered consciousness. He knew his magic-frozen legionaries would be able to look after themselves, once dawn restored them. He rode hard, yearning to outrace the happenings of that night.

He rode on, expecting at any minute to feel the bite of age at his back, the pains lacing up his legs, the flesh withering while he watched. None of it happened, for a while. . . .

He was just entering one of the city gates when the dove fluttered down to perch on his wrist. It tilted its head, looked at him with one pomegranate eye, then changed. Smooth white feathers darkened to dirty brown, the bright red eyes a glittering black, the bird itself dwindling in size until a sparrow peeped and hopped along the back of his hand, pecking at the reins.

They passed beneath the shadow of the gate. The stone sparrow fell from Brutus' palsy-stricken hand.

Epilog

The old man knew that he had come to a town by the smell of the place and by the fact that the earth was packed down harder under his feet. He didn't know its name, not that it mattered: All these Judaean towns were pretty much alike.

And yet he felt sure that he ought to ask the town's name. He knew there was a reason for the uncounted days he had passed on the road, the nights like this one spent cold and hungry. He couldn't recall where his journey had begun and sometimes he lost sight of where it was going. There had to be a reason for it, but if so, it had flown from his mind, leaving behind it nothing but an ache and an urgency.

I must find the town, he thought, stumbling on. *But— Which town? And why?* He found no answers; only the small, insistent nub of a memory that had otherwise crumbled away. It laid hold of his peace and tugged him forward, though each step was pain and there was nothing before his eyes but milky mist.

I must find the town.

Hunger raked his belly. He dreamed of bread, a house of bread, its walls made all of loaves hot from the oven. They shone before his almost sightless eyes like the Pharos beacon, bread transformed to light. There was a great light shining just ahead, a golden ankh held in a great lady's hand, a star. Even through the fog dimming his vision he could see its brightness.

He leaned heavily on his olivewood staff and dragged himself onward, step by step, until the pain became too great. He swayed in the middle of the street, breathing hard, until a passerby moved more by expedience than kindness hustled him out of the way. His groping hand felt the rough surface of a poorly daubed wall and his nose filled with the smells of beer and wine: A tavern. He slid his body down the wall to rest.

Someone was singing inside. The voice reached him through ears that often felt as if they were crammed with tufts of wool. He could barely make out the language, let alone the words, but the tune was sweet. *What was that?* he wondered as a lone word startled his ear with unexpected clarity. *Did I hear 'Illium'?* But then the singing ended, and he heard nothing except the sound of merry, half-drunk voices and many cups being thumped on wood. He closed his eyes and hoped for another song.

The old man sat with his back to the tavern wall and his legs splayed out before him. It was no wonder that the next man out of the tavern door tripped over them and went sprawling into the dirt.

"Watch where you're at, old man! Can't you find someplace else to be drunk?" The aggrieved party spoke Aramaic with more enthusiasm than mastery, and with an accent that shouted *Roma!*

There were times—times that grew increasingly more rare with every day that passed—that the mists clouding the old man's eyes parted. They did so now just long enough for him to see the face of a fairly young soldier in the uniform of the legions.

The old man slowly drew his skinny legs up to his body, wincing with the effort. "To be drunk requires that I have the price of a drink, young cockerel," he replied in Latin.

The soldier gaped. "Your pardon, sir. Are you a veteran?"

"Mmmm. Maybe I was. I forget."

"Wait here." The younger man ducked back into the tavern and came out again carrying a cup of wine. "Here," he said, smiling. "Just on the chance that you are a veteran. It'd be bad luck to let you go thirsty."

The old man drank the wine in short, rapid gulps. Most of it sloshed out of the cup and dribbled down the grizzled whiskers on his chin. When it was all gone he said, "I may not remember if I'm a veteran of the legions or no, but I *do* remember wine tasting better than that."

"Best I could buy on my pay, sir." The soldier sounded sheepish. "I could've done you better if I hadn't given a coin to that singer in there." He jerked his thumb at the tavern door. "Did you hear him? He *was* fine. Sang about the fall of Troy so that you could almost smell the timbers burning, see Aeneas walking through the blaze with his old father Anchises on his shoulders, his little boy by the hand, while his mother Venus looks down from Olympus and weeps." He sighed happily, once more the willing captive of a song. He blinked, coming back to the present, and added, "There's beer to be had too. I can bring you some of that. Or are you hungry? They sell bread and—"

He tried to keep the weariness from his voice, but it was so hard, so very hard! "Young man, your kindness shames me. And here I haven't even thanked you for the wine. They say that it's expected for the young to neglect good manners, but when the old forget them as well, the world's just waiting to end."

"Could be, sir. Each day seems to bring us a fresh load of troubles. The Parthians are stirring again. The way they go through kings it's astonishing they've got the time to bother us, but they manage. Clever bastards."

"Stirring?" The old man pricked up his ears. "Stirring how?"

"Mostly raids on the trade routes, sir, and a few of the bolder lords have made strikes against the farther trade cities. My centurion says something ought to be done. Not that we'll do it. There's trouble enough brewing right here in Judaea. They say King Herod's on his deathbed. The gods know that that family of his will tear the land to shreds until Roma steps in to wipe their arses for them. Meanwhile it's wait, wait, wait."

"It always was."

The soldier laughed. "So you are a veteran after all!

Look, my name's Gaius Junius Pulcher. You come back with me to camp and we'll see you rested and fed."

The old man shook his head slightly, even such a small gesture shooting nails through his veins. "I must go elsewhere, young man."

"Yeah?" He sounded surprised, but not scornful. "Well, where's that? I'll see you get there safe."

"Do you see that light?" A hand more bone than flesh pointed at the brightness hovering in the heavens.

"Yeah. It's hard not to. One of my messmates, old Septimus, has gone crazy since it showed. He claims it's a sign that the gods are angry and we're all doomed. Mind you, when we ask him what it is we've done lately to make the gods any angrier than normal, he can't say. He just hollers, 'You'll see!' and dashes off to make another sacrifice. If the cooks don't catch wise there won't be a live chicken left in our mess, and that's a fact." He snickered. "So, it's the light you're after?"

"There will be a town. I must find the town. I must, I must—" The old man's limbs began to shake and his lips were cold.

"Hey, easy there, I'll help you find your town." A strong hand patted his back with remarkable gentleness. "Your town and your light *and* a good méal in our camp afterwards, into the bargain. Up we go!"

The old man felt his frail body being lifted effortlessly up into the air. He came to rest on the younger man's shoulder. From his new perch he could see the light even more clearly, and when he glanced down he found that he could see the soldier's face with perfect sight. It was a fine, handsome face; easy to understand how this man had earned the cognomen Pulcher.

He almost looks— The old man's thought seeped away.

"Do you know?" he said. "Your name is— Well, I'm alone in this world but if— I like to think that if I ever *had* had a son, I might have named him—"

"Now, now, didn't I just tell you to take it easy? Save

your voice, sir, save your strength. And who's to be sure you haven't got a son somewhere? You're a soldier of Roma!" Gaius laughed out loud, then asked, "Ready, then? Hold fast, off we go." He started down the street.

"Bright . . ." The old man lifted his face to the great blaze in the heavens. It filled his eyes and suddenly he could see the silver pinpoints of the other stars again. He thought he would die from the beauty of it all. "It looks as if it's all afire," he gasped in wonder. "Like a city caught in flames."

"Troy herself, eh?" The young man chuckled. "Don't worry, Father Anchises, you're safe with me." Pleased with his jest, he began to sing a soldier's song, taking the road to the light.

END